Fresh on Her Majesty's Lobes

A Very True Account on the Life of Piss Dingle

by Ward Geit Fung

Telling of Contents

2

Part III
A Quest of High and Mighty Goodness

Foreword by Ward Geit Fung

Though it should not need mentioning, I will mention it, as I see that hatred is easily roused in my time: the following account has been set down to ease tempers, and bring folk together in the bond of Passian grace, instead of furthering the curse of inflammation which now spreads across our Lobes. Many of my contemporaries have read these pages and told me that I am not of sound mind to think that my manuscript could ever bring about any benefit to society at large, but yet I believe it might. To some, it most certainly will. To those who are slow to condemnation, those of patience and appreciation for the art of metaphor, they will find deep joy in the loins of this draft.

But for those who are quick to anger, who spout steam from burning heads after a criticism against their view is spoken, I should say this account will bring about plenty of violent toils.

Perhaps this work should not be contemplated for how it will fare in the short term, however, against the minds of those who scream but do not listen. Perhaps it will enjoy a better life in the farflung deeps of time, when all the world has settled and learned to embrace all breeds with a friendly diddle of body and mind. If only I could travel to such places as did those Fortunate Few who lived in the Time of Enchantment, some 600 years ago. How the lands have fallen since then, and how the anguish now roams.

Let this tale be a beacon for times to come. Whether we ever reach the former heights of our glory, or whether we continue to live and die enslaved to prejudice and pride, let this account on the Prime Days of Piss Dingle, namely when he first comes to the world stage, 'fresh on Her Majesty's Lobes,' first of the Dingleites, serve to inspire and amuse all that read on.

4

Reference Timeline with Folk and Lobe Listings

The Original Dingleite Party Sanctioned by Fundrik
Luber was, in 3334:

1. The Honourable Piss Dingle
2. Windal of Klontug
3. Brooth Dimfether
4. Carvin Cong
5. Ward Geit Fung
6. Lady Victory
7. Swilly
8. Marc Tempull
9. Deng Lu
10. Siddlebok
11. Puup Gargeri
12. Wode Punling
13. The Girl Perfection
14. Urtain Piik
15. Dorak of Pagosa
16. Jernander Skug
17. Fi Fernin
18. 23 Unspoken Women and Wermen

Then Joined in Fyninfer were:
41. Rick Cottontree
42. Tibsmith

Then Joined in the Bowels of Lakewood were:
43. Inder Sohn
44. Dunly Moan
45. Kang Joon
46. Lord Cuomo, their Liberator

And Rejoined at Athragal was The Good Skin Toot.

The Lobes of Hakamena, from East to West:

Harlobe: Here lies Rich Mahogany Supremacy, and the towns of Tugpikkle, Rayce and Ho Spleen Ho.

Narlobe: Here lies Rich Mahogany Supremacy. Very small, but housing the Lobe Capital of Essen.

Yonderlobe: Sparsely inhabited. People of all breeds do as they please here.

Farlobe: Here lies Rich Mahogany Supremacy, and the town of Little Fools and Tree City, along with the regions of Flatfinger and Athragal.

Westlobe: Here lies Tanfolk Supremacy, and the sacred place of Lidion, as well as the Forest of Arches, Sesterball, and Dingle's birthplace of Murder Creek.

A Simplified Timeline of Lobian Politics as it Pertains to our Tale:

3327	Url Skulfing defeats Miet-Boosh.
3330	Bahmoeth Burden defeats Skulfing; Skulfing steals The Choosing.
3333	Leg Randy kills Piss Lip; Bahmoeth Burden defeats Skulfing; Skulfing assassinates Burden.

Some of our Characters, to be Kept Straight
M. denotes Mahogany, T. denotes Tanfolk, P. denotes Paleskin

(the Honourable)	Piss Dingle.	M.
(the Good) Skin Toot	His pal.	T.
Ward Geit Fung	Myself. Their chronicler.	P/T.
Carvin Cong	Elderly cousin of Dingle.	M.
Swilly	He's magic with the flute.	M.
Lady Victory	Actress and warrior.	M.
Wi Tan Pree	Wise, tall, large, deep.	T.
Rick Cottontree	A reluctant Dingleite.	P.
Deng Lu	A zealous Dingleite.	P.
Tibsmith	Lover of bowels.	T.
Brooth Dimfether	Large of body and song.	M.
Fundrik Luber	High Judge of Ho Spleen Ho.	M.
Jidbilly	An actress.	?
Feekro Dential	An actress.	?
Empress Hakamena	Of the Hayamese Empire.	M.
Miekpanse	First subordinate to Skulfing.	T.
Grandbor	Of Skulfing's High Deeplove.	M.

Fendyrd	High Deeplove. Disemboweled.	T.
Huivz	Fendyrd's replacement. Skinned.	T.
PARPINFOHZ	Skulfing's famed assassin. Burned.	M.
Leg Randy	Recreational political assassin.	M.
Piss Lip	Skulfing's Opposition in 3333.	M.
Bahmoeth Burden	Skulfing's Opposition in 3333.	T.
Carpis	Proprietor of the Deep Tickle.	M.
Slivvery	Countess of the Deep Tickle.	M.
Jic Topper	In Council of Sound Logic.	T.
Dunly Moan	In Council of Sound Logic.	M.
Kang Joon	In Council of Sound Logic.	T.
Inder Sohn	In Council of Sound Logic.	T.
Katario	She who raped Dingle.	M.
Flod	One who was killed unjustly.	P.
Dark Chevron	He who killed Flod unjustly.	M.
Rockhard Werman,	Chief of the Heart of Rockdom.	T.
Lobe Minister Url Skulfing	An evil thing from the stars.	

The Dingleite Charge, at Lidion in 3336, Consisted of:

1. Lord Cuomo of Costerwall
2. The Honourable Piss Dingle of Murder Creek
3. Ward Geit Fung of Dolerenn
4. Jernander Skug of Essen
5. Inder Sohn of Tipidan
6. Rick Cottontree of Fyninfer
7. Tibsmith of Fyninfer
8. Unspoken
9. Unspoken
10. Unspoken
11. Fi Fernin of Little Fools
12. Lady Victory of Ho Spleen Ho

4747474747474747474747474747474747474747474747474747

This book is dedicated to Tirna, who minded not my heinous ways.

"Let there be passion in the pits and terror in the trenches."
—Rallying Cry of the Dingleites

4747474747474747474747474747474747474747474747474747

Prologue and the Deed of Pass

Let me take you back, to the dawning year of 3323, when old Piss Dingle roamed along the Essen, drifting here and there between Yonderlobe and Harlobe.

These were the names— along with the Farlobe and Westlobe— given to the lands in Glitharog, after that ancient kingdom had fallen. The mythos of our primary man Piss Dingle the Younger has come to be celebrated chiefly in the Yonderlobe and so I shall swiftly describe its borders, they being the Craun in the west and the Essen in the east, so that its form mimicked the curves of a very thin woman.

These places were— from about 2800 to 3200— the Lawless Land of Lobes, where in the vast green places of the western world men governed themselves by their own nature, which was predominantly heinous. But as the vast Hayamese Empire rose in the south, taming their own sands and then rising into the fertile fields of green, they colonized the Lobes. This was done and declared by 3214, when the Empress Caracos fashioned herself as Overlord to all lands from Excelsior to Lidion, or from Harlobe to Westlobe as those places would now be called. All who live in the graces of these fertile lands still pay tribute to the the Empress of Hayaman (who in my time was Glorious Hakamena, who was far too glorious to deal with any of the problems in the Lobes for as long as she reigned). Despite this tribute and acknowledgement of their servitude, the Lobes are nonetheless free to administer their own Choosings of Ministers, which is a trait unique to our society, as far as we know. But the intricacies of our politics will later be spelled out; now we must tell a quick tale of Elder Piss Dingle, a man with Rich Mahogany skin that signified his supremacy compared to other breeds in all but one of the Lobes.

As the elder Piss came walking down into a forest dell, he saw the company of three men, knelt before a fire, with another figure lying horizontal, hands tied behind his back, and a dirtied white sack over his head. So low against the ground, and with clothes that had been dirtied by the soils, that the elder Piss almost passed on without even seeing him. When he realized there was indeed a captive man lying helpless on the ground under the hands of these three forest folk, he gave a tip of his corn-fashioned hat—

"Good evening," spoke the elder Piss, then raising a friendly hand.

"More than good," replied one of the men, who had a hand on the neck of the captive, "For we're about to have a feast of entrails."

"You're welcome to join us," said the second of these men.

At that moment, the elder Piss knew it was time to move on. And so he took strides away, with his back towards this group of forest-dwellers, but a whisper in the wind bid him halt. He sighed, bit his lip, and turned back to the questionable fellows.

"And whose entrails might we be feasting on?"

The leader of the threesome tapped his knuckles against his captive.

A further question from Old Piss Dingle: "And does that captive werman... mind, that you're to be feasting on his entrails?"

"Believe me, if you saw his face, your sympathy would be voided."

"Well let's put that theory to the deed then." And he motioned for the kneeling man to lift the sack off his captive's head. He did so, and Old Piss Dingle saw that the man held against the forest floor was a white-fleshed

11

Dikenian, a "Paleskin" as they are commonly known in the Lobes.

"You see now?" asked the third of the threesome. "Just a Paleskin. So move along, or help us carve him up and roast the good gut good."

And the elder Dingle could not argue with that. He had no appetite for entrails, having just eaten an hour ago, and so he continued on his path, though he altered course to walk up and away from the threesome, instead of following the dell as he had planned.

As Old Piss Dingle made his way back home in the gathering dusk, he assured himself that there was no malice in any of his actions that night. In fact, they were not actions at all— rather, the lack of actions. And he knew that the holding back of deeds was always the safest of options, for there was no trouble to be had in leaving things undone. He turned his mind towards lighter topics, such as how he would soon be lifting and pressing upon the paws of his dog in harmony with the music which would come from his wife's sloot.

But as Paleskin screams filled the forest air, Old Dingle's mind was drawn back to his talk— however short— with that Threesome. If it had been a man of Rich Mahogany complexion, he would have been compelled to act, to be swift and heroic. If it had been one of the Tanfolk, he might have even been persuaded to act in a middling fashion, if his conscience was up on its game. But thankfully, thought the elder Dingle, the captive had been a Paleskin. And with that all sense of obligation was up out the rooftop, for everyone in those lands knew that Paleskins were nothing to fret over.

They had been slaves for centuries, ever since Jasper of Dikenia sold his dignity away to the foul queen Melizar, back in... the year 2320 was it? And in the west of the world their servitude was held until the year 3303, making for 983 years of enslavement. The year now being 3323, they had been free folk for a mere 20 years. So logically, thought Elder Piss, that breed of folk ought to still be relishing in the fresh feels of freedom that they had only recently won.

Yes, he reassured himself, he had done no wrong. Sure, he might have been able to lash out upon the Threesome and attempted to free the Paleskin— or at least further intervened in some way— but such a thing would have surely led to trouble. And certainly there could be no optimal outcome for the captive Paleskin no matter what his course of action. The threesome would have prevailed in any case by right of their obvious majority, and the Paleskin, if not eaten by that particular threesome, would have met a similar if not worse fate within days or weeks, for that country was not a welcome place for men of their complexion.

"Yes," spoke the ever constant voice in the mind of Elder Piss on his walk home, "interference would have made great harm for myself while doing nothing grand for any involved. That Paleskin was forever doomed and any show of resistance against his Rich Mahogany oppressors would have been quite futile." This was only common knowledge in those days.

In walking away, he had crafted the optimal outcome for himself. And this sat fine in the conscience of Elder Piss after many hours of reconciling his thoughts, such was the idle ideology of the day. Elder Piss abhorred trouble, and so did all around, all those who were of mahogany complexion in the land of Rich Mahogany Supremacy.

But sooner than one may have guessed, did the loins of change swiften, bringing about winds that would shake the thoughts of men, and seek to crack the foundations of ancient institutions and firm prejudice, so long thought to be indicative of natural law. I will not say that the change was brought about through the will

13

and deeds of one man alone, for it is likely that these winds of passage spoke to many thousands at once as they are ought to do, but for my part, the change is clearly represented in the tale of one: Piss Dingle, son of the Elder Piss whose life we have described here in a brief episode.

Unlike his father, Piss Dingle the Younger would not so easily allow his thoughts to be tamed with feelings of helpless ineffectiveness. He would not be content to endorse the conventional customs of his age, and would not be fearful of a fruitless conflict. He did not abhor trouble; on the other hand he welcomed it into his court and wrestled with its beating breast.

Piss Dingle was one who would rouse the Lobes, and awaken in them a sense of dignity for all breeds— Mahogany, Tanfolk, and Paleskin alike— so that they might begin to live as one, distinct yet with equal regard, within the Passian race. Let us now speak of his tale.

After providing context to a particularly strange statute that will bring about the root concern of the first chapter.

"All thee as I see, residents of this province we do call Harlobe, with the Essen in the west and the Sashites in the east, bound between Narlobe and Farlobe, I address you here today."

—These were the opening words of Miekpanse of Marcunnel, first subordinate to Url Skulfing, elected Lobe Minister of those realms, upon the delivery of what promised to be a grand declaration addressing the woes of the land—

"We here today face a crisis of monumental disgrace. Our numbers dwindle, our children weak with impotence. Not a town today may count more in its youth than in its elder line. So where does this leave our future? Should war ever break out between Narlobe and Farlobe, perhaps led on by those rapine breeds far off in the Westlobe— which eventually of course will come to pass— we will have none to defend our way. The way of the Harlobe, lobe which lies closest to the Mother Country, dear Hayaman, cast aside and buried by the West! And it may not be so close as the other side of the Essen."

Here the faces in the crowd fled a true concern.

"Yes, if we do not harbor these precautions and act with sound reason, we may find ourselves living in a world of white. Yes, the Paleskin Man stirs freely in the Westlobe, where the Tanfolk breed has always reigned supreme. In a manner of great nonsense they find favor in the white skins over those that hold power in all other parts of the world— they accept the pale while shunning the Rich Mahogany! We will not attempt to further unravel their sick line of thought. But rest in the truth that if ever these fiends of the Westlobe cross the large curves of the Craun, and then the thin curves of Yonderlobe, and still then pass over the Essen into our own city of Ho Spleen Ho, they will find a reversal of fortune! For those intruders we might reinstate old customs, no?"

And there was riotous clammer in the stands.

"For those invaders we would surely show the strength of our ropes, for they ought to be reminded of their place in the Lobes of Hakamena, these great territories rising up from the Motherland of Hayaman— where Lady Law and Old Order be our only guide!"

And by this— Lady Law and Old Order— of course everyone knew that he was only applying them as they gave advantage to the strong breed of the Rich Mahogany Man, which in those parts sought to trample other breeds always into subservience. Miekpanse continued:

15

"In order to preserve the dignity of Old Order and dearest Lady Law, we must be diligent. We must act on our shortcomings, which today concern the curiosities of our rising generation. Yes, to you who have left your nest, and now seek out the road that you will travel the rest of your lives, I speak. You, WOMEN, have been shy of your wermen's advances. Wermen approach— I have seen it— and you will refuse them outright, even should it be a proper approach! Let me tell you, this is not a match to how my father and mother behaved.

My father was a man of standard proportions, and so he found a mate with little fret. All those of standard proportion did in his day. And thus we in Harlobe came to be strong, plentiful in our offspring. Had my father lived today, however, or even in my time of youth— he would have found the breeding grounds changed. I speak to you, Women of Harlobe."

And here he made many low-browed looks, locking eyes with women, giving them guilt.

"Women of Harlobe, no longer do you elope with men of standard proportions, who make standard inquiries. You have risen above, have you? Do you think that you have grown all that much better in the span of two generations? That you are all now worthy of only the courtship of exceptional men? Do not turn your faces from me."

Just off the stage, a man called Fendyrd crossed his hands with a smile, as did one called Grandbor (or Grand Bor, as some chroniclers have styled him). They will come to figure more in the coming chapters, but for now let it suffice to know that they were there gladly by the side of Miekpanse as he gave this monumental address, scorning the haughtiness of women. The speech continued:

16

"Is there one woman among you who would rise and explain to me why you have not by this time in your life mothered a child? I know your numbers are resounding. Wheat of every nane of you have held off in these matters. When a werman of standard standing approaches you, I am told you shrug him off— or rather, that was the practice twenty years ago. Today you grow BITTER at the approach. You will not stand to be looked at. If you should catch one of standard proportion stealing looks at your high graces you tell them to depart without a second glance. And why?"

Let it be said needlessly that a vast number of women in the crowd were made quite uncomfortable now as Miekpanse called out their growing sense of self-worth.

"Ladies of Harlobe. I understand. You crave those of exceptional proportion, such is the way of the world. But more than half of you are not deserving of such and I ask you again, why do you scorn those of the standard kind? Why do you condemn our people to an age of infertile distress while nations around grow plentiful? Why do you dwindle our numbers?!"

He slammed his hand against his podium. Deep in the shadows to his side, the image of Url Skulfing crept back into darkness. He was the source of power in those Lobes— Harlobe, Narlobe, and Farlobe— yet his appearances were kept to a minimum. Many peoples in his Lobes adored him as of yet, for he had kept silent on a great many things. He spoke fervently on the need for Rich Mahogany Supremacy, for this was a popular thing among the Mahogany, but on issues that might not prove so unanimously splendid to his followers, he left in the hands of men like Miekpanse, Fendyrd and Grandbor. This tonight was one such occasion, and while the wermen in the crowd agreed with what was being said, many women recoiled, to hear their customs brought

17

into question. Slowly over the course of the night would their entire concept of social liberty be brought into question (and eventually dismantled).

"My father, had he lived today, would not be able to obtain a wife. He that was perfectly fine and acceptable in yesteryears would be today seen as inadequate. I see it everyday, and it is shameful. Fine wermen, with fine occupations, and fine strokes of intelligence— they come to you, looking for affection, and you turn them down. You swoon to be in the arms of the exceptional, but I am afraid not nearly enough of us can claim that distinction."

But here Miekpanse took a brief pause, remembering that his lord Url Skulfing had bade him to always express the people of his Lobes as nothing short of exceptional, the greatest of all folk. And so he amended his words gracefully.

"Of course we are exceptional. As a Lobe we are exceptional. Far more so than any other land. But you— women, you— believe that you are supremely high, enough so to deny the approach of wermen you consider to be standard, even when they are exceptional, as all of us are. And now we live in a land which— while vastly exceptional— has hardly a young lad to speak of. If we continue down this path, in fifty years we shall be ancient and decrepit all."

He shook his head, hung low, and dropped a tear upon his notes. To his left, Fendyrd the gatherer of crowds closed his eyes and shook his head, lamenting the unborn and the dead potential for a rising generation of Harlobians.

"It is not too late. It is not too late for the Harlobe. Yes, we are the most exceptional of lands, and we will be for all of time. But we may not be, should we keep down this path into twilight realms. If you.... women... continue to adore yourselves to no end and hold off your willingness to wed before your time has turned to crust and crack— you will be the end of our Lobe! Do not be the end of our Lobe."

He pressed his lips and let his head swing as a pendulum. With every swing of the head, cheers began to grow in the crowd and soon a plethoric applause was at hand.

"Do not turn away suitors because you do not deem them high enough to your absurd standards. Do not push them out of taverns, to wander dark and lonely streets in the twisted hours of night. Rather, be goodly as is your call! Be right in the ways of your predecessors, be men of kindly warmth and hospitable nature! Open your arms to the werman of Harlobe, they mean you no harm! They wish only to continue the line of their people, of our people!"

Screams of approval and howls of ecstasy filled the looming night.

"In a most perfect of worlds, every woman and Werman might be lucky enough to find and elope with one whom they find to be most exceptional, and all would be happy in their monogamous dealings, peaceful in their simplicity. But that world is not upon us, and many of us are ugly. Many of us are of ill proportion, with stammering lips and dimmed wits. Do not condemn us to a life of loneliness based on these shortcomings. If you do, we will find ourselves dead as a nation within the century."

And here he flung out a vast proclamation on a wide scroll, the parchment of which rolled off the stage, letting it be known to all that this was not merely a speech of passions, but rather a calculated introduction to a very real decree that would dominate lives in Harlobe for quite some time.

"To correct this sinking course, the Url Skulfing has proclaimed that a DEED OF PASS— to be lawfully

19

obtained in our courts— now be required, in order to decline an invitation to intercourse."

Gasping sharp inhales filled the silence.

"No longer, women. Will you be able to dance about like happy deer in playful woods, evading bowmen as they long to puncture you. When those bowmen come, you will now act as my mother and her mother before, reaching up into the latter times of our folk. Dignity will once again thrive. We will have children, and love. In our society, these will now find their place among us."

Already had various pockets of women begun to weave their ways out of the crowd. But Miekpanse riled the wermen.

"Boys of Harlobe, you all know of the fine wines you've harbored in your mind. For years you might have kept desires for those wines locked away, knowing yourselves to be less than exceptional in their eyes. But tomorrow, recommence your pursuits. Think of all the Urkas and Kambars that denied your advances; they will do so no longer. For now it will be against the will of Url Skulfing. Now it will be against the will of Lady Law and Old Order. So go out to them. Go up to the doors of a Loddy or Nola, go seek out an Urmi or a Kwalska in a tavern! And if it does not come to violence, then propose to them a child. If all of you do this, if all of you mate— then in no time at all we will become a Lobe worthy of name once more. Though we have always been, and always shall be, exceptional."

As this marked the end of the proclamation, so it will mark the end of my prologue.

PART I (JUAN)

FOUNDATIONS OF GOODNESS

Chapter I
The Rape of Dingle

Now at last we come to Piss Dingle, the Younger, as he was in the year 3333, at the age of 24.

Concerning his appearance, he held a passive stance with a passive Mahogany face, with his lips and cheeks his most expressive parts, never failing to express the true nature of his countenance. The brows of his eyes, too, would often rise in accordance with his feelings. He was an expert in Corn Fashion, wearing shirts of woven multi-colored maize, though this sadly went unappreciated and in some cases altogether unnoticed by the folk of the Harlobe, who had no cultural inklings towards Corn Fashion whatsoever.

In the warming days of Sexarion, when for the first time that year the nights did not bring a chill, and when at last the trees were fully clothed in green, Piss Dingle stood in the stream. The Stream of Tugpikkle, we may call it, for the stream had no name, nor any use for name, for the quaint town of Tugpikkle had but one. There would be no confusing it with another stream.

There, Piss Dingle dealt with Bare Cod for a living. Now, to those unfamiliar with the town of Tugpikkle, which surely accounts for the vast number of my readers, I will sprinkle quick seeds of telling: many in Harlobe had never heard of Tugpikkle, for it was quite small, with short of a thousand souls, but those in the towns around its immediate perimeter knew it to be quite charming. And the thing that gave Tugpikkle its charm was that all the fish... there in the Stream... were all dressed up... as little men.

So the nature of Piss Dingle's occupation, then, was to go into the Stream and find all the bare and naked Cod, fish who had either escaped generations of diligent dressers or who had been born afresh and outside of the

Birthing Pools (where dressings were habitually performed before releasing the Cod into the Stream). Dingle then would keep keen eyes pointed down at the Stream, watching as hundreds of Cod dressed as little men would go swimming by, and every hour or so he might find one without clothes: a Bare Cod. And then he would put hands or devices into the Stream, and he would catch the fish, and proceed to dress them up as little men.

This was a dignified profession in the town of Tugpikkle. For those who dealt with the Bare Cod held up the very charm of the region; without ensuring that the Stream was filled with fully-clothed fish, the charm would be lost.

On this cool and pleasant morning, an emissary of Url Skulfing approached the Stream, where Piss Dingle stood among mild rock and rapid.

"What business do I see transpiring here?"

"Uh... it's my job to catch—" and here he attempted to snatch a naked fish, to no prevail. Then he gave up and gave the emissary his full attention. "It's my job to catch the naked fish and put them in cloth."

"And what is your name, good lad?"

"Piss Dingle."

"Yes," replied the royal emissary with a nod of the head. "That sounds like a name worthy of your task."

"Huh?"

For Piss Dingle always had a hard time hearing men over the sound of the rushing waters.

"I only said that what you're doing sounds like something that a Piss Dingle would do!"

"And who are you?"

"An anonymous royal emissary, in the employment of the grand Lobe Minister Url Skulfing."

Now Piss Dingle rose out of the stream, wiping his hands dry. He looked the emissary up and down, confused as to why he might have sought him out.

"What be lovely?"

"Many things be lovely, especially now that Miekpanse hath ordered the DECREE OF EASE. Now children will be here in these lands once again, and that will be lovely."

"I don't like kids," replied Piss Dingle, for he quite frankly did not.

"But this is a matter of security, of Lobian pride," continued the emissary of Skulfing. "And you have been summoned, by the one called Katario."

And suddenly Dingle's eyes grew large. He had known Katario, since early days of youth in the town of Murder Creek. She had followed him then, into his Tugpikkle days, always teasing and offering up hints of goodness. Finally after years did Dingle break down and see her to be adequate, and they walked together to a lovely bridge, under which freaks would blow on their pipes. But after some weeks of bridge-walking, Katario pulled back, departing swift and sprinting for great hills, leaving Dingle alone and wondering why she had even bothered to catch his affection in the first place.

Then passed many more years, and Katario returned, having found no great happiness in the hills and knowing only failure. She entreated for kind sentiment from Dingle. But at this time, Dingle recoiled, for Katario had grown far too large. He left her in much the same way as she had left him. And now, to his great surprise, a royal emissary brought back that name from out of shadow, slamming it into his face and washing all his features with it.

"You do know Katario, yes?"

"Yes. I know Katario," spoke Dingle, with as little enthusiasm as ever a man did have.

"She wishes for your goodness," smiled the emissary.

"She will not have my goodness. I'm holding onto my goodness til I come across the right lady. She is not the right lady."

And Piss Dingle started back into the stream—

"The time has come when men will not be so choosy in their affairs. It has been decreed! The Decree of Ease states that the desires of any suitor who approaches must be fulfilled. You must meet with this Katario, and you will then be at her mercy."

"That whale has no mercy."

But then a troop of SKULFERS appeared in the woods, on both sides of the Stream, come to take Dingle to his doom. Skulfers, of course, being the loyal forces of Url Skulfing who filled his Lobes with the authority needed to ensure law, order, and fearful loyalty. These patrollers of unrest were always upon their horses, and often times armed with long tubes, the nature of which was then unknown to all, for those who had briefly known the nature of the tubes now found themselves dead.

The Skulfers escorted Dingle to a small inn, where Katario waited with a shaking leg and hip-bound hands. She looked clearly upset with him, as though she had any reason to be, after ten years of absence following his desertion of her following her desertion of him.

"Dingle," spoke the condescending Katario.

"No," objected Dingle on the spot. "I will put no part in this."

"Oh but you must," went on Katario, looking more to the Skulfers than to Dingle. "For it is law now. For the preservation of our Lobe."

"If matches like you and I are to be upheld then the Lobe will rightfully burn. Can you imagine a child

25

born of our loins? The thing would be too hideous to behold."

Here the royal emissary whispered into the ear of Piss, "If she wishes to bed, you'll have no recourse."

"That's a load of Cod dropping. No-path can that be the rule of the land."

"It is the rule of Url Skulfing. It is the Decree of Ease, that all who wish to produce offspring will be permitted to do so with tremendous ease—"

"There is no tremendous ease with this woman! See her well as she stands! I could not find my way into her chambers, it would take weeks and even then quite frankly my life squirts are not strong enough to penetrate those halls. It would be a fruitless endeavor."

"All the same, Dingle, she desires your flesh."

"There's a way out of this. There has to be a way to avoid this evil fate."

And here stepped forward the smallest of the Skulfers present, a man of the book who sympathized with Dingle's plight.

"There is a way, dear Bare Cod dresser. There is a Deed of Pass, which may be obtained through the courts, and if you receive it within fourteen days of the request to make men, you will be allowed to decline the request."

"Great. I will take one Deed of Pass."

"You must apply in Sanklode."

"Sanklode?!" exclaimed Dingle, "That's all the way in Narlobe!"

"The Narlobe is near. That is why it is called Narlobe."

"Well I'd better leave now then! It'll take me nearly a week just to walk there."

"We will escort you."

Piss Dingle certainly had no wish to be carried over the border into Narlobe by the Skulfers, and so he asked several more questions until the optimal method of obtaining a Deed of Pass was revealed. He would dictate a formal plea to a scribe-boy, who would then pass the plea along to a ring of messengers, who would carry the plea to Sanklode, to be obtained and then ridden back to Tugpikkle. Dingle was assured that the circuit of riders took an average of two days to reach Sanklode, and then two days to return to Tugpikkle.

There would be no problems in obtaining a Deed of Pass then, thought Piss Dingle. And so he relaxed himself, and spent the next several days in the home of his grandmother— where he resided most often— making joy with puppies and puppets, both of which were abundantly deep. During those few days Dingle did not even think to dictate his plea to the local scribe-boy, for he had his grandmother's house all to himself upon his grandmother vacating to a mountain trip with fellow elders, and Dingle was nought to pass up time spent alone in a quiet, lovely house.

Four days had then passed, with ten left to obtain the Deed of Pass, when Dingle sauntered over to the local scribe-boy Scart Parter.

"What took you so long?" asked the boy called Scart. "You live just down the road but already you've diddled away four days in the allotted fourteen day period."

"Do you wish for my plea or not?" said an unamused Dingle, before listing all the reasons why he ought to be able to hold the right of denying Katario's demands. These reasons included but were not limited to her previous manipulations and transgressions, as well as her condition of being a wee bit massive. Scart Parter shook his head with wide eyes, but transcribed the plea all the same, wishing Piss luck in its acceptance and then passing it on to the Ring of Riders.

With haste a great messenger rode swift and out of sight, and Dingle opted to never think on the matter of Katario for the rest of the day. He strolled down to the Stream, and began searching for pure and naked Cod, as was his lot in life.

Did he aspire to more meaningful ends than the ones he found himself facing? Of course, but he didn't long dwell on these things in those times. Piss Dingle had come to accept his position as a Bare Cod Dresser in the quaint village of Tugpikkle, and he found a certain degree of happiness in its comfort. He had once dreamed of being a great hero of the stage, wherein he might be applauded in showhouses all round the bout for punching men who could take it, and performing ghastly rituals of mutilation within the bounds of acceptable practice, but these aspirations were at their end. He knew that all those who fought onstage were gifted the privilege by their predecessors who had also found a living fighting onstage, and there were few outsiders welcomed in.

Therefore he would be content to linger in that stagnant place. While he stood in the Stream looking down at fast moving currents, he knew that— unlike the currents— he would not be going anywhere. He longed to follow the Stream, to see where those waters led, but more than all he just wished for a life of comfort. And that he certainly had in Tugpikkle, and in the home of his mother's mother.

On the ninth day of the allotted fourteen day period to receive his Deed of Pass, a messenger returned to Tugpikkle from Sanklode. Dingle excused himself from his grandmother's table, to go out and meet the messenger, expecting to receive his Deed of Pass. But the messenger handed back the original plea, to the frustration of Piss.

"You forgot to sign the plea."

And so he had. But no matter, Dingle was not concerned. Still five days there were, and the Ring of Riders took only four days to make the circuit. That made for an entire day to spare. He signed the plea and sent the messenger back on his way.

Nonetheless, on the twelfth day Dingle began to feel a growing dread in his breast. On the thirteenth day, the dread moved to his loin. On the fourteenth day, still the Deed of Pass had not arrived. And now Katario planted herself outside Dingle's window, waiting for night to come, when she would have full right to force herself in and thrust Dingle upon her. Our protagonist did not wish to have his grandmother's home tainted by such vile fluids, and so he walked across town to the home of his father, Elder Piss. As he walked, Katario followed, pleading with him to penetrate her willingly.

"Katario, no. By an act of free will this will come about never. I don't pity you; you're the one who ran for the hills."

"Do you know what I endured by the sea? Do you know how I toiled away years of my life? My job was to pull the intestines out of living whales."

"Well that is awful. Really. But that does not give you the right to molest my body." And with that, Piss Dingle ran into the home of his father, seeking reprieve from the troubles of the outside world.

The troubles on the inside were not much better, for immediately upon entrance he was caught in the middle of one of his father's rants on the inferiority of the Paleskin man.

"There's rioting and looting!" he exclaimed, showing his son the scribbles of news that had come from the town of Rayce.

"Well, is rioting and looting so bad as murder? Because I heard that a Tanfolk lad in Rayce was killed."

"That's

29

"Well... it keeps happening. And there seems to be no effort to stop it."

"Url Skulfing is not the man who killed that Tanfolk— Flod, or whatever his name was."

"Well you're right. Skulfing did not kill Flod. Skulfing is the Lobe Minister, and performing outright murder would be about the only thing that would break his spell over his followers. But Skulfing has not condemned the killing of Flod."

A bit of context for this conversation: recently in the town of Rayce, a Paleskin by the name of Flod sat upon an idle carriage, blowing on his pope next to a lively market, merry with the joy of holiday. Rich Mahogany were always with keen eyes looking for suspicious behaviors of the Tanfolk and Paleskins of Rayce, often demanding punishment of light-skins for the same activities that a Mahog might enjoy freely and without reprimand.

On this particularly fateful day, a passing Mahog spotted a pile of clipped coins in the carriage upon which the Paleskin Flod sat, and took it upon his moral authority to inform a local Skulfer. The Skulfer, upon hearing that the accused was Paleskin, decided on his guilt in an instant, and gathered a force of three other Skulfers to apprehend the man called Flod. They gave him little chance to explain himself, and upon the first show of his resistance to their will, they brought him to his belly and crushed his neck with their knees, until his breathing stopped.

Off-put by his father, who saw more fault in those who protested the killing of Flod than the original sin of the killing of Flod itself, Dingle sought reprieve in the home of his mother. This was, as always, more than equally frustrating.

30

"What are you doing with your life?" was her immediate question most days upon seeing her son, who she felt should at all times be occupied in hard labors of toil, and whenever she her son not labored in hard toil, she criticized him. "Time to figure out what you want to do with your life," she would say every time she saw the boy taking a sit.

"I have a task, Mother! You know this! I am the Dresser of the Bare Cod. It's a dignified thing— well, around here anyway.

Simply seeing his mother was always enough to make Dingle's blood haste rise, and he questioned why he had come. Peering outside, he remembered he had come because he needed only a place within doors to hide, for Katario owned the streets, and the Skulfers strode by her, waiting eagerly to apprehend Dingle and oversee the commencement of forced love.

Mother Dingle asked what Piss was so shaken over, and he replied in a weak voice—

"There's a woman who wants to make men with me tonight."

"You should be happy," was his mother's response to the rape on his horizon. "It's a long, lonely life ahead of you. Are you ever gonna bring a girl to wife?"

"Yes Mother, you make it sound so easy, I know you were wedded three times over by the time you were my age but I'm not like you. I'm not... appealing to those who—"

"Have you even been trying? To meet someone?"

Indeed Dingle had been trying, but that is a tale for another time, and we will not even begin to delve into petty romantic affairs, for this is a chronicle of war between societal ideals, and above the simple workings of the plagued minds in those like Mother Dingle. No matter, the conquest of passion was not the issue at the forefront of this night. The issue at the forefront of this

31

night was simply to receive his Deed of Pass, so that he might not be made a conquest by the lust of Katario, who sought to pummel his loins with her round thighs and fist.

      The Deed of Pass had not come.

      And so the hands of Piss were bound, and he was led into the stable where his body would be molested. I will not give details, but it came to pass.

      After being raped by Katario, Dingle went to the house of his Grandmother Dingle. There he held little hope of being cheered, but where else was he to go. It was better than wandering the streets of Tugpikkle or going back to the home of the Elder Piss, or of Mother Dingle. Compared to those routes, the home of his mother's mother was a roaring haven of peace.

      Indeed, any man less fortunate would find that place to be an indisputable paradise. At the door one was greeted straight away with the lovely sound of chimes, ringing gracefully and harmonious in the wind, but never to the point of annoyance. Upon the opening of the door — which itself was a cause for excitement, for its glass was of great color and a radial design, crafted by the finest of smiths— one found a tall and open space, stretching back a greater distance than most men held in the whole of their homes in those days. The roof was high and vaulted, high enough that three men could stand upon shoulders and only then touch it, and slanted up towards a sharp peak in the center of the space. Also worthy of mention was the fact that this roof was of a consistent plaster, not the type of rotting and crumbling wood that one would find in the shacks of all Tanfolk or Paleskins throughout the land.

      Also, the spoons were laced with gold.

Dingle had hoped for some time alone in that temple of a home, to reflect on his molestation, but solitude was hard to come by in those days. Dingle's Grandmother was fine company, and vastly superior to the generation she had given rise to, but every odd day she would say a thing equally as unsettling on the mind of Piss Dingle. Today she happened to be complaining of a young Tanfolk girl who had taken a few breaks from labor at the local tavern where they both worked.

"I guess those people don't have the best work ethic, is that what you'd say?"

"That is not what I'd say," said the young Dingle, quick to disassociate himself with such a silly phrase indicting an entire breed for the shortcomings of one individual.

"What would you say then? That those people are just up-down idle?"

"Well... you're talking about the actions of one girl. A young girl at that. There are other Tanfolk people in the world besides this one young idle girl. So why bring all of them into your judgment of work ethics?"

But his grandmother was not listening, for in that time little thought did she put into the things she said, and even less thought into the things she heard. Young Piss Dingle too moved on from it, for it was not the worst thing to be said, and a thing so in line with the thinking of all the Mahogs in Harlobe. To the Rich Mahogany men in those lands, the Tanfolk were seen as acceptable but inferior, which was a better lot than the Paleskins, who were outright despised. And this was the nature of those days.

The nature of these present days are much the same, despite what anyone might say, though the changing wind has certainly come. It started with a soft breeze, and has since grown into the kind of swift gale that will push you back if you walk against it, and try it will to pluck the hat from your head if you don't hold it down.

We will speak now of the initial wind, the soft breeze as it were that started to pick up around that year 3333, started by many but formally recognized as a movement when it was championed by the Honorable Piss Lip of Tree City beyond Cumpear.

But before we tell of him, we must speak of his opponent and the downfall of all that was right and honest in our lands— that tall and powerful freak reigning from the Fortress of Essen, Lobe Minister Skulfing.

Chapter II
Url Skulfing

There are many things to be said of the Lobe Minister Url Skulfing. None concerning either his character or countenance could be considered less than heinous. But let us start with his surprising appearance, so that we might be able to visualize him in flesh before delving upon his deeds.

The first thing that one might notice about the Url Skulfing was the fact that he was impossibly thin. At his narrowest point, one might form a circumference with just two hands around, and to make this picture even more horrifying, he was also quite tall. And so if one did manage to get close enough to Skulfing to place hands about his waist, a long and narrow head would be looming above, held aloft by such a disproportioned stem that all commented daily on the great wonder that his body did not simply snap in half when he bent. Indeed, the mid-section of his frame was so compact that one could hardly imagine there being enough space to fit any one of the essential bodily organs, let alone all of which he surely must have had. The apparent smallness of his inners, then, raised the constant question as to whether Url Skulfing was truly a werman, or if he was some creature of ghastly design sent from deep in the other world.

Despite being comically thin, the shoulders of Skulfing were quite broad. Of course no one ever saw his shoulders— except Piss Dingle and perhaps some others who did not live to recount the experience, as we will come to see by the end of this tale— for Url Skulfing's shoulders were at all times covered by thick pads of royal violet, or as some might say, "purple."

And he had a fake chin that was so obviously fake as to make all the people in the entire world question to what avail his fake chin was held.

But perhaps the most revolting of his physical attributes was that this creature of alien design had legs which seeped an ice cold fluid, blue to the eye and glowing in dark places. Strange.

Now onto the character of Skulfing, which was quite frankly even worse. All of his character was worse, all his person vile and even evil when held to common terms. Yet I should not play with such words of insult, true as they may be. For it has been to my side's detriment, to attempt to expose Skulfing for nothing more than what he is. In using harsh words against him, it only proves to further strengthen the resolve of his supporters who worship him.

For the greatest quality which Url Skulfing undoubtedly had was the power to tickle men (approximately one out of every two) into an enamored state of adoration. If he had not obtained such a cult of loyal servants, we would not today be speaking of him. He would only be a side mention, a fool in the body of a farce, for who else upon this world seeps ice cold fluid from their loins? This would be the main talking point in his life if he had only existed as a vile praiser of hate and corruption, dreamer of praise of power. But this is not the case. He did amass great swarms of very real following, and has thus come to be a strong wave in the course of our histories.

Not all men, of course, fell victim to the admiration of his courts, but those whom he fingered with rash appeal could never be pulled from his side. Those would do unending service, even after Url Skulfing cast them apart and provided no further incentive for their loyalty. Still they would serve him with an unbreakable fealty, granting unto the tall and thin beast with legs of seeping fluid lavish gifts and glory.

I will tell a quick tale to confirm my prior passage in gruesome detail:

In the Narlobe, smallest of the Lobes but home to its administrative capital in Essen, there was a table of round demeanor, the "Rounded Table" of great renown, famous all the world over. Famous for its bold ideology that any who sat at such a table would be of equal standing, that all who graced the Rounded Table were of one sacred body.

It was this Rounded Table, which Skulfing made to be squared.

When he first laid ass upon his seat, he made calculated and conscious action to place a boar's head in front of him, so there could be no dispute that he was seated at the head of the table. And then he ordered his Skulfers to make immediate preparations for this ancient table to be carved so that his seat would bulge out ahead from the lower sphere.

"But the point of this Rounded Table is that there is no head," spoke Fendyrd, most loyal and beloved of all Skulfing advisors, he who had lost limb and lung performing physical combat on multiple occasions for the right of his lord to carry off daughters and turn them to whores.

Url Skulfing protested, with a silent shake of the head. Fendyrd continued, "My Lord, this is a most ancient table. It has come from the Mother Nation of Hayaman itself, and has been here since the very day those armies overtook Essen, and began the spread of the Lobes."

Url Skulfing did not care for history. He did not appreciate tale, or legend, nor Passian dignity.

Fendyrd had his bowels torn out, a clean cut across the waist by PARPINFOHZ, styled as that great King DANE of Angelon in that all his letters were tall.

PARPINFOHZ, lanky pole of a servant as he was, slid upon the floor, putting his hands up to Fendyrd's gut and beginning to pull, as one might milk a cow. Slowly yet smoothly did Fendyrd's shimmering bowels slide, and PARPINFOHZ gave him a moment of reprieve, so that he might speak while his bowels were squeezed by one who enjoyed the feel of them.

"Highest Lord," gasped Fendyrd, "Have I not been in the company of your Deeplove for longer than any in this room? Have I not endured combat and disgrace for your triumphs? Have I not traveled through wind and rain without rest to carry forth your designs? You should be licking through stone for me after all that I have done, yet here you are, demanding your boy PARPINFOHZ to play with my inners!"

"I will find one to do my will without question," was Skulfing's response, so content to disgrace and murder one who he indeed should have been licking through stone for. PARPINFOHZ milked all of Fendyrd's bowels, before the Rounded Table that was soon to be squared, and a Tanfolk from Westlobe called Huivz was summoned swiftly to replace Fendyrd.

Some might think it odd that a Tanfolk would be admitted as one of Skulfing's higher-ups when the entire point of his administration was to rebuild a dominant Mahogany Supremacy. But, you see, Tanfolk are in the supremacy of the Westlobe, and since Huivz was a Tanfolk of Westlobe origin, his supremacy was easily translated across Lobian borders.

In the time of our tale, the greatest schism in the Lobes of Hakamena was between those who had

38

Deeplove for Skulfing and those who were given an even deeper sense of dread and gross feeling by his approach. In those days, the number of his Deeplove was high, and we on the side of his Opposition were only slightly lowered. But the sound of his Deeplove was uproarious, and they were louder than the fierce winds, and so it seemed as though all the world was in Skulfing's Deeplove, while only a mere seeming pocket of sanity remained in us who resented him. So while the number of Skulfing's Deeplove and we in their Opposition was nearly identical, the Deeplove of Skulfing managed to make the numbers seem much greater apart, and as though they were the overwhelming majority of Lobian men.

I have laid the basic picture of this schism, but now must begin to pour evidence on my claims, as to why I and many others hold Url Skulfing in such disdain. It begins, naturally, which his rise to recognition as a leader of the Lobes, in the year 3327. This was a year for the CHOOSING OF THE REIGN, an evolutionary new phenomenon which was fairly new to the Lobes, and was wholly unheard of in large kingdoms such as Ilandia. There, and in most other lands of Elaptirius, power was established and passed from generation to generation within the same line.

In the Lobes of Hakamena, however, the bold offspring of the Kingdom of Hayaman chose to administer their governance quite differently. Every third year, the Leader of the Lobes was held to the judgmental eyes of the people, and if he did not pass their test, he was cast down, not into hell but into the comfort of a normal life.

A new Minister was then chosen by the Choosers, who were chosen by common folk. In such a way, the Lobe Minister was chosen indirectly by the citizens of the land, and the citizens called this "good enough," for it was a compromise by the great mobs of peasants— who wanted to hold direct choosings of the Lobe Ministers— and the delegates of Hayaman, who would have preferred to be in complete control of who would administer the Lobes.

In the year 3327, Lobe Minister Miet-Boosh Markeyn was held to the aforementioned eyes of the judgmental Lobefolk. Now Miet-Boosh was not remarkable as a Minister. But as least he was one. At least he did the job. And during his nine years as Minister he preserved a sense of peace and dignity in his Lobes.

Yes, there was well warrant for criticism. Miet-Boosh had performed costly campaigns of conquests to the north, held small traders with a touch of contempt while gifting advantage to their worldly superiors, and held forty wives in his chambers, which many considered a gush of lustful excess.

But, to counter those criticisms, with his wars Miet-Boosh was following the age-old custom of conquest that had never been strayed from. In favoring worldly traders over those stationed in localities, he too was merely adhering to the norm of societal conventions. And at least his forty wives were all wedded to him by consent. They sought out his chambers. And all the while, Miet-Boosh held the Lobes in a state of prosperity, a land of neighbors friendly towards all— even Rich Mahogany toward Paleskin, for Miet-Boosh was of the mind that outright prejudice was most undignified— and an ongoing state of peace.

All that Url Skulfing would provide during his tenure was a farce of Peace Dangle. He swore in 3327, year of his rising, to strive hard for the greatest Peace that was ever known west of the Sashites. He swore to do away with all the ill practice of "dirty" men like Miet-Boosh and his lot, in turn restoring the Lobes to an ill-defined state of former greatness, that had apparently been achieved at some distant point in the past but now lay dead under the stench of progress.

But of a much more key note, Url Skulfing swore to uphold more than all else the dominance of Rich Mahogany Supremacy. To those rich and of Mahogany flesh in those lobes— Harlobe, Narlobe, and Farlobe— Skulfing spoke in full force, appealing to their buried desire for the Tanfolk and Paleskins to be put back in their place.

For many of the Mahogany, hatred had not come into mind. Very few of them hated anyone, as the far-Opposition would come to claim. Rather, the vast majority of the high Mahogany breed in those Lobes were simply grown tired of too much progress at once— albeit spread over the length of a generation— and were sick of the swift change in their society. Perhaps they did not hate the light-skinned breeds, but they hated how they themselves had been robbed of their place above them in standing. Just forty years prior the institution of slavery had ended, and the Rich Mahogany had lost their place as physical masters. Skulfing sensed this vulnerability and fear of the loss of supremacy among the Lobians.

He was wise in the ways of deviance, for he gathered his support by masking his own shortcomings and accusing others of those same shortcomings. Skulfing had displayed all the corruption and lies of Miet-Boosh and more, but by accusing his adversaries of even greater corruption and lies, Skulfing was able to make half the people miraculously forget that he was a culprit of the things he denounced. The common rule that one should not denounce others for a thing which he himself partakes in most vigorously... apparently did not apply to Skulfing in the eyes of his Deeplove, who either did not believe the report of Skulfing's crimes, or did not care.

Of his many rivals, Skulfing said they were all too rich to have any real care for the struggling peasants of the Lobes. He, on the other hand, would "moisten the dry land." He could be trusted to hold the interest of all peasants, so he said, for he was one of them.

And all the world could clearly see he was not.

It was to be seen by any who had half a working eye, for Skulfing arrived to his platforms in silver robes at the head of massive processions, with up to eighty women ever changing— twice the number as Miet-Boosh ever held in his private chambers. Even if one had never heard the rumors of Url Skulfing's descent from above, they could clearly see that he had a suspiciously large amount of wealth. On such rumors of his origins we will now speak.

The rumors told of how he had arrived on Overlind, from a cold void in the stars, landing upon the hill of Kuntrif Mar around the year 3300 in a fallen egg, covered all in gold plating. His egg was lined with blazing red strips of metal, that came and went as a heartbeat. He was first witnessed to emerge in his full grown state, by goat herders who shortly thereafter went blind. A great fortress was built up on that spot, with alarming speed, and was completed in 3314, the same year that Url Skulfing's name began to spread across the Lobes as one who could share secrets of fire and flame, and this enterprise made him presumably even more vastly wealthy than he was when he supposedly landed upon Farlobe in a gold-laden egg.

Of course, then, Url Skulfing was not truly of the interest in bringing wealth or any kind of prosperity to his Lobes at large. In actuality he sought the powers that the Minister held, so that he could better go about increasing his own vast wealth that he had stored across the lands, wealth that was already several times more numerous than the wealth of entire villages.

This being considered, one might assume that the people of the lobes might come to view Skulfing as something of an enemy, or at least come to terms with the truth that his interests and their were not at all the same. But indeed, even if the people of Hayaman's lobes had come to this realization, still many of them would not have relinquished their support of Url Skulfing. For it was in his great charisma— not a kind or enthusiastic charisma, rather a relentless energy of stern and high-chested anger— that Skulfing forged great ranks of followers known as the Deeplove.

He knew that his followers would never turn against him in earnest, but to be extra cautious, and to garner a larger allegiance at the same time, Skulfing diverted all mention of his own affairs and spoke only on the suspicious affairs of Tanfolk and Paleskins. All attention was put to those outside breeds, which were both very much present in the Lobes but not to the extent of the Rich Mahogany (in actuality, the number of Paleskins and Tanfolk together numbered about half of the Mahogany population, but all manners of state and cultural significance were carried out chiefly by Mahogs, giving the impression of a far greater Mahogany presence).

"They are thieves, molesters, burdenous. While some, I assume, are not deserving of nine arrows in the back... all of them are, however, deserving of at least five."

And his supporters would laugh.

Such was the standard rhetoric that would spew from the mouth resting between the broad violet shoulder cuffs, always keeping the eyes far away from his own private dealings, always keeping them on the smaller criminal affairs of individuals from a different breed, and those singular affairs would come to define the breeds of Paleskin and Tanfolk in the mind of the Rich Mahogany.

In this way, Url Skulfing brought together the Mahogany people of his lobes in a mutual aversion for the other breeds living within their lands, and this is where their eyes rested. In this time, a man of Mahogany complexion might go about wrongdoings most easily, for the sheriffs were not watching closely in their direction. But Tanfolk deeds would not pass by without the highest discretion, and indeed the smallest offense for them was caught and taken into the courts, to be punished to the highest extent of the law.

Speaking of law, it was laughable in the time of Skulfing. Laughable, at first, when one considers the absurdity of it. But then sorrowful, and only inspiring laughter in the most evil of men, when one considers the impact on actual lives that these times held.

It was said that in the interest of protecting the good Mahogany peoples from the raging wickedness of Tanfolk and Paleskin, Url Skulfing brought in his own regime of mercenaries, to police all towns and roads. These were the Skulfers, and they operated in a manner of high prejudice and thought not of justice, at least not in the way that it is defined by the greater part of the world.

For justice to the Skulfers did not mean that a wrong is atoned for in an agreed-upon manner, and then set as a standard for like wrongs. Rather, to the Skulfers, a wrong committed by the Mahogany was to be forgiven, whereas a like wrong committed by either Paleskin or Tanfolk was to be punished heinously (mildly heinous for Tanfolk, devilishly heinous for a Paleskin).

To give a concrete example, we will speak on the flowery Cudnut leaf. Surely I need not explain to most of my readers, but for the straight and naive of you, I will spell it out. Grind the Cudnut leaf, and light it ablaze— inhale this and you will go lovely in all ways. In the dark ages of wood and cave, people would use the Cudnut leaf at all hours without thought, but in more modern times societies have grown away from its use. In the Golden Age, now marked 600 years ago, before Feenisall of Doncrethi ripped down the shining towers and doomed us all to lives of darkness, use of the Cudnut had actually been done away with fully as far as we can know. It is largely frowned upon as uncivilized today, yet many men (almost all, in fact) of the Mahogany breed will make use of the Cudnut, and there is no outright condemnation for it.

Skulfers would come across Rich Mahogany wermen, women, children with a full pipe of Cudnut— all the same, the Skulfers would look the other way. But in the presence of Tanfolk they would scour, noses large and eyes peeled sharp, for if they saw— or even caught word— of a Tanfolk with a drop of Cudnut, they would bring said man in for many nights spent in cages. There was no question of it. They said they were only upholding Old Order, that any man found with Cudnut be placed in cages so that they might out-root the evil from within. Of course, these Laws of Cudnut were really only applicable to Tanfolk, and for no good reason other than pomp of the victor.

And to Paleskins, the crime of Cudnut bore an even worse fate. These unfortunate Paleskins would have their skulls opened up delicately, their brains then to be poked and scratched, with scalpels and knives, in an attempt to regain the knowings that were lost in the late hours of the 27th century.

In the past decades, nothing had really been learnt from opening the skull of a Paleskin. Yet the Patrols loved doing it; it kept them amused, and gave them an otherworldly sense of godlike authority, to be

45

able to penetrate and annihilate a man's mind completely with just a few lingering taps of the finger, or a brash fall of the hammer. When the standard Patrols were integrated with the new Lobe Minister's Skulfers in the year 3327, these skull openings became more numerous, like a drug to the Skulfers, to the point where a Paleskin would flee for the woods upon the very approach of a Skulfer, for fear of a naked head, even if no wrong had been done.

Yes, it is strange indeed how such a murderous self-righteous regime came to be uplifted among the Lobians. They themselves were an alien breed in that land, with an alien ruler of their choosing, but still they voiced evermore on their hatred of aliens. Skulfing knew that the people of Narlobe, Harlobe, and Farlobe were not as sharp-witted as they thought themselves to be. He knew that their attentions could be easily diverted, and so he consistently diverted all their attentions to the Tanfolk and the Paleskin, even though his own crimes far outweighed the entire register of wrongdoing committed by either breed.

Remember, though, that a great deal of us did hold a heavy disdain for Skulfing, and opposition grew increasingly throughout the first six years of his reign. Fair men of great deeds and spirit rose up to counter the tall beast, which only served to anger his heinousness. For all that appeared fairer than he, he sought to do away with completely.

Concerning those he sought to do away with completely, we cannot help but think to include the Company of Sound Judgment. These were a group of Lobe Counselors that stood firm in the face of Skulfing, always touring about the land despite the danger it entailed, and always brave in criticizing the vile man even as Skulfers stood near.

I have gone to the length of gathering some of their words, so that you might hear from them, contemporary words from the wise men of Sound Judgment who spoke truth in those dark times.

In the words of Inder Sohn:

"How much longer are we as a Lobe-land doomed to follow this giant blue twig-man? I'm sorry. That's not — that's not a valid criticism. I shouldn't attack his appearance— although he attacks the appearance of others— and it's not fair to the other men of our lands who are incredibly tall with blue skin. Which there are none. But I'll move on: what are valid criticisms of this Lobe Minister are his consistent calls for the spread of hate and violence.

Now you might say to me, 'Inder Sohn, I don't see the Minister actively doing this things. I don't see him going from town to town, attacking Tanfolk or Paleskin, or telling others to go out and do so.' But it's what he's not doing here that speaks the loudest.

Instead of denouncing these acts of cruelty, he seems to be supporting them. When Skulfers executed a string of Tanfolk men without judicial process last month, Minister Skulfing did nothing to condemn this. To the contrary, when pressed to react, Minister Skulfing said they were the 'finest of stock.' And he was referring to the men who murdered the Tanfolk. Tanfolk who had committed the most petty of crime, if any crime at all. When asked to respond to the killing of the Tanfolk, Skulfing said nothing."

Now from the tongue of Jic Topper, on the eve of 3330's Choosing of Reign:

47

"Here we are, not even a day after the casting of ballots, and I have news from the capital of Essen: the Lobe Minister, saying... that he— won? He did not win. I would just like to make that clear. Because we are still tallying the results. I cannot fathom why the Minister would claim this— well, I can fathom perfectly why— but will anyone believe him?

Again, I know the answer to this, perhaps the question I should ask is if anyone should believe him. After all, this is a man who has spent his three years as Minister lying on a six-times-per-hour basis. Perhaps he is now— prematurely, mind you— declaring victory because he sees no clear way of legitimately obtaining that victory? Perhaps he believes that— by saying he won— his Deeplove will believe Him and hence do anything to make sure he does win, even if he has not been chosen by the will of the Lobians.

Whatever the result of this Choosing, needless to say this is a disturbing move by Minister Skulfing, one that may end up leading to a loss of faith in the way these Lobes conduct public Choosings. May he burn in Hell."

And here he gave his podium to Kang Joon, hard at work tallying a town's worth of votes, who could only be bothered to give a quick "We're not done here."

And now from the mouth of Dunly Moan:
"I don't... understand. I don't... see why these men continue to follow him.

Year after year, he shows his hand. Year after year, he shows... that his supporters are disposable. To them I say: do you think he actually cares about you, or your best interest? No. This is the same man who swore to fight for the wealth of miners and tenders and keepers, all across these Lobes, then turned around and taxed

48

them double while handing out privileges to local lords. This is the same man who rewarded his most loyal followers— Fendyrd and Poomp Yu— with positions at his Squared Rounded Table, only to replace them both with Grandbor and Huivz as soon as they dared to question his methods. Fendyrd was even disemboweled.

Mm-hm. Yeah. How's that for compensation.

This is the same man who, a night before his election three years ago, endeavored to beat a man senseless, in front of an intoxicated crowd. But the crowd didn't care. In fact, they loved it. And those are the people we're dealing with.

The people who... despite knowing that Url Skulfing has lost... will continue to say he won. That Burden lost. Even though we all know Burden won. Won by the same margin that Skulfing beat Miet-Boosh by three years ago. Skulfing called that victory a landslide. But now— now that he appears to be losing— he goes ahead and tries to take the Lobes down with him.

He's so small. He's just... so, so small. And I say that not in a way to diminish his physical stature, which is absurdly large."

And after hearing these words spoken against him, Skulfing declared war on the likes of Sohn, Topper, and Moan— of this, we will be reminded in a later chapter, when these brave counselors of the realm will once again come into play.

It was now a warm evening in the month of Sevallia, and Url Skulfing sat at his desk with his customary number of cups— always five, and filled as such: the first with water, one with milk, one with ale, one of a sweet and surprising juice, and the last of literal flame. And as the heinous Lobe Minister took turns with a sip from each cup, he bathed in boiling mud, reading chronicles of far distant lands, chronicles that spoke of an elusive, threatening force— not posed by an army, or even that which could be seen.

The threat was that of the Crown Sickness. And the more Url Skulfing heard of this Sickness, the more he smirked in silence.

Chapter III
The Dark Wiggles

It was known as the Crown Sickness to knowledgeable ears. But as it slithered from its starting place in the deep of Ilandia, this quiet plague took on a new name, one indicative of its most obvious symptom: the uncontrollable spasms of the genitalia. In addition to spasms, the Crown Sickness sometimes caused an itchy groin, or death.

There was no remedy for this curious phenomenon, and indeed all the ministers and clerks of the land could see only one sound precaution: to wear a simple cloth over one's genitals, for it was from the genitals that the infectious vapors emerged, and in the genitals that the infectious vapors took hold.

By the High of Wethember in 3333 this regrettable misfortune had reached Harlobe, and the reactions varied from the frantic to the incredibly calm. Piss Dingle, as in all things, held his everlasting calm. He would hold his guard and keep his eyes diligent, regarding all developments in the understanding of the Crown Sickness and how society around him would deal with its coming.

Mother Dingle, however, would listen to no voice except her own on the issue. She had become a lover of health and longevity in recent years, in light of losing her father to a devastating illness. And so she had come to believe over the course of the last four summers that she was more adept in the ways of healing, and she had more than a few words for the encroaching of the Crown Sickness.

She did not believe it was real. She found the tellings of thousands dead to be unfounded, and a lie spread by devious spreaders of misfortune.

What follows is an egregious conversation taken from real life, between Piss Dingle and his mother, reconstructed by the best efforts of his memory. It is a sad thing to know this talk was held in earnest, but let us try to laugh and find some joy in the lopsided scale of wits which the Passian race often times displays:

"What's really going on here?" asked Mother Dingle to her son on a lovely Nanethis day, for she expected that all the Crown Sickness— should she decide it to be real— had been concocted as a conspiring of evil forces. And if, as she foremost expected, the Sickness was simply a nonexistent fiction that was spreading near and far, she expected that to be a conspiring too.

"What do you mean Mother?" asked Piss Dingle.

"I mean what's really going on here. Why are they telling us people are getting sick?"

"I suppose because people really are getting sick."

"Then who's behind it?"

"The... same forces that have made men sick for centuries."

"Then why is this such a big deal?"

"Because it's come up out of nowhere and we haven't an idea for the remedy, and it's taking a surprisingly deep number of lives."

"Bears have taken more lives. Why aren't we doing something about bears?"

"Well, we did. That was already taken care of many ages ago. For the most part they've been herded over the Urf into the Bear Stretch, so there are very few bear assaults now."

"But they still happen. Why doesn't everybody get worked up about that?"

"Because there's about six a year. And if one does get killed by a bear, the town certainly does react.

52

Twenty folk rise up from the village and don't rest until the bear is skinned and danced upon in the square. Anyway, you're welcome to go out and help the bear crisis if you'd like. But while you're at it, you might consider putting a cloth on your crotch when you're near folk because it's quite a simple thing to do and it can prevent something very nasty from happening. Why don't you wear the cloth?"

And once again, a topic all at once random and unrelated was brought up by Mother Dingle. "Do you know how many starving children there are in the world?"

And Dingle hesitated, trying to see if there was any path in her line of thought. Indeed she had not answered his question. So he put to her a new one: "And what are you doing for the starving children then?"

But Mother Dingle did not answer this— "I went to the market today with a free crotch, just as I always do. Just as we're intended to."

"Do you get looks from the people at the market who are doing the decent thing what they've been told to do?"

"I don't know. I don't look at people."

"You don't look at your fellow man?"

"They're all wearing crotch cloth."

"All except for you, yes."

"Why would I look at someone with a cloth on their crotch?"

"Why wouldn't you? They're the ones doing the right thing."

"It doesn't help!"

"How would you know that?! How many studies have you conducted?"

"Why would it help? How is wearing a cloth on your crotch going to help anything?"

53

"Because the Crown Sickness is driven by sudden ejaculations; it infects people through the crotch. How, then, would covering your crotch not help?"

"Because it's not actually happening."

"Just because you don't know anyone affected doesn't mean it's not affecting people."

"But why would you assume it's affecting people if you don't see it happening?"

"Because I've heard it's happening. People talk. They spread knowledge and news—"

"Yeah. The people spreading the news are the ones who want us to panic."

"Why would they want that? If there wasn't reason for concern—"

"Because the doctors and medicine men are the ones behind this. They're giving us the Sickness."

"Why would medicine men want to make folk of their nation sick?"

"Because the world is sick. Men are twisted."

"Not four minutes ago you were singing a song about how you believe that there's goodness in everyone —"

"There is."

"Then why would doctors— people who have devoted their entire lives to the study of helping people — go large and beyond to make people sick, and in some cases kill people?"

"Where else would this have come from?"

"I'm sure there's a much simpler, natural explanation. So, since you're asking these questions, you've accepted that the Crown Sickness is real then?"

"If it's real it's because the doctors want to kill us."

"Well, Mother, I say again— you don't actually believe people are good if you believe that medicine men are the ones behind the thing that is killing many, many people."

"It's hardly anyone."

"Hardly anyone that's dying? The numbers rank over ten thousand in our towns alone."

"But that's hardly anything compared to the amount of people there are."

"Why would you compare it to the total count? Why would you compare anything to the total count of anything? Why must it be a comparison? Suddenly ten thousand dead doesn't matter to you because it's not half of all the people living on this earth?"

"Well people die from so many other things— more people die of other things than those who die of the Dick Wiggles! Why should we have to sacrifice now when we never had to sacrifice for dying people before?"

"It's hardly a sacrifice! It's putting a strip of cloth on over your cunt."

"And why do we do that?"

"We've been over this."

"So what if we get it. All that's gonna happen is a little tickle."

"No but that's the point— most likely nothing all that bad would happen to us. But these precautions are not about us, it's about protecting the odd amount who would succumb to such a thing as this."

"Then it's their fault for not taking good care of themselves."

"So people deserve to die if they're not healthy? If their bodies aren't well-equipped enough to fight off this Crown Sickness? Is that how you felt about your father when he died? That he deserved to die because he was an unhealthy man?"

"He wouldn't have died from this."

"Sure. But why do you still lament in sorrow over losing him? His life numbered one. He was one life. And you yourself just said that ten thousand lives is nothing."

"The people are dying from other things. It's not the Dick Wiggles."

"The Crown Sickness is a facilitator. It weakens the body and allows other things in, so really it is the true killer. And of course it happens often enough— the genitals go black, really, really, pitch black— and then they crack, and crumble... turn to dust. And the whole patch just falls off, exposing the lower entrails."

"That doesn't happen."

"It does though. There'd be no reason for men to make up such a gruesome detail. And is not wearing a simple strip of cloth around your waist a fair price for possibly preventing someone around you from receiving that evil fate?"

"I will never wear a cloth over my crotch."

"Not even to save a life?"

"I don't have it. I won't get it. It's not coming here, you are freaked for nothing."

"It's already here, Mother. I'm not freaked, but it is here. It's in the Stream— men I have worked with in close quarters have had it. We probably have it right now."

"I will never wear a cloth over my crotch."

A long, defeated exhale from Piss Dingle... he knew this argument was futile, and so he resigned the fight with one last piece of knowledge.

"Ya know, Mother, covering those parts is not unheard of. Those who practice safe concern for others in these lands are not the first to cover the front of their loins. Some 700 years ago, before the time of Fingerlobe... it was absurd NOT to cover your dick. It was unheard of not to conceal your vagina. When Fingoy laf Turope Phertes came down out of Fart Funger, he

56

looked ridiculous, wearing pants with a hole in the middle to let his flip hang free. All those around him concealed their flips. But things change. Fingerlobe became a legend, and men began to dangle free in his honor. But now it's time we go back. Maybe not forever, but at least until this Sickness departs. You are very selfish indeed if you will not change a mere portion of your mode of dress in order to care for those around you."

"I do care for those around me."

"Then why do you not care if they get a terrible ailment?"

"Because ailment is a part of life."

"It doesn't have to be. You can wear the cloth."

"I will never wear a cloth on my crotch."

Still more and more knowledge of this bizarre plague would roll in, more and more findings, but still firmly planted was Mother Dingle in her view, and never would she falter from it. She couldn't, she had planted herself too deep in that plot. And her son returned home from the Stream one day, very frustrated indeed.

"Mother. For twelve hours straight I am forced to wear a cloth over my crotch. In a stream of all places. Yet you cannot even do it for two mikkin minutes."

And he resigned himself to his chamber, where he spent much of his time in that month of Nanethis dreaming of a better time, a time in the future, when he might bed numerous women all within the frame of a few weeks.

But Mother Dingle would have none of this idleness, even after a full day of work in the Stream, and she let her son know—

"Perhaps you should focus less on your idle time," said she, though the 'perhaps' came across in a tone as to denote that it really had no place in the command.

And of course Piss Dingle shot back in anger for he was tired and desired nothing but rest, and of course Mother Dingle thereafter tried to erase that which she had said by simply asserting that it had not been said, but Piss Dingle knew better. This was the way of things in her house. It was likewise that things transpired in Skulfing's court: facts were dismissed in favor of whatever was felt in the moment. Memories were not kept, lessons were not learned. There was no true dialogue, only the resounding voice of Skulfing or, in this case, Mother Dingle.

And then, as happened many times before, Dingle resolved on a retreat to his grandmother's home — a home true and right— but thought he would add a graceful note of departure:

"I have followed your every command thus heartily up til now, Mother, but this I will not do. I will not rid myself of my idle time while I continue to labor in the Stream. If my idle time must go, soon too will I."

And he thought that a winning time to take his leave, but his Mother continued on with the Crown Sickness—

"It's all a bunch of pump-loaded cock. When's it going to be over?"

"When they find out what they need to plug us with."

"Ha! Plugs. Severance. Clippings. Those things don't work! Why do they still cut off our tails when we're babies? How long has it been since tails gave us any problems!?"

"Well Mother, they no longer give us problems... because we sever them to make them less severe."

And this was true. The long-held tradition of severing side-tails at birth greatly diminished the chance of side-tails ever causing problems for the Passian race ever since. But Mother Dingle never took the time to correlate cause and effect; rather, she just cursed at folk any time she felt inconvenienced.

Grandma Dingle's home continued to prove a faithful refuge in those days, and there she spoke words of well comfort to the disheartened Piss.

"Your mother... doesn't know how to stop. She can't take any time off, not for herself, not for others— and if she sees you being idle, she doesn't know how else to respond. But you need that time, yes. You've been tasking along. And you'll continue to task. But it's important to relieve yourself.

"That's the one good thing they say that has come of this Dick Wiggle, that people have gone back to finding ways to relieve themselves. They've begun to remember things that are important in one's life... mainly living. And not being consumed by Sickness. The protection of others, so that others might not succumb to these Dick Wiggles. They've found that we do care about each other."

"Not in the case of my mother."

"Well, no. People react differently, to everything it seems, for whatever reason. I mean it's not so bad to wear a strip of cloth down there. I wouldn't want to do it all the time, but yes, for the sake of other people's health... I don't see why it's so hard for some. In time your mother may come to realize her foolishness, but then again she may not."

And Dingle laughed along with Grandma Dingle. He took it as a sign of goodness, for just recently he had remembered his grandmother to have been one of those who followed the mentality of her neighbors, whatever it may have been. She had bought into the discord sown against Tanfolk and Paleskin, and had chosen Url Skulfing in the 3327 Choosing and again in 3330.

But it was in the course of the 3330 Choosing, when it was clear that the Lobes had chosen Bahmoeth Burden and not Skulfing— when Skulfing fought the courts and ripped the choice of the people up from under them— that she began to turn from Skulfing. Edged on by a newfound love of peace, right, harmony, justice, sanity and sense, Grandma Dingle had taken new counsel with those of lovely relation, and thus opened her eyes to the demon that was Skulfing.

She now supported the one called Piss Lip, chosen by the Opposition to duel with wits for possession of the Lobes. But of course, everyone feared that even if Piss Lip was able to obtain victory over Skulfing, Skulfing would surely not admit defeat. And since he had already compromised the courts and stolen the Choosing three years prior from its rightful victor, what chance was there that Skulfing's reign would come to an end in that year, 3333?

Still, Dingle felt optimistic. If one as simple as his grandmother could have found enlightenment over the course of six years, then surely the sentiments of the greater Lobians were also being turned against the tall and powerful freak. Surely the Lobes would see goodness rise again.

If not, perhaps there was something he yet could do.

Chapter IV
Leg Randy and Piss Lip

Elsewhere and months ahead, off in the far land of the Farlobe, a man called Leg Randy was tall too. Tall and thin in the manner of PARPINFOHZ, with the same Rich Mahogany complexion, but far lacking in the freakly tallness of Url Skulfing.

This Leg Randy was known all about his town, a little town called Tree City, just beyond the reach of Cumpear, and south of the Titfall Dig. He was one of those folk who everyone knows, for everyone must know such a man, so that they might avoid him at all costs.

Yes, Leg Randy was one of those, who meant no harm and had no real discernible vice in all his days. Yet he would bother the folk of Tree City beyond Cumpear beyond compare, in a way that is well remembered:

The manner is which Leg Randy operated— so it was set down by the town's chroniclers— is that he would approach with a fair greeting and a tip of the hat. But then the approached, usually filled with dread already, would find their leg magically swept up in Randy's arm, or the other way around. Yes, sometimes the victim's leg would be swept up by Leg Randy, but even more appallingly, Leg Randy managed just as often to have his own leg swept up with the arm of his victim. And this was done daily, to be endured by any who had not the heart to flee at Randy's approach.

How Leg Randy achieved this successfully on the unwitting limbs of those who knew him not is a curious matter. He must have had some enchanted skill with arms, that it is a great wonder he was not called Arm Randy. But for the vast majority of his leg-sweepings, it was no longer a matter of skill.

It was no longer a surprise for the people of Tree City beyond Cumpear. They had come to expect a leg-sweep every time Leg Randy drew near, and it was just one of those things. Whether it was right is still being debated in courts down to my own time. Is such an act a crime? Is it true and honest harassment to continuously sweep the legs of one's community? Even if done just once? How many times must a leg be swept in order for it to be counted as wrong?

Is it still wrong if it's done as a jest or in the name of good fun? Must consent be obtained for a sweep of the leg? Is such a deed worthy of punishment? Is it even worthy of mention at all?

None of these questions were ever asked of Leg Randy, nor was he ever brought to court. And if he had been, truly the habitual leg-sweepings would have been overlooked, for Leg Randy was— in the year 3333— to commit a far more startling atrocity.

Piss Lip was the hope of Skulfing's Opposition in 3333. He was of Rich Mahogany skin, so he was not automatically hated by the Mahogs, and he held a kind sympathy for Tanfolk, so he was also overwhelmingly supported by that breed over Skulfing, who hated them.

It was the lovely green month of Tanariat, two months before the Choosing of the Reign in Duchallia, when Lip had completed his tour of the Farlobe, giving great impassioned speeches on why the Lobes must overthrow Skulfing, but do so in a way that would be both diplomatic and respectable. He returned now to his home village of Tree City beyond Cumpear, and spoke to familiar faces, kind and real:

"—We all know this already, but Skulfing has ripped a hole in these Lobes. All communications with our friends, in outside lands, have been severed. This is a

62

man who, to deflect suspicion and criticism from his own deeds, will accuse his rivals of the same things which he himself is guilty of. He accuses his opponents of corruption, despite being himself the most corrupt of all earthbound men!"

"He's not a man!" was shouted out by various voices in the crowd.

"Indeed he's not a man," returned the honorable Piss Lip. "To say he's a man is... well, it raises eyebrows. Anyway, back to my speech.

"Despite his eternal greed, he says that we who are trying to balance the wealth are crooked, only in it for ourselves!

"Despite his unending lies, he accuses us of spreading lies about him, when our 'lies' are only the very words that he speaks.

"Now I have spent time in the courts, overrun by the Deeplove and their Skulfers. Let me tell you that these people are operating on a completely different set of facts."

And great hoots of agreement and praise trickled from the crowd.

"They do not want to face reality. They will not come to terms with the fact that Url Skulfing was not chosen as Lobe Minister in 3330, and for the past three years we have been living under the rule of a tyrant who will not accept the reality that his term is done. That is why we must show them this year, that the Lobes have changed! The Lobes have become wise, to the fact that the Lobes of Url Skulfing's, are not the Lobes we want for ourselves."

And men wept to hear such goodness descend from the lips of Piss Lip and they were uplifted to know that he would be heading the Opposition against Skulfing, his Skulfers, and the Deeplove. With Piss Lip at the fore, they could not lose. Hope was deep within them rising.

Piss Lip was a true werman of the people, and he met with his followers after his speech, touching them lightly for they all loved him and wished for his touch, and it was a consensual pile of feeling.

The bold Lip was, however, relieved to be out from that mob as he walked along the winding cobblestone path out of town, up a great green hill, towards home. From the top of this hill he could see a familiar figure, rounding up over a hill in the distance. Piss Lip knew this figure, for all in Tree City knew the figure of Leg Randy. But Piss Lip was so honorable and kind, that he did not run the other way. He felt good upon that night, and so he would oblige Leg Randy in letting his leg be swept up as always.

Leg Randy approached as he always did, merry and of high spirit, marching down the hill with arms flailing and hands flapping militaristically. He had swept up the Honorable Piss Lip's leg many times in yesteryear, but not since Piss Lip had become such a famous politician.

Piss Lip smiled and laughed heartily as Leg Randy came near, joyously playing along with the Tree City ritual— "Ah, Leg Randy! A long time it's been! Yeah, no, I remember— I remember the thing. My leg or your leg this time?"

But Leg Randy put both hands on the politician's head and pulled it down with such force, cracking it upon his knee, which he brought up with tremendous vigor. Then Leg Randy grabbed Piss Lip by the leg and snatched it so suddenly that the affable saint landed on the path with a crack.

The unwarranted violence ended not there, for Leg Randy twisted Piss Lip's leg as far as it would go. What happened next is still debated contentiously: he either dug his claws into the leg and tore out the shin, or laid his teeth into the calf and ripped out the muscles with his mouth. Then Leg Randy remembered that he had cones of beef in his cottage nearby, and so he ran away with newfound purpose.

Piss Lip, bleeding in many places, cried out for help. It was not long before a crowd reformed, around the heinously wounded Mahog member of the Ass Affiliate, the affiliate leading the charge against Skulfing and his Snake Affiliate.

"Who has done this to you?!" wept folk in the crowd.

But so honorable was Piss Lip that he would not even cast blame. As he lay there dying, many feared that the culprit of this assassination would never be known.

But in one of the great curiosities of modern history, the assassin returned to the scene to finish the murder, which had already been effectively done. Yes, Leg Randy bolted back through the crowd, now holding two large cones of beef from his cottage. Although Piss Lip was already so close to death, although Leg Randy could have lived out his life as an anonymous killer, he came back proudly to show all assembled that he was nothing short of terrible.

To end his stunning act, Leg Randy smashed his two cones of pounded raw beef against Piss Lip's ears. These cones of beef were hard, and so when they came together it produced the same result as if Piss Lip's face were to have been smashed by two boulders. The honorable man was no more, and it took great containment for the crowd not to rip apart the assassin Leg Randy then and there.

And so it was that Leg Randy was declared an outlaw, terrorist, and— even worse— a fiend.

All was thrown into havoc upon the death of Piss Lip. Just two months from the Choosing of the Reign, the Ass Affiliate was left leaderless. They had put all their manuscripts in one monastery with their beloved Piss Lip, and the Opposition against Skulfing now looked to be dead.

What was more alarming to many was the fact that a Rich Mahogany man— and one of such high standing at that— had been killed. This was not a thing to be done in those days. Of course it's not a thing to be done today either, but now there is at least some consensus that assassination is wrong on all fronts, regardless of breed.

Killings of Tanfolk and Paleskin were far more permissible in the times of which I speak. It was not uncommon in those days to hear the words "get murdered" under the breath of the Rich Mahogany, directed towards the Paleskins of Dikenia. For the Tanfolk, especially since they were in their own Supremacy of the Westlobe, such a phrase was harsh. "Get thrashed about violently" was the more acceptable thing to say to a Tanfolk if one was of Rich Mahogany flesh.

But violence against Mahogs was a thing wholly forbidden by all, and that fact that Leg Randy, a fellow Mahog, had killed another Mahog did not sit well at all with anyone. It certainly posed questions— was the violence condoned by Url Skulfing against Tanfolk and Paleskin coming to condone violence against fellow Mahogany? Were all breeds now subject to equal terror and insecurity? Powerful legates set to work examining the rationale and motivation for Leg Randy's assassination, and what implications it might hold for the future.

66

Such an absurd event was later discussed at length by Piss Dingle and his pal Skin Toot in my presence, and although it requires a jarring jump of time, I will include it here, as to confine the tellings of Piss Lip all to one chapter. I apologize to those readers who might be put off by the sudden and unexpected inclusion of Skin Toot, chapters before we come to his proper introduction. But for now, so that we might hear their conversation on the subject of Piss Lip, let it suffice to be known that Piss Dingle and Skin Toot held the deepest affection for one another, far deeper even than that ancient love between Domis Foke and his dog Large.

In many ways, the characters of Dingle and Toot— or Piss and Skin— were interchangeable. One was Mahogany, the other was a Tanfolk, but both had lived as both the dominant and submissive breed for equal parts of their lives. Dingle had been raised in the Westlobe, where he as a Mahogany man was not of the dominant breed, and then relocated to Harlobe in his third decade, where Rich Mahogany Supremacy reigned. Skin Toot had also been born to the Westlobe, where he as a Tanfolk was of the dominant breed in those parts, but moved in his third decade to Farlobe, where those of his flesh were profiled under the same Mahogany strength.

In this way, both Piss and Skin— or Dingle and Toot— had both experienced what it was to be part of the majority breed and the scorned minority breed within their lands, and frankly they didn't seem much different to them. They were likable and dignified enough to have never been targeted by breed-fueled acts, but at the same time had been utterly friendless and passed through most places unnoticed, despite being two of the most remarkable men in all the world.

The world would soon come to know of their glory, but this talk happened near the start of their friendship, as they still rode about the neutral place of Yonderlobe, unbeknownst to all of any standing.

Here is their conversation on the unfortunate death of Piss Lip, as they spoke of it while on beastback, riding through woods near the Lone Lake (which rested between many other lakes):

"You ever wonder what drives folk to kill?" mused Piss Dingle upon beastback.

"Or what stops him from going through with it?" mused Skin Toot, also on beastback. "For instance, a fellow of mine was living in Marcstown when the honorable Bahmoeth Burden was passing through on his campaign for the 3330 Choosing of the Reign. And this fellow of mine— Urndi, I believe he was called— looked out his window, and saw that Burden was directly below him. Oh, about thirty strides below him. And he told me his thought thereafter: 'I could drop a brick on Burden. I could drop a brick on the leader of the Ass Affiliate right.'"

Here Piss Dingle laughed, and Skin Toot went on: "And I thought to myself, well, if someone was in that position... and they really had nothing going for them... why not? You would at least be famous."

"You would definitely go in the manuscripts."

"Yes, and that close to a Choosing of the Reign? You would single-handedly change the course of history — of Lobian history at least."

"That certainly wouldn't have helped his vigor," laughed Dingle, referring to the elderly state of Bahmoeth Burden, who was controversially wrinkled and silver.

"Well no, it would've killed him. If you dropped a brick from— Urndi was thirty strides above. If he had dropped a brick from that distance?"

"It would kill him," conceded Dingle.

"It would kill a young and able person! How much more so that old decrepit Burden? Killed nine times over I should think."

And the beasts they rode upon strode down a hill tunneled over by tree, losing sight of their lake.

"There is a twisted logic to that though," continued Dingle. "I mean, your friend— this Urndi. He has his life ahead of him, he has yet to accomplish great things— but what if you were old, and not a flick going for you? Just some old... nothing?"

"Right, and this hypothetical Old Nothing might then look around, think to himself: 'I have no wealth, no kin, I reside within these plain walls quite thinly spaced... and there's a nominee for the Lobe Minister!' Even if you supported him, you might go ahead and think, 'Well, I like the guy— I even want him to be Minister! But if I kill him... if I kill him... I then make a name for myself.'"

"Or you could just be a nobody."

"Right. One might seize the opportunity, or let it go by... as my friend Urndi resolved to do. Now for the rest of his days he will think to himself, 'I could have easily killed Bahmoeth Burden.'"

"'I could've easily sent the entire Ass Affiliate scrambling— for weeks— trying to come up with a new candidate for the Choosing of the Reign.'"

"And then people would be coming up to him every day— 'why'd you do it?!'

'I was upstairs; he was right below my window; I had a brick.'"

"That could've been him! What's this guy Urndi doing now?"

"He's just making apes."

"Which is fine— but he's not the guy who killed Bahmoeth Burden."

"That he is not. That he is not. And I'll remind him of that til the end of time. Every time I see him I will call him the Man who Could've Killed the Burden."

"But didn't. There would've been books written about him, man!"

"Yes, yes—" continued Skin Toot, "because it is such an odd thing to do. Men would always look for the motivation. Why did he do it? Even if he just did it because he could, as we have been suggesting here."

"Yeah, there would definitely be people who wouldn't accept it was just a random act."

And they laughed heartily on the idea of one of their friends having feasibly been a political assassin in a world not too far from their own. And at that point, I interjected that such a thing had recently come to pass, in this world, with the merciless killing of Piss Lip by the fiend Leg Randy, which Piss Dingle and Skin Toot had not yet heard of.

"No... you're telling me this actually happened?" asked Toot.

"Don't you tickle us on, Ward Geit," went Dingle, "You actually heard this? From a credible source?"

And I held my position, that yes indeed I had heard the news from Farlobe of the honorable Piss Lip being brutally murdered at the hands of a certain Leg Randy. Here I thought my companions would change their tone, and speak solemn of the lost life, especially one so noble as Honorable Piss Lip, whom both of our friends had admired in life.

But it was not so. Ever keen on throwing a good laugh upon a dark topic, Piss Dingle and Skin Toot continued on through the woods, merry as the birds of Trankle Plooce.

"Well that's hilarious," went Dingle. "What are the chances that you and me are here talking about some guy who could've killed an important Lobe leader, and then we find out a very similar thing literally just happened."

"Makes me feel a great pity for my friend Urndi," went Toot. "For he could have truly put himself in the famous position of this Leg Randy three years ago, and now Urndi will be forgotten while Leg Randy's name lives. For no one will remember Urndi, he who COULD HAVE killed Burden."

"No. Not at all. Now they'll only remember Randy, the one who DID kill Lip. Damn. What if this Leg Randy... what if he was that guy?"

"The one we've been dreaming up who just kills a politician for no real reason?"

"Yeah, what if Leg Randy is him?"

"Well as nice as it is to think that, I have a feeling his actions were probably much more politically charged. One does not simply kill the Honorable Piss Lip on a whim. What's the consensus from Farlobe, Ward Geit Fung?"

And here, finally given again a moment to speak for myself, I gladly took it, for getting a word in with these two was difficult at best: "The current consensus is that there is no consensus. Nobody has any idea why this Leg Randy so maliciously killed the good Piss Lip."

"Ah— my point exactly!" exclaimed Dingle. "I bet he was even in the same Affiliate as Piss Lip. Speaking of that, you ever wonder how the Affiliates got their animals? Snake and Ass? Did they choose their animals for themselves? Were either of those ever a respected animal?

"No, I'm pretty sure those are the worst of the worst in terms of pre-conceived animal notions. I mean, last time I checked, the Ass has always been... the least respected animal. And the Snake has always been... well, called evil, deceitful and a humiliation that can't even walk because it has no legs."

71

"Right. You got a slithering freak and a beast that everyone mistreats, for Affiliates' associative identities. Someone else must've chosen these animals."

"They probably chose each other's."

And as the subjects of my manuscript continued to muse endlessly on why things are the way they are and guess as to the random motivations of famous heinousities, I asked them if I truly must transcribe the whole of their talk, feeling that it had already by this point become superfluous and redundant. They said they would peel my urethra if I dealt their conversation an omission, and I so I have come to include it. Many of their words between the prior talk and of that below— when they had realized they were lost in the woods on the cusp of dark— have been lost to time (or my own refusal to include such endless dialogue in an interest of salvaging the dignity of my work), and for that I received not a peeling of the urethra, for I stated my intentions were pure, but rather only a shaving of the foreskin.

"Yo... do you have ANY idea where we're going?"

"Remember, we came this way!" replied Skin Toot.

"I remember going through that, yeah—" remarked Dingle, referring to the tunnel they just passed through.

But soon their pleasant remarks grew to slow confusion, and profound silences, until Skin Toot erupted in a fury of self-condemnations as their horses refused to go any further.

"So we're lost?" asked Dingle.

"Well, in my defense, it's not our fault that we lost the lake. When you embark upon a lakeside trail, the assumption is that the trail will follow along the entire length of the lake, and will bring you back to where you started."

"The assumption is then also that the lake is round."

"The Lone Lake is round! It's just, when these other lakes are factored in, and paths veer off in strange directions— I should have known better. I knew we had never passed under a tunnel on our way here, and therefore should've had no need for passing under a tunnel to return. But now dark is upon us, and our horses have made their minds to stay, so we must hasten on with legs!"

And so they ran. As the sun disappeared, the woods along the Lone Lake grew lightless, and strange croaks and flutterings were heard all around.

Pants were abundant. And sweat flew in all directions with the wind. Yet Skin Toot still cursed himself and attempted to defend his folly, letting out weak vocalizations between his labored huffs.

"I like to think of myself as a navigator! What kind of a navigator— I've lost all faith in myself. But really— what kind of trail is this?! When we got to that other lake, there were no signs whatsoever! No signs to say 'you are going to an entirely different lake.' Someone could've let us know. Or at least there should be some better indication of how far it is. Because I suspected too— 'oh we're heading up to the other lake' but I didn't realize there was so much space between! Because on a map there's no perception, no indication of 'how long would it take to walk from here to here.'"

And they were both nearly dead with the exertions of their sweaty bods.

"You know what's good about this though?" asked the panting Skin Toot, trying to retain optimism.

"What's that?"

"That you could be a woman. And if I was acting this way in the presence of a woman, I definitely would NOT be getting thrust tonight. At all."

"Yeah."

"I wouldn't even be getting a second glance."

"Right, because I had a good time tonight, but this walk was entirely too long. If I was a woman this would be the end of things. I wouldn't even keep on with you down the track— I'd do what the horses did. I'd stop back there, in the pitch dark, and huddle up waiting for the dawn, cursing your name the whole night through."

Eventually we did find our way back to our carriage, in the deep dusk— a sticky hot one at that— and all our skins were wet with the sweat.

"Oh... mik you, Lone Lake!" Shouted Skin Toot back in the direction of the winding trails. "You made us late for... well, it's a good thing we did the ride after dinner. If we would have done this ride before, I don't think there would have been a dinner."

"I'm pretty fricken exhausted," agreed Piss Dingle. Then, cracking up, "It was fricken dark in those woods."

"Yes, while there's still a little light left— in general — but when you're in the woods—"

"I'm assuming those were frogs that were chasing after us?"

"Yeah, there was some deep and evil rustling behind."

"I didn't bother to look back."

Chapter V
Exiled from the Stables, and Virtuous

Harking back to the month of Nanethis, Piss Dingle had failed in all of his endeavors. He had been haunted by his rape that could have prevented if only he had obtained a Deed of Pass, but then he began to turn his anger towards the powers that had decreed a Deed of Pass necessary in the first place. And then he was drawn down into further anger by men like his father and mother, who supported the forces of Skulfing and their reasonings.

Often times a conversing would play out as such:

"Mother. How can you support a man such as that? He's vile."

To which Mother Dingle might reply along the lines of, "He's going to be the one who cleans up all the corruption in the world."

And then Piss Dingle would logically respond "But he is the one who is bringing all the corruption."

"No, he's going to drain the seeping refuse that has so long plagued our courts."

"Well then why hasn't he done that in the six years that he's maintained power?"

"Because half the Lobes have not accepted him as the true Minister."

And this was because three years prior he had stolen the Choosing, so there was much call for him to not be accepted as a valid Lobe Minister. This brought to mind Dingle's conversation with his mother three years ago, when Mother Dingle felt certain that Skulfing would continue to rule the Lobes despite being declared the loser of the Choosing:

"He will still win yet another reign and another after that."

"But the choosing of the reign is over," protested Dingle, who at that time had still faith in the democratic process of the Lobes. "He did not win, yet he pretends as though he did. In this way he is acting as four-year-old child, raised without dignity nor the knowledge of scarcity."

"But he must serve a second term. For then he will drain the seeping refuse that has so long plagued our courts."

Of course it came to pass that Skulfing did take second term, but he did so by destroying the courts, and in his three years, still he did nothing to "drain the seeping refuse." Yet on that day in 3333, Mother Dingle was still convinced that Skulfing must serve yet another term, for this time he would surely drain the seeping refuse.

"How can you trust a man who will not follow rules himself to be charged with charging others to follow rules?" asked Dingle. "All my life you've been setting down rules for me follow, saying they were drastically important, but now you follow who pays no mind to any rules whatsoever, while you yourself no longer follow rules."

To which Mother Dingle spouted on still, but never making a coherent point. The boy Dingle could take such things no longer, and so abandoned his post at the Stream and gave those he knew a quick notice of his departure, telling his mother that he would no longer follow her rules, and would leave swiftly.

"Where will you go?" asked his mother.

"Oh, you know me. I won't go anywhere. I'll just walk, and wander, and then keep walking, and my wandering may take me to an open grave. And then I'll crawl inside, and fall asleep. And with any luck, a gravetender will come along and bury me, and all will be done."

And upon hearing this, and seeing his son depart with his most precious possessions, Old Piss Dingle himself resolved to have his heart stop its beating. In this way, the old Lady Dingle was deprived of both her husband and her youngest son on the same eve. Heartsad she was for but a time, for soon she realized that now there would be no watching eyes in that wooded dell, and so she was at last free to act as she would on her eldest.

Piss Grobe does not figure into this tale, but as an aside let it be said that he on that night started a new branch of Dingle men, when he lay in bed with his grieving mother.

Piss Dingle intended to head due west, towards the fabled Yonderlobe, lying over the Essen River. Of all the Lobe-lands of the Hayamese Empress Hakamena, the Yonderlobe was the only one yet free of her jurisdiction, left to be governed (or, rather, not governed at all) by the Native Tanfolk, who had lived in those regions from time immemorial. There, our friend Dingle planned to seek out life anew, all his own, away from the prying eyes and judgments of his own kin.

He made brash expulsions of the throat as he went, slapping his knees in a jolly manner, for this was a jolly time. All he knew was being left behind, with the world opening up before him in a bush of green clover, extending the full length of the great valley that rose up before him. Such was the beauty of the southward road from Tugpikkle to Rayce, which was now on his left side as he started the westward trek. But that westward road — the one that bridges Tugpikkle and Ho Spleen Ho— was one of a flat and treeless nature. Brutal would be the sun and joyless the views of that walk. And so Piss

Dingle here amended his route for the first time. It would not be the last.

For when the corn-dressed werman reached the town of Rayce, he was met with the signature words of that place— so similar and predictable among all who traveled through that place, that they were soon after the establishment of the village come to be known as "Raycisms." And the Raycisms were much the same in all taverns of the town: that their holy idol Thirusaca had willed it that the Empire of Hayaman spread north and west, displacing all peoples that had inhabited the lands prior, and establishing their mark as dominance divine.

An arrogant man in a tavern spoke the following upon his hearing of Dingle's trek:

"Believe me man: you want nothing to do on the west side of the Essen. Nothing but Tanfolk on that side."

"But are the Tanfolk really that bad?" asked Dingle. He spoke with confidence, as if asserting that he knew for a fact that they were not bad— but then he felt the eyes upon him. "I mean, I've never met any. I'm just not sure is all."

And all at once the tavern folk laid upon him, without invitation, hours worth of anecdotes and Raycisms on the subject of the Tanfolk.

"They are violent beyond cause. The whole lot of them. They'll attack and skin ya for a good morning. And worse yet, lazy and loafing! All of them! Unwilling to act when a foreign power walks up into their land. They sit in their huts, just waiting to be mauled over, swept away in such little time as if they were nothing at all. For they are cowards, unwilling to stand and fight— unable, for it is their sluggish nature!"

"It seems as though you've made a contradiction," spoke Dingle.

78

"What do you mean?" asked the man of Rayce.

"Well, you say that ALL of them are idle cowards, unwilling to fight, and at the same time, ALL of them are violent beyond cause."

"Well of course that means that some all-of-them are idle, while the other some all-of-them are violent beyond cause."

"And what would determine the cause? Who is to say their violence is 'beyond' that cause?"

"They'll take women and children from their beds! Tie them up in strong-held cloth and set their arms ablaze, so when they open up the cloths there's nothing left to their limbs but bone!"

"But haven't the Rich Mahogany burned entire Tanfolk villages? In that case... killing women, children, wermen too— and also pets and property?"

"That leads into the Third Inferiority," spoke the man of Rayce, nodding with shuttered eyes and speaking as if this were all a direct science. "That the Tanfolk are dumb. Lacking all intelligence. Dense and mindless, without wit and foresight. You know why this is?"

"I'm sure you'll tell me."

And indeed the man of Rayce did. "It's because— amidst all this— amidst our Empire scratching off their hut-lands, amidst our companies brushing off their raiding parties as if they were gnats on our jackets... they still do not submit. This is a mark of folly...! Of pure and utter farce!"

And he leaned back on his chair, putting out a hand for all those standing at the bar to join in— "Of pure and utter farce!"

And swiftly the man of Rayce leaned forward again, grabbing Piss Dingle by the collar and looking him dead with one eye: "Now you tell me what they are, if not dumb, to resist a nation such as ours?"

"I suppose that would make them dumb."

As Dingle walked the streets of Rayce, his mind had not been swayed much from before his time in the tavern— seldom are the minds of men swayed in such little time, despite the strength of various arguments. And the arguments of the men in the tavern were certainly not strong, so Dingle still held nothing against the Tanfolk, thinking them neither idle, violent beyond cause, nor dumb. However, the repeated tales of surprise raids in the Yonderlobe plains did pose a growing concern in Dingle's mind.

Little faith could he place in the tales of Mahogany men in their taverns, those who had likely never stepped leg outside the Harlobe, but still a fool he would be to start a new life in the Yonderlobe if it meant risking a hungry Tan man in his shed upon some unexpecting night. What would he do if such rumors and gossip actually had a basis in truth? If he with his small but adequate Mahogany fortune crossed over the Essen and purchased a modest home amidst those lands, would he be a target for those peoples dispossessed?

Yes, Dingle viewed his own sums of currency as small, and any home he made for himself in the Yonderlobe would be modest by his own standards. But to the eyes of the Tanfolk, he would be rich beyond reckoning, in a home highly enviable, and so he did fear what all the Rich Mahogany in the Harlobe feared: that he would wake up to a noise in his shed on some dark and starless night, and with a flicker of the candle see a tall and slender Tanfolk up against the wall, silent as Kezhil-Hai. Upon the stopping of the dread-filled heart, the Tanfolk would then leap forth, thrusting spear into the shocked arms of a Mahogany foe, and then take his speechless victim to his horse, bringing him back to a circle of huts where never light would be seen again.

This is not the fate Piss Dingle fancied for himself.

So he decided against setting out west for the Yonderlobe, at the time being. Instead, he walked back up the road whence he came, for he did so much love that Green Valley. And then, being so close to home, decided to peek back in for just a moment, to see if anything had changed in the last set of days. As soon as he set foot back in Tugpikkle, he was called out on the streets for his insolence in seeking out a journey, and ridiculed for the stoutness of his trip. His jog turned to a sprint for the doors of his mother's house, and upon bursting in and finding his mother and brother nude upon desk, sped out with even greater speed than he had sped in with.

And so he was obliged to reside again in the truest home he had known, at the house of his grandmother there in the comely town of Tugpikkle, where all seemed at peace, but great turmoil was brewing just under its pot.

Now we all know that Piss Dingle was not one for political debate in those early days. He believed that things remained in their optimal position when such topics were left alone, for they only led to bad ends.

But on certain occasions, when one spoke out in high pride on things that were so clearly wrong— in all definitions of the word as he had come to know— Dingle found that he could not stay silent. He found a certain pull within him to speak, no matter how ill-equipped he was in his voice, to speak out against evil words and to attempt to serve the truth and right of things. Such an occurrence often came to be in the presence of the Old Maid.

Dingle sat now in the presence of the Old Maid once again, as he done in days of old, when she was not so old and not so vile. But now as she sat amidst a company other elders, spouting contempt for all in Skulfing's Opposition, Dingle held his tongue, remembering the last time he had engaged her in debate...

It was 3330, just after the Choosing of the Reign, when it looked as though Bahmoeth Burden had won, for indeed he had. Yet all of Skulfing's Deeplove cried out that Skulfing had won, for by his own admission he was the victor.

"You don't just go to bed on the night when Skulfing is ahead, and wake up to find that suddenly he's not," sternly said the Old Maid.

"You do though," put in Dingle. "It happens all the time and it has happened again. Just because Skulfing is ahead one night doesn't mean he's won the entire Choosing. Not all the votes had been counted on the night of which you speak. If they had, then the Choosing would have been over. But there were more votes to be tallied, and it turns out that those remaining votes tipped the scale in favor of Burden."

The Old Maid was livid. "We haven't had a fair choosing of the reign since the Yu CongMo."

"How do you come across this knowledge?" asked Dingle, for he was truly curious. Ten Choosings had taken place since the Choosing of Yu CongMo, and he had never in all his life heard anyone made an accusation of rigged Choosings, not in the least going back thirty-some years.

"I feel it. It is true. The choosing of the reign is not a fair choosing," shouted the Old Maid.

"Then we're simply no worse off than any of the lands around. Ilandia, Acstrivium, Hayaman proper—

not one of those places even consider the option of having an election. There the ruler simply is. The people have no say in it at all."

"The same goes for here! Our people have no say."

"But we do though," argued Dingle. "You have just come to think we don't. Because Url Skulfing says so."

"Skulfing is in the right."

"In the right for saying the Choosing of the Reign is rigged? Just because he hasn't won?"

"It is rigged! This time around people are up with their arms all over the Lobes!"

"Because Skulfing is making it so! But crying out that it was unfair! Even though everyone believes the process worked just fine when Skulfing was chosen. Things have not changed in these three years. The only thing that has changed is the victor."

Not wanting to get caught in her true folly, the Old Maid reconvened with her fictitious fact.

"As I said— this Lobe has not held a fair Choosing of the Reign since the election of Yu CongMo!"

"If you believe the system is always corrupted, then why are you especially upset this time around? Because your preferred man did not win."

"It's not that. It's that his enemies have not given him a fair go."

"If his enemies truly wished to stifle his power, they would not have allowed him to assume that power three years ago. Nor hold it for the entire course of the three years."

"He has been stifled now because he now has more enemies."

"Exactly right, Old Maid. He has abundantly more enemies. And those enemies are those who have voted, and cast him out of his power through entirely fair means."

And here the debate might have been ended if the same laws of logic that dictated Dingle's mind dictated that of the Old Maid, but logic is not an objective thing. It takes a different form in the mind of many, and so the debate would never end, not until the endings of time, when from that point on all men will live inside the confines of their own individual kingdoms, in vast palatial sweeps of the everlasting mind.

We jump back now to 3333, as Dingle attempted to hold his tongue while the Old Maid preached on an even more heinous topic, that of the killing of Flod at the hands of the Skulfers in Rayce. The Old Maid at first applauded the Skulfers. Yes, the act of killing Flod might have been excessive said she, but at least the Skulfers had attempted to serve justice in prosecuting Flod for smoking the dreaded Cudnut.

Dear God, Dingle was on the brink of losing his mind. How much longer could he stay silent?

"You know," said the Old Maid. "If those people don't want to be harassed by the Patrols, they shouldn't engage in that type of behavior!"

Dingle could no longer hold his tongue. That was fast.

"So you'd be happy if they had killed your grandson?" Asked Dingle, and all eyes were suddenly turned towards him. Here it was, him being faced down by greatest fear: that of being of controversial amidst an opinionated crowd. But, even under this tremendous pressure, Dingle managed to make his point:

"Your grandson smokes the Cudnut daily. Your grandson deals in Cudnut, demands the affection of women with Cudnut, and was even caught in the middle of a knife-fight over Cudnut last year. The Patrols arrived and broke up the fight, as they ought to. But they did not kill your grandson. Yet today you hear of a Paleskin in Rayce, who was merely accused of smoking Cudnut, and he was murdered, yet you find this to be fine."

"Well, yes. It's a terrible thing that's happened. But worse things are happening now as a result of it. You have Tanfolk and Paleskin burning taverns all across the Lobes!"

"So the loss of property is worse than the loss of life?"

Of course the Old Maid would not come out and say it outright. But through her dodgings she was communicating a resounding "yes."

"You don't understanding what's going on," countered the Old Maid.

"Look, I comprehend it well. Our flesh is of a rich complexion. And so we are the Rich Mahogany, but does that really mean we can drive the less fortunate to the tune of our own wills?"

Here Dingle excused himself, to go again into a self-imposed exile, and all through the night before his second departure he overheard in the Stables what the company in the midst of the Old Maid spoke of when one of breed sensitivity was not around to make conjectures and criticisms.

On the appearance and worth of the Paleskin they made no concessions:

"Take a stretching gaze at them. They are hideous. Their disgrace of form knows not a single bound. So white they are that their green inners shine brighter than the skin. White is weakness, pale is pain, and let us keep it that way, as it has been for as long as we have known."

And this kind of talk only amplified under the rule of Skulfing. Now one might very well assume that such a disastrous regime would only last but a week in lands where true justice was to be upheld. But in Hayaman's Lobes, it was going on six.

Six years had now passed without great incident since Skulfing's election— that is, an incident that brought all the lands into battle— but the tensions of unrest were now simmering large. How could they not, when all the air was filled with the spewing hatred of a leader concerned only with pushing suspicions and ill thoughts away from himself and onto other breeds of men? The seeds of distrust and high prejudice were sown, and very soon they would begin to bloom. Oh but it were that those seeds might blossom into flowers, but all know that seeds of prejudice give rise only to war.

Chapter VI
Piss Dingle Stabs the Countess

With the killing of a second Paleskin by the hands of Skulfers within weeks of Flod, the Lobes erupted into flames. All towns now felt the heat of the Opposition, those who demanded justice for the murdered Paleskins, and they implored Lobe Minister Skulfing to address his Lobes on how the crisis was being handled.

When Url Skulfing stepped forward to address the masses, he did what was expected of him.

He did not address the grieving, the lamentations, the pain of those were tired of being seen as less worthy of receiving life's graces. He spoke only of the destruction that those same people were now causing— and though the lootings were brought on by only the most eager of Tanfolk, Skulfing made it sound as if the entire breed were engaged in spreading flame. He made them out to be Caldar reincarnated, the very devils that the Rich Mahogany wished that they were. He spoke not of their peril, not of their strife, only of their wrongdoings. And as he denounced their lootings, he refused to acknowledge why the lootings were occurring in the first place. It was as if he assumed, or wanted his followers to assume, that they were simply looting for no reason at all— that it was their nature to burn and steal, and defy Old Lady Law, even though it was his own Skulfers that had begun the tradition of defying law for years.

And so the Opposition was further enraged, and brought about further flame, edged on with the eternal picture of Flod being suffocated on the ground by Dark Chevron. In all honesty it was the image that did it. The image that stuck in everyone's mind— easily recalled, not easily dismissed— that caused an uproar that would not be silenced. For Paleskins had been killed by Skulfers many times before, but this particular killing had been a step too far for many.

Flod had provided no real threat. Yet the Dark Chevron and his fellow Skulfers put unto him the most excessive and humiliating treatment, forcing him onto the ground for a drastic sweep of time, and putting their knees to his neck. Such an image made the allegory very real: the Mahogs in Skulfing's Deeplove were declaring their absolute dominance over the Tanfolk and Paleskins, and the Opposition would no longer stand for it.

As so they put forth riots, and the Skulfers retaliated. Retaliated with bone and arrow, against even those who just stood by near the rallies. Hundreds of bystanders were blinded with stones thrown at their eyes, yet as word of this spread, still folk like the Old Maid declared, "If those people want to be obstructers of justice, they deserve it!"

In the Large of Nanethis, Piss Dingle set out from Tugpikkle a second time, bitterly regretting his weakness which allowed him to give in to the urge of return. But this time Dingle held fast to the westward track— no matter how flat, and how uneventful— until he came to the city called Ho Spleen Ho. Here was an altogether different population than that which he found in Rayce.

Unlike the majority of the population of Rayce, who despised the Tanfolk and Paleskin to no end, the majority of Ho Spleen Hoyans were supremely sympathetic to the oppressed breeds of Harlobe. Dingle found this refreshing. Refreshing to be in the company of those who, like him, cared for the plight of those less fortunate.

He found Ho Spleen Ho to be refreshing for about four days. He found work in a tavern called The Deep Tickle, under the management of one called Carpis. But then Dingle began to be extremely aggravated with the total lack of moderation in that place, and the judgment which he himself received for not being active enough. For the peoples of Ho Spleen Ho were intense in their goodwill, radical as some might say, and if one was not out on the streets acting on behalf of justice at least twelve hours of the day, it would be called insufficient.

Now we all know Dingle to be a lover of equality and a hater of oppression, but he was moreover a lover of peace and minding one's own business. So when he was targeted daily at the Tavern where he found employment, for using his afternoon to sit and draw instead of burning about the town in protest of the recent Paleskin murders, he felt a bit uncomfortable.

"You only feel uncomfortable because of your high privilege," spoke Carpis, the tavern owner, who was actively involved in the daily riots of Ho Spleen Ho. "Now ask yourself, Dangle, what better use could your time be serving than sitting here making doodles?"

"Look, Carpis," replied Dingle, "First of all, it's Dingle. Second of all, I've had a rough year. I just got away from a very judgmental place where I was scorned for taking any idle time at all. I've been working all year in a Stream, I got raped, and nearly all my family seems to be on the side of the oppressors. I don't like it, but that's how it is. Now I came here to seek some reprieve."

"Did you say you have family members who support the Skulfing regime?" asked Carpis.

"I— yes."

"You should kill them."

And Dingle's eyes fluttered a few moments.

"Seriously?"

"You should consider it. How else will we rid the Lobes of their kind?" asked Carpis the Radical.

"Oakay— you see what's happening here? You're becoming your worst enemy. By saying we should just go and kill our enemies, those are the same tactics that the enemy uses! The kind of tactics that you abhor! If we give in to those hateful methods, the Lobes will be at war until one side is annihilated, and the way the board stands, both sides are pretty evenly stacked! Look, I understand the rioting and looting. You guys are pissed, I'm pissed too. It's even in my name. But if you're gonna continue to go out rioting this much, the Skulfers are gonna continue to retaliate until there's a full-out war and that'll be no good for anyone."

Carpis just shook his head, with squinted eyes full of judgment— "You just don't understand."

"Alright, I've had enough of this place too," said Dingle, and he got up to leave, but was stopped in his step as a lass of godly proportion entered in.

Now there are many in the world who claim the title of countess. A countess of Ploobis, a countess of Fetherstrok. But the countess that we will now speak of, that which Piss would have dealings with, had come to be called the True Countess, for counting was a part of her occupation, and she counted where other countesses did not. And, as earlier stated, she was of godly proportions. This was, above all else, the thing that kept Dingle rooted to that radical tavern for two full weeks of his life.

The Countess counted the coins in The Deep Tickle, and for her Dingle would feign any amount of militant passion for the violent downfall of Url Skulfing. Over the course of the next few weeks, into the month of Tanariat, Dingle gathered favor in the eyes of the True

90

Countess by going out with Carpis and setting fire to toy shops on the edge of the city.

"I dunno, is this really helping anything?" asked Dingle.

"We are sending a powerful message," replied Carpis, as he looted the place dry.

Later on, the march took a turn for the manor of Ho Spleen Ho's Captain of the Patrol, who had served the region long from thieves, killers and molesters. But due to his inevitable recent association with the influx of Skulfers into the Patrol, the people of Ho Spleen Ho now saw the Captain of the Patrol as an enemy. They marched on his manor, soiled his fields, and then demanded the Captain step out into the night.

Then Carpis stepped forward, loudly demanding things be done that the Captain had in that instance no means of doing, and then smacking the Captain in the name of Justice Truth.

"Hold up Carpis, I thought we were the ones against violence," said Dingle as his employer continued to lay hands all over the Captain.

"We are against the violence administered to Tanfolk and Paleskin," shouted Carpis, as he flicked his fingers all upon the Captain.

"This guy's the Captain of Ho Spleen Ho. I'm pretty sure he's trying to help."

"What has he done to help in the last ten years? His help has not come quick enough."

"Well I don't think this issue was ever brought to his attention until very recently—"

"This issue has persisted for generations, and we are now done with the civilized way of progress."

Dingle shrugged. "Alright. I mean I get it. You're upset, and maybe this kind of thing's a natural response. But I just don't think you sticking your thumb up this guy's nose is gonna get you the results you're looking for."

Upon hearing of Dingle's participation in the riots, the True Countess — Slivvery, as she was called— took notice and began to speak with him.

"So Dingle... I hear you were be-uhmmed as to why Carpis assaulted the Captain tonight."

"Well. A little."

"For generations the Rich Mahogany Man has been violent towards Tanfolk and Paleskin. The Mahog will prosecute one of light skin on a whim, and so they do not dare fight back. That is why it is OUR place, we the Mahogany who seek to serve Justice Truth, to tip the scales of equality."

"Ah, I see..." pondered Dingle, "So it's just cross-breed violence that upsets you. Going out to beat up fellow Mahogs is just fine to you."

"To those who have held power and stood by idly, yes. Now Dingle, I've heard you have relatives. Tell me, why aren't they here fighting for the cause alongside you?"

"Isn't it enough that I'm here? Isn't it cool that I believe in your cause?"

"Don't you have sway over them?"

"No. I wouldn't say I have 'sway' over my family members. But I will say this: my grandmother used to be on Skulfing's side and she's come over to the side of Lip, so that's something! Isn't it?"

"How could she ever be on the side of Skulfing?"

"Well... I'm sure she had her reasons, but the point is she's not now. People can change. People do change, if and when they realize they've been wrong—"

"We don't need people like her on our side."

92

"But then... how are you gonna get more people on your side? The way to do that is to make Skulfing's Deeplove see that there's nothing real to love about him."

"People who are worth saving will have seen that all along," sighed Slivvery as she put away cups. This puzzling idea held a firm conviction over her.

"But those have seen it along are not those you would seek to save— look, half of these Lobes are still in Skulfing's grasp, are you saying they're a lost cause?"

"They're full of hate and prejudice."

"Well so are you by the sounds of it!" is what Dingle wanted to say, but he stopped, for the True Countess was quite hot. Instead he just nodded.

"I wouldn't expect a Rich Mahogany man from privilege to fully understand," said Slivvery after the silence.

"Um... you're Mahogany too."

"But I have the mind of a Paleskin."

"You have the mind of a— but isn't the whole point of your movement that minds and personalities aren't confined to breed? That Paleskins, Tanfolk, or Mahogs don't have any kind of collective 'mind' and every individual's thoughts are unique? And I was born in Westlobe, where the Tanfolk reigns supreme, and there we Mahogs are somewhat frowned upon by the Supremacy."

"Don't try and hide your privilege."

Thus Dingle endured the difficult talks with the True Countess, who stood on the exact opposite side of things from his mother, yet he felt as though he was talking to the same exact person. Perhaps the Countess was some sort of mirror image of Mother Dingle, bearing a completely flipped ideology yet with the same immovable sense of authority, as though everything she said must be praised as truth. And Dingle decided that he would stick it out in that Deep Tickle place for a few more days, to see if any pleasure could be brought from it.

In those weeks spent at the radical tavern in the changing town of Ho Spleen Ho, Dingle reflected long and hard on where he was and how he had come to be there. His home of Tugpikkle had largely turned a blind eye to the great atrocities going on in the more peopled cities of the Lobes, but at least the individual folks he knew tended towards the good of the world, and would judge most things on a circumstantial basis.

Here in Ho Spleen Ho, all was led by doctrine. There were charismatic leaders at the forefront of movements, and all that they said would be followed by mobs without question. And there was only ever room for one Truth at a time. The example I will use is that of the Crown Sickness. When the Crown Sickness first reached Ho Spleen Ho in the month of Fevariat 3333, those in great favor cried out that none were to leave their homes. And the people listened. This was good, in my view, for it showed the rallying together of men for a common cause, the cause of preventing needless death and ailment while news came in from Ilandia as to the true nature of that disease.

But in the month of Sexarion, just one month after all had been told to stay within walls for the good of all, the death of Flod changed everything abruptly. Suddenly Justice Truth had to be carried out immediately, and the One Objective flung rapidly from that of preventing the Crown Sickness to that of avenging Flod. In the eyes of the Ho Spleen Hoyans, there was no middle ground. Either one went out and avenged the death of Flod, amidst the masses, or one was worthy of criticism. No matter if people were still on edge about the Crown Sickness— that had been the Truth of Fevariat. Of course the Crown Sickness still lingered, but the Truth of Sexarion was that Flod had been killed, and everyone now was to swiftly forget about the Crown Sickness. As a result, hundreds in Ho Spleen Ho lost their lives due to those infamous Dark Wiggles that month.

Yes, it was a beautiful thing that so many people rallied together in the name of one who had fallen at the hands of wicked Skulfers, thought Dingle. But why was it that they couldn't still adhere to precautions regarding the Crown Sickness and not be criticized? Why couldn't one stay safe within doors, mind one's own business, not partake in destructive deeds, and still be seen as standing on the side of the Tanfolk and Paleskins? Dingle certainly held sympathy for the Tan and Pale. But he didn't feel obliged to go out yelling at the top of his lungs, nor did he care to hold a torch and intimidate those who were not of his same mind.

In his rush to leave home, Dingle now realized he had made a grave error with stopping in Ho Spleen Ho. Actually no— it was a blessing that he had stopped in this equal city of freaks. For it made him realize that there are freaks on all sides.

On every issue, in every pocket of the world: freaks abound.

Was there not a place, then, where folk were not freaks? Was there not a place where man could live in a tranquil harmony, showing mutual respect to one another, and not giving way to extreme shows of rage and vengeance? This is where Piss Dingle longed to be.

He would find it soon, thought he, but first he had that godly proportioned Countess to attend to.

Dingle stood behind the True Countess for a spell, one night towards the end of his employment, quiet and still. She was cleaning cups, and when she did not turn, Piss Dingle took out a little dagger from his pocket and held it up above the shoulder of the True Countess. When still she did not turn, Piss Dingle lowered his dagger into her shoulder, gave a little prick, and then pushed it down an inch before pulling it back up.

Now many who have doubted this tale take this as evidence of its folly, for all the women they know— or any woman in general— would yelp about in pain upon having a dagger slipped down into their shoulder, or at the very least acknowledge the puncture before it went a full inch deep.

The True Countess, however, did not. Still she did not turn, not until Dingle said his fateful line:

"Well, that's not quite where I wanted to stab you, but it'll do for now."

And immediately after it fell from his lips, Dingle knew it to be a mistake. It was a wrong thing to say. And the True Countess merely turned slowly, and stared at him with cold, cold eyes. He had faltered immensely.

The incident of Piss Dingle laying a dagger in to the True Countess' shoulder would go on to haunt his steps for all days to come. It would grow to be the greatest blemish on his character, and an easy arrow mark for all the enemies of future Dingleites, who wished to discredit all that blossomed for that one great man. Could he even be called great, if he had in truth done this terrible and sick deed? Truth did not even matter to the many. Just the fact that he was accused of this non-consensual stab was enough to undo all his life's work.

Indeed Dingle's greatness was in later years brought to question, when this "stabbing" of Countess Slivvery came to light among the masses. He himself said it was merely a poke— that he had merely 'poked' the Countess Slivvery and said "that's not exactly where I wanted to POKE you, but it will do for now." But we will remain there in Nanethis of the Year 3333, where the story is transpiring in its due course.

The next day— the day after the suggestive stabbing, that is— Carpis approached Dingle with a touch of scowl. "Dingle boy. You've got something to say?"

And at first our protagonist had no honest idea what Carpis could be on about. "I believe you have a confession to make," restated Carpis.

But Dingle shook his head, "The only thing I have off the top of my head is my confession for the love of Corn Fashion," and he motioned down at his clothes made of corn. But then he remembered. Oh yes, he remembered.

"Oh, this isn't about—?"

"You stabbing Countess Slivvery?"

"Stab? Stab?! Did she say that?"

"She said you came up to her from behind, stabbed her with a knife, and suggested you would have rather stabbed her in a more obscene location."

"Wha—?! That's not— oh, well, sure. Some of that's right. Didn't use a knife— used my finger, so there's that. A minor detail that's actually pretty important. Not even the nail of my finger. It was a tap. And it wasn't even in a lewd tone, it was just— playful."

"You came up from behind."

"Well— yes, that I did. But again, it was one of those 'ah, you didn't know I was here, and now I'm here' sort of things, or like a 'eh, we're being friendly because we're such good friends now.'"

Carpis was having none of Dingle's stammers, excuses, or reasonings. In the eyes of his judgment, Dingle's deed stood on the same ground as a prolonged molestation.

"One does not stab another without first obtaining due consent," spoke Carpis, "and one then certainly does not go on making lewd comments in impure suggestion thereafter."

"It was a tap! You're saying I can't ever tap someone on the shoulder?"

"Only in the most dire of circumstances. When one considers the context in which this act was carried out, I should say you have done a rape."

"Wait, Carpis, now I'll admit what I did was uncalled for. I'll apologize profusely. I will never tap someone on the shoulder again in my life. I will certainly never make a lewd suggestive comment as long as I live. But to equate what I did with rape? I've been raped. I was raped in Sevallia. Just two months ago. And believe me, it was different than what I did to the Countess."

And with a deep sense of humiliation, remorse, anger, and feeling as though he was never given a fair chance to be heard in that place, Dingle quickly gathered his things and headed for the door. As one leg stepped out onto the street, he turned quickly, realizing that he must at least attempt to leave that bastard Carpis with a stinging phrase in his mind, one that would haunt him til the end of time, one that was so cleverly divined as to intricately weave together all the things that needed saying.

"Deep in your loin it's fart!" is all that came out of Dingle's mouth, but it was good enough despite being awful, and he hurried down the street, leaving that man forever in that place and never to be thought of willingly again. And as he strode out into the night— he remembered the place he had originally set out for, before being discouraged by the Men of Rayce: that peaceful place called Yonderlobe. Yes, he had heard tales of skinnings and drownings and stonings and burnings and men being frequently feasted alive, but he had also heard that the mentality of those in Yonderlobe was quite lovely.

Men of the Yonderlobe were said to be the most carefree of any people, and that is what Dingle craved. He was done with this life of politics, of high-handed folk aspiring to absolute right and wrong, and never contending that there might be a little of both in every situation.

And thus did Dingle, so enthralled with the idea of becoming one of Yonderlobe, walk the entire length of the night, north along the River Essen, through the towns of Tallshaven and Klontug west of Deep Tug, until he came to a bridge that would lead him out from Harlobe.

There was no turning course. Piss Dingle would now swiftly become the One True Fiend of the Yonderlobe.

PART II (TOGE)

A PLACE OF DEEP GOODNESS

Chapter VII
Skin Toot

Piss Dingle tooth-tongued his way merrily over the bridge across the Essen, for he could not whistle, but still he was in want of some merry joy to accompany his crossing from Harlobe into the Yonderlobe. Yes, this was a geographical and political change as denoted by our maps, but for him it was also to be a change in the stages of his own life— one for the better, one without shame and guilt of his own breed's wrongdoings on both sides of the coin.

But his sloppy tooth-tonguing came to a halt when he saw that the bridge did as well, for near to the Yonderlobe side the bridge was smashed clean apart, the rubble of stones lying down visible in the water below, sticking up above the rippling current. The chasm lying now before Dingle looked a distance too great to leap, and he thought it better not to risk and see. A better alternative, he thought, was to simply ford on across the river, for he could see it was not deep at all in parts, since the fallen stone rubble from the bridge rested above the water line.

Leaping from rock to rock, Dingle made it to the middle of the river, and then ran out of rock. "Oh Supreme Lord Horlio, Lord of the Stars and Hence All That Exists! Is this how I come to end?! If so, I guess that's alright. That's fair."

And he was about to step off the last rock, and be carried downstream, up to that fabled place called Brundlecock in the Darkwood. But a voice called out to him, seemingly from up above— "Get down on your belly."

In truth the voice did come from above, be it only about two meters above where Piss Dingle now stood. For over upon the Yonderlobe bank was a

Tanfolk, standing up on a ledge of thick gold sand and showing root, his arms crossed, seen intermittent behind green leaves.

For the greater part of the Rich Mahogany of Harlobe, seeing a Tanfolk face amid the leaves of virgin forest would mean a certain stopping of the heart. But for Piss Dingle, one of a more rounded mind of well-meaning, it made for only a mild start, which cured itself almost instantly.

"Hey what be lovely? I'm kind of stuck here."

"Yes, and a I say again, get down on your belly," projected the Tanfolk.

Piss Dingle questioned why he ought to.

"So that you might ford easily across the river."

"You want me to crawl across the river bed— under water— on my belly?"

"Dear Lyvierfania no— don't try that! I mean that you'll be able to easily walk across, for the River Essen goes shallow as the Suns begin to dim. But before that you'll be subjected to the Mid Morning Rise, which is happening right now."

"So I picked a foul time to come to Yonderlobe?"

"Most foul. Any other time you could have attempted your crossing and found greater ease. But hear this, for I seek to give you aids. Aids that will make you live. The rock you stand upon. That rock's name is Duke. Now if you lie down and embrace Duke with an unfaltering loyalty, he will serve you with far longer swaths of life than you would otherwise have! So go flat. And if you wrap your legs around that adjacent rock Piddle, you'll be right fine."

And so Piss Ding took the counsel of this Tanfolk, for little choice did he have. The waters of the Essen rose, and Dingle struggled hard to keep his head above the rush as he held onto Duke with his arms and Piddle with his legs. Ancient murk rushed under and over him, for the Essen was a brown river, old with sediment and all the lifelings smaller than the dust, who like to crawl up living tubes such as the urethra.

After an hour or so, Dingle's torment from the ancient river ceased, and the waters fell, revealing much more of the rocks than had previously been visible. Upon the Tanfolk's insistence that he would not now die, Piss Dingle stepped off of Duke, and fell into the Essen up to his neck. In truth, he almost did die, for he could feel his steps sinking into the thick mud of that elderly stream, and if he had not been quick about it, he very well could have been swallowed whole by such mud, as many have become lost in that way.

"Well you're not late," spoke the forest man of tan complexion as he helped Dingle up off the slope of newly exposed mud, and onto the sandy ledge of the Yonderlobe bank.

"That's good," replied Piss Dingle, confused. "Am I expected?"

"One of your kind has been expected— not you in particular, but it's you who's come."

"Yes, I have come."

"Why? Have you come."

"I've heard great things about this Yonderlobe."

At this the Tanfolk laughed. "You have surely not. Over in Harlobe they do not speak well of us, unless you are not in the company of the mass morale?"

"I— no. You can discount any assumption of me being one with their mass morale. Their mass morale is that you're all criminals and violent barbarians just by nature of living. And the second morale is that everyone from my own breed not ascribing to their views is worthy of death of destruction."

"And you don't believe that?" Here the Tanfolk leapt down from his root ledge, and held up a dagger, exposing his teeth.

But Piss Dingle held great composure, even though in his heart he did begin to worry, that perhaps the Tanfolk were to be feared at all costs and that this one might skin him for leisure. "I don't believe that."

And the Tanfolk dropped his dagger in the dirt. Then flung open his arms. "I bid you welcome to this Lobe then! Skin Toot."

The first part of the phrase Piss Dingle understood just fine. But the last two words puzzled him, and he put his ear forward again inquisitively.

"Skin Toot," said the man, placing emphasis on the Skin. "Or Skin Toot if you'd like," placing emphasis on the Toot.

Several more moments passed, and then Dingle was hit with the snap of standing. "Oh, it's your name! Skin Toot. Got it."

And since we have now revealed the name of Skin Toot I must give him a brief description of his appearance, which is easy as he wore no clothes besides a belt. On his clavicles were crowned two large leaves of the elm, while thin leaves of the ash lined the spheres of his breast. Massive maples were slapped onto the cheek of each ass, while his low-hung flip was sheathed with a cap of the Pendalese palm, curious for its rarity in those parts. But most proudly were there oak leaves round his belt, and oak too upon his face, namely tucked behind the ears.

And so the leaf-clad Skin Toot led Piss Dingle along a narrow winding trail through green bush and branch—

"And what do you wish to be called?"

Now this was a strange question to Piss Dingle, who all his life had been asked 'what is your name' instead of 'what do you wish to be called.'

"My name?" asked Dingle, full of uncertainty and dread, for truly he had dreaded saying his name all the days of his life.

"Indeed, speak it."

"Well back in Harlobe, and over in Westlobe from where I hail, I was given the name Danreid Alemonah."

"Do you wish to be called that here?" asked Skin Toot, sensing the discomfort that saying the name had given him, and hearing the 'ums' and 'uhs' that filled its telling.

"Hm, I suppose not. Never cared for the name. I find it dumb. So I guess you can just call me Piss Dingle. That sounds better."

And henceforth, the one known by law in the Lobes as Danreid Alemonah of Tugpikkle and Murder Creek Before, came to be known as Piss Dingle evermore. Skin Toot asked if he was rightly sure of his choice.

"No, I'm sure. Piss Dingle is what I will be til the Falling of Hell and the Rising of Better Things. Can we change my father's name while we're at it? And my mother, and her mother? Can they all be Dingles now?"

And of course that is how it came to be. So we are unsure of the respective names for any of Dingle's relatives, for whenever pressed by chroniclers, he would insist that they were all called Dingle, even though he himself was not so in the beginning.

Now Dingle and Toot walked across a log that lay fallen over a shallow trickling stream, even though finding balance upon the log was in truth harder than it would have been to simply walk across the Ankle Deep Creek. As they traversed the log, Dingle spotted a large dwelling of stone, three storeys high with boarded windows. It was old to be sure, and the stones were in places beginning to break away from their old order, but it was sturdy and warm nonetheless.

"Is that where you dwell?"

"We are not about living in dwellings of stone," replied the loins of Skin Toot.

"Then who lives in that stone dwelling?"

"Not one. It is wholly unoccupied."

"Well that's a bit of a waste, isn't it?"

"Indeed. And why should we dwell in a bit of waste?"

"That's not— I mean, the stone house looks fine! It's a waste that nobody's living in it."

"Right again, why do you think we speak different? It's a waste that nobody's living in."

"But see, that's not what I'm saying. I'm saying, the waste is not the stone house. The waste is that—"

"Yes, the waste is THAT. And therefore we do not live in that."

"What do you live in then?"

"The forest, naturally."

"So you'd rather sleep in the woods than in that stone house?"

"We do not live in the woods, Piss Dingle, we live in the forest. Squirrels live in the woods and you will see them pop in and out of their woods most frequently. Men are too large and deep for such things."

And true to Toot's words, Dingle soon— once he started looking at the hollow places in the trees— saw the little heads of squirrels and chipmunks, peeping out to see the man of Rich Mahogany skin come from Harlobe. He felt a flick bit unwelcome, as though the forest creatures knew he was a foreigner. But of course this was an insecurity of his own mind and not that of the forest creatures. Perhaps.

Skin Toot blew new life into the talk as they turned off the wide track and began penetrating deeper into the trees—

"Well anycourse, I'm glad you forded your way before the end of the sexen day. So guess who does not get fingered?"

"Um, me?"

"Yeah, you don't— you don't get fingered."

"Well then who does get fingered?"

"Someone gets fingered."

"Next person who's late?"

"Precisely. If, for example, the bringer of our meal doesn't bring the meal when we want it, that chap will be fingered 'til the end of time."

"Seems a little harsh of a sentence."

"It is by design. Tell me Dingle, can you think of anything worse than being fingered 'til the end of time? Besides... being dealt other-worse-things 'til the end of time."

And Dingle pondered the matter.

"I don't know, anything until the end of time seems pretty rough."

"I'm amending the question. Either you be subjected to any number of heinous tortures for a fixed amount of time— say twenty days— or you're fingered for ALL time. Which do you choose?"

And Dingle pondered still.

"I mean it's up there—"

"Indeed, the finger is far up—"

"I mean 'up there' in terms of things you don't want to become of you. You know, it cuts, it's terrible— and of course I have no experience with this, but I imagine it would just get boring after a while. At first it's horrific, it's terrifying... but then you'll just be asking if you can do something else— anything else— besides having this finger put up your—"

107

"Sir Dingle, I do believe you are missing the idea. Of course you've never seen how we go about this so you are not to blame, but when I say fingered 'til the end of time I do not mean that it is a constant act of unending torture— no, the finger is not repeatedly brought up and down while you are left to do nothing else with your time. To the contrary, you can do anything and everything that you might otherwise do, go about your business at will but just know that everything you ever do from that point forward, there will always be a finger inside you."

"Oh! Well in that case, as terrible as it sounds, you'd probably get used to it."

And there was a nod of consensus between both Dingle and Toot, who had now come to be on the same track of understanding with their conversings on the custom of finger-unending. But for the sake of cementing the understanding, the usual allegories and metaphors came next in to play.

"So, well, it's kind of akin to having a tongue in your mouth," spoke Skin Toot.

And Piss Dingle immediately picked up the allegory— "Right, and you forget! You forget that it's in there until you're actually thinking about your tongue."

"Exact! Now think about the tongue-less societies of our world and all the others. They're probably just now having a conversation not unlike our own, and they're saying, 'what could be worse than being tongued 'til the end of time?'"

"How awful would it be to have a thing in your mouth? Besides your teeth, just a long wet hunk of pink. Just sitting in there."

"But yet that is our reality! Damn. Now you've got me thinking that it's a form of punishment to have this tongue in my mouth, and gah I've gotta get it out."

"Right, it's gross. It's a gross thing to have."

"I'll bet somewhere in the High Above, in one of the worlds Thala traveled to in Godsong, there was a race of creatures that would find it odd to have tongues put in the mouth. And I'll wager that same species might very well have fingers naturally placed in their asses."

"Yes, and one day we'll meet and they'll think our tongues are horrifically disgusting, and then they'll show us the fingers in their asses—"

"And then we'll say that in our land, it's a punishment. We only put fingers there if men are late."

"Mm. So— this is all hypothetical right? Because you've been using the word 'you' when describing this stuff and looking directly at me—"

"Never be late and you'll never have to worry."

"That is certainly a relief to hear. But tell me, Skin *Toot*—"

"*Skin* Toot is certainly better to my ear."

"Sorry, Skin Toot— I just have to ask what your customs for dealing with... those abstaining from men-making are?"

"Is this a crime that is more relevant to you, Lord Dingle?"

"Well. Let's just say I didn't leave Harlobe all for the change of scenery."

"You refer to the Decree of Ease? We have heard of its effect, slowly but really news comes through these woods from the other side of the Essen. Tell me now of your plight."

"Yeah, so... this girl comes out of the past and the only thing that's changed is now she's a wee bit massive. Still the same old treachery in her deeds. And she knows that now because of the Decree-veez she can force me into bed and no one will stop it! In fact they'll make sure it happens, the Skulfers stood watch at the door and held me down on the bed!"

"Sounds like you have more reason than most to despise the Decreeveez."

"The Decreeveez can go to Darkwood and the Deepest Pits for all I care."

And Skin Toot put kind fingers of reassurance on Dingle's shoulder—

"Aye, fret not my lard. Here we will do you no harm for abstaining from men-making. Here you'll never be punished for doing nothing."

"Those words are excellent, for doing nothing is what I intend to do for a very long time."

And for a deep spell of days, nothing is exactly what Piss Dingle did.

He sat outstretched on a bed of ropes between trees, just above the Essen, on a bend in that river, overlooking the border of Harlobe across. He was served fruits and fingers upon wood platters, but unfortunately, his food arrived in a timely manner, and so for those two weeks he would not have the pleasure of having his curiosity fed, for none would be fingered til the end of time yet before his eyes.

"So what's your story?" asked Dingle to his forest host on one of those uneventful morns.

"I have more than one, surely. That question is far too broad for me to make any serious poke in it."

"Fine then. Let's start with this: why does one call you Skin Toot?"

"From the sound that protrudes out of a skin flute, one supposes."

"Are you... in any way like that sound?"

"No more than any other man. But my forefathers found comfort and joy in the sound of a skin flute, the skin toot as it were, and so they wanted—

110

quite naturally— to have a hint of that same joy when they looked upon me, I'd wager."

"And how do you pass the days, Skin Toot?"

"In sorrow, mostly."

"I mean, what do you do to meet your ends?"

"Not a thing, anymore. The Unspoken care for me and all of my ends."

"Convenient setup you have, then, to keep you from being upset. But before you encountered these Unspoken?"

"Well, I don't much like to go back to those days. But because you're an honest friend, I'll tell you true. Pardon the hint of shame that's sure to read in my voice, but I— I used to deal in Stocks. Comparing the Stocks. Of men."

"There's no shame in that."

"There is though. For the Stocks I refer to were of a lifetime breed. Life-long stocks. Of solid excrement."

And here Skin Toot went on to describe the true nature of his job, which up til now had been completely unknown as a profession to the mind of Dingle. It is too sorrowful to report in full, so I have omitted some passages at the expense of being fingered til the end of the month. But I will retain the knowledge that the average life-long Stock of a man could amount to the size of ten horses stood up and put together, and in these Skin Toot would dive for anomalies and trinkets, and compare the weight with Stocks of other men on scales. This was all done to for the sake of satisfying the curiosity of wealthy elders, so that they would leave life knowing how much waste they had produced in their time.

Making wagers on life-long Stocks of Excrement was also a desperate way for a peasant to miraculously find wealth in their twilight days, and this aspect of the

111

job Toot enjoyed, for to bring happiness to those on the verge of death who had never known such a thing was a mighty treat indeed.

But still Skin did not like to remember those days.

"And how was it that you made your own ends, Master Dingle?"

"Please. Call me Piss. But as for myself, I dealt with Bare Cod for a living."

"You don't mean the undressed fish, those that swim the streams of Tugpikkle?!"

"I mean exactly that."

"Is it a job of great fulfillment?"

"Like all jobs it answers only to your frame of mind. Some days I would feel disgraced to be wet, disgraced to be touching and failing to touch the scaly and slime-ridden beast, then demeaning them all the further for the joy of our town's amusement. But other days I would feel well enough, knowing that if I were not in that position I might have been in one worse— at least I wasn't pulling the intestines out of living whales, as I hear is done on the southern shores of the sea."

And Piss Dingle and Skin Toot made a fond embrace, to drain out the twitching memories of the past.

"Now there, now I've gotten to know my host."

"A host? Is that how you're thinking of me?" asked Skin Toot.

"Well— you haven't forced me off this land."

"What right would I have to? I was given this land by none, for this land was held by none. Stay here and lie atop the tree as long as you'd like, but this inactivity may rot you inside and make you large."

Dingle didn't care. The idle time was what he had been craving for some long years, and he went on watching the River for a further spell of days.

112

It was then the twelfth (or douchen) day of Lurvarion, and Dingle had laid upon the Kind Tree for about two weeks. But then a wind blew true something that gave Piss a mind to rise: the smell of meat. Pork and bark, is what he smelled. And as Skin Toot arrived with a daily platter of fruit fingers, he found it strange to see Dingle on his own legs.

"You've risen early," spoke Toot. "Could it be that you've reached the limit of your idle time?"

"We hold to a certain phrase back in my parts, Skin: we hold that it's never too late to meet one's neighbors."

"Oh, and share in their feast?! Is that what you're expecting, Piss? You smell the pork and bark."

"Well, I— I haven't had a solid cowbed in a full lifespan of the moon."

"And what makes you think my Unspoken are well enough in flame and platter to serve up mighty cowbeds?"

"I'm just craving a cowbed is all I meant. I make no presumptions on what it is you folk here eat."

Skin Toot glared long and hard, hard and long— hard and hard and long and long— at the fiendish Dingle. But then he went friendly.

"You have a firm unwavering countenance, that ya do Dingle. And so I'm beginning to take a kind eye towards you. But before I take you to meet my Unspoken company so you might mooch of their meats, do one thing for me do. Put up your pie, and I don't mean your baked crust."

"Then I guess I don't know what you mean," spoke the confused man of corn fashion, who had only ever known pie to be a dessert of baked crust.

113

"Your pie is that stump that you balance on! Hanging on down there at the bottom of your jam! Ya do know what jams are?"

"Oh. Sure. I know what jams are. Are you talking about— my body?" For indeed Piss Dingle had not heard the words pie and jam in reference to Passian anatomy before.

And here Skin Toot sighed, and placed hands— or hams, as will be seen— all over Piss Dingle's living corpse. With each slap of his ham, Toot listed off the equivalent in his own folks' dialect for the various parts of the Passian body.

"Farheed, tit, jew, nooz, hole, nake, hams, jams, pies, drips of moonlight, drops of starlight, cups, bobes, tarts, purrnice, hor, eez, feese, shooldarz, chevy, airs, leeps, stormac, burly, kees—" and he tapped Piss Dingle on the chest, "and in there's your core."

And then he slapped him on the ass— "And that's your feast."

Thus did Dingle come to know the new terminology for the ports of the body, all according to Skin Toot and his tribe of the Unspoken.

"Ah, now I see," said Piss Dingle, "why my people think your people are bizarre as rock-hards."

"And you haven't done the thing which I requested some moments ago."

"Oh, my pie. Right. Apologies, I was distracted when you sprung forth twenty new terms for things I thought I always knew the names of."

And Piss Dingle reluctantly raised his foot— or pie— onto the tree stump.

"Off with your boot, Dingle."

And Dingle, even more reluctantly, removed his boot.

"Thank the gods of which there are many," sighed Skin Toot. "Your second drop of starlight is just as long as the first. If this were not so, we would have to operate. Or you be shunned from this place forever. But you are not deserving of the genocide that my Unspoken like to impose."

"They... impose genocide on people if their first toe is taller than the second?"

"Yes, for that is wrong. You and I have met their standards and so we will not be killed, now let us go on to meet these lovely folk."

And he led Dingle along the trail, then shortly after veering off into the woods. After a few great strides, they stopped in the shallows of the wood, just paces away from the trail, at a young narrow tree that had a great birth defect: it was growing completely bent.

"Now tell me what we should do with this and you will partake in the largest feast you've yet had in your life tonight. I cannot say it will be the greatest, but the largest yes."

"You want me to... tell you what to do with this crooked tree?"

"I'll let you feast if you can tell me what we do with it."

"Well... just let it grow?"

"Well on course we intend to let it grow! We're not choppers of trees in this wood!"

"Oh. Then... what are you asking?"

"What do we DO with this tree? It's a special tree to be sure! Can you not see that?"

"No, I— it's very special," muttered Piss, nodding his head with extended lips. "Very special."

"We call it 'Bended Tree.' For it is quite bent. And that is why we believe it deserves some sort of purpose in life."

"Well you could always disembowel someone on it. Lay them back against the curve of the bark."

115

Skin Toot's face grew wide and tall. "And with that, my sacred Piss, you have earned your keep."

"My dinner, you mean."

"Dinner sure, but a bed as well!"

"And who says I want to be staying all that long?"

"Well, you've stayed fourteen days and nights, doing nothing but sitting upon a branch and looking out upon the Essen. You might spend forty now once you make into the shallows of our woods."

"Of that I cannot be certain."

"You'll be off then, after the meal?"

Piss Dingle pondered, and seeing that Skin Toot might already be quite fond of him, thought it might be advantageous for him to stay, and saw the possibility of milking his favor.

"It seems to me, Skin, that you desire me to stay more than I've any such desire myself. What will you give me to take up residence?"

"An army. Of Unspoken men, so that they'll never speak harsh words against you."

"Well, an army that grand sounds too large to pass up."

"I'm not guaranteeing that they never argue. But they have their own way. Their way is not of words."

"Ah well then you'll have to offer me something else."

"You could name the place?"

"It doesn't already have a name? You haven't named the place you live in?"

"I had a name in mind but the Unspoken threw up guts when they heard it; I took it as a declination but as they are Unspoken, they could not suggest to me a better alternative."

"What did you endeavor to call this place?"

"I was thinking Skin Village."

"Yes that's awful. How about Dingle's Dagger?"

116

"Sounds as if you want the place to be remembered for yourself. And your dagger— do you have one?"

"No but I'd like one."

"And why's that?"

"So I could use it to impose my will in naming this place."

"The scene has just now played across my mind and there will be no need to bring it into this world. Henceforth we call this place Dingle's Dagger."

And as they approached the Camp of the Unspoken, the smell of pork and bark filled their nostrils thrillingly.

"You said you were craving Cowbed?"

Piss Dingle nodded, but Skin Toot's head shook the other way.

"We will give you things far better."

Chapter VIII
A Meal of Roasted Cunt

"How many men do you suppose to surround you?"

This was the question posed to Piss Dingle after his eyes had been bound, upon approaching the place Skin Toot called the Dark and Wonderful Deep— a rounded forest clearing in that place which was soon to be rechristened as Dingle's Dagger.

Dingle opened wide his ears, and— hearing nothing but the near breath of his companion Skin— took what to him sounded a reasonable guess: "I suppose there is none but you around me, Skin, and that you will now poke me with blade to spill my bowels, and roast them before me. That is the best guess I can venture as to why you led me into the quiet Dark and Wonderful Deep, without the use of my sight."

Skin Toot laughed aloud. "They are quiet! They are very quiet. But alas you share this space now with 42 others besides myself, and they are the Unspoken, for they do not speak."

Here Skin Toot removed the blind from Dingle's eyes, and the first thing to be seen was a Dad Pole.

"What am I seeing?" was Piss Dingle's response, and a natural response it was.

"We call this a Dad Pole," informed the good Skin Toot as he patted Dingle on the back. "It is where the Unspoken tie their fathers when they have become too old. As I understand, it's been their custom for nine generations."

"Why do they hold this custom?" asked Dingle to Toot, as he looked up the tall pole, seeing three old wermen bound near its peak.

"That I do not know, nor seek to find out."

"Is this not what one might call an evil custom?"

118

"It is quite conceivably an evil custom."

"Then why don't you do away with it? Are you not their chieftain, and claim to be the Master of these Unspoken? Do you not wish to uproot evil customs?"

"You forget where you are, Lord Dingle. This is not Harlobe, Narlobe, Farlobe, nor Westlobe! This is the YONDERLOBE. And here we do not judge. Here we tolerate. And therefore the only custom we hold is that it be necessary to uphold all customs, whether they be conceived as evil or right, and that is why we have peace."

"So never mind the peace of those poor old men, whose sons have thrust them up the Dad Pole."

"I would not dwell too much on their plight. For, as I have spoken, the thrusting of fathers up the Dad Pole has gone on for something like 300 years, so really those elders have nothing to blame but themselves. If they had wished to avoid, at all cost, the evil fate of being thrust up the Dad Pole, they could have left these woods long ago. But they stayed. And so one might presume that they were either looking forward to this obscene tradition, or they were too dumb to make flight when it was possible. In either case I do not pity them. Just as I would not pity you if you had languished in Tugpikkle for the rest of your days."

"No, I do see— if I had stayed in Tugpikkle and languished I would have had none to blame but myself. But I have come now, to a better place."

And just as he said this, an elder fell from the top of the Dad Pole, and let out wails of brokenness as he cracked upon the ground.

"You see now, that when prompted only under the most severe circumstances, the Unspoken will make use of the voices that the Deep Lord hath granted them, though they sound not intelligent at all."

119

And to shut the wails protruding from the broken father's neck, Skin Toot tossed up a large branch from the ground, and battered the elder to the forest floor with a fell swing. Relieved to be once again amongst the quiet of the Dark and Wonderful Deep amidst Dingle's Dagger, Skin Toot spread his arms with welcome.

"Come now, and drink of my cup."

Many thoughts tickled about Dingle's mind as he sat to table, with Skin Toot to his left, and thirty-nine Unspoken folk to his right. He had just witnessed the casual killing of one old at the hand of his host, and he wanted very much to judge this deed. But Piss Dingle went to war within his mind, remembering how he had longed to escape the world of judgment, and that in Harlobe he had faced vexing frustration to the point of insanity from both sides of his judgment. So now the long-traveled Dingle chose to at least entertain the notion of peace and tolerance granted by his host, and to accept the custom of Dad Poles as just one of those odd, regrettable things.

Now he lifted up his cup, which was lined with thick hair— beast hair, it must have been— and he objected to its feel.

"I don't like this," spoke Dingle of the cup and the milky juice inside.

"It is not for you to like, it is for you to drink."

And so Dingle put it all to stomach— the cup too, for he could see all around the table devouring the cup of beast-hair after its liquid had been consumed. "What is there for me to like, then?"

And the Master of the Unspoken rocked from side to side with a stupid gesture of hands as his arms were raised. This signaled for the Unspoken to serve the fruits and meat of their twelve course feast.

"What is the occasion for this great feast?" Asked Dingle of his host.

"It is the Eve of Cotimas, dear Dingle. As the moon reaches its summit, we will enter into that holiest of days, the thirteenth of Lurvarion, that which marked the arrival of Supreme Lord Horlio amongst this land when it was yet called Glitharog."

"I don't know what any of that means, but I'll give it toleration."

"Ay! Spoken true like one of the Yonderlobe—" and Skin Toot toasted to Dingle's goodness.

After a plethora of standard meats, a dish was placed before Dingle which made his curiosity and judgment come rushing back. For now on his plate lay what appeared to be the sacred temple of a woman, cut out from the body and served as food. Nausea ensued.

"And what do you think of our delicate dishes?" asked the host.

"Well," spoke Dingle, raising a hand to his mouth, and choosing his words carefully, not wishing to offend, "I can see why those across the river find you to be uncivilized brutes."

"Have you not seen one before?"

"No, I— I've seen one. Remember, I told you I was molested but weeks ago?"

"Perhaps you had shielded your eyes."

"I know what this is, Skin. I'm just confused why it's on a plate."

"It is their custom—"

"And it is an evil custom."

Skin Toot smirked and shook his head. "Evil? How so?"

"To cut out any part of a person's body to serve as a delicacy is, it's just beyond society."

121

"These meats were obtained through the most civil of means, I assure you, Lord Dingle."

"Yeah? And who was civil enough to let you cut out their womb and serve it in the middle of a feast?"

"That womb before you belonged to one called Sand. I know this because whenever I asked her name, she would lead me to the sand— this is how the Unspoken give me their names. I did nothing to cut Sand's body when she passed, it is all done by those around you. It is their custom. If you must know why they do it, look to them, and not me. Though I suspect you will not grow to understand them so soon."

"Fine. So these Unspoken Paleskins are completely outside the reach of civilization. They are violent to no end, and because we're in the tolerance of the Yonderlobe we just need to accept it, right?"

"Violent to no end— how do you mean?" asked Skin Toot with a puzzled face.

"How else has this vagina come to be on my plate if not by violence?!"

"It is only the natural proceeding of their lives. Many of their women know that they are of great taste and therefore take it upon themselves to sacrifice their bodies come old age, in honor of the Feast. There was no violence done here. Only a willing sacrifice."

And here an Unspoken Paleskin set down a platter before Skin Toot, lifting the lid on a tall tower of man-flesh, sprinkled with spices and surrounded by green lettuce, with colorful juices trailing down the sides.

"Likewise, the wermen do the same. If you would feel most uncomfortable in partaking of the feminine roast, feel free to trade with me and instead devour this erected masculine phallus."

Dingle opted to work on that which was given him, and left his host to his more pointed dessert.

"I still don't know how I feel about this," gagged Dingle as he chewed on, this being his first foray into cannabalism.

"Think of it this way, Lord Dingle: the elders who chose to end their lives on Cotimas Eve desired for you to enjoy their meats. Now, if you do not enjoy them, their sacrifice will have been in vain. There is much to enjoy, so I plead with you to swallow."

After the Feast of Cotimas was finished, Piss Dingle cried in a corner of the woods. Here Skin Toot continued to comfort him, and attempted to explain away his guilt:

"The meats you devoured were given of pure consent. You know the importance of that word, Lord Dingle. Is it not better to eat what you consider to be a heinous meal if it was given of pure consent, than to do anything else without the gift of consent?"

And it was Skin Toot's allegory of consent that made Dingle finally begin to feel at home within the Yonderlobe. Yes, all of the customs of the Unspoken were bizarre to no end. Most of them were considered heinous by any who claimed to be part of an advanced society. But Dingle saw that all around strove to uphold these customs by consent, and they were joyous in their rites.

It was as Skin Toot had said: anything done by consent, however egregious in the eyes of a privileged Rich Mahogany of Harlobe, was ultimately better than anything that would be done without consent.

"So the law of Yonderlobe in tolerance and consent," spoke Piss Dingle in the bright of Cotimas, as they rode upon asses.

"It truly is that simple," nodded the good Skin Toot. "These asses tolerate our asses, and so they consent to have us ride them, and so this Yonderlobe, Land of Tolerance and Consent."

"But which takes precedence?" Here Skin Toot was confused. "I mean," continued Dingle, "What if someone in this Lobe were to be intolerant? Would their consent still then be valued?"

"Oh! Yuh-durga-durg. I see. You ask the question I've longed for you to ask. What becomes of those evil men from Harlobe and Farlobe, who find their way wandering across our borders?"

"Yes. What becomes of them?"

"Well, if they are tolerant of all things given consent, as you are, we welcome them in. As we did for Swilly."

And here a tall and slender Mahogany flutist leapt out of the woods and pranced about Dingle, who was startled to the point of collapsing.

"This is Swilly, our resident flutist, who is not shy of skin."

"Not shy of yourself?"

"Well, yes, but also the skins of those who find their way into Yonderlobe who are intolerant. Once we have proof of anyone's tolerance, their consent is then discarded with. Such is the joyous simplicity of our land."

And with Swilly fluting about with a charming tune, Skin Toot led Dingle to a wood chest, which he flung open, revealing a the entire chest to be full of skin. Dingle gave out great vomit.

"Are you intolerant of our methods whereby we deal with intolerance?" asked Swilly.

"No— no no!" yelped Dingle. "I'm tolerant. I'm tolerant of all the customs driven by consent in these lands!"

124

Swilly laughed joyously at the crack in Dingle's voice, then brought his flute back to his lips, and pranced about, back into the woods.

The sight of the chest full of actual skin haunted Piss Dingle for the better part of that Cotimas in the year 3333. But again, as he reflected upon it, he saw that there was nothing so evil about it. The evil had been done by those who had crossed over into Yonderlobe, seeking to bring their prejudice and intolerance along with them, tainting the free spirited nature of that land. Being there was no high authority in this Lobe, it was only natural that law and justice be meted out by individuals, and Dingle certainly preferred the simple logic of Skin Toot's justice to anything he had seen back home.

Here, anything would be tolerated as long as it was driven by consent. But as soon as one showed any sign of intolerance, or if one committed an act which was not driven by consent, they would then be subject to total punishment (the kind which here usually took the form of a skinning).

As Dingle came to this realization, he began to recall his old childhood dreams of using his body to no limit, of crusading against injustice by way of harsh physical prowess, and showing all the sway that his body could have on enacting monumental deeds. For too many years had he given way to the norms of others Lobes, where violence was only condoned against Tanfolk or Paleskin. For one of Rich Mahogany flesh to be violent against one of his own breed was unthinkable.

But now Dingle did desire to use his great physical strength to demonstrate the virtue of equality and justice. And he told it to Skin Toot the day after Cotimas—

125

"I've been thinking about that chest full of flesh. And I think, that I want to do... the most heinous things, ever. Against those who deserve to be mutilated. I only worry that word of these mutilations will cross either river, and mutilations are severely punishable in both Harlobe and Farlobe."

"You're in luck," replied Skin Toot. "For little that ever happens here finds its way to the knowledge of those in other Lobes."

"But at the same time I want an audience. I want that. I want the world— the entire world— to know exactly what I'm doing. And be horrendously appalled."

"You sound a bit like Fingerboy, I dare say. Going out publicly to bring deep acts of violence against those you deem to be foes?"

"Look, Skin Toot— we are going to overdo Fingerboy in all his fashions. All of Fingerboy's deeds will pale in comparison to what we do."

And now Skin Toot was beginning to see that Piss Dingle was altogether a wilder beast than he had reckoned. Now he would have to be reeled in.

"Look, it's one thing to have the yearly skinning," explained Skin Toot. "If an especially rowdy and disrespectful man crosses over the Essen onto our side of the river, with him we can do what we please. But we can only keep at it as long as it keeps quiet. We can't make this an affair worthy of legend, because as soon as we do, the Skulfers will cross over and then we'll all be burned up."

"We will be a mobile force, both stealthy and silent in the deep of the dark."

"Still, Dingle! We can't go around bringing death down upon those who are in the Supremacy of our neighboring Lobes. That won't be tolerated."

"But see, I can do that. Because I'm one of the Rich Mahogany myself; I can get away with skinning my

126

own race. Well, not really. But you're right, you certainly couldn't get away with it. Because your folk are 'lower'— not saying I believe that— but the Mahogany Man does. So you need me to be the glorifier behind this. I give this entire plot validation. Without me, you're just a lot of Tan Folk committing atrocities against the Rich Mahogany Man."

"Ah, yes!" shouted Skin Toot, his voice growing in thunder. "With you at our front, we are not just a barbarous group of heathens! With you at our front we are a statement, an ideological force as well as a brute one!"

And so it was decided, that Piss Dingle would become the head of their defiance, and they would as Fingerlobe (or Fingerboy) did in years past, dispensing justice as they saw fit in that primal place of astoundingly common law.

Now men of Arnindol came to the place called Dingle's Dagger, to attend a council convened by Skin Toot, who hoped that they could all join forces in rising up against their Rich Mahogany oppressors. But the Tanfolk of Arnindol were up in arms as to why the place was suddenly called Dingle's Dagger.

"It was not called Dingle's Dagger the last time we were here, Skin!" shouted Meil Cummax, a broad and boisterous Tanfolk with dirt upon his whole, the leader of the Arnindol party.

"Last time this place was called nothing!" shot back Skin Toot. "Other than the Dark and Wonderful Deep. Rejoice for we have a leader among us now! One who is willing to take the fight to the men of intolerance that every day now cross our borders. And best of all, he is Mahogany himself! So we will not be so quickly swept aside; if we follow under him and he is taken to trial, the

127

Mahogany leaders will find more sympathy in him. He is our man."

But Meil Cummax was not of accord. To his fellows of Arnindol he spoke, "I do not like that fraud Piss Dingle. He enters in with words of promise, offering aid and to lift us up out of our toils. But is that not our own right to do? If there is any to lift the Tanfolk out of torment, is it not the Tanfolk themselves? We must be our own deliverers, and not depend on one from the camp of our rival."

Here Piss Dingle arrived with firewood. "Ay! Got the firewood— you guys speaking ill of me?"

"They are, Lord Dingle," nodded Toot regrettably.

"Look, I get it. Meil... Cummax? That's your name? I understand. The Rich Mahogany— my breed— has been terrorizing you and the Paleskins for centuries. You want to rise up from their tyranny. But remember I am not one of them. I crossed over into Yonderlobe by my own accord, and now I seek to help you."

"We don't need your help. We Tanfolk will pull ourselves up by our own stamina, as we did in Westlobe."

"Well, Tanfolk have always been the Supremacy in Westlobe. So really your allegory should be that you'll pull yourselves up as the Mahogany did in Westlobe, which... hasn't happened. Again, I offer you my assistance, as one who currently stands as an equal in the eyes of the Rich Mahogany."

But Meil Cummax would not stand to be under one of the same breed that he so despised, and so he took most of his men back with him to Arnindol, where they would form a group of outright militarism to face the Mahogs head-on. They would be known to history as the Arnyndoline. What few of them remained there with Skin Toot in Dingle's Dagger would come to be

128

among the first DINGLEITES, along with the Unspoken Paleskins residing there in the woods.

That night, the first Council of the Dingleites was formed, and all present agreed to follow the command of Piss Dingle and Skin Toot, and spread forth across Yonderlobe in search of intolerance and men who did not hold regard for consent. These would then be brought to Dingle's Dagger with haste, to be dealt with in merciless manner.

All rejoiced to be part of such a bold new venture, and they made merry under the stars to the sound of Swilly's flute.

As the flute of Swilly sounded out, bringing thoughts of seduction into the minds of all, Dingle cast eyes onto a lovely woman seated alone, perhaps ten years his elder. He did not wish to have any incident remotely resembling the tragedy of his actions with Countess Slivvery, so far the longest of times Dingle kept his distance. But at last when many had gone to their tents and still this lady lingered, Dingle asked if he could take a seat next to her. Invited to sit, he brought up a topic that they would surely hold common ground in: the agreement that Lobe Minister Skulfing was in all ways atrocious.

"That man is the worst, is he not?"

"I doubt anyone here would argue with that," spoke the lady (now, the name of the lady has come down to me as many things throughout the years— all from the same source, that source being Dingle himself, who apparently couldn't remember the girl's name. Ann-Maurice it was, when first he told me. Shortly after he said no, the name was actually Anna-Leece. Changed his memory was again, and the name was then for a time in his mind "Aneese." Among others were Anna-Reese,

Anticreece, Anal-Ice, and Ann-Martee. We will call her Ann.)

"Some days I wonder if all the hatred in the Lobes could just be tamed— perhaps not quelled entirely— but lessened to a significant degree if that one man could just be made rid of."

"Well surely he's the largest of our adversaries," spoke Ann, "But after he's gone we'll have years of genocide yet to carry out."

And here Piss Dingle saw that it was the Countess all over again. "You mean, you won't rest until all prejudice and intolerance is completely stamped out?"

"Wouldn't you? Justice won't be justice until everything they stood by to enable is done to them."

"So you're saying you would round up my mother, and my grandmother too if her ideals didn't match yours entirely, and do to her the things that some of the Mahogany have done to the Tanfolk and Paleskins?"

"Tell me of the things your grandmother has said."

And here Dingle listed some of the insensitive comments his Grandmother had let slip in the past, despite her best intentions.

"If you can't see her as being problematic, then you're part of the problem."

"Now I'm part of the problem? I'm the one who suggested this initiative of retribution, now I'm part of the problem if I wouldn't condone it stop

"Where would you have it stop?"

"Well I have you not go after the likes of folk like my elders. She's not engaged in any crime, she's a kind person—"

"Kind only to her own kind."

"But doesn't that count for something? If you would go about doing unto half the Mahogany what half the Mahogany did to half the Paleskins, doesn't that

130

make you just as bad as the half of the Mahoganies that you wish you to condemn?"

And at this Ann was puzzled. She then stressed her desire for peace, but to Dingle it sounded to be nothing more than "We need peace, as long as I'm always right."

"Look, I'll lead this group of Dingleites until we see the veil of hate lifting. We take out Skulfing, and I have no doubt that the problems of these Lobes will begin to correct themselves, and they'll we'll have the same peace we had before."

"But that's what you don't understand," scolded Ann. "To you, the world was at peace before. Yes, Skulfing made things worse for everyone. But to us, we were never content. To us, contentment is not something to be regained, it is something to be discovered. To you, this battle ends with Skulfing. But to us, we will not stop fighting— we cannot stop fighting— until we've achieved equality."

Her words were of passion and clearly she believed what she said, and Dingle would have done better to have just respected her view and let it be. But Dingle was dumb, and still he wanted to make his point —

"Look, just don't go after my grandma is all I'm saying."

Ann shot him a glare of contempt.

"And you should be happy I crossed over. What would you guys be doing now without me? Huh? You'd still be in Arnindol. Because a group of Tanfolk rising up agains the Rich Mahogany is a farce and you know it. But because of me, you all might stand a chance. And I will lead these Dingleites with vigor until we have Url Skulfing on his neck, just as his Skulfers had Flod on his neck... but after that I don't know."

This did nothing to relieve Ann's anger.

"Url Skulfing's heinous. Just be happy that I— a Rich Mahogany from Harlobe— am sticking my ass out to help put an end to his heinous ways."

"You seem to be a heinous man yourself."

"That I do not dispute. But I have no plans to run for public office. And that's the greatest difference between a bad man, and one who must be put out of his ways."

"Don't forget to wet the beds," spoke Skin Toot to Fur Dirks, one of the Dingleites, when all the tents had been taken and only a few hours of moonlight remained. And at this remark, Piss Dingle was curious, and so followed Fur Dirks through the trees to a dell full of flattened stones.

"Why do you follow me?" asked Fur Dirks.

"I am dying to know what you're about to do," replied Dingle.

"No, you are dying to fulfill your pact with nature — that all things granted life upon Overlind are indebted to give back what Lyvierfania has given."

"Well, yes, I suppose that is the reason why I am literally dying. But I'm following you because I am entirely wondering why Skin Toot told you to wet the beds."

And Fur Dirks lifted a finger, then lifted a bucket of water out from a nearby stream. With his long arms he thrust forth the bucket and the thick round of water hit the flattened stones. Within moments, the stones began to grow soft, and Piss Dingle's brow moved up and then down.

"Now the men of Arnindol may rest easy," sighed Fur Dirks as he pressed the palm of his hand in the moistened stone of mush— a rising of water emerging up around his fingers as he did so.

"I will not be sleeping on any such thing," spoke a defiant Dingle.

But he did, and then the night passed on.

In the wide of afternoon, Piss Dingle was awoken by a heavily stimulated man of the Unspoken. He shook Dingle, slapped Dingle, licked Dingle with long strokes of the tongue, and at last Dingle began to beat shit out of the Unspoken, for he knew not how to communicate with him.

"It is not a complex thing he wants from you, Lord Dingle!" shouted Skin Toot as he emerged down the path. "So do not harm him anymore. Now come. And see what is glorious upon this day."

He led Dingle to the top of a wooded crest, and pointed down at a freshly uncovered pit, where a finely-dressed Tanfolk wandered about, looking for means of exit.

"Who's this?" asked Dingle genuinely.

"He's not one of ours. Crossed over at dawn, riding swift from Harlobe, fording the river on a valiant stallion."

"So what? We're not gonna kill him. He's one of you. He's Tanfolk, I thought we were after privileged Mahogs like me."

"Take a look at his attire. He's one of wealth, that's for sure— by the looks of it, one of Skulfing's Deeplove to the highest degree. I'll wager he's a Tanfolk of Westlobe, where that breed reigns supreme."

"Oh... so you want to..." and here Piss Dingle gulped, realizing that the last several days had all been talk. Sure, it had been joyous to speak of skinning foes and bring adversaries to gruesome doom, but now that he saw some such man helpless down in yonder pit, he grew sick in the stomach once more.

"Fret not, Lord Dingle. We will first put him to the test."

And here Swilly dropped down into the pit, himself now dressed in regal attire. "What would one of Skulfing's Deeplove be doing here in Yonderlobe, I wonder?"

"Truth be told, I was expelled from his presence. He did the same to Fendyrd after years of service, but I never thought the same would become of me."

"No? Why should you have been any different?" Asked Swilly, dressed in Skulfer attire and speaking in a regal voice.

"Because I did everything for that man! I turned my back on my own principles, stances I had held since youth! All went tumbling down so that I could carry out every whim of Skulfing, and when he sent me across Lobes to speak with his followers, I did as he would have me do. I knelt down and licked their muddy dick bottoms, put honest tongue against the underside of those foul things, but alas it would not suffice.

"For Skulfing's supporters have not been growing in number. He has not won any new followers in his last terms— if anything, he hoped to retain all he had, but the Opposition has been on the rise. Skulfing knows this. That Piss Lip is set to win the Choosing!

And so Skulfing asked me to go cross-Lobes once again, only this time to speak with the Counters of the Choosing with all my intimidation, and to persuade them to count in favor of Skulfing no matter what the outcome. This I will not do. This my conscience will prohibit. For in two months, there will be a Choosing of the Reign, and if Piss Lip is meant to obtain victory, I cannot stand in place of his destiny."

"So, let me here confirm," replied Swilly. "You stood by Skulfing for years, yet this is too much? Now that he aims to steal a Choosing for the second time?

134

For surely you adhered to similar deeds three years ago, in the Choosing of 3330."

"Yes, fellow Skulfer, it is true. I was the integral piece in the re-election our Great Minister Skulfing, for in truth the counting was in favor of Bahmoeth Burden three years back. I rode against the Counters, setting fire to their halls, putting old women to the sword for doing nothing more than engaging in this broken Lobian democracy."

"It appears as though it would not have been broken, had you not helped to smash it," pointed out Swilly.

"Yes and to what end? Still I finish as Fendyrd, expelled from the favor of Skulfing upon my first word against him."

"Only you do not finish as Fendyrd."

"That is right," nodded Huivz, finding this as cause enough to smile. "For Fendyrd had not the foresight to flee, and was swiftly disemboweled. I, on the other hand, was already halfway out the door when I denounced Skulfing, and with my steed in hand I mounted, racing fast across Harlobe til I came to the Essen, where I knew I would be safe. For the Yonderlobe is home to wary men like myself, men like you, who have grown tired of Skulfing's regime, and I do not doubt you will guide me through these lands so I might find my way back home to Westlobe."

"You are right in one of those things, Huivz," smiled Swilly, as he placed a hand upon the shoulder of Huivz, "You will not share in the fate of Fendyrd."

A swarm of birds erupted out of the trees, soaring quick for quiet, since the woods of Dingle's Dagger now filled with the shrieks of Huivz.

On Bended Tree, this former chancellor of Minister Skulfing was bound and nude, most disgracefully.

Piss Dingle watched on with a sense of obligation: this was the world he had committed himself to, and he could not look away, no matter how he wished to.

By his side stood Swilly, playing a bouncing melody merrily upon the flute, as Skin Toot stepped forward with knife in hand, to take the flesh from Huivz — in the same manner as skin is peeled from a deep and juicy fruit.

Chapter IX
Master of the Unspoken

In the prisons of Ho Spleen Ho, the fiend Leg Randy was given massive pleasure, day after week, as confused and frantic word-seekers flooded to his cell—

"Why did you do it? Why did you kill the Honorable Piss Lip?"

And every time, Leg Randy shrugged the questions off with apathy: "I dunno. Thought it would be neat."

Or sometimes he gave a secondary answer, which was little different, "I did it because I could. I thought it would be a neat thing to do."

And obviously word of this unexpected stroke of good fortune reached Lob Minister Skulfing, that his primary adversary had been dealt with in so gruesome a manner. Skulfing— like the vast majority of those in the realm— felt that certainly this Leg Randy must have acted out of some sort of enfueled rage, or on behalf of a bold political agenda. He simply would not believe, the same as others, that Leg Randy would have killed Piss Lip out of sheer randomness, on a whim as it were.

Yet Leg Randy insisted there was no real reason for the killing. He had not planned to kill Piss Lip; he didn't even feel a great desire to kill Piss Lip. To the contrary, Leg Randy admired Piss Lip, as did all the peoples of Tree City beyond Cumpear. But when that beloved man was visible upon the hill, unarmed and without guard, Leg Randy had felt a sudden impulse: that it might indeed be neat to become a political assassin, if only for that night.

And so prison is where Leg Randy now resided, given no rest from folk who pleaded to know the true reason for the killing, when in fact all truth had already been spoken. To placate their curiosities, Leg Randy began to make up a different story every time, and all who spoke with him grew mad.

Still, Lobe Minister Skulfing was quite certain that this Leg Randy must be liberated to join his cause. Regardless of reason of logic, this Leg Randy had indeed rid him of his chief political opponent, and for that Url Skulfing was prepared to obtain the service of this freak. And so he dispatched that loyal executor of his deeds, PARPINFOHZ, to liberate Leg Randy from his cell, so that he might be brought to Essen, and made to do deeds of a similar striking mischief directly for the Leader of the Lobes.

I am told that PARPINFOHZ did not wish to set Leg Randy free. This is understandable, up until this point PARPINFOHZ had been the sole executive in Url Skulfing's line of executioners, and was rather pleased to be seen as first and foremost. Strings of jealousy no doubt took hold, as this Leg Randy had single-handedly done away with Skulfing's rival in a momentous strike. Who was Leg Randy to take upon such a feat for himself?

Of course the fears of PARPINFOHZ that his office would be eclipsed were unfounded, for Leg Randy refused to even depart his cell for the fortress at Essen. But PARPINFOHZ tied him to a horse all the same, for it was his task to bring this one-time killer into the presence of his lord.

"You have done me a great favor," spoke the voice of Url Skulfing upon his rounded throne in his fortress at Essonoth. "One that no others were capable of."

Here PARPINFOHZ objected, saying that he would have been all too willing to kill Piss Lip.

"But you, my loyal executioner," explained Skulfing, "had you done this deed all the Lobes would be in revolt, for it would have been clear that you had been sent to do my bidding. Thanks to this bold... Leg

Randy... we now have our rival dead, but all the world thinks it to be nothing more than an accident. Of course we know better. Tell me the true place of your allegiance, Randy."

"I don't really have any allegiance," shrugged Leg Randy. "I just thought it'd be cool to kill him, so I did. Won't do it again. Well, because I was successful the first time. So I wouldn't be able to kill him again. But all the same I won't kill anyone else."

"You will serve me in other ways then?"

"No thanks."

And the negotiations went on as such deep into the night, with Leg Randy stood firm against Skulfing's offers, and all the while Skulfing viewed the vexing man with an immovable sense of reverence, for nothing could remove the fact that Leg Randy had so heinously murdered Piss Lip, and this was pleasing to the Lobe Minister.

We depart now from the wicked scene of treachery, which was so placed to set up later things, and return to the jolly presence of the ones we love. But we will not find them where we last did, for on the day of which I write their home of Dingle's Dagger was all spilled out.

Piss Dingle and Skin Toot were now on the move, to another Lobe— the Westlobe, if you must know. And as they approached the Deepshallow of the Craun, which would lead them out of Yonderlobe and into Farlobe, two men stepped to the edge of the ledge, which looked down into the ravine forming the border between those Lobes.

The men were them. Them here being Piss Dingle and Skin Toot.

"Why do they call this place Deepshallow?" asked the first man, who was still Dingle. "I would just venture to call it Deep."

"The gorge is deep but the water is shallow," replied the second man, who was still Toot. "It is thus named to avoid confusion with the Shallowdeep, which you will find on the southern side of Little Fools."

"Which be the easier to pass?"

"Well surely you can see the river Craun would give us no trouble at all with the crossing here, the water being hardly knee high. But the valley is too deep."

"Yes, that's the problem."

"Whereas the Valley of Shallowdeep would be but a hop down and up, only there the waters are so swift and relentless that they'd swallow you down lovely. So the road for us is that which cuts across the Craun at the town of Little Fools."

And Piss Dingle grumbled to hear they would need to step back into civilization, however brief. For living in the Yonderlobe the last several weeks he had become quite the Bastard of Beard— that is to say a barbarian. He was come to be made of unshaven sweat, and his mouth had not opened wider than an inch in many days, for the only one he spoke with was Toot, and Toot did not mind to decipher blatant mumbles.

"Maybe you cross over at Little Fools and I find my own way over the river," mumbled Dingle.

"What? What's that?" laughed Skin Toot. "Your mumbles are fine back home but we draw very near to Farlobe, where men won't have it. And you in your abundant skill might find a way to leap the Craun, but that is not what shall be done. We won't have the founder of our Dingleite company jumping off to death or misery with a broken leg, when a crossing is all too simple at the next town."

"Look, I don't mind walking a little further is all."

"Why walk further? We're almost to the town of Little Fools now!"

"Alright, here it is. I have unfond memories of that place."

"Unfond memories? Of Little Fools?! But the place is so very hospitable!"

"I do not see it as such," shook Dingle, with a blatant disdain for the place. For as I was later informed, he had spent a regrettable four years in the town of Little Fools to pursue his learnings, while in transit between his birthplace of Murder Creek and Tugpikkle. There he had been consumed by an unwilling solitude while all his peers form broad coalitions, and when at seldom times he ventured to speak, his words sounded of pure shit which wrought only embarrassment and valid reason to then judge harshly the one who had up til then only been guilty of silence and seclusion.

But enough of Dingle's prior doom in Little Fools; he spoke of it rarely and if it is ever to be explored in depth it must be in a work of his own, should he ever learn to write himself. Now we proceed to Dingle's second doom of Little Fools, to where he was lured with pork.

"This is how they get you," ranted Dingle as he nibbled upon that pork. "They make you go through their town. Whoever came up with Little Fools— it's a brilliant idea. Just center a town around a bridge that people are gonna have to use if they want to get across the river without walking fifty miles in either direction."

"If only our own Dingle's Dagger was so favorably situated, as to command the passage of visitors."

"What are you speaking of, Toot. We don't ever want My Dagger to become a place where people are forced to go. We want to keep them out. Why'd we leave?"

"Have you truly forgotten?"

141

"I... know we've been walking for two days but I've completely lost grip of where we're going and why we were. Which isn't all my fault. The way you described it was very unclear and convoluted."

"I will not argue that our present journey is full of masterful convolution," spoke the good Skin Toot, and then he sang: "While it is right that I am truly he, the Master of the Unspoken, I am not so by my own power, nor by right. I hold that title in return for the tribute which I grant to He my Overlord, He who holds the very lives of my Unspoken folk in His breast. And I take you now to Him, so that He might transfer my authority unto you, so that your excellent lordship will be in all ways Master yourself of my Unspoken friends, under only this Overlord who is grand and tall and lovely. Lovely and large, large and deep like a dog. He is Wi Tan Pree, and he lives amongst the stones: deep and glorious rocks of Lidion, where that great battle of old shone true like death! And if you are lovely as lovely boys are, you may find this Wi Tan Pree gifting you other things besides! For he is deep in the ways of grace, and lovely things will he bestow upon lovely, lovely boys. But beware of the shops on the skirts of those lands, for many a man will they catch, offering pipes of great promise! They are far more spendy, than any pipe I have ever seen, and simply at no greater... quality."

And the song was finished.

Piss Dingle stared a good few moments at Toot, to make sure he was done. "So this guy's gonna give me stuff?"

"Only if you're kind and lovely."

"Pff, you know me. My loins exude those things."

The passage through the town of Little Fools proved not as swift as Dingle would have liked, or as

Skin Toot had promised. This was because the work of shuffling thirty-some Paleskins— Unspoken, at that— through the Farlobe border was challenging in those days: Skulfers kept a keen eye on the bridge, ever ready to whack the cream out of any they saw with lack of pigment in their skin. They needed only a reasonable cause in the eyes of the law, and these "causes" were often times stretched to apply to even the narrowest of suspicions. Yes, if there was any suspicion at all— if a Paleskin raised his voice in an unsuitable manner, or if a Paleskin showed up with a questionable cloth concealing the genitals (though this is what was requested to combat the Crown Sickness)— this would be seen as enough to warrant a Skulfer to pounce.

Needless to say, a forest-dwelling lot of thirty-some Unspoken Paleskins from Yonderlobe would then be enough to warrant an immediate execution under Skulfing's regime. So before Skin Toot crossed over, he gave explicit instruction to his men that they were to only cross over the Bridge of Little Fools one at a time, or two by two. And each pair was then to place a hour's wait between each crossing, so as to avoid all sense of suspicion. It is sad that suspicion was thus defined as people walking across a bridge in group-like fashion, but then again this group was indeed a band of warriors looking to uproot Mahogany Supremacy in the Lobes, so perhaps it was understandable from the point of view of those in the high seats of power.

For the remainder of that day (21 Lurvarion 3333), Piss Dingle and Skin Toot sat at the pleasant tables of various taverns along the calm of the Craun, keeping their eyes ever on the great bridge, where their white companions sauntered over one by one or two by two, every hour or so.

"I do hope nothing evil becomes of them," trailed off the voice of Dingle as he shifted his eyes from the bridge to his drink.

"Well, I'm sure a few will be picked off before the night's through, but that's the peril of journey. Can't expect to step outside your door in dangerous times and not face the chance of death."

"But did they know the chances of death were slightly higher now that Skulfing's got his Skulfers patrolling the Bridge of Little Fools?"

"Well I didn't even know that. Haven't been to these parts in years, not since I took up residency as a Toot of Dingle's Danger, you know that."

"But you did communicate to them that the Farlobe has now become treacherous to them?"

"Let's speak of other things. What'll you have your main in?" Asked Toot, motioning to Dingle's menu.

"I'll have my main in tits."

"You forget we're not back home. We'll have to enjoy food of the Farlobe: if a child can't touch it, you can't eat it. Those are the rules they swear by here."

And so Dingle settled on the cat-core main, whereby the grilled heart of a cat was served to him with onions. Skin Toot ordered the milk shells on ice.

"Anyway, lovely country we'll be heading up on in two day's time, Athragal."

"What's in Athragal?" asked Dingle unemphatically, for he knew the Farlobe to be nothing more than flat and dry, devoid of all interest.

Here a man walked in from out of nowhere, making a heavy-handed claim. "They have the best countryside."

"The BEST?" asked Piss Dingle, in skeptical disbelief, but the man who had made the claim so unexpectedly had already gone. "Pff, you hear that Skin?

144

Some fool of Little Fools thinks Athragal's got the best country."

"I would agree with him. They do have the best countryside."

And Dingle raised his brows high at Toot. "We talking about the same Athragal? Flatfinger Athragal?"

"Well, yes, Flatfinger is at the top of Athragal, but there's more to Athragal than just Flatfinger. Much more."

"Flatfinger was the flattest, most boring... place I've ever been to. And the landscape never changed. All the way from Watercross to Little Fools. Just an entire Lobe... of flat."

"Ah, you took the Enterlobe. For you did not think to travel but a few miles south, where you would have found the most pristine valleys of gentle rolling hills that you will ever see."

"You're giving my dagger a tug."

"There is no tug. There is only truth in that which I speak: the winding road of Athragal, that which dips under Flatfinger, leads you through the most glorious hills imaginable."

"Then screw my father," huffed Dingle, "Made us take the Enterlobe. Still, I can't believe that it's the best. The best countryside you've ever seen? How can it be the best when just a miles north is the worst?"

"Men are often surprised to hear it, but the greatest gems of our earth are hidden just out of sight from the places that are oft-traversed."

"Oakay... how good is it?"

"Would you not rather find out for yourself? Why ruin the freshness with words of foresight."

And in truth Dingle was beginning to thirst with desire for this so-called glorious countryside, while at the same denying that it could ever be as grand as Toot was making it out to be. But their travel plans would sadly be abruptly changed, for before the night was through, four of their Unspoken friends would be either murdered or taken into custody by the Skulfers. Three of these were stopped on the bridge for daring to go across as a trio, and a threesome of Paleskins was great cause for alarm in the eyes of the Skulfers. The fourth was brought to death as he danced across the bridge holding a stick— a broad stick he used variably as a walking pole and as a thing to be waved about in the air. The Skulfers knew that they could evade scrutiny by the quick killing of one such as this; if their deeds were criticized, they could simply inform the courts that the Paleskin held that which could be deemed a weapon.

In the town of Little Fools, Skin Toot quickly assembled his Unspoken friends at the meeting spots he had instructed them to go to, but they were growing ravenous and shaky with anger upon learning the fates of their four unfortunate companions. Skin did his best to calm them and inform them that they must leave the town of Little Fools swiftly; if they did not, there would be greater trouble to pay.

And so they left in the night, but a lookout on the West Gate of Little Fools caught sight of this wailing crowd of Paleskins as they made their way out. He informed the Skulfers, and a great chase was made, for no mob of Paleskins was to be permissible in the Farlobe under Skulfing's new laws, for fear of Paleskin riots. Mahogany riots had been deemed just fine, and in fact a thing of great pride— all young folk of the Rich Mahogany breed were encouraged to riot, for whatever they saw fit. But a Paleskin riot would not do.

Necessity, then, obliged the Dingleites to lift their pace and their legs, and to huff on at a jog through the entire length of that dark night, lest they be overrun by the Skulfers who now pursued them.

"Good Skin Toot," panted Piss Dingle, out of breath as he struggled to keep up with the swift Unspoken, "I don't think I want to see the glorious hills of Athragal like this. It's not right. It's not good timing."

"Any fool would agree with you! That is why we have altered course. We now make for the High and Low Road— yes, the plain High and Low Road that marches straight towards Lidion in the Westlobe which will prove to be a quicker jaunt. Our eyes will be deprived to take that way, as we will not see beauty, but also will our eyes be spared, for they will not be put out by Skulfers if we do yet hurry."

"And both ways lead to the same place? This... High and Low Road?"

"Yes, both roads lead to Lidion, once great capital of the Kingdom of Alyinen, shining tall amidst the prairie... now all their structures have gone, collapsed through either time or dismantlement, but the Redstone Valley remains, and this was always the most beautiful anyway."

By some great miracle of Horlio, the Dingleites ran the whole night through, and were not overcome by their chasers. In the morning, they again dispersed, those of light skin making for the Low Road, while Piss Dingle and Swilly— the only two Mahogs currently in the party— took the Farlobe High Road, as was customary.

"Tell me Swilly," spoke Dingle upon the High Road, "Have you been to this place called Lidion?"

"I have, but speak another word of it I damn well shan't."

"Is it true that all their tall structures from the Age of Enchantment have collapsed? All of them?"

"Well, the Fortress remains. In ruins. But that's a wide yelp from what rows of glory used to welcome those who travelled to that Westlobian oasis."

And here the talk was temporarily closed, for the Farlobe was subsiding into Westlobe, and therefore the High Road and Low Road now crossed and switched places. Those on the Farlobe Low Road— Tanfolk and Paleskins of inferior breed— now rose up to take the Westlobe High Road, for their breeds were now in Supremacy. And likewise, the Mahogany men on the Farlobe High Road now moved on to the Westlobe Low Road, for their Supremacy was no longer a thing in this Lobe.

"As I was saying," continued Swilly, "Up the road here a few miles you would've been welcomed by the stunning towers of Lidion Vargis, two shimmering towers of golden yellow, reflecting all the suns' rays like a dancing pool of piss. Those towers would've been here."

And Swilly pointed to a bare spot on the flat land, where there was nothing.

"And just beyond, right about there— was a broad temple with four sides rising to a single peak, just as bright and shimmery, but all black."

Here Swilly pointed to the place of the ancient pyramid, which was now occupied by a mound of trash and the startling remains of livestock.

"And a mile or so beyond, a sprawling fortress with rounded turrets, a palace of a thousand colors, built of finest stone, cut and polished to make every man feel a king."

Here Swilly pointed to the place of the ancient fortress— which was at least something. The ruins of that landmark stood tall enough, only a fraction of its former height, but no room was enclosed. It was only sparse walls, here and there, with old decaying stone that were falling out of line, with the vines of the earth overtaking its ancient glory.

"And last of all was the Little Village. Well, they called it the Little Village; I reckon it took in more folk than any of our modern towns in the Lobes. You can see up here it's now a pit."

And indeed the Little Village was now nothing more than a pit; a pit because the scavengers at the end of the Age of Enchantment made it so. They had dug out every last acre of old achievement when those days had reached their end, carrying the structures of higher society out with them and taking them off to their pitiful communes of disgrace. Dazzling wonders such as Lidion Vargis had risen up in the course of merely a century (the 27th century, of course) only to be completely undone in the following century, and nearly forgotten by the next.

Now in the 33rd, all of it was a distant memory, known, yes, by the likes of Swilly, or anyone who cared to dig through the old books, but never to be seen in its enthralling grandeur. Piss Dingle thought this sad, and laid down a quick prayer that his entire life might be a bad dream, and that he would wake up in the arms of that comforting 27th century, where all was possible and towers stood shimmering in the sky, for all to enjoy and take part in.

But alas, Piss Dingle truly did live in the year 3333. But it was not all cock-dismal, for Skin Toot was right: the Redstone Valley did remain, and this was the most beautiful of it all, anyway.

Dingle found it to be strange— for miles in every direction was a flat grassland prairie, which then without warning gave way to a long and curving row of these massive chunks of red stone. Just before the stones, or "Lidion Proper" as one could call it, the High Road and

Low Road of Westlobe met up, and so did Dingle and Swilly with the rest of their company.

Skin Toot now led Dingle to the edge of the Redstone, where they looked down to see a drop of about twenty feet. Not treacherously deep, but at the same time deep enough to inspire a feeling of greatness.

A collection of smooth narrow paths curved all about the place, weaving in and out of trees and boulders. And of course, the sound of a contented waterfall gave off a calming sound in the distance.

"That be the sound of the Falls of Harl," smiled the good Skin Toot.

"Great. Now where's this Wi Tan Pree so we can get our help?"

"Help is not what you have traveled to seek," spoke a voice calm and deep, from inside the rocks.

Dingle turned apprehensively, taking the voice to be some dirty trick left over from the Age of Enchantment. But it was no trick; the voice was true, and the man it belonged to strode now out of a deep crack in the mighty rock. The man was as he had been advertised: large and deep, tall and true... wise and lovely.

The man was Wi Tan Pree.

"You have been knocked off your guard by the introduction of my deepness. Let me say again what it was I said: help is not what you have traveled to seek."

"Well I certainly thought it was."

"No. You have come to seek my approval of this venture. I give it now my blessing, and you will be henceforth glad that I did."

And Dingle was amazed that such a thing could be so easy. "You sure? You're just gonna approve it without us saying anything?"

"I was informed of your journey by a letter sent by Ward Geit Fung."

150

"So me and Skin Toot are gonna wreak some massive havoc on the Yonderlobe. We're gonna be jumping on bare bowels and shit. You're fine with that?"

Wi Tan Pree gave Dingle the smuggest face of all wisdom. "I trust your venture, no matter how heinous, is a necessary thing, in bringing about... what needs... to be brought about. So go now. Go forth. Go... with my blessing."

A spell of time passed as Piss Dingle looked firm at Wi Tan Pree with head bent and brows low, ever still as Skin Toot swayed from side to side, chewing the air and drifting his own eyes to avoid feeling the oak-ward sensation. At last Dingle spoke.

"You better be giving us more than your blessing. We're not leaving with just that."

And so Wi Tan Pree drew forth a smile, and led Dingle and Toot silently towards the edge of the rock towers, down a winding stone staircase— the Staircase of Joy, as all should know— into the little valley, where a well-paved path snaked between trees.

"Your dagger is rusty, Lord Dingle."

"Yeah," retorted Piss, passing it off with pride and confidence, "It's meant to be like that."

"I think not," spoke Pree, knowing better. "Rust be a sign of farring age, and farring age be a sign crumbling effect. At any rate, such a dagger is not so strong as you may wish."

"It's strong enough. Many a throat have I pierced with its blade."

"Here in Lidion we define the word 'many' as more than six. Do you stand by your statement?"

"No. But that is only because my pal Skin Toot tore me away from my business, to come and find you in your small but holy valley."

"You words are of cock," smirked Wi Tan Pree. "But it matters not to me; go, go back to your dealings on the west-banks of the Essen. Try as you will to cut the throats of men with an ever-rusting knife. In mere weeks you will find it grows harder and harder— if you have not already felt its change. Soon you will have to push with might just to penetrate the skin. And that gives your prey an advantage: in the extra moment that it will take for you to end their life, they will have squirmed or twisted their way out of your grasp, and you might come to have your own blood drawn by a rock to the skull, or a twig in the eye."

"Fine, give me a new dagger."

And here Skin Toot stepped in to apologize for the bitter sting of Piss.

"It's the clouds, they've made him unkind."

"Strange," laughed Wi Tan Pree, "For I and my folk find it is the suns that make us sluggish and unkind. We adore the clouds here, it is the only way we find the strength to rise and carry through the days in pleasant stance."

"Yes, we as a people are very much not alike," said Dingle bluntly. "No matter what they might now be saying in Ho Spleen Ho."

"But there is nothing wrong in being not very much alike," nodded the wise and tempered Wi Tan Pree. "The danger comes either in assuming that there is, or beginning to think that we are so much alike as to warrant like behavior."

True to his hintings, Wi Tan Pree presented Dingle with a host of shining daggers, which he pulled from a narrow chasm between great slabs of redrock.

"You just keep your blades lying inside your rocks? Shouldn't they be locked up in a chest of... of some kind?"

152

"You speak as a true and affluent Mahog, ever fearful of what one might do, while here we think only of what people will do. There are none here with ill intent. What will one of our folk do upon finding a sharpened knife in the crevice of a rock? You might— out of fear— say that 'oh, he might wound us.' But it has not happened. Instead, they use the blades to cut through food or cloth, and there is nothing wrong in that."

"Sure, no one's used these for violence yet. But you wait."

"We will wait, Lord Dingle. Perhaps it will happen while you are here, for after all, your company is the only in our midst that has ever partaken of violence. A mark of your breed, I might think."

"Wo-kai!" exclaimed Dingle, a bit provoked. "I'll admit, the Mahogany are... quick to anger. But we hear far more tales of Tanfolk violence than that of our own —"

"Those are the stories, but they are untrue. Yes, in recent years, Tanfolk have become violent towards the Mahogs as the Mahogs drive them off their own lands, lands that we have resided upon for generations. I think it is only natural."

Skin Toot, sensing a rising hostility on its way, backed up against the redrock, fitting himself into the narrow crevice.

"Not so hasty," retorted Dingle. "The Mahogany conquests are one thing; sure, Tanfolk violence might be warranted there. But you can't be saying that your breed were never violent themselves before that."

"There has never been a murder in this valley since the time before time."

"But over in the Farlobe," recited Dingle, raising a finger, "In that place called Moysinthy? They would

153

murder folk every week for the sake of ritual, before the Mahogany marched over and put an end to that."

"Well, to that I say, that the Tanfolk of the Westlobe are far different than those of the Farlobe.

"I'm just speaking of Tanfolk in general."

"Well don't." And Wi Tan Pree began to walk away, turning back and interjecting, "Don't speak of any color of flesh in broad strokes, for it is without point."

And Piss Dingle bowed his head, silent. Still Pree went on.

"Did we not just speak of the natural variance among men? The variance does not simply stop with flesh. There is not a color that defines character. And character is not defined by color. Now you might very well see similarities among 'breeds' as it were, and you might point them out if you mean to be humorous or well-intentioned. But to speak of flaws in the Passian race and assign such flaws to an entire breed, it is the most base of all stupidities."

And he took his leave. Dingle, with wretched head still low, did not even turn to look as Skin Toot slowly moved forward out of his crevice.

"For a moment it did look like that was about to rupture into a mighty brawl," nodded Toot.

"No," sighed Dingle. "He's too well-tempered for that. He finds the strength to walk away, while delivering his sermon with such fluent words, elegant and concise. Perhaps it is he who should lead our cause. He who should carry the daggers. He who should change the tide of the Lobes."

But Skin Toot shook his head and nudged Dingle's side. "If he carried the daggers, we'd never have any corpses."

"And why do we need corpses? If we take bodies from the Mahoganies, will not the Mahoganies continue

154

to take bodies from your folk, and at an increasing rate? Will it not be war for all time unending?"

"If this world were right and fair," spoke the peculiar Tanfolk to the peculiar Mahogany, "Such things could be carried out in words. Wars could be fought in the Talking Places and the right verdict would flush out into the streets. But men don't see the connection. Their own lives are null-affected by the preachings of richer ones who spend their days wrapped up in debate. The makers and the farmers, the merchants and the cooks—they're the ones who make up the near whole of society. And they're the ones we're trying to reach. Listen they will not... to the great strides that might be flowing out of Talking Places. They need to see things."

And for a moment Piss Dingle gleaned an honest bit of wisdom in the tender eyes of Skin Toot. But then he continued.

"They need to see with their own eyes, their kin burning bright and hanged from the branches of oak and ash, as they have done to us and the Paleskin. The children need to see the innards of their fathers being pulled out slowly, as your rapist Katario once did with whales, so they might know what's in store for them if they don't change their ways. The Rich Mahogany must cast aside her richness; it is time for the Tanfolk man to rise. And rise we shall."

Piss Dingle let out a whistle at the intensity of his friend's words. In all truth, they gave him a bit of a scare.

"I find it odd, Dingle, that you have not yet tried out your new toys," spoke the large and deep Wi Tan Pree, looking on as Dingle fingered his collection of polished daggers.

"And how do you know I haven't yet tried them? Your eyes have not been on me all of the day."

155

"Believe me, I would know if you had thrown one of those mighty blades."

Dingle looked all around. Not much of a target anywhere in sight. "There be no one in my sight worthy of receiving it in the neck."

"Why don't you try a tree?"

"I was afraid that, in your supreme reverence of the trees, you might find offense at me daggerin' one."

"We love our oak and elm and ash and spruce, but all of those you see in our midst are strong enough. They will feel the strike of your dagger and rejoice, for to them it will feel as a tender tickling upon their hardened bark."

"Wo-kai." And Dingle rose, readying his dagger by its tip, eyeing up a tree with squinted face and beginning well his form. "Watch about now, don't want any ripped-up vein should this toss go awry."

And he let the dagger fly. It twirled through the air, tumbling over itself forty times before striking the tree. And as it struck, a sound of explosive thunder, crushing stone and sudden avalanche filled all of their ears.

Dingle and Toot were astonished. Wi Tan Pree laughed, bringing merry hands together.

"I am completely without speech," spoke Dingle in an ironic contradiction.

"Is it not the most magical thing you have ever heard?"

"It's probably the most surprising thing I've ever heard."

"The daggers produce a sound which in old days might be called a 'car crash.' They are old, very old these daggers. Fresh from the Age of Enchantment! And therefore they speak. Thunderous words of their own. They are among the last of those relics."

"If only the structures of that century had found a way to last as long as these daggers," smarted Lord Dingle.

"If ancient structures are pleasing to you, come with me now, and we will see a thing to be seen," smiled Wi Tan Pree.

And so they walked through wooded lowlands for some time, until the land opened up before them and they beheld a tremendous work of architecture. Rising above them were two great bridgeways, tall beyond the reach of thirty men, and stretching across the River Dan, though the mid-sections were fallen down long ago. They were monumentally tall, so tall as to be denoted "fricken huge" in the Annals of Stone.

"This is... the tallest thing... I have ever seen," whispered Piss Dingle, struck by wonder, a figurative tear streaming down his cheek.

"The structures of Lidion Vargis were much taller," spoke the blatant wisdom of Wi Tan Pree, giving Dingle a pat on the back. "These are but roadways."

"What cause— what cause did mere roadways have to be so tall?"

"Cause? Well, no cause at all. They could have been built just off the ground. But men in those times were proud and capable, and so they built their roads to be a hundred strides off the ground."

"Why are there two? One for Tan and Pale, one for Mahogs?"

"No. Of course not. When those bridges were built around 2712, there was no great difference between the breeds. Petty prejudice, within the minds of every odd individual perhaps, but nothing built into society. Their world was lovely in that way. All laid claim to the same rights of life, and had an equal shot at bettering themselves. But to answer your question, there's two of them because of what they called 'tree-fuhk.'"

157

"Tree-fuhk, Master Pree?"

"Tree-fuhk is what came of so many people all wanting to go to the same place at the same time. And even they had the fastest mode of travel— brilliant shells of a swift and terrible speed— sometimes these shells would get backed up, and men would get very angry. The double road was then, a means to prevent tree-fuhk from spilling over and killing those who were traveling the opposite direction. On one roadway, folk would go east, and on the other, folk would go west. So that all the shell on one's roadway would be, ideally, traveling in the same direction. Tree-fuhk still proved to be deadly, but far less so."

"It's quite brilliant."

"Many things in those times were brilliant," sighed Wi Tan Pree with a smile. "Those were the times of Fingerlobe."

"I call him Fingerboy."

"But of course. Surely you read of his deeds in the childs' manuscript, that which has more pictures than words, that which has corrupted his name and presented the disembowelings as lovely and rose-scented."

"Judge me not."

"Before you go, there are two matters more," proclaimed the tall Wi Tan Pree to Dingle, Toot, Swilly and the Unspoken, after a sensual night spent in the calming midst of the Falls of Harl, amongst that oasis of the Redrock Valley, in the haven of Lidion Proper.

"The first," continued Pree, "is this dead deer. Preserved and petrified, his fur and bone grown quite stiff. Stiff enough to handle, without your hands tearing it into a crumbling paste, as is often the case when one attempts to handle a corpse of long dead issue. Yet light enough to lift with little effort."

158

"Well, praises!" said a mighty puzzled Dingle, scratching his hair. "What am I supposed to do with the dead deer?"

"Do as your instinct dictates, should ever the time come when your fingers find themselves without a dagger ready."

And then Piss Dingle gave his secondary weapon a trial, lifting the aged deer carcass off the ground, easily for it was indeed quite light. In a single moment the deer was high above his head, and then twirling through the air.

"Lovely. And the second thing?" asked Dingle.

"Yes, the second matter is also of great importance, and it concerns the storehouse on the edge of our land. There are pipes there that you might purchase. Go. Buy them. With whatever coin you have brought."

Here Skin Toot bowed his head most graciously, and he went in haste to buy many pipes.

Chapter X
In the Image of Almighty Fingerboy

Now I believe it is time, at the beginning of this tenth chapter, for me to introduce myself, for those who find themselves still reading.

Forty-five minutes before I came into this tale, on the 15th of Lurvarion, there was a conversing between Dingle and Toot that went as such:

"Say, the Good Skin Toot, I do believe we are on our way to achieving great and terrible things."

"I do concur, my Honourable Piss Dingle! The world will shake from our loins and rest forever changed."

"Well if that's true, then we ought to find someone to set our conversings to script, before we forget completely what has transpired in the past weeks."

And so the admirable men went about the near places, searching for one with the full-fledged qualities of comprehension, wit, as well as knowledge of letters and their craft. The road was not an easy one, for— be it no mark against their intelligence— the Unspoken lot truly could not read nor write. Swilly could not write. Nor could any of the Dingleites that had come from Arnindol.

But among those in Dingle's Dagger that day— two days after the Feast of Cotimas, when all were still monstrously fat— there sat a stranger, in the corner of the place, holding fingers with his fingers.

His name was Ward Geit Fung, and it was me.

The Good Skin Toot approached me then, and said to me, "We're in search of a chronicler, one to set a record of our deeds and send it forth to the masses."

"We need you to send our deeds far and wide," clarified the Honorable Piss Dingle.

"I could do that," said the one who was me.

"Well this is our guy!"

And a great set of terms were put forth, after many questions on their part. For my part, I told them my entire life story, how I was one paid to walk about in the background of city streets, doing things of no consequence, so that great administrators could display the goodness of their streets when royal inspections came round. I then spoke of my tasks concerning letters and writings, which include but are not limited to:

—An account to find the number of days between the birth of myself and the birth of all those I meet.

—An account to rank all the reigns of kings and tales.

—An account to record all the nighttime eyelids, or 'dreams' as they are sometimes called, that I have any recollection of.

—An account to align each day of the year with an occurrence in my own life, spread across the many, many years.

—An account to reorganize the passage of time, so that the numbering of years is more suited to the events that have transpired therein.

Of these numerous accounts, Piss and Skin were most impressed, and felt ever certain that I was the one destined to sing of their deeds. Yet through my own folly I let pass that I had once— only once— done a foul murder, and this brought them some uncertainty.

They took to whispers, and I could not make out their words. But then Skin Toot asked me loud:

"I'm sorry, did you say you murdered someone?"

"It was but one murder. Not some one. Just one."

"Was it heinous?" Asked Dingle.

"I..." was how I started out, as though I could make it seem to be a friendly murder, but I gave up the charade with a shake of the head. "Well yes. It was."

Dingle and Toot exchanged their glances as they are ought to, but they needed their chronicler.

"Anycourse, I'm sure it wasn't that heinous. I shouldn't have suggested that word. It's an extreme word. Tell us of your murder, Ward Geit."

"So— and just to be clear, this is someone who deserved it— but anyway, I..."

And my deep friends put their lobes in close.

"I snuck up to the house, and barred the doors. Then barred up the windows. Then set it ablaze. With her— she who deserved it, mind you— and her werman friend... and her family inside."

Upon hearing the extent of my heinous murder by flame, I saw Piss Dingle and Skin Toot turn their heads slow to face one another. They stared long, and I heard their voices say something to the effect of 'Oh damned and furry excrement.'

And they paused.

"But he's still the guy, right?"

And I was relieved, for they were not going to let my crimes disqualify me from employment as their scribe. But Skin Toot was not so eager as Dingle, and he leaned in close, whispering in words I could just barely make out. They went something like such:

"Look, nobody else here can read or write. I don't like it either, but... what are you gonna do."

"Right, right— but he's trying to make it sound like this girl deserved to be burned inside her own home."

"Well, she probably didn't but he's— he's trying to get the job! What else is he gonna say?"

"Why don't we ask more about his reasoning for burning this girl and her family alive?"

"Because then we'll just come to hate the guy."

"Right, and then we'll have no one to sing of our deeds."

"Our deeds aren't gonna be the best either."

162

"Not to some people, no."

"Arsony's kind of funny too sometimes."

"Typically not when people are trapped inside the arson ground."

And as this went on, I became discouraged. Not wanting to waste their time any further, I asked for a verdict. And as I did so, I held up a scroll of my penmanship, struck down with elegant strokes of thin line and deeply smooth curvature.

They looked at me, decided of their choice.

"Full pardon," was all they said.

And so I leapt in my heart, frolicking in this second chance that had come along a most unexpected of roads.

In the afternoon, as we rode along the Park of Sainthood, they spoke of tales and how theirs would soon be better than them all.

"We're gonna have the best tale, don't you think Dingle?"

"Our tale... will be the tale that everyone speaks of... until the end of time. So marked with complexity and chilling sophisticated violence, that the full-grown will revel in it. It will truly be a tale for the full-grown, and none younger than full. But at the same time, children will love it."

"They will find it massively appealing as well," chimed in the good Skin Toot.

"Where would you like me to begin tonight when I first set pen to parchment?" was my first question.

"Uh... well, I suppose the front. Start at the front, right? Tales ought to be told from the beginning."

"Absolutely false," was my response. And I then went on to tell the true way that tales ought to be told, if they are looking to be in league with the best:

"Stories should be told always from the start, but that start need not be the beginning. In fact, it's poor

163

form if it is. I've learned that the best formula is to begin far left of center, and then to jump to the catalyst, proceeding with a jump back to explain the context of preceding years, then jumping right but not all the way, then further right past the center to a great incident, then further yet to provide an anecdote for said incident, then back a few months to the center, then back far left again to provide context for a present conversation, then proceeding forward as normal for a good bulk, and then jumping back a month or two to explain a character that was up until that point left out, then back to the center, where we proceed until there's a broad, broad sweep of time, which then proceeds until there is cause to go back for a quick explanation of how things came to be as they are and to provide the suspense that is needing to propel the tale towards its point at the furthest right, and then of course ending with the end."

"You're dumb, Ward Geit."

"Such a method of storytelling has been proven time and time again!"

"Who would ever think to do that much jumping left of center?"

"The very first storyteller in all the world! As the Scribe-Boy of Parpishaly saw fit, and rightly so, when he set to paper the first and greatest of all our epics, recording the deeds of Clarfon Both in the Second Age."

"How do you know there weren't tons of tales before that, and the Scribe-Boy of Parfishinee wasn't just tired of being conventional, so he said 'watch me make a big mess out of this tale.'"

"The Clarfonath is the first tale written, and therefore sets all conventions."

"First tale that we know of."

164

"Anyway it's a mighty old tale and my point is only to prove that my conventions of storytelling are not so bizarre—"

"Who's still reading things from the Second Age anyway?"

"Well I prefer the Fifth Age to be honest. Many great feats and heinous deeds to be seen in the old Kingdom of Angelon, driven to the banks of torment in the War of Haegos. Back then one's adversary was clear. There was no debate among sides, no wondering as to who the true enemy might be."

"The same could be said of our current time!" shouted the good Skin Toot. "We know our enemies well enough."

"And how is that? How would you know your enemy if you saw one?" I asked.

"Easy enough. Our enemies are those with prejudice towards Tanfolk and Paleskin; those who support the evils of Url Skulfing."

"But that is my point, Skin Toot. You cannot tell these things simply by looking at one. You cannot read guilt on a man's face, nor sense one's true allegiance from afar."

"Trust me, the supporters of Skulfing are easily known."

"Even then. Do all of his supporters deserve death? To be smote down with indiscretion, no matter why they lent him support or to what degree? Would you put half of all people in these Lobes to death for simply falling into line with the leader?"

"Alright, Ward Geit, perhaps you've got me. Perhaps our enemies are not so clearly labelled as the Haegosians were to the ancient Angelons. But Dingle and I have been in talk with a fellow who will help us to define those who we ought to be diddling with blade, against those who will receive nothing more than passing scowls from us."

"Oh?" I asked to the Honourable Piss Dingle.

"Yeah, I know a guy from back home. We call him Carvin Cong."

And so the one called Carvin Cong, who resided in Deleras just beyond the northern border of the Lobes and was of relation to Piss Dingle, was sent for. He arrived at the place called Dingle's Dagger on 4 Duchallia 3333, having no idea what it was he had been summoned for, except that there was payment involved.

"So what is it, cousin? Why have you paid me to come all this way?" asked Carvin Cong to Dingle upon his arrival.

"We have need of one who can talk to our enemies, to discover if they truly are enemies or not."

"We? Who's this we?" asked Carvin as he dismounted from his horse, removing his velvet gloves and stroking his thick white beard.

"I am comprise the other half of that 'we!'" shouted Skin Toot, running from out of the woods— to the disgruntled alarm of Carvin Cong, who was getting too old and uppity to be a fan of men leaping out of the woods at him.

"Ha! A Tanfolk. Now I see why the sum was so large. Hmph." And Carvin Cong's tone was demeaning.

As he went to grab his belongings from his carriage, Piss Dingle gave small affirmations to Skin Toot, who was beginning to think that this Carvin Cong was a real tangledick.

"No, he's not— he's not bad once you get to know him," whispered Dingle. "He's just had a long ride."

"He seems to hold contempt for my breed, Dingle. I thought the whole point of our outfit was to stamp

166

that out of the world. And you think we should be receiving help from the likes of which we ought to be stamping out?"

"We ought not to be stamping out my cousin, he doesn't really mean to be cross. That only proves why he's here; we need full knowledge of our targets before we kill them. Otherwise we might just be killing folk on a bad day."

"Well if it's just a bad day he's had, I'll try and cheer him up!"

"Don't, Skin."

But as soon as Carvin Cong returned to them, indeed Skin Toot did pull out a charming ditty from his throat, that wondrous night in Yonderlobe.

Carvin Cong
With a carving song,
Went carving 'long,
But carving wrong!

And he was done.

A few anticipating moments lingered on, but when those gathered round knew with certainty that the extent of the ditty had been sung, they burst out in praise. Carvin Cong was not impressed at all. In fact, so offended was he by what the Tanfolk claimed to be high honor that he swept Piss Dingle away into the Smalltree Talking Place.

"You think they are clever? Truly do you think they are clever Piss?"

"I never said they were clever," shrugged Dingle. "Just that they're not deserving of having their homes burned down." And he and Carvin walked into dark seclusion.

"Well not many are deserving of that, sure, but those are deeds of the prior century," reasoned Carvin.

167

"How often have you heard of such things happening in our own lifetimes?"

"Well, it's true half of the peoples in Harlobe have turned against their feelings of superiority. And they are now held to be the moral front. So while the half that still goes on hating the Tanfolk in their hearts have still a mind to do heinous deeds, they now go on quietly about it. They do not wish to be condemned by the other half of their own people, and so their true mind is hidden. This does not mean that we have eradicated the notion of prejudice altogether."

"I'm not speaking of prejudice," retorted Carvin. "I have prejudice. Every man upon these Lobes harbors some prejudice or other in their bones. I am speaking only of unspeakable acts of violence—"

"And there you prove my point. Acts of violence against the Tanfolk have become 'unspeakable,' and therefore people do not speak of them. So they very well may still be happening. We, perhaps, are simply unaware. Because we do not hear of things that people do not speak of. This is why we need a spy."

And here Carvin Cong realized that his own intellect might only be pumping arrogance into the starry night sky, and so he allowed his friend Dingle to go on, elaborating on all his plans and reasonings. And thus Carvin Cong was employed in the service of Piss Dingle and Skin Toot, to be their spy in the woman-curved regions of the Yonderlobe.

On the 18th of Duchallia, Carvin Cong returned to Dingle's Dagger, after spending near two weeks traversing the Yonderlobe, in search of ripe bastards for his cousin to plunder.

"What news from Greater Yonderlobe, dear cousin?" called down Dingle, for he was at present standing atop a tall tree.

"I have seen things. Much," nodded the spy of the Dingleites.

"Things much you have seen," spoke Toot solemn.

"Do you know of the bridge that stands one single stride above the little ripples, in yon Fickling Stream?" asked Carvin of Skin.

"It can hardly be called a bridge, but yes, I know the one."

"Yes, the cause of its crafting can surely only be accounted to by the boredom of children. But the bridge is fine for leisure, and I'll often sit upon its planks to let my legs dangle off, and have my legends swing back and forth, the tips of my legends brushing against the cool rushing water—"

"Wo-kai then, Carvin! How often do you dangle your legs from that little bridge? How far deep, exactly, have you been in the Yonderlobe? Or have you just been splashing about the Fickling Stream? You've been gone two weeks! And now you come back with tidings from a place two miles down the road, which any of us could easily have strolled down to today by chance? What are we paying you for, Cong?"

And here Dingle climbed down his tree cautiously yet in a hurry, should conflict erupt between his cousin Cong and pal Skin Toot.

"I come back to you now with great news, do you wish for it or not?! Damned toot of the skin."

"It's Skin Toot. But yes. Do go on."

"So then. I was sitting on the bridge— never you mind how long— my legs dangling off, and all of a sudden, up comes this horse. And a man upon. 'This is no bridge for a horse' I laughed. But then he says he needs to get across the stream. I tell him to have his horse step beside the bridge, that the water is less than an inch deep, and his horse ought to step down and up from the bank with great ease. He says 'no, my horse does not like to step up and down, but rather to walk on an even scale at all times.' I say, 'well, I suggest you go back from whence you came then, and consider getting a new horse, because the only place you'll find an even scale at all times is Flatfinger, and you're not there.'"

"I know where this story is going, old man. But I suppose you'll go on with it anyway."

"I told him not to try it! Told him there was no way that lovely little bridge would support his fat arse and horse. But this cosh of a horse master was naughty and went right on, the bridge snapping as soon as the horse stood in its center."

"What's this?" asked Dingle, now stepping up to Cong and Toot. "Horseman fell in the stream?"

"Yes, a perfect target for you two I must say; you'll never find better, that lad's helpless."

But Dingle rubbed his face with his palm. "Cousin. Why... do we have cause to assault this man? The way you've told the tale makes it sound as though he was just trying to get across the bridge."

"Well we had a bit of brawl with the words. He wasn't a nice man at all."

"You're not a nice man, Cong!" said the good Skin Toot emphatically. "Does that mean you deserve our wrath?"

"Right, like I said when you got here," sighed Dingle, "we've employed you... to find men who are truly atrocious, and need to be eliminated from this earth for the greater good. We're not looking to kill for the fun of it; we're not looking to kill folks who are already having a miserable day."

"Well geez, did I leave out the most important part? I suppose I did— this horseman was dressed in full Skulfer!"

"What— what do you mean dressed in full Skulfer? You mean he was in a Skulfer's uniform?"

"That's right. Better go get him before he manages to crawl up out of that stream."

And Skin Toot sheathed up a dagger, this being all the evidence he was in need of. "Alright, I'm ready. Let's go get the cosh mik."

"Hold on, Skin," exhaled Dingle, looking to be a bit more rational. "Now, cousin, it's true we are not lovers of the Skulfers here, but going about and causing violence unprovoked is not the thing I'm looking to make my name in. Is there anything else that was... criminal, or especially revolting, about this Skulfer?"

"More importantly, what color was he?" asked Skin Toot.

"He was Tanfolk like you," admitted Cong.

"Oh. Well then we shouldn't kill him."

"But he was a Tanfolk of Westlobe!" rumbled Carvin Cong, "And that means he's more deserving of death than the Mahogs of Harlobe and Farlobe."

"Fair, fair," nodded Toot, "Well in that case, you'll have to kill him, Dingle. I can't kill one of my own breed."

"What?! Why not?! You killed Huivz! I'm the one who can't go about killing Tanfolk! I'm Rich Mahogany, how would that look in Harlobe to have a privileged man in the Supremacy killing one of the inferior breeds?!"

"Oh right, right— no you're right. I got confused for a moment on the proper etiquette of breed-motivated killings. You're very right. I'm Tanfolk, so I kill the light-skin, you're Mahog so you kill the rich-skin."

171

Carvin Cong laughed hard to see the way in which Toot so timidly recounted his error, and approached with a praising hand. "I will not see you as my equal, but my sympathy for you is growing. It's there."

"I do not like that Carvin Cong," spoke Skin Toot, as soon as they had left the presence of that white-bearded Westlobian Mahog.

"And he does not like you," replied Piss Dingle. "But this is not about liking one another— such things are overly sentimental and not practical for the current age. This is about getting a job done. And obtaining a mutual respect between peoples, in both the eyes of everyday folk and in the courts of our Empire, in justice and in life. Once we have achieved those ends, we might start towards 'liking each other,' and by that point we might skip over friendship and land directly in love." — Piss Dingle raised the back of his hand to Skin Toot's cheek, but did not let it land— "Now let us go rip apart bellies of Raycyst men."

And they veered off into the narrow trails of the forest, towards the Fickling Stream, where indeed they heard the agony of a Skulfer who had fallen down the gentle slope of the little creek, along with his massive horse.

"Think of it this way," whispered Dingle. "The man's as good as dead anyway. We'll simply be easing his passing."

"Mm, well..." pondered Skin Toot. "I'm not much of an easer of passings. That's not why we've joined forces, at least not in my view. I'd like to have a bit of fun with him first."

Dingle put low brows on Toot. "At least find out if he's evil at heart."

"That's part of the fun, dear Dingle."

172

And then Skin Toot spoke aloud in the trees, projecting down upon the miserable Skulfer who was pulling himself slowly up the stream, with tired arms and mangled legs. "You there! Skulfer of Westlobe! Do you serve in Harlobe or Farlobe?"

"Stationed in Harlobe, but now en route back home for a family gathering," spoke the voice of the Skulfer lying in the stream.

"Any tales to speak of regarding the trampling of fellow Tanfolk in those parts?"

Here the Skulfer would have to tread carefully. While he was Tanfolk himself and had always felt a proud superiority in Westlobe, he had since been conditioned to see the Rich Mahogany of Harlobe as superior to the Tanfolk there, and so while he did not wish to speak ill of the Tanfolk— for he himself was one — he felt a great need to speak to the favor of the Mahogany. And as he was a Tanfolk with intolerance of the Mahogs now fighting for the strength of Mahogany Supremacy, his very existence was not much more than a contradiction.

All that the Skulfer could think to do now was to take the side which the voice in the woods would most likely be in accord with. This particular voice in the woods sounded to be from the mouth of a Tanfolk, as indeed it was, and so the Skulfer's dialogue played out accordingly: "You have me wrong, boy! I'm a Skulfer by trade in Harlobe, sure, but I've done no wrong to the Tanfolk there! I'm a man of Westlobe!"

"Then you laid hands upon your fair share of Mahogs then?" asked Skin Toot, playing to be pleased.

"Oh but of course! Those dirty dark bastards, how they have the nerve to declare themselves in Supremacy east of Westlobe—"

And here Piss Dingle stepped out of the trees, revealing himself in full: "Yes, how do we have the nerve?"

"Oh, well sir I've misspoken! Of course I— well, being from Westlobe I can't help their own policies, but I assure you..." and the Skulfer laughed uneasily to himself, changing his tactic, "that as I served in Harlobe I was nothing short of loyal to Lobe Minister Skulfing. And of course that means persecution of the light-skinned bastards there."

"Persecution of what?!" yelled Skin Toot as he too revealed himself.

"Oh what the hell," muttered the Skulfer.

"Is this concerning to you? Never seen a cross-breed friendship before?"

"Are you that dense?" yelled up the Skulfer, who now saw this was just a set-up to kick a mangled man in a stream. "Of course I've seen friends of a cross-breed nature— I'm a tan goddamn Skulfer in Harlobe! All my comrades are Mahogany!"

"Doesn't excuse the crimes against my people," spoke Skin Toot, stepping closer.

"Your people? Your people are my people! We're the same damn breed!"

Here Skin Toot turned to Dingle, who had much apprehension in his eyes. "Better get it over with before he says more, think I'm beginning to see his side of things. If he says anymore I might come to like him."

"What was that?!" screamed the Skulfer. "Are you gonna help me up or not? As you can see I've fallen off my horse and cracked my legs!"

But the two founders of Dingleism were absorbed in their own faces, about to take a deep plunge into their own destiny.

"Am I not speaking loud enough for you?!" shouted the Skulfer, not knowing those words to be his last.

"That uniform speaks loud enough," spoke Skin Toot with resolve, and then hurled a rock at the head of the wounded Skulfer.

The next twenty-four seconds seemed to be the longest spread of twenty-four seconds in the memory of either Dingle or Toot.

"Well, that... certainly didn't seem too heroic," said Dingle at last.

Skin Toot breathed, and tapped his hips along. Finally he concurred. "Yeah. But you heard him speak. He was certainly a far cry from good."

"We might be a far cry from good too."

"Yes, well, in that case, should a pair of forest vigilantes spring up out of the woods to murder us here and now, I wouldn't complain."

There is a certain corrupted copy of my manuscript where exactly that then happens— upon the speaking of these words, a pair of remarkably similar forest men pop out from the trees to kill Piss Dingle and Skin Toot on the spot, by strangling them with goat entrails, and then drowning them in cold blood. That copy of the manuscript has come to be called the "Ironic Account," but that is not this copy. This copy proceeds as follows:

"We'd better get his body back to Bended Tree so we can carve him up and decorate our woods with all of him in a thousand different spots."

"I'd say we could have Carvin carve him, for that word play would be glorious, but I know he will object."

And indeed Carvin would have no part in the carving of this dead Skulfer.

"You sure, Carvin?" asked the good Skin Toot, who was not so very good upon that day. "You're the one who told us to go after this guy."

"Yes, I did... and after our brief talk on the bridge I imagined I would revel in the sight of him dead. But now I pity him."

"Fret not. He can't feel this." And Skin Toot laid into him with blade on Bended Tree, soon spilling out all upon the forest floor, as a pumpkin is cleared out hollow.

Over the course of that evening, the Unspoken hung the bowels and the flesh and the bone from bush and branch, and a sign was erected which read "Skulfers Beware."

Carvin erected a second sign which read "Skulfers Have Ware" and I, myself, erected a third sign which read "Skulfers Be Aware." And so it was that our haven of Dingle's Dagger came to have bloody decor.

Three days passed and the Honorable Piss Dingle came to see that there was nothing honorable in the way he and Skin Toot had disposed of the Skulfer in the Fickling Stream. He came to me, seeking guidance, and I told him words, words which are written here:

"You speak much of the Age of Enchantment, Lord Dingle, as if you long for it, when you have never known it. You have heard of its pleasure, yes, and seen but few of its monuments. But alas I say, these are not in truth the essence of what that Age stood for.

"Yes, the Age of Enchantment was one of towering structures, of glistening pools and shimmering lights, but more so it was a time of great temperance. Of tolerance and talk, all of which you crave but without knowing how to obtain it. For the glories of that age will never be reobtained should you go about, seeking to restore them through violence! By attempting to impose your will upon men by way of death can do nothing to restore the old order of things.

176

"Your methods, your mission... is exactly what brought down the towers you so admire. That Enchanted Age that you idolize was sent crashing down by the very philosophies you now seek to employ, and we are still living in a world of its consequences."

"How can we rebuilt, then?" asked my Lord Piss Dingle. "How can we put the world back as it was, when all men were seen as worthy of a base respect and dignity, and when the common will was to rise up from the earth in splendor, rather than turning the peoples against one another?"

"Sadly, I think the only remedy for this is time," said I. "In time, we may come to rise again as a people. If folk like you and Skin Toot continue on, making friendship, spreading laughter among the Lobes... perhaps mixing the breeds here and there... sprinkle these merits down upon your children, and have them repeat. In but four or five generations we may be in short order for the fall of tyranny—"

But I was not able to finish my last phrase, for Dingle was throwing up arms.

"Five generations?! You gotta bring my kids into this— who even knows if I'll have kids? Twist-a-diddle and tug, man! I was really leaning in there, with your talk of changing my philosophy and all, but then you gotta go and say the fruits of my seeds won't come up for five generations?"

Needless to say, my words had served only to rile the passions of Dingle, who stepped out to lick his fingernails in order to relieve himself.

Still, I was able to get one thing across to Dingle on that night: that he ought to suspend the notion of crusading for vigilante justice at least until the Choosing of the Reign had been decided, for it was to be decided quite soon. In just three days, folk of the Lobes would casting their votes for either Url Skulfing, incumbent of

177

the Snake Affiliate, or Bahmoeth Burden of the Ass Affiliate.

One will remember that it was Piss Lip of the Ass Affiliate who was to be challenging Url Skulfing head on — many hopes rested on the honorable Piss Lip, but he was grotesquely assassinated, seemingly on a whim by the one called Leg Randy. This indeed had sent the Ass Affiliate into a frantic frenzy in the weeks leading up to the Choosing; in the end, they went with what many considered to be a most sound option in Bahmoeth Burden. After all, many suspected that Burden had in fact won the Choosing of 3330, but was not allowed to ascend to Minister's office, for Url Skulfing then simply sacked the courts and retained his position.

This year may prove to be different, many thought. Members of Skulfing's Opposition had been in deep with the courts for the better part of the year, reinforcing their structures and creating defensive strategies to protect the integrity of 3333's Choosing of the Reign. With prior chances of foul play thus being removed, the Ass Affiliate trusted that if Bahmoeth Burden had garnered more votes than Skulfing in 3330, he could surely repeat the move in 3333.

As it turned about, they were right. But the process of confirming the Choosing of the Reign took some three weeks, and it is worth noting that in all that time, not a single murder took place in or around Dingle's Dagger. Lord Dingle and Toot simply stood back and waited, leaning against trees and learning the secrets of the flute from Swilly. And when news reached them on the 15th of Leskarion that Burden had officially been declared Minister of the Lobes, they gave him the nine cheers while at the same time lamenting that now there would be no more murders.

For there was a thing deeply innate within both Dingle and Toot, that was a product of our age: the primal lust for carnage. They would both speak invariably of peace and order, justice and mild manner, but I would see in them every day a very subdued desire to stir up conflict. It was never outright, and by no means overdone; it was a simplistic, passive violence that they pursued. Once that carried no malice or ill will, nor hatred, nor anger. They just wished to be rash for the fun of it, and to have cause enough to engage in brutal dances of the flesh. This is my analysis of them.

And so, with Burden rising to the highest office in the land, all hopes of their dark escapades of the night, brooding among the forest and halting the deeds of evildoers seemed extinguished. For Burden now promised to right all wrongs, and set well to all the evil customs of Skulfing.

As he accepted the charge of his office on the 18th of Leskarion, he addressed the masses in Essen. The masses were all wet with the tears of grace in their eyes, and sobbed to see the shadows of oppression receding behind this old and glorious Tanfolk elder. He spoke to all upon that night who could call themselves Passian: hopeful, optimistic, true, loving words of strength, but not of pride, of passion, but not of arrogance. He called for the end of hypocrisy, the end of alienation, the end of lies, the end of hate, and sang out a call to silence all the demons that Skulfing had relentlessly released. To this the crowd gave him far more than the nine cheers.

And so history appeared to be correcting itself upon that night: the fierce and fiery twilight realm was now giving way to immensely pleasing mists of soft rain, glorious cloud and abundant shade. Red was giving way to green. And dark things were giving way to all that was deep.

But it was not to be.

3333 was not to be the end of Skulfing.

I write now with new lines for each sentence.

So as to relay my deep sorrow at what unfortunately must come next.

For it still pains me to this day.

To think back upon the awful fate of Burden.

Who did not deserve his fate.

Or of all the people in his crowd that night.

So happy and hopeful, for that future to come, so close to their grasp.

For they, too, did not deserve what came next.

The Lobes were so close to obtaining its rightful redemption, and turning a page on Skulfing forever—

When PARPINFOHZ leapt onto the stage in the middle of Burden's speech and put his third finger deep into the sockets of the Lobe Minister's eyes.

Blinded, Burden would have fallen— had PARPINFOHZ not continued the attack, as the cheers of the crowd below turned to sudden screams of horror, shock and dismay.

PARPINFOHZ murdered Burden long upon the stage that night, and he was not stopped, for as he went on, a blinding gas filled the whole of that place. The capital of Essen was under assault by Skulfing's Deeplove, and they flooded down amongst Burden's supporters, shuffling them out of the city by force. Then did the Deeplove of Skulfing lay siege to the Grand Court itself, last standing structure on that side of the world to be built of glass.

Skulfing's Deeplove rammed the Grand Court all into the night, with every strike a deafening roar of anger, the voice of the mob would not be silenced. The glass began to crack and the Deeplove flooded in, with such barbarity as had not been seen since the days of Domis Foke in the 28th century.

As glass rained down, the Deeplove of Url Skulfing picked it up with their bare hands— caring not for how deep it cut them, nor how the blood flew freely from their palms— and with this glass they struck down all members of the court, who had dared to declare Burden as the victor in a fight he so clearly won.

The judges and magistrates pleaded with Skulfing's mob, trying to lay out in basic terms the tenets on which democracy rested. The Deeplove objected, crying out that Skulfing was the rightful Minister. But still those of the Court stood strong to their rightful convictions, explaining how Burden was the true Minister, since he had been CHOSEN— it was the will of the Lobians that had chosen a new Minister. To this, the mob shouted that Burden was dead, and indeed he was, assassinated by PARPINFOHZ. They demanded of the Court that Skulfing then be granted his powers back.

Still the Court refused, and this was what provoked the placing of glass from their temple to their throats. Yes, the Deeplove of Url Skulfing was so driven to madness, that they rushed willingly to their greatest city, in order to tear down its temple, object to the principles on which their society operated, and then fill the bellies of those who sought to ensure the survival of that society, with glass.

Upon hearing of the events which transpired in Essen on the eve of Burden's inauguration, Piss Dingle and Skin Toot, as well as all others in Dingle's Dagger, were... well, we were all a bit enraged.

Any hope of Dingle now settling down into a passive life of licking fingers now subsided into the clear notion that yes, more people were going to die. And not just the innocent victims of Skulfing, his Skulfers, or their Deeplove. No, now there was clear cause for action: there had to be casualties from the evil side as well. And many casualties, to match for the atrocities committed in Essen.

181

Shouts were screamed, screams were shouted, howls were cried and cries were yelled, making the company at Dingle's Dagger appear to be no better than the mob at Essen. But Dingle restored order, and told Carvin Cong to be off straight away, to be back by nightfall, with the whereabouts of the first wicked men he could find.

Carvin did not disappoint. At the setting of the suns he rode back swift into the forest clearing, the words falling from his white beard:

"There were two men I heard in the deep trees of Anaria. Rich Mahogs, speaking ill of two Paleskins, who had found the favor of women, where they had not."

"Calm yourself, Carvin, take a drink," said Swilly, offering the old Mahog a swig of water.

"Of the Paleskins, these Mahogany pricks said they said they were stealing their women, as if they themselves owned these women. As if women were things to be owned at all!"

"It's a common thing I've found," nodded Skin Toot. "Rich Mahogany wermen not finding success in realm of woman, and then taking this anger out upon other breeds."

"Quite," huffed Carvin. "In the last moonlife I've found that to be the most common cause for rage against the Tan or the Pale: fear of them having more appeal in the eyes of the Rich Mahogany Woman."

"Then it comes from a place of insecurity. Much of this 'hatred.'"

"Now is not the night for deliberation. Not the night for discussing why Mahogs hate Tannies or why Tannies hate Mahogs. Tell us more of these pricks, Carvin."

"They're called Poonzu and Fitarse— both part of the Deeplove. Both on their way to meet with old Han Dass tonight."

182

"Old Han Dass?" wondered Toot. "Swilly, how do I know that name?"

"Han Dass is that bloke what deals in bear skins. Other tiny skins. Some say he trades women too though, there could be some truth in it."

And Dingle and Toot made bold preparations as the dark tickled in. I approached them, giddy as an upside puppy, for all this excitement was the first taste of action I had been amidst since I lit that house ablaze.

"Do you wish for me to come with you?" I asked my Lord Dingle.

"I think it'd be better for you to write an accurate account if you only have our words to go by."

"I... don't think that makes sense at all. Hearing an account from would certainly be less reliable than if I were there myself."

"Fine then. Come along with men."

And so I rode with these two great heroes into the night, as stars begin to spread their fingers above. I offered them great embellishments, so that whatever happened upon that night— 21 Leskarion 3333— it might rank among the most glorious in all recorded nights of godly deed.

"We don't want any embellishments, Geit Fung. No liberties of your own making. You will write our deeds exactly as you see them."

In a fine forest clearing, made up with rich table and cloth, a tall Mahog called Han Dass stood tall, yelling out bold insults into the night. Two wermen also of the Rich Mahogany race— Fitarse and Poonzu— stood by, joyously clinking to their superiority.

"That be true though, oh yes that be true. The only reason the Tannies find favor is because they're so oppressed. The ladies pity them freaks. It's the sorrow in their weak-ass hearts. If we was in, what, the time of Fingerlobe? Back when the world made sense? We Mahogs'd be getting all the wombs. Fifty out of fifty. The Tannies and the Pales would go extinct."

"But then we'd have no one to be better than!" whined Fitarse.

"You're not tugging! So you've got those eyes on those two ladies. Them ladies think they're in love with your Tannie boys, but they're not. They just sad. So you give me the furs, I'll get those Tannies out the way for you. For another bucket of furs, I'll even get them girls right here in the woods, tied up and down. I only have one question—"

But the question was never uttered, for a moment later the despicable Han Dass was struck hard by Dingle's dagger.

"Now there couldn't be a more annoying way to witness a killing," was the response of Fitarse, who shook his head with aggravation. "Now we'll never know his one question."

And then a second dagger hit his friend Poonzu, sending him to the ground.

"What enchantment possesses this dagger," wondered Fitarse aloud, "that it makes the sound of such obnoxious thunder."

"It be the sound of a 'car crash,'" spoke Dingle from the trees. "And it is so endowed for it comes directly from the Age of Enchantment, when blades could be made to give sound. Would you like to hear the sound a third time?"

"I suppose I would!" Shouted back Fitarse, playing it cool in the face of his incredible fear, for death truly stood just over his shoulder.

"How's that?" asked the voice of Dingle, stepping forth.

184

"Well there truly wouldn't be anything more annoying than killing a man's friend and then leaving him alive for a great many days to dwell in the trauma," laughed Fitarse, uneasily.

"Well we wouldn't want to be annoying," smiled Dingle, and he was about to throw his third dagger, when Skin Toot stopped him.

"No, Master Dingle. He wants you to kill him."

"Yes, he said so. That's why I shan't disappoint."

"You don't catch my meaning— he says it'd be annoying not to be killed, because he knows it'd be even more annoying to be struck down next to his companions."

"I realize this. That's why I'm being gracious and about to hurl this dagger at him, so he'll die in the same matter as his comps."

"But why? Don't you think we deserve to give a more heinous death to one of these blokes? After all, they're heinous men."

"I dunno, isn't it bad enough— or good enough— just to throw the dagger and let the blood fly as the neck bulges out grossly?"

"No! You stay!" and here Skin Toot was shouting at Fitarse, who had started to shuffle away into the trees.

"I'm not about to stay and seal my fate as you two tannie-lovers debate the means of putting an end to me!"

"How's this," put forth Dingle, "You stay there and I'll hurl this dagger at your head— it'll be done in two seconds. If you dash off into the woods, we're gonna have to chase after you and then it'll get real heinous."

"Will you give me a stride's start?"

Dingle and Toot exchanged a conferring glance.

"One stride start. But if we catch you, we'll stab you up your ethra."

"My ethra? What in Snick's name's an ethra?!"

"Your ethra!"

185

"You mean 'my urethra?'"

"Yes but I'm not about to go along saying 'your urethra.' It's redundant. No need to say the 'yur' twice."

"Might I suggest using the word 'the' instead of 'your' then? That way you can still say 'urethra' and folk'll know what you're talking about!"

"We'll stab you up the urethra? No. Still don't like that. Sounds like I'm saying 'the your ethra' and that's just as bad. We'll stab you up the ure! How's that?"

"Well I see what you mean but I still don't like the idea much."

"Very well. You've made your choice then? You'll stand still for this dagger?"

"Will you take heed of my final words, and report them to my people back in Deep Tug?"

"Absolutely not, for you're a Raycist ass-pit."

"Fine then."

And Fitarse put out his arms, sooner accepting death than to relinquish his strong prejudice. Dingle then let his dagger fly— and it missed. By quite a bit actually.

"Now I'm confused," remarked Skin Toot, "Because you hit the other two from many strides away." And by this point Fitarse was already bolting into the woods— "Can't say I'm disappointed though, cause now we're in full right to stab him up the ure."

And Skin Toot dashed along into the trees as well. Were it a mere leg race, Dingle's companion would have never caught up to the Raycist of Deep Tug, but here Skin Toot pulled out a whimsical instrument, one that he would hence be known for in bringing down his enemies: two round balls, tied together by a simple piece of rope.

Skin Toot tossed this ball-rope contraption towards the running Fitarse at a distance, and by the grace of God he was tripped up by their strike. Two

186

great celebratory howls filled the dark forest air, and a few moments is all it took for Dingle and Toot to catch up with Fitarse, and stab him up his urethra.

In this way, Fitarse, Poonzu, and Han Dass were all suspended from the realm of life on that eve in Leskarion.

The jaunt home towards Dingle's Dagger was done in no great hurry. The horses swayed from side to side in a slow saunter, and neither Piss nor Skin did anything to hasten them along.

As they rounded up over the gentle peak of a breasted hill, they felt suddenly closer to the stars. Indeed, they were a full forty strides closer to the night sky than they were at the base of the hill. And such contentment at being so much closer to the stars made Skin Toot yawn. And his yawn made Dingle fear he would soon be nodding off, so he interjected the peaceful silence with a harsh— "Dude, what were those balls back there?"

And Skin Toot snapped his head up erect, and shook off the sleep from his face. "You mean my ballropes?"

"Yes. Why do you have them?"

"For the sake of distinction. I can't go around throwing daggers, or else people will think I'm you. That this is all a one-man job.

"Mm."

That night, Piss Dingle and Skin Toot slept on sacks full of shit, for these were the best on which to sleep. It made for a very soft and flexible padding, and therefore their nights were full of comfort.

But Dingle could find no repose on this night, and he turned this way and that upon his shit sack.

"What bothers you?" asked Skin Toot.

"The manner in which I stabbed that man up the ure. I didn't even know his name."

"It was Fitarse. And then there was Poonzu and Han Dass. How do you not recall?"

"Wo-kai, the Skulfer then. The helpless one we killed in the Fickling Stream."

"Dear Horlio, are we still on that? You knew he was a man of deep prejudice so did his name even matter?"

"I don't think I can carry on as Fingerboy did. I fear I have remorse and more of it may come."

Skin Toot sighed, bringing up the atrocities carried out in Essen.

"Do you remember the days when Deep Love referred to nothing more than the eternal bond between man and dog? I remember those times. They were not long ago. Yet today the term's been corrupted. Deeplove refers to a cult, a gathering of wrongdoing, headed by the most evil creature to walk this world since Caldar. And that Deeplove just sacked the town of Essen, MURDERED the Court and the new Lobe Minister, and now we have at least three more years of Skulfing to endure."

"Yes, it's awful, it's horrendous, it sucks like one large and ugly. But we're here in the Yonderlobe— peaceful land where stars spread like fingers. And we've just committed the same atrocities, albeit on a much smaller scale. Yes, we're doing it to avenge the sins carried out at Essen, but does our intention even matter? For the murder of three ass-pits has done nothing to take away the shame of that night, nor will it do anything to prevent further sins from happening. If anything, we've just contributed to the growing wages of sin all the world over."

And with this revelation, already, after but a single chapter, Piss Dingle laid down the daggers that he had only just begun to use.

Chapter XI
The Failure of Winning Victory

"So the tale's done then?" asked Skin Toot, upon seeing Dingle's daggers catching purposeful flame inside a large firepit.

"I think the length was adequate enough. There are better ways that we must put our skills to use."

"Aye, it's a hard task to rid the world of injustice. Let us go and find women, so that we might find more success in that realm of conquest."

And they sang great songs as they vacated Dingle's Dagger for the town of Ho Spleen Ho. There, Swilly knew of men, and men of the woman kind no less. For wise was Swilly of the arts concerning ladies, and he was graced from the earliest days of his life with the undefinable charm which lures them to dark chambers. His powers of sad action were only doubled in recent years by his prowess with the flute— indeed, folk would flood from far to hear the lovely sound that blew whenever his lips struck upon the flute-hole.

The presence of Swilly, then, was all it took to assemble a crowd of some ninety-five admirers in the Inn of Ho Spleen Ho, where they would put on gay performances in its theatre for a spell of months. Swilly could have conceivably taken all ninety-five to his private quarters, but modest as he was, he took only sixty-three— that being nine for each finger, considering Swilly had lost three fingers in the Skirmish of Bottom Lass Peat. This left some thirty contenders at the Inn, able to be courted by myself, Piss Dingle and Skin Toot, and to the great surprise of all of us, we were all in some way successful.

The measures of our success are questionable. Asked today if our courtings that night blossomed into glorious fruit, no doubt all three of us would say no. But at the time, it seemed as though we had made a win, for indeed each of us embarked upon small intimacies within the subsequent frame of time, and that is more than we could have hoped for. I will now go on to provide brief accounts of our respective winnings that came about after that night, which quickly turned into failures.

I will start with Piss Dingle, as he is the protagonist of my tale, and his winning failure by winning the favor of a lass called Victory is the most consequential to our present story.

Dingle saw the Lady Victory from afar on the first night when Swilly's Theatre Brigade was assembled at the Inn of Ho Spleen Ho. And every night thereafter, Dingle would cast eyes upon her when he could, but for a week or so he only saw her from the eyes up. For in the midst of their gay performances, she was reserved and sat behind a raised desk, so that the eyeline and forehead was all that Dingle could admire. Still, it was a grand forehead, and an even more enchanting eyeline. So enchanting was the eyeline that, when it stopped appearing on the stage altogether after about a week, Dingle felt compelled to seek it out after an especially gay performance. He found it now behind the curtains, providing assistance with the ropes.

"I miss your eyeline," said the honorable Lord Dingle, going for the most simplistic, true and inoffensive thing he could think to say.

The Lady Victory, of course, knew what he was speaking of— they had locked eyes many times on the stage. But she feigned to be surprised, and not have any idea what he could possibly mean. "My eyeline?"

"Well, when you were on the stage and sat behind that desk, I— from across the stage— could see you but only from the eyes up."

"Then how do you know you're talking to the same person now?"

And Dingle put up his hand, to compare the eyes and forehead of his memory with the eyes and forehead that stood before him now. "Same eyeline. Same forehead."

"I possess a large forehead. It's quite ridiculous."

"Foreheads be best when they be large. I count the trait of tolerance as one of my strongest, yet a small forehead is a thing that is most intolerable. And how much might it cost to kiss such a forehead as yours, which is large but not to a fault?"

Now, there may have been much dialogue between Dingle's initial approach and his line of her forehead, in fact there almost certainly was, but this chapter ought to be swift and my hand is already aching from all the long-winded aspects of this tale. Let it suffice that the forehead proposal of Lord Dingle was the crux which tilted the Lady Victory towards his favor, though she still would not tumble for him quite so quickly.

"My forehead is large and large to a fault."

"Does that mean it would cost more to kiss than an average-sized one?"

"Certain things are priceless."

"Um... what does that mean? It's without price? I could kiss it for free? I wouldn't want to rob you, such a forehead is clearly worth a startling sum on account of its startling size."

"You do instigate."

"Sorry. I would very much like to do that at some point in the future though, regardless of cost."

"Tell me about yourself," spoke the Lady Victory, steering the talk away from her forehead. "Tell me of your passion for acting."

"My passion for acting is roughly equivalent to my passion for raccoons, which is neither large nor small."

"Interesting analogy."

"And what passion do you find to be most deep?" asked Lord Dingle.

"Aside from the obvious, which is making sure my cat has all she needs, I can never seem to read enough."

"Ah! And there is where I will win your favor. See that lad over there? The one talking to Jidbilly? That's Ward Geit Fung. And he can read, as well as write. And he is writing an entire account of my deeds."

"Dear God. Be your deeds that impressive?"

"My deeds are the kind which ought to be witnessed in close and private quarters."

And something to this effect was enough to gain Dingle access to Lady Victory's close and private quarters, that being her small apartment in the main of Ho Spleen Ho. There, upon entering, Dingle immediately brought up Victory's forehead, once again.

"So about that forehead."

To dampen Dingle's thirst, the Lady Victory put a towel around the top of her head, so that any forehead lust would be extinguished. But Dingle tried to defend himself, thinking she had got the wrong idea.

"Look, I'm not— I'm not truly after your forehead. It's not all that appealing to me. I just thought it might be an appropriate place for a first kiss, being that it's of the more innocent ports, and we have a strong foreheadial connection, as the first several times I saw you, all I saw was forehead."

"And eyeline."

"Well if you would have me kiss your eyes I certainly would."

But the Lady Victory shook her head, and instead lifted up the cat which roamed about as Duke of that place.

"You can kiss Alliver."

The cat's name was Alliver. Yet what Dingle heard were the words "all of her."

"All of her?" asked Dingle, seeking confirmation.

"Yes, Alliver," replied the Lady Victory. "If you want to kiss me, you'll have to kiss Alliver."

"All of her?" asked Dingle, still mistaking the name "Alliver" for the words "all of her."

"Yes, go ahead. Kiss Alliver, she'll love it."

And Victory seemed to be quite serious.

So it was that Piss Dingle took the cat in his hands, at first holding her at a distance and frowning, then moving the fur closer to his lips. And for several long moments, he kissed the cat. All of her.

Victory just watched on, amazed. A frozen look of smug surprise, on the verge of breaking out in a display of the hilarity that was.

"Is this— is this good?" asked Dingle after kissing the whole of the cat.

"Better go a little longer."

And so it was that Dingle kissed all of Alliver for something like half an hour, before finally being granted permission to give the Lady Victory one peck upon the forehead large.

Weeks went by in that place, and Dingle stayed for the sole purpose that every day he was permitted to kiss one spot more, granted that he licked all of Alliver thoroughly before.

But then there was cause for contention, which began— as it often does— over a matter of breakfast. It is odd that a matter of breakfast should have ever come to bother Dingle, for Dingle is well known to have not cared for breakfast in the slightest. He did not eat it. He

194

had no strong opinions on it. And therefore he thought that matters of breakfast would never become a point of contention. That is, until the Lady Victory did a very contentious thing, concerning grace and breakfast.

For on the morning of their return to the theatre where they found their present employ, Dingle stood in a corner, doing nothing. He was not hungry, for he was seldom hungry in the mornings, and therefore he did not venture into the breakfast line, nor put forth the effort to create a plate of breakfast foods. But Lady Victory stepped forth, giving him a plate full of breakfast unexpectedly.

"I didn't know what you liked, so I grabbed a bit of everything."

"Oh, well that was nice. Thank you very much."

And it was nice. It was a nice gesture, for Victory to give Piss Dingle a bit of breakfast.

But then she began to yell out, garnering the attention of all in that place, all who were still tired and shaking off the sleep of dawn.

"Actors of this theatre in the Inn of Ho Spleen Ho! Do you see what I have done? I went out of my way, to fill up not just breakfast for myself, but breakfast for my friend. I do this because I am a good person. You ought to do it too. It's not much to ask, that fellow folk— working together, breathing together— be aware of the needs of our neighbors. Dingle here takes a good several hours to truly wake up in the morning. Until that time, he is not well. Look at him. There's no life in him at all. He stands in the corner, idle and ugly. For whatever reason, he does not nourish himself before the lunch hour. So see what I have done— it was not too much a burden, so I took it upon myself, to grab some extra food while I was in the line... so that I could give him... breakfast. It's an important thing to do."

195

And she went on, bragging and lauding herself as the perfect example of Passianity, that she would go out of her way to bring breakfast to one such as Dingle. And after that day, the deed was never done again.

Never again did she give Dingle breakfast.

After making such a big deal out of her generosity on its first and only occasion, for all to see, it then subsided into nothing. And from that point on, Dingle— who had never cared a snap for any sort of breakfast— began to wonder why she was not giving him breakfast on any other occasion. But he got past it. It was only breakfast.

Later on in the week, the Lady Victory saw two young Mahogany children, wandering about the street below her apartment. She gasped and got Dingle, pointing down with furious finger.

"Look at that!" She exclaimed.

"Um... children?"

"Wandering about by themselves! The parents ought to be locked up."

"Well, it's fine for now, isn't it?"

"This is not fine. How can you think this is fine?"

"Well, it's not 'fine'— it's not a good thing that these children are out about wandering the streets, but we shouldn't fully blame the parents—"

Victory's expression was of the deathful rage. Dingle changed his tune.

"I mean that yes, we can blame them— they should know where their kids are— but perhaps we shouldn't be so quick to judge and condemn them. Perhaps they are searching with tremendous vigor as we speak, and the children, crafty as they are, happened to slip out at a bad moment."

"Don't look for reasons to excuse the heinous crimes of these parents."

196

"You don't know the parents! How can you even be certain that this is a crime? How can you accuse people of being heinous in a situation you know next to nothing about?"

But the Lady Victory called upon the Skulfers, and the wandering children were rounded up, to be sent to a better home, and the parents were sentenced to time in jail.

The following week, a situation of startling similarity occurred, albeit with a Paleskin child.

"Oh," said Dingle, shaking his head, looking out the window. "Another child on the loose, should we presume the parents have done great wrong and call for him to be rounded up and put into a better home?"

"How dare you speak that way," said Victory, slapping him hard.

And now Dingle was truly puzzled. "But... this is the same situation we were faced with last week—"

"You know the Skulfers would punish the Paleskins no matter what the reason for this child's wandering. How do you not get that?"

"I'm just— it's just that you ripped two kids away from their parents last week because you saw the children roaming the streets. How is this any different? A child is roaming the streets. The parents are not around. Last week you called the Skulfers knowing the Mahogany parents would be punished for allowing the same thing to happen— you didn't give those parents the benefit of the doubt."

"Our Mahogany breed garners enough benefit."

"Well, true as that may be, last week two parents were thrown in jail and had their children taken from them. We now see the exact same scene outside our window, the only difference being that the child is now pale. Isn't justice meant to have the same implication when the cases are of a similar nature?"

"We live in a broken system," said Victory, shaking her head.

"Then... why not try to keep it functioning as best we can?"

And they argued long that day, the Lady Victory seeing her way as nothing but right, despite her blatant contradictions in why the same action was in the present time acceptable for Paleskins but condemnable for Mahoganies.

Enough of Dingle and Lady Victory. It is time to tell my tale of breast and courtship.

I began my time in Swilly's theatre venture as a dancing stream, twirling about with reeds shooting out water from all sides. Therefore, I came to be quite unpopular from the start, and something of a thing to be avoided. Regardless, I have given praise every day of my life since my arson, in that I remain free— a blessing that I attribute to my cutting off the broad tip of my flip, which I believe, in addition to serving my prisonly sentence, was penance enough in the eyes of God. Since then I have taken on the philosophy that all avenues of desire ought to be strolled upon, and all doors of potential opportunity ought to be at least knocked on.

I take rejection quite well, being always pleased that I at least put forth respectable effort to make my interest in a thing known. It would bother me greatly to have the slightest chance of obtaining success in a thing and not to head after it in some fashion. Therefore, to all the charming creatures of Swilly's theatre company, I sent out bold letters in attempt to glean where my prospects did lie. If anything, a good deal of them should have found mighty impress with my admirable skill with the pen.

"My wish is to tickle you in dark places.
Might I obtain that wish?"

was the letter that I sent out to the six winds. Rather unfortunately, it was given the nine cheers by none.

I sent out a second round of letters, with slight tweaks to the wording, but of a similar gist. Still, it looked as though my luck would be rot. These women, perhaps they sensed my days of arson. Perhaps they simply could not read. These are the two most logical reasons I can glean for why for my letters were so apparently ill-received. So I went about a new tactic, which was to simply speak light with one who I one day found myself speaking light to.

Her name was Jidbilly, and she was just fine. She must've have found myself just fine as well, for we soon found ourselves in her apartment, which was less than fine, but it had a nice view.

Upon gathering the details of her birth, I did a quick run with the arithmetics— "995."

"What?" asked the simple Jidbilly.

"995 is the count of the days between our birthings."

"Is that strange?"

"Why would it be strange?" I asked. "It's strange that you think it would be strange."

"Well I can't fathom why you would make note of the calculation," returned Jidbilly, "or why one would venture to make such a calculation at all."

As you might well assume, I followed up this conjecture with a complete telling of all my ventures in the way of records and documentation, but it must've all gone straight out the other end of Jidbilly's passages, if we take into account what happened next.

For at this point, my two hired boys shuffled in quick, drawing little attention to themselves, but still failing to divert all attention, for they were full grown men sweeping across the floor to the corner of the room, no matter how crouched in their discreetness. On the other side of that dwelling, they set up easels and parchment, taking out their pens, ready to write of all the deeds and words set forth upon that good night.

"And what... is the purpose of those two boys?" asked Jidbilly, sitting up in bed, giving me a tone that was the least friendly of all her prior evening tones.

"Well, isn't it apparent from what I've told you concerning my records and documentation? Those are my scribe-boys."

Jidbilly did not speak, nor did she remove her eyes from their apparent target of mine.

"Windal Klontug and Jernander Skug are their names," I continued, tearing my eyes from her, for they now made me quite uncomfortable. "Windal comes from a respectable line, as does Jernander— he claims to trace his lineage back to the famous Skoogs, those with the double-o, he's since replaced the same sound in his name with a sing 'u'; the lad can't stand double letters, nor can I. Anycourse, they will be watching and listening throughout the night, and setting our actions to the sheet. Where, God willing, our deeds will never die, and the events of this night will live in the halls of fame, for all eternal days to come."

Jidbilly with this was not fine.

And so she chased Windal of Klontug and Jernander Skug from our presence, and said I ought to apologize, though I knew not what for. I had explained my position— that I am a chronicler, a keeper of records — and to let a night of passion go by unrecorded is among my greater fears. Indeed, the thing I hate most in life is the crime of forgetting, of letting truth pass out of all knowledge, putting flawed fragmented memories in their place.

Hollow memories are a fine thing, yes, but they are no substitute for the truth, full and uncorrupted. That is why I write, when all is fresh in the mind, and when I am predisposed, have others take down the words in my stead. Because if things are not taken down as they transpire, time will soon forget, and the past will become nothing more than a faded recollection, foggy and flawed.

That is why, after Windal and Jernander were expelled from Jidbilly's chamber, they held to the order of business, and positioned themselves just outside Jidbilly's window, so that still might make out every moan and sigh of passion, so that they could in turn be written down and made eternal.

And of course there were sighs and moans, which the lasher of my pubes has censored from this account, and that is fine by me, for records of that sort are meant to be wholly of a private nature, and have no business in a widely circulated tale. They are for my personal use, to strengthen my own recollection, but allow me to say that it was the debate between whether one particular sound was a "ah-uhn" or a "woo-huh" that gave exposure to my scribe-boys. Windal thought Jidbilly had made a clear ah-uhn, while Jernander had heard more of a woo-huh (I, for my part, remember it as a "wuh-hah," which just goes along to prove my point: memory is flawed, and all that can be must be documented in the moment of its happening to avoid a further diminishment of accuracy).

So Windal and Jernander went about arguing in the bushes outside Jidbilly's window, in whispers of course, as to whether she had gone and done an ah-uhn or a woo-huh. Jidbilly caught them, and banished all the three of us from her presence, evermore.

That will be the end of this, and for my part— while I enjoyed the company of this Jidbilly in that time — I do not regret our parting of ways. For anyone who would have such a problem with truth being put to words... anyone who would rather inevitably forget all the passings of their life than choose to remember... is of no great interest to me anyway.

We have heard of the shortsighted conquests of Dingle and myself in the months of our employment with Swilly's theatrical group; mine was of no real consequence one way or the other, Dingle— being the passive lord he is— was annoyed as he slowly peeled back the layers of Lady Victory, yet found ways to ignore her faults.

But Skin Toot, oh the dear Skin Toot, fared worse in these matters than any lad before or since. For the lass who attached herself to Skin Toot was none other than Feekro Dential, and why she was called that will soon come to be known.

At first, Feekro appeared to be bearable, even cute in the eyes of Toot, as he wandered about the stage in the middle of a crowded scene in their performance. He carried about a long fruit, and would test affability of his colleagues in how they would react to his approach with the fruit. Most gave it no mind. But Feekro Dential loved— simply adored— whenever Skin Toot came along with the fruit. And she laughed the cry of real true laughter, not just the feigned laugh of those on stage, but the laugh of those who are deeply taken.

This should have been a warning sign from the start, that any woman who would laugh so hard at such a stupid thing as fruit would probably not prove to have the most complex of spirits. But Skin Toot gave it no deeper thought; he was only pleasantly surprised to see that Feekro Dential was responding so well to his constant approach with the fruit.

And so the long fruit opened up a doorway for Skin Toot straight into the Realm of Damnation, or in literal terms, Feekro's dwelling.

Skin Toot was ecstatic to gain access to Feekro's apartment for the first time— for it had been a great while since such a thing had happened, and he was still thinking of Feekro as one who was cute and full of well humor. But upon seeing the inside of her dwelling, my friend Toot immediately had dark forebodings that his association with this lady would soon bring certain doom.

For Feekro's dwelling was a prison. Not in the literal sense, but very much in the figurative, for there was but no place to readily move. Little as the furnishings were, there was still only space for a few strides, and that was the end of it. A chair for reclining, yes, but no table. There was no space for that— a table could be brought in, but it would have to be at the expense of the chair.

There was then only one room adjacent, which housed the bed of Feekro, and the bed— although not even that large of a bed— took up the entire width of that room. It was a narrow, hollow space of bare white plaster, with no windows nor pipes for which to tame the air. The nights would be dreadful, for on the standard type, the room would draw so moist in its heat that Skin Toot found himself completely without cloth, and still burning up in pulsating bouts of sweat. And on the other kind of the night— the kind that blew cold winds— he would find himself unable to gain the previously dreaded heat, for lack of blanket and sheet in that bare cell of misfortune.

And there was a chirp in the halls. A dreaded, painful chirp which sounded out every half a minute, one that Feekro would do nothing about, nor even acknowledge hearing herself. But it bothered Skin to no

203

end, to the point where he lay up half the night, and often had to press his hands hard against his ears to stop the noise of that evil sound.

All of this might have been forgivable if Skin Toot had a lovely view to awaken with, but as he pushed aside the curtains, he saw only dirty glass, a series of iron bars, and beyond, just overhead, sacks of trash hung from the neighbor's stairway.

This lack of a view, space, or breathable air too, might have been forgivable if the lady who leant hospitality to Skin had been a lady of charm, wit, or godly features and proportions, but here too he was struck by misfortune. For this Feekro, Feekro Dential, was a lass he found now massively intolerable. But as he was said to have set forth his deeds in the mode of supreme toleration, he ventured to tolerate her presence for as long as he could.

For one thing, her face began to change soon after they met. Whether it was a real change, or perhaps just a change in the mind of Toot (the kind which can be even more potent), one can not be sure. But the pleasant face Skin swore to see upon that night when he approached her with fruit on the stage: that was never to be seen again. Now it was that Skin Toot could hardly look at her. For her eyes were large now, too large, and many have protested that large eyes are never a bad thing— that large eyes are the most appealing. This is often times true.

But the eyes of Feekro Dential were eyes that were large in all the wrong fashions: large like an over curious hawk, large like an ever-watching grandmother who would not rest until all desires were attended to, large like a scary aging child who had never made it to the land of adolescence, and was also incapable of grasping complex thought. Her nose was too long, thin and sharp, but many have noses less than perfect, so we will not judge her harshly for this. But when that nose was paired with those eyes— which it always was— yes, she was terrifying.

For a thing of a separate nature, Feekro's taste in tales was most appalling. She championed tales of a tasteless violence, loud and bloody but without reason, motivation or sense. And of Skin Toot's own tastes— which of course included tales of grand symphonic violence, the kind set to sweeping movements of depth and glory— she said she had no interest. Tales of "anything history" (and she did indeed use that precise phrase) she found to be nothing short of boredom.

Upon one night when Skin and Feekro could at last decide upon a tale to read together which they both found to be marvelous, it turns out the essence of the tale swept full above her head.

And on top of these horrendous missteps of judgment, the lady Feekro Dential spoke at all times (to Toot at least) in a fake rodential voice. Yes, that is why she came to be reported to me as nothing else but Feekro Dential. At first, the good Skin Toot had assumed that her high-pitched rodent's voice was only her God-given natural tone, and therefore would not venture to mock it, for many men are cursed with ill voices, and they cannot help it.

But upon one day of dreadful revelation, Skin Toot — feigning sleep into the noontime hours, as he often did to avoid speaking with his host— overheard a conversation that Feekro held with a friend. As she spoke with this friend, her voice was surprisingly fine. Not the best voice, but far from the worst. There was a bit of a strange accent, but the pitch and tone and rhythm were all bearable. It was a real voice.

But then as soon as she saw the pitiful Skin Toot to be awake, she sat back down upon the bed, and cradled his head in her arms, and began to speak once again as a quiet old rat-nurse. Why did she do this? Why did she insist on speaking so at all times to the poor Skin Toot? Could she not sense in his voice the immense sound of dissatisfaction, of displeasure and even downright aggravation?

For Feekro Dential truly spoke to Skin as he was a child in need of nursing— in need of nursing from a giant squeaky rodent, apparently— and she chose to act the part of a nurturing grandmother. This was not a role which inspired great attraction.

It revolted Skin to no end.

The things Feekro chose to say revolted Skin to an even greater extent— all day long, in the night and in the morning as well, Feekro would torment him with continual stroke and whisper in her faint, squeak of a rodential voice: "What do you want?"

And Skin Toot would often reply with nothing, he wanted nothing.

"Mmm... are you sure?" went the mousy curse.

Skin Toot was sure. He wanted nothing. He dreaded whatever it was that constituted something, and therefore he truly wanted nothing.

"What do *you* want?" asked Skin Toot, more annoyed than anything with the fact that Feekro would not simply come out and say what she clearly wanted. Rather, she kept asking and asking in her fake rodential what SKIN wanted, when clearly Skin wanted no such thing.

For Skin Toot, like all the Dingleites, was supremely submissive in matters of intimacy. He desired one who could take hold, demand orders, and give out fierce commands. He could not stand this weak and simple host, always asking questions and dealing out

206

ridiculous apologies where none were warranted, always looking for Toot to make some bold move that he had no intention of ever making. And it was her denseness that was most infuriating, for clearly anyone could see that Toot was uncomfortable as could be in his position. After making it abundantly clear that he "wanted" nothing other than sleep, why was it that this host still insisted upon his staying? Why was it that she continued to stroke him, continued to ask what he wanted? Why did she continuously speak to him in the blatant voice of a rodent?

The dying Skin Toot took up these concerns on a walk with the honorable Piss Dingle, after tolerating Feekro for an unbelievable spell of days.

"This is odd to you too, is it not? The fact that she persists? Continuously stroking, even when I turn my face? Clearly I'm not enjoying it. My moans are not sighs of satisfaction, they are moans of pain. And then she has the audacity to ask what it is I want. And I scream inside my mind that I want for her to stop everything fake and rodential at all costs, but of course I'm too polite to call her Fake Rodential, or to outright deny her of the pleasure she seems to receive from serving me. She seems to be a sad aging woman, despite looking like a child with impossibly large eyes, and I dare not take from her the only joy she seems to have."

"The fake rodential voice is the part that gets me," spoke the puzzled Dingle, still trying to process the extensive list of his friend's complaints. "At least she doesn't order you about."

"I wish she would. I wish she was capable of any show of strength at all. But those big adoring eyes are all there is, apart from that haunting rat's voice. I try to be the antithesis of politeness, now abstaining fully from kind words, in a hope that she'll do the same. But she's too damn polite, Dingle. She's got etiquette beyond

207

cause! And those damn apologies, those cosh damn apologies."

"She apologizes too much?"

"She apologizes for everything, everything except that which she ought to: keeping me hostage in the dark and assaulting my body. But no, she'll apologize for accidentally tapping me, or for walking across the room when she thinks me asleep, or moving my things when she needs a seat— why apologize for such useless things?!"

"Just to tug on you by the sounds of it."

"If she apologizes for no reason one more time, I swear, I... am going to give myself something to apologize for."

"Gonna give her the Ward Geit treatment?"

"Oh, don't joke about such heinous things. But do take the matter of the chirp. There is a thing that truly drives me mad. But she will not apologize for that no matter how many times I mention it! I lay it into our conversations subtly— 'oh, there's that chirp again, doesn't it bother you?' But she's never once said sorry for that, much less informed the lord of her property!"

"Some folks aren't good at taking hints."

"No, and that's the real problem, isn't it? I don't want to be so directly bold as to be outright insulting, because that would be unavoidable if I told her the truth of things. At this point, I'm just so... incredibly amazed at her density, that I just keep upping the 'hints' to see how long it will be until she realizes, that 'oh, perhaps I am driving Skin to the grave.'"

"Well there's gotta be some good that's come from you dwelling in her chamber, you said she had a large collection of tales?"

"Yes, but sadly the ones that have substance all go directly over her head. Last night I read aloud both 'Stirring of the Oak' and 'Sunright Road.' Both great classical works with some real depth, and after I was through, I said 'You know, those make a good double read. A lot of thematic similarities between the two.' But she spoke only of the aesthetic similarities, and even then, ever so briefly. Nothing of the story. Nothing of the darkness, deep and true, that lies at the core of both those tales. Nothing on what those stories actually mean — because Dingle, I do not think she understands what those stories mean."

"No, probably not, if she's as simple as you make her out to be."

"She was giggling as I read the last pages of Sunright Road."

"Sunright Road's a pretty serious tale if I remember right, especially at the end."

"Indeed it is. A tragedy about an aging woman who can't come to terms with the fact that the world has rejected her. A prisoner to remorse and solitude, she holds a young lad prisoner in her halls, oblivious to the fact that he wants ultimately nothing from her. As I read those pages, I felt for certain that Feekro would come to make the connection between those characters and our very similar situation, but as always there was no sign of comprehension that I could see."

"Ha, you are like the guy in Sunright Road. But at least he got a whole estate to dance around in. You're just stuck in her tiny apartment by the sounds of it."

"No, you're right, she has no wealth to speak of. The guy in Sunright Road enjoyed the spoils of the lady's wealth and still found room to complain. So I think I'm well within my rights to vent about my peculiar prison."

"No, I think you're absolutely within rights, it sounds awful."

"It is beyond stifling. Whenever she puts her face close to mine, I am suffocating. I turn on my side, away from her, and she strokes me, I scream out in my mind: 'Danaria! Help me Danaria! Save me from this pain.'"

Danaria, of course, being the old and eternal affection of Skin Toot's life, who was unfortunately far too godly for the likes of him.

To counter the increasing attacks of Feekro's lips, Skin Toot thereafter ceased cleaning his own mouth, and piled in odious foods, to protect his face from any potential assault from Feekro's tongue. He feigned to be asleep at all times, and soon this took a toll on his being. He was then for the longest time increasingly tired, prone to headaches and a stiffness in the neck, and the purpose of life itself drained out of his knowledge. In this way, the joyous and tireless Skin Toot was transformed truly into a thing he was not, at the hands of Feekro Dential.

For the entirety of the months of Uanethis, Togallia, Thracember and Farethis, we committed no murders.

We embarked upon those romantic affairs, and while we succeeded from a certain point of views, in many other ways we all found failure.

But there in Ho Spleen Ho we rested for a spell of months. We slept and we chilled. For the winters in that part of the world are not the least bit friendly to men out of doors, and surely there were no doors in the woods of Dingle's Dagger; that is why we felt compelled to stay in Ho Spleen Ho for the winter, in what dwellings we could find.

Farethis brought an end to the snow, but it also brought us into court.

Now we feared not just for our sanity, which had been threatened by women, but also for our physical lives, which now stood threatened by the like of Lobe

Minister Url Skulfing— who still held power, despite being voted out by the people for the second time the previous year.

"Tell me Lord Dingle, do you find it easy to kill those of your own race?" asked the Grand Judge of Ho Spleen Ho, who had caught wind of Dingle's deeds in Yonderlobe. His name was Fundrik Luber.

"I suppose it's easier than killing those of a different breed," shrugged Dingle, standing below the great stand of the judge.

"And why's that?" asked Luber.

"I'd feel mighty guilty to kill someone of a different breed."

"Then it would be the place of someone of the tan complexion to go about crusading against fellow Tanfolk? Someone like Skin Toot perhaps?"

"Yes, Skin Toot could do it, but I myself would not feel right in slaying a Tanfolk."

"You felt right in the slaying of fellow Mahogs though?"

Here Dingle hesitated. Surely this would be the response that would land him in jail.

"I was acting as Fingerboy would have. For I believe justice is not being served by Skulfing's administration— rather, the opposite is being done. Peoples are being terrorized. The capital under siege. Our method of governing put into doubt."

And there was a vastly uncomfortable sweep of silence, for none were yet sure how this Fundrik Luber would see things.

"You do know that Fingoy laf Turope Phertes— better known as Fingerboy to you— was the greatest villain ever known to the Empire of Hayaman?" spoke Fundrik Luber, High Judge of Ho Spleen Ho.

"Yes but one nation's villain makes for another's hero— he is seen as such by Tanfolk and Paleskin."

211

"Why do you side with them over your own folk?"

"I could answer your question with another question, but I won't, because that's the most aggravating of all things. Ah, flick it, I will. I put to you, good Judge Luber: why do you feel that both Tanfolk and Paleskin alike be treated as inferior— subservient even— to the Rich Mahogany breed?"

And all in the room gasped at the audacity in the straight-forward manner which Dingle pressed upon the judge.

Turns out, their fears were unfounded, for Fundrik Luber, like the vast majority of Ho Spleen Hoyans, was on the side of the oppressed. He had turned long ago from the side of Skulfing, how much more so when that beast managed to stay in office long after his term expired. And so there was great laughter from all except Dingle, who was peeved to have been summoned to court when all Fundrik Luber meant to say was 'good job.' There was yet more that Luber had to say, but this took place in private, after the mandatory proceedings of the renegade court:

"Now for the true reason of your summons, Master Dingle," spoke Fundrik Luber, opening his door to a pink and sweaty messenger, searching hard for breath.

"It has happened again," panted that pink messenger, sweat pouring out of pores. "Not far from the place were Flod had his neck crushed by a knee."

"Oh dear Horlio, what is it now?" asked Skin Toot, who had insisted upon accompanying Dingle to this meeting with Fundrik Luber, as did all other familiar Dingleites friends.

"In the town of Fyninfer, upon the plains of Flatfinger, a dispute broke out between two Mahogany women. A small dispute, I learned not even what it was. But a Paleskin comes about, with good intentions I'm sure, to help resolve the conflict. Anyway, no crime in that, whatever means he may have used to attempt to break the fight."

"So this Paleskin was trying to help then, in a simple manner of speak."

"One might say. But we all know that a Paleskin trying to do good— trying to do good for two Mahogs no doubt— is a thing that seldom ends well in this country, and it wound him up with seven arrows in the back."

"Seven arrows?"

And there was a silence, as all took into account the picture of seven arrows striking a man in the back. The image simply didn't compute for many.

"Seven arrows?" they all spoke again.

And it was confirmed by the messenger. But how could such a thing be stated as fact? Even the most vile of evil-doing Mahogs could flee a crime and only receive two or three arrows at maximum. But for one not even doing wrong— for the Skulfer had arrived upon calls concerning the two fighting women— to receive seven arrows? It was beyond excessive. Clearly those Skulfers were making a deliberate statement in the amount of arrows they fired. One would assume they were looking for all-out war.

"Was it not a thing that could have been settled with words?" I myself asked, founded dumb to the messenger.

"I reckon it could have been, indeed should have been, for as I said, the Paleskin was doing no wrong. But from my understanding, the Skulfer— Tem Lomin he was called— arrived and saw the raised voices of three individuals, with arms flailing, and he saw the chance to kill a Paleskin. So he did so with—"

"Seven arrows, so we heard," muttered Carvin Cong, his hand scratching his long white beard.

"Anyway the Skulfer hasn't faced a lick of prosecution; he knew he wouldn't. After seeing the lack of action taken against other such Skulfers— those that killed Flod, Rice of Rayce, Braelor, Fair Lindo of Castle for example— this particular Skulfer surely had no fear in taking the life of yet another Paleskin. He knew damn well that if he was questioned, he could say he felt threatened, he could say it was a violent situation, that the Paleskin was acting defiantly—"

"But none of this is true, there was no defiance from what I'm hearing," I noted. "The pale man was running away, after doing no wrong, and still let fly this Skulfer did: arrow, then arrow, then arrow, then arrow, then arrow, then arrow, then arrow."

And here there was a sudden change in both Piss Dingle and Skin Toot. Skin Toot— who had ever been eager to fight— grew discouraged, and felt a tug of discouragement, that no matter how hard he tried, this evil would never be quenched. But Piss Dingle— who had ever til that point been reluctant to fight— grew now enraged, and felt that he must suddenly leap to action.

"I'm going to find this Skulfer and I'm going to put seven daggers into his back," growled Dingle to Skin Toot.

"I wish you luck."

"Will you not come with me?"

Here Skin was silent. And here there was an important scene, so I and my scribe-boys sat crouched by the door, giving our friend intimacy yet recording their words all the same.

"After all your vigor in the woods, and the killings of retribution we made all along the Yonderlobe? Has it now faded from even you?"

Skin Toot sighed, and let his feelings flee:

214

"Our lives are at a crossroads, friend, and I believe we are now heading in different directions. Now it is you who will carry the vigor, the thirst, the call for vengeance... and I will take for a peaceful life. I do not wish to end unwell in a clasp of Mahogany fist, or with arrows piercing my flesh— I understand, all these things might happen anyway because of the lack of pigment in my skin, but be it not so likely if I laid low in places minding my own business."

"You've become discouraged, Skin."

"And wouldn't you, Lord Dingle? Picture yourself with my skin. You in the skin of Skin Toot. And you hear that all those like you were being murdered across the land, sometimes for no reason at all, and the men who carried out those murders were upheld as heroes. That they are the representatives of law and justice, and they see your life as not only unworthy of being protected, but a thing actively sought out to be terrorized. Picture yourself in a land where your life is seen only worthy of being ended."

And Dingle nodded. He would do no more to steer Skin from his path, for his mind was well spoken and of sound logic.

"Well I understand your concern. I won't pressure you. We must all cope with these dark times in whatever way our souls command."

And Piss Dingle and Skin Toot held a tight embrace of parting.

Thereafter, Piss Dingle set upon drawing out a new mission, one that was clear of goal and purpose, strictly organized this time: not just a streak of random killings in the woods, no— now they would go after those truly responsible. There were direct targets to be taken: retribution to be paid by the Skulfers who had acted out

215

such undeniable acts of injustice, and still roamed free under the lawless tongue of Skulfing.

Still a tad bit unsure of his place in all this, Dingle did as good boys do and sought the permission of the judge Fundrik Luber, so that he might feel better about going out on a deep crusade of blood. An so, on 26 Farethis, 3334, our favorite judge laid down our favorite verdict.

"To go about at will, punishing in most heinous deed all those who would impose harm upon the breeds not found to be in Supremacy... and specifically the likes of Dark Chevron, killer of Flod, and Tem Lomin, killer of the Fyninfer Paleskin by way of seven arrows..."

—There was a hush of anticipation—

"Myself, High Judge Fundrik Luber, and the grand jury of Ho Spleen Ho, grant you full right."

PART III (THRACE)

A HIGH AND MIGHTY
QUEST OF GOODNESS
BOTH NOBLE TRUE AND GLORIOUS

Chapter XII
Spread Them Wide

Piss Dingle sat upon a flowery chair in Watercross, that storied place of enchantment where two great rivers switch direct with one another's path, and there he thought of wind and philosophy. For much of his path he had been guided by whims of the breeze, first pushed along by the need to escape his own conditions at home, and then led by a blinding rage of all the injustice burning through the land.

Now he would be quiet, and still, and watch the ripples on the river, which will give concise answer to all questions if the words of the Godsong are to be trusted. It would turn out to be a defining day for him.

The particular river Dingle now sat watching was the Tom Ball Wade. I make this distinction, for the waters of the Craun also pass through Watercross, and although the Craun and the Tom Ball intersect briefly at a single point, by some strange enchantment their waters do not mix. From their meeting at Watercross, the Craun continues on to the northwest with its wide and brown tendency, while the Tom Ball goes on a northeasterly trail, retaining its deep blue majesty.

Try Dingle did to keep his eyes on the flowing water known then as the Tom Ball Wade, but he found it difficult after short time, for a bear was diddling round on the bank, with the air of a drunken merchant. "Get far and quick," thought Dingle, who found it hard to concentrate on the river while this inebriated bear was fumbling and fondling on an undecided course.

After ten minutes of conscious avoidance, Dingle realized the bear was still no further on from where he had been last time he looked, and the temptation to watch the bear grew too grand. Casting away his resolve to watch nothing but the river until his philosophy ran to him, Dingle began to watch the bear, and it was then that his philosophy ran to him, and pummeled him down with fist.

Why could he not call this bear friend?

Here we must take a short side step to explain the history of Beardom in the realm of western Elaptirius. Perhaps there were always equally hostile towards Passian men, but in the time of the great blooming of men, reports of bear-violence became all the more prevalent. Throughout the Dark Days when Caldar strode along the West, bears were of little concern. To have a child eaten every now and again was no real bother, for the constant malice that men faced under Caldar and his forces were a far greater terror.

After Caldar's defeat at Risenwood, however, men began to grow soft once more, as will always be the case when great adversity is removed. After a century or so, the bear had now risen up to take Caldar's place in becoming the great enemy of men. Village folk would now hold councils (I speak now of times around the year 1200 or so) concerning the egregious bear, dark devil wrapped in softest fur. They gave the creature a new name— Crothantheng— so that they would not have to utter the word 'bear.'

And in their sole joint enterprise that has come down to us in knowledge, the peoples of Glitharog and Gandrypool joined together to rid their lands of Crothantheng, or bears.

The forces involved are said to have been greater than all the men sent to battle Caldar combined, which is sad, considering Caldar was a powerful leader of armies bent on systematically enslaving the earth, while the Crothantheng were just bears. Regardless, the folk of Glitharog and Gandrypool were successful in driving all the bears of the western world into a small area of land, bound by the Urf in the east and south, the Woods of

219

Chipperin and Niswana (then Kind) to the west, and the Tredellian Valleys to the north.

This perimeter housed the 'Bear Stretch,' and it is within this unremarkable swath of country— with long gentle hills, yes, but never a tree nor stream— that all the bears in Elaptirius were confined. Guards were set upon the borders of the Bear Stretch, and stayed for a thousand years. But by the year 2001, they were no longer needed; the bears of the Stretch had come to know this was their place, however sad and dismal, and there they would stay.

Every now and again, a lone bear might come wandering down and out into strange distant places, such was the case with the bear Piss Dingle was seeing now. All the way south and west to Watercross had this bear come, and Dingle applauded him for that, now that he was thinking clearly, and not content just to watch the damn waters of the Tom Ball Wade.

Now Dingle thought of all the sorrows that bear-kind had faced in the past millennia. Were they incredibly hostile towards folk? Sure. But to him, it seemed as though the bears had never got a fair chance at being understood. Perhaps there could have been a way for the two lifelings to exist harmoniously in the past, instead of resorting to war and conquest, and the pushing and confining of one to the far extremities of their home. Perhaps amends could still be made; perhaps such things were folly, but they were nice thoughts to have.

And here Deng Lu came forth to hasten Piss along, for Piss Dingle had now been sitting by the Tom Ball Wade for upwards of an hour. You may be struggling here, and frantically racking your memories, to recall just when and where Deng Lu came into play. Truth be told, this is the first time I write of him, but we will shortly jump back to his proper introduction. I begin this chapter with the Bear Incident of Watercross only because it is the fine and proper way of telling the tale, as indicated by CLARFONATH— perfect tale of old— and since I strive to be a perfect writer, I must follow its form.

So Deng Lu comes up to Piss Dingle.

"Hasten yourself or it will be the end of our friendship."

"Oh Deng Lu, mere weeks ago you were so pleased to be joining my company."

"For you promised great things, Lord Dingle. That we would be enacting divine punishment on the Skulfers who took the lives of my Tanfolk and Paleskin brothers."

"You exaggerate, Deng. You have no idea how closely you're related to such men. But I see your point — you have greater sympathy for them because you are of a similar appearance. Very well. We will go to slaughter them soon. But look at this sight wonders."

And Deng Lu stepped forth, looking down at the waters of the Tom Ball Wade, seeing not the drunken bear that fumbled and fondled beyond.

"It's just the Tom Ball Wade. We've been looking at it for three days."

"Do you not see the drunken bear?"

"What is drunk on I wonder... no matter. You keep an eye on it and I'll alert the Skulfers."

At this Dingle was struck by flicks of hypocrisy, and he grabbed hold of Deng Lu's arm.

"Now you mean to approach the Skulfers? Willingly? The same brood that you curse day and night? Then you do not stop to think that some of them might be kind, or useless— that they are all but monsters. But you are only too happy to summon them when there is a bear by the stream."

"Well who else is going to rid the Tom Ball of that drunken Crothantheng?"

221

"Who says the river needs ridding?" Asked Dingle, but he received only a firm look from Deng. "You too, Deng? Why must all this land be so hateful towards the brown furry beast? You know the name 'Crothantheng' is antiquated, and, well, insulting to the bear."

"The Crothantheng knows no better. It belongs either back in the Bear Stretch, or out of

"How do you know this bear comes from the Stretch? Perhaps it is a free bear. Perhaps it was merely a bear longing for the deep fruits of liberty. At any cost, does it do any harm?"

"Not now, but wait til a child goes walking by, and that Crothantheng snatches up her leg with its teeth, and rips the torso aside with its fiendish claws."

"Perhaps all we need to do then, as a race, is keep our distance."

"Why do you take the side of the bear?"

And here the conversation began to truly baffle Dingle. For Deng Lu had such a fiery passion for bringing about the equality of his own breed at any cost, but would do nothing for a creature so similarly oppressed. To the contrary, Deng Lu failed to even notice that the bear was oppressed at all.

"How can you be so passionate about the Paleskin cause but so blind to the troubles of other creatures?"

And Deng Lu was monumentally insulted.

"You ask how I am so passionate on the Paleskin cause? Are you not champion of the cause yourself? Why then do we call you leader?"

"That's a good question, why do you? I wasn't exactly born to lead men. I'm only just now beginning to develop my philosophy; that's why you've caught me staring out at the river and then at the drunken bear."

"Who needs philosophy, we're on a campaign!"

222

"So you'd rather just act, just do— and muse on the reasons why you did what you did after the time has passed?"

"That's how the Skulfers do it. They kill the white folk right off and stop to think of what they've done only afterwards, if at all."

"Deng. You know my place in this. I am against Oppression— and all oppression, not just oppression as it relates to a single group."

"Fine. Bear Lover I'll call you. But the bears will have to wait; my people are being slaughtered now. And it's now that we must act."

But still Piss Dingle kept eyes on the calm moving waters of the Tom Ball Wade. By now the bear had wandered on. Piss Dingle then spoke a quiet defining passage, and though interrupted by Deng Lu several times throughout, simply kept speaking at a consistent tone and rate.

"I move slowly, Deng... if there's one I'm learning about myself it's that I have a tremendous streak of patience. And if there's one attribute I now hold higher than all others, it's that of thought and reason. In this pivotal time in our history, I feel strongly that care should be taken to prevent the making of perfectly avoidable mistakes. Hatred and rage, abounding on all sides, even within this company. If we follow that course, we may find our work never to be done. And if we're not careful, we may come to find new orders of oppression built up in place of the old as soon as we have accomplished our aims."

"What the cosh is that supposed to mean?" asked an aggravated Deng Lu.

"I don't yet know. I also advise patience and compassion, above all else." And Piss Dingle rose, his calm body at odds with the fiery views of Deng Lu. "And it is beyond me how you can be so rashly impatient at a time when we are not even aware of our enemy's' location; as soon as we know where he is, we may then hurry on in haste. But until then, do not attempt to hasten me when there is no hastening to be done."

To clarify our position at that time, we were the First Order of Dingleites, sanctioned by the High Judge of Ho Spleen Ho Fundrik Luber to go out into the Lobes and do away with ex-Skulfers who had committed heinous crimes driven by the prejudice of breeds. We were numbered 42, and though the Honorable Piss Dingle did not even bother to learn all our names, I have taken an account, and will list them for the sake of thoroughness. In addition to we who had been with Dingle already for many months (we being myself, Carvin Cong, Swilly, the Lady Victory, and 23 remaining members of the Unspoken) there was also now Tibsmith and Rick Cottontree, two men we had picked up in Fyninfer, one a woman and the other a werman. Those we had received by the rallying of Fundrik Luber numbered twelve, they being Deng Lu, Brooth Dimfether, Marc Tempull, Jernander Skug, Fi Fernin, Siddlebok, Puup Gargeri, Windal of Klontug, Wode Punling, Dorak of Pagosa, Urtain Piik and Perfection.

And so we were all there waiting in Watercross for a heading. The location of the ex-Skulfer Tem Lomin was known soon enough, when a messenger rode in with the news, and all we Dingleites gave him the nine cheers. Then the time for haste had come.

"By loin and by groin we will find this Tem Lomin, and show to him a new tale of justice," laughed Carvin Cong darkly, who now stood near to the young Deng Lu on near every occasion, for their shared love of vengeance against the Rich Mahogs brought them close together.

224

We set out then on a northerly route, up the Tom Ball Wade, meaning to cross west when we came to the ending of the River Del, which we would then follow to the north and west until we came to Wesdel, that being the village where Tem Lomin was last sighted. And so, after a week of slow travel and rest, we Dingleites were at a swift pace once again, the fire rising from our bottoms into the starlit sky.

Absent from the party now, however, was the memorable Skin Toot. He resided now in Aslut, prosperous community of Paleskin enterprisers, thriving in the southernmost reaches of Athragal. And so, for lack of anyone fonder to talk with, Piss Dingle would often approach me, as I have always had an affable approachability, though many have taken it for the nature of a reserved crooked creep.

"I'm surprised you're speaking to me by your own will," I remember telling Dingle.

"Well there's something I've been looking to discuss, but I've found most of the men in our company — rich-skinned, light-skinned or otherwise— to be a bit hypocritical on one matter."

"You wish to speak to me of the bear?" I inquired, for I had heard Deng Lu's ranting about what was now coming to be known as Dingle's Folly— his apparently deep passion for Beardom.

"Look, I don't like bears that much. I don't know why people keep talking about it like I'm obsessed with them. I just— just think they should be free! Free of the confines of the Bear Stretch. I mean, I wouldn't mind seeing a bear every now and again on the road. I'd be a little scared at first, but you'd get used to it! We just need to learn how to be around each other again."

I laughed and gave Dingle a healthy pat on a place unspeakable.

"You cannot hide your love for those creatures. I'm afraid we all know by now."

"What do you mean by now?! I only saw the damn bear a few hours ago and said nothing of arousal."

"Words travel swift by the mouth of Deng Lu. And his words carry a great persuasion."

"Well these rumors must be quelled before they become deep-rooted truths in the minds of our men. I will mount a tree and speak to them."

"I advise against that," I advised against him, "For if you bring the matter up at all, these men will see how uneasy you are concerning the subject, and will be convinced all the more of your ravenous hunger for bear fur and flesh."

"What's this I hear of bears?" came a voice from behind, a voice that Dingle had forgotten to be now part of his company, so quiet and soft-spoken as it was. The voice belonged to a certain Rick Cottontree, and instead of bringing him into the fold without his proper introduction, I will not leap back to the time a week back when Piss Dingle met the lad at Fyninfer.

Dingle and myself, along with Carvin Cong, the Unspoken and a host of fifteen others— Deng Lu included— gathered by the High Judge Fundrik Luber for the purpose of carrying out retribution on naughty Skulfers, came to the town of Fyninfer on the unremarkable plains of Flatfinger.

As soon as we arrived, I remember how passionately Dingle spoke on the awful country. It was as though he mistook me for Skin Toot— often times I would hear those two ranting on about a random thing that suddenly struck them as lacking in quality, while avoiding topics of real consequence. We had come to Fyninfer to search for Tem Lomin— he who had shot a

226

Paleskin mercilessly in the back with seven arrows— but Dingle spoke not a word on that man. Instead he sent out the eager Deng Lu to quest the village folk, and then turned to me to complain about the awful country.

"How do people live here? Could you live here?"

"I— it looks quite peaceful," said I, turning to look at the quaint round-houses, all built in a circle around a central town hearth, with a communal stock of food, fluid and firewood.

"Don't look that way!" exclaimed Dingle, and he took me by the shoulders and turned me to look at the bare country on all sides. "There. Tell me your thoughts on this."

"I can't," said I, after a moment's ponder. "For there's nothing there."

"Nothing where?"

"Anywhere."

"Exactly," nodded Dingle. "Now that'd be all fine and well if the village had a name that struck a chord with its province of Flatfinger, because that's telling. That lets people know before they come, that the land is flat. That's a reasonable name. But to call this place Fyninfer?! Completely unacceptable!"

"Perhaps the folk have a good reason to call it that after all. Snag one," I suggested.

Dingle snagged the first villager he could find, and it would prove to be a fateful snag. "You there— you call this place home?"

"I've doed for as long as I did live."

"Oh god. They're a stupid lot too. Can you speak proper, Boy?"

"Sorry, my lord. I can. It's just we have our own dialect here in Fyninfer."

"What do you call yourself?"

"Rick Cottontree."

"Uproarious."

"Praise you kindly."

"Now tell, Rick Cottontree," continued Dingle, "Why do you call this place Fyninfer?"

"I? Well I calls it Fyninfer on account of it being the name. But those who named it? Named it so because it's fine and fair—"

"It is not fine and fair! To say this place is fine and fair is to say that fish have cocks! They don't! I've dressed them."

"I'm sorry you don't like the village, my lord. I thought it was a fine place to grow tall."

Here the Honorable Dingle and I shared many glances, holding in our giggles, for this young Rick Cottontree had no idea of the humorous innuendo he had just made. After some time of enduring our snickers, he asked for the matter.

"What is it that's snickery?"

"I don't suppose you've been over to the more peopled places in the Lobes," I began, holding in my laughter, "but in such peopled places, to say 'grow tall' means to, well..." I regained my composure. "City folk tend to think of head to foot as length, and hip to hip as width, so tallness then..."

Still Rick Cottontree was clueless.

Dingle helped him out by demonstrating the meaning of tallness, by putting a hand on his chest and pulling it outward. This did not help.

"So growing tall... to you... means that your chest, falls out?"

Dingle rolled his eyes and told me to get down on my back. I did so, and Dingle motioned down at me.

"See, the chronicler lies on his back. If he continues to lie on his back, there is but one way for him to grow tall."

"To put his arms out before him?"

228

Dingle slapped himself on the forehead. Clearly Rick Cottontree had no mind for organs of the loin. But no matter— these make for the best traveling companions, for they seldom complain of lust and thirst. So we laid out an offer to Rick Cottontree.

"You want me to come with you where?" he asked.

"Anywhere that naughty Skulfers lurk."

"That's a vague response. Now I've heard that there are plenty naughty Skulfer about in the world now days—"

"You best believe that," spoke Deng Lu passing by. "Just ten days ago a Skulfer killed a man by way of seven arrows. In this very village."

Rick Cottontree seemed shocked. He looked behind, at the tightly knit village of about forty homes, all close and within plain sight. Dingle and Deng were notably appalled.

"You said you lived here? How—"

"Forget it Dingle," went Deng, "This boy is clearly a drifter."

"Right, there's no way you're gonna live in this place and not hear a guy get shot seven times."

"Well I go on long walks for decent spells."

"Still. You'd hear about it when you got back."

"No. Not necessarily," spoke Cottontree, quiet and slow. "I'm quite sheltered. Even for one of Fyninfer."

"Sheltered from proper speech no doubt," critiqued Deng Lu, "But living out here, that's not necessarily a bad thing."

And on that sudden, Dingle— who had been having deep fun with Cottontree up to that point— began to take the side of sympathy, and condemned Deng Lu for his rudeness.

"If you lived out here all your life I bet you'd be something of a dow-facing tree yourself. Now go and do not return until your task is done."

With salty lips did Deng depart, and then Dingle and I apologized to the mild-mannered Cottontree.

"But no, you should come with us. You seem to be very kind and deep, and those are the kind of men we're looking for. These Unspoken Paleskins that I've acquired by the grace of Skin Toot are not at all deep, and the Tanfolk that I've acquired from Fundrik Luber are not all that kind. For you, having both qualities is a high virtue."

"It's nice to feel wanted," mused Rick Cottontree. "But my place is here... in the place they call Fyninfer."

And once again Dingle, riled by the name of that place so flat and barren, raised his voice to a stronger tone that it usually took.

"Fyninfer is a shit-land, and it will be called a shitland forevermore by map-makers and chroniclers. Back me up here."

And I backed up Dingle's point, for I agreed with him: "Neither hill, nor a single tree, rises up from the land in all that can be seen. Rick Cottontree, if that be your true name... there are better places in this world. Places that are not flat. Places that have trees, and wonder."

"You speak a word unfamiliar to me. Trees, what is this?"

And then it was decided.

"You're coming with us," ordered Dingle. "You cannot have lived twenty years and not know what a Horlio damn tree is. Come on. Pack your cloth."

"I do not doubt that a 'tree' might be wondrous to behold," spoke Cottontree, biting his lip and wringing his shirt with his hands. "But there are reasons why this place is called Fyninfer."

"Name one."

"It is both fine and fair to have such a sense of security. One might look out for miles in all directions...

230

to see the coming of winds, or men. It is impossible to here be struck by surprise."

And there was truth in this, for one could turn in a full circle and view nothing but flat... barren... nothing. Yet this flat and barren nothingness could indeed be viewed at an unbroken range of ten or so miles, which is nothing short of notable. So it appeared then that Rick Cottontree truly did feel a sense of belonging amidst that desolate gathering of huts called Fyninfer.

"I will not rip you from the place you call you," spoke Dingle with a respectful tip of his corn-fashioned hat, and then he said many more words of heart tickling invitation. His words were long-winded; skip over them if you must. But if you do, know in your heart that you are disgraced for your incompetence with the written word.

"I apologize in honest and in earnest for the rude insults I've regurgitated on the whole of this land. But do take my offer in sincerity: if you would like to see greater things— I promise they do exist— then you are more than welcome to become a Dingleite. We are a group of men with common purpose, to end the tyranny of Url Skulfing's Skulfers, those of the Old Patrol who have been corrupted and now carry out raids and killings on folk on account of their skin not being dark enough. I sense that you may wish to come with us, but fear and comfort hold you back. You like the village of Fyninfer because you feel safe... but how safe do you feel knowing that a Skulfer rode in days ago and shot one of your breed seven times with no just cause? I take it you fear the concept of rolling and winding roads, never knowing what comes next in a country of varied landscapes. But that is the thrill of life! To set out on a road amidst valley and trees? Nothing is more worth living for. It may be slightly more treacherous, but not by a long margin. The world is treacherous. If your time should come to be

231

struck down or hung up, vile forces can just as easily descend upon you here. There is no army of Fyninfer. If the world decides to dispense with you, it will be done and done quite easily. In fact, I would argue that you are very unsafe in this place! For if you have enemies, sure, you could see them coming from ten miles away. But what do you do at that point? Run? They could trap you on all sides. Being able to see for ten miles across also means that you can be seen for ten miles across. You are an easy prey here in Fyninfer. Come with us and I will show you towns set on hilltop, or in gentle dells of the wood, set by riverside or in lands with all three! These folk have options when it comes to their defense. And more importantly, their people have joy in their hearts. The joy that comes from simply existing in a place worth living! Places of beauty, Rick! Come with us."

"No thanks."

And with that, Piss Dingle stood, ashamed that he had just shown so much overwhelming vigor at trying to get a young timid nobody to join his crew. I gave him comfort.

And then we were all set to leave, for Deng Lu had finished interrogating all of the village folk, and found that none of them were harboring Tem Lomin, nor did any of them have any idea to where he had fled.

"These simplesons are as flat as the land they've built their huts on," huffed Deng Lu, removing his hot iron gloves.

"You questioned them thoroughly?" asked Carvin Cong.

"I am beyond surprised that the girth with which I performed my inquiries did not give rise to any piece of knowledge. And yes, each of the huts were searched entirely, as you can see by the exteriors a full sack only takes about sixty counts to perform."

232

"Then our quest is ended," exhaled Cong, ready to just throw in the gloves there and then.

"We do not end until have done what we set forth to do," put down Deng with great resolve. "Dingle. Where do we go from here?"

And all eyes looked to Dingle, for he was the leader of the Dingleites, a fact which he still oftenly forgot.

"Oh! We, uh... let's go to Watercross. I dunno."

And with that, our party of Dingleites gathered their things for the trek to Watercross.

"Watercross, eh?" asked Deng Lu, putting on his hot iron gloves once again.

"It just uh... sounded like a nice place. Haven't you ever wanted to go?"

"I was under the impression by his High Judgery Fundrik Luber that you were a man of action. Not a man of pleasure."

"Is it not possible to be both?"

"Very well," smiled Deng Lu. "Why not spend the night here then? Milk what treasures we can from this stop."

"What the hell treasures are you talking about?" asked Dingle, but then he knew Deng Lu meant women.

"Oh. You want to... well, I don't know if that's the kind of thing Fundrik Luber would approve of."

"It'll be no raid. I'll keep a strict eye on that. Only the ones that want it."

"You've found one who 'wants it' then, I take?"

"Mm-hm. She's called Tibsmith, and she's agreed to come with us. A mighty fine lover of bowels she is— taking them out, that is."

"Oh! Oakay. That's cool," nodded Dingle, just ready for Deng Lu to be out of his sight.

As soon as he had gone, a startling finger tapped on Dingle's side—

"Damn you Fung!"

But it was not Fung. It was Rick Cottontree.

"I've reconsidered. I'd like to come."

Dingle stood completely baffled. "What proved to be the alteration of your mind?"

"Just thought it was time I left this place behind, to see bold new places with trees."

In reality it was because of a girl and a girl alone. The one called Tibsmith, who he had just heard would be joining the Dingleites. Truth be told, it was Tibsmith that had kept Rick Cottontree chained to the village of Fyninfer all those years. Though he never spoke to her, and only seldomly spoke in her presence, he felt the highest meaning in his life was to be near to her, and quite plainly that now meant following her on a grand expedition across Elaptirius.

"Well we're glad to have you as a Dingleite! You are fine with the risk, though? There will be great risk for all of us ahead; as I said, lands beyond this one are varied. Roads that wind, roads that curve, roads obscured by shadow and pit."

"Well it's about time I took a risk," spoke Rick Cottontree to the ground, for he often looked there, "After all it is my name."

"Your— what? I thought your name was Rick."

"It is. But back when the letter 'c' was serpent-like, the name Rick sounded like Risk. It's only recently that folk say it like 'Rikk' and I don't want to be bothersome with correcting them on something so unimportant as... my name."

"Poor Risky," I lamented, and then Risky (as I called him as a pet name) brought up his grounded head.

"I will take the risk of your travels on the condition that Tibsmith be brought before you and fully initiated tonight after a vigorous interview— one that lasts the whole night— so she is not allowed to sleep."

234

An odd request. But we obliged, none of us thinking at the time that little Risky might have had stirrings for the tall and dominating Tibsmith, for after all, little Risky had not even been able to grasp the fact that 'growing tall' is the same as having a penile erection.

This brings us back to the present. Now you know of Rick Cottontree, or Little Risky as I fondly refer to him, and of his Shitland called Fyninfer, and his wrenching for the Lady Tibsmith, who was tall and loved the thought of pulling out bowels.

"What's this I hear of bears?" Rick Cottontree had said.

"We are not speaking of bears!" yelled out Dingle for his own sake. But then, seeing that he was talking to self-doubting Cottontree, he brought his voice down to a gentle tone. "Don't you think that bears could be something of a friend to man?"

"I'm not the one to ask. I've only just seen hills and trees for the first time," spoke Cottontree plainly.

"And what do you think? Is the world not more lovely than you could have possibly imagined?" and here Dingle motioned grandly up the road they were ascending, alongside gentle slopes with trees dotting their tops.

"I mean it's great and all," shrugged Cottontree, "But don't you think it'd be better if all the trees were taken down and the road flattened out, so we could see for miles in all directions?"

"Go from my side."

And Rick Cottontree bowed with an apologetic "Yes my lord" and fell behind once again.

Just miles north of Watercross, they were now approaching the Border of the Lobes. Once they passed through the Lobian Gate, they would be in a completely new land, one free from all jurisdiction of the Hayamese Empire. It was a thing that made many of the Dingleites rejoice, especially the more vocal of the bunch, namely Deng Lu.

"Can't wait to get out of this fecalhole," he would say, and "Just miles away from a better place."

"Hey man, why you hating on the Lobes so much?" asked Brooth Dimfether, a deep broad-shouldered Mahogany man who often hung around Deng for amusement.

"What is there not to hate about the Lobes? Prejudice on all sides. Corrupted forms of governing. A rise in violence, oppression, a failing and a faulty definition of law and order perpetrated by dumb dumb folk."

"I guarantee you will find those things all over the world," smirked Dimfether. "It's not just the Lobes."

But Deng Lu maintained that he was nothing but full of glee to be leaving the Lobes behind.

We then paraded by the Lobian Guard, who were only concerned with folk coming into the Lobes, and had no interest in our reason for leaving. We crossed under the Arches of Salt, and then found ourselves in a nameless land, for there was no authority over that stretch. At best it could be described as Garigal, but even when that region was commonly known as such, it was not an official name by any means. Garigal was simply what outsiders called the place, for it was full of so-called Garigs, they being fierce and and unassociated with any established order. Like the bears of Elaptirius, perhaps they were only hostile because they were being entrenched upon.

Anyway, as soon as we were out of the Lobes, the road grew thin and the grass grew tremendously tall.

Deng Lu was the first to complain.

236

"How's one supposed to walk on a track this small — it's barely a path! And who has been cutting the grass?"

"Nobody by the looks of it," laughed Brooth Dimfether.

Upon hearing Deng's complaints, I sped up to him, so that I might recall his former arrogance at being so happy to leave the Lobes.

"I will be first to point out that someone indeed has been cutting this grass, and the width of this narrow path is the best you'll get this side of the Tom Ball. Soon the track will be gone, and we'll be left to wade through chest-high blades."

"What of the Road to Deleras? You spoke of a road!"

"Aye, the Tom Ball is the road! But our company be all too poor for river vessels."

"I'd rather swim the Tom Ball than trudge through chest-high grass—"

"You say that now, but you also said that things would be far better outside the Lobes. I'm beginning to doubt the things that escape your teeth." I was especially proud of this remark, and it even garnered a ten-thronged tickle from Brooth.

Bitterly Deng retreated back to Dingle, who spoke to Cottontree concerning the prospects of renaming the Tom Ball Wade.

"I'm sure there was a good reason," resigned Dingle. "I'm sure Tom Ball was a real person in years gone by, and probably a good one too! But now no one knows his name. No one knows who Tom Ball is. No one in this company knows, no one at Watercross knew."

"Well the Tom Ball's a mighty river," explained Rick Cottontree. "You got people all the way from the Sestarions to... who knows where, calling it Tom Ball. I don't think you can just start calling it something else."

"That's gonna be the one defining thing of my life," mused Dingle. "If all else fails, I'm gonna rename the Tom Ball River. I'll at least call it a river. What is a Wade? No one wades in a river."

"What would you call it ideally?"

"Something pleasant. Something inspiring. Maybe the Bear... something. Bearman? Bearfriend?"

"I knew it—" and it was the voice of Deng Lu sneaking up behind Dingle, "You're wet freckles over them. All you can talk about—"

"No, no! You caught me by chance there, but we weren't talking about bears, we were talking about renaming the Tom Ball."

"To the River Bearfriend?! The only the folk of this river would agree to that is if you were the last of them."

Deng waited for Dingle's reply, but all he got a shivery jump. To what cause? A small serpent that slithered quick along the ground, right between Dingle's legs and onto into the tall grass.

"My, that serpent seems to have given you a start. Do you love them?" Inquired Deng Lu.

"I don't hate them, if that's what you're implying."

"But do you love them? If I were to pick up the next one I find— and there will be many in this untamed weed— should I hold it out to you as an offer of good will?"

"Look, Deng, there'd be no good will in that from my perspective."

"But don't you believe that serpents have been wrongfully oppressed as of late? The victim of a nasty prejudice?"

"Ah, I see what you're trying to do here. You don't like bears, I don't like serpents. Let's just leave it at that."

"But tell me Lord Dingle, why don't you like serpents? I'm deeply curious."

238

And it occurred to Piss Dingle that he never truly considered why it was that he didn't care for serpents. He asked Deng, rather, why it was that he admired them.

"I admire the snakes of the earth for they are always subservient. They have no other means. Crawling on their bellies, at the feet of their masters... I feel a certain fondness for them, for they know their place. I feel good having them under me, knowing they will not rise."

"They cannot rise. If they could, they almost certainly would."

"Still. Whether by choice or not, they are the embodiment of submission. Does that not please you, Lord Dingle?"

"Not one bit. I do not think that creatures should be made for submission. Perhaps it is because I feel the urge towards submission myself... but only if I choose it. It should always be a choice. For me, seeing a serpent slithering beneath me makes me all too uncomfortable— I feel that I should be in its place. I do not like anything at my feet, for I belong on the ground myself, at the feet of something greater than myself."

"This is all too good to hear," spoke Deng Lu, thinking to himself. "One day surely you will renounce your title of Leader of the Dingleites?"

"I would never grant power to you, Deng Lu."

Deng chuckled— "I did not ask for such a thing."

"I can read through your words. I have heard you saying of the fallen Tanfolk, 'may they rest in power.'"

"Yes, because power was denied to them in life!"

"Would they not rather have peace then? In death, is not peace the greatest of all things? In life it was power that robbed them. The power of men is that which causes tragedy. Why then would you wish 'power' upon the dead who have died as a result of such 'power?'

Power is the ultimate corruptor, and it should not be granted to any man so lightly, even in death."

"We all crave power, Dingle."

"And here I thought we all craved peace."

"We all crave one 'P' word or another," I proudly put in as my piece.

As the suns began to set, we all grew weary as we took the high steps through ridiculously tall grass. According to the calculations I had laid out, we would soon be gazing upon a small cluster of trees, in which we could conveniently spend the night. With light disappearing fast, Brooth Dimfether joked that he would use my body as a torch if we did not reach the Cluster by nightfall.

Fortunately, we came upon the Cluster just moments before Sa-Thren's final farewell.

Unfortunately, as we all piled into the trees on the narrow path, a bear leapt out from behind a tree.

Fortunately, Dingle had been secretly hoping to catch sight of another bear the whole living day.

Unfortunately, he did anticipate his encounter to be one of this close nature, nor was he prepared to think clearly in such a situation.

Thank the dear Lord Horlio of All the Stars that the bear merely snatched up one of the Unspoken. It was terrifying, surely, but it gave us all time to flee down up the hill to our right, that which led to the river, which at this point was curiously held between two stretches of high land. The bear did not follow us up the slope, and none of us were sad at the choice of meal the bear had chosen. That is not to say that bear no longer concerned us.

"I think it's very clear what must be done," whispered Deng Lu, "One of us must dispense with the Crothantheng."

"Um, that bear is no longer a threat."

Obviously this remark came from Piss Dingle, as he was now clearly and most certainly the only member of his own party to have a blatant love for bears, both physically and spiritually.

"Dingle. Don't give in to this folly," whispered I to he.

"No, I mean it. For too long— too long have those creations been treated like animals! They are... soft. And large. Full of prowess. With kind faces. And lovely arms. The kind that could cradle you and not let go."

"Hey Dingle, go offer yourself up then," suggested Deng. "Go on. Go kneel before your master."

And Piss Dingle strongly considered it.

But as it were, the bear simply sauntered off after having devoured the poor Unspoken. Then the Dingleites were split: half wished to take the counsel of Deng, and chase after the bear so that they might be rid of any enemy, while the other half listened to Dingle and decided that having left, the bear was now of no real danger.

"Look, the bear's not hungry anymore. It swallowed an entire man. We're good."

And this was logic that persuaded them to leave the bear in peace. They moved cautiously over to the Cluster, and set up their tents within the trees. Some of them endeavored to climb and spend the night in the branches, for the fear of Crothantheng was still quite present.

"Ah, you guys are a bunch of tongue-for-cocks," brushed off Dingle as he set sack upon the ground. "If that bear comes back, I'll show you all how to get down with one."

And muttering soft sensualities, he fell reached the realm of sweet slumber.

Of course the bear did come back. She was still well satisfied from her Unspoken meal, however, and so she kept to the low grass at the bottom of the Cluster, rolling around for lack of anything more productive to do.

This rolling of the bear did wake up a certain light-sleeping Dingleite, and it was Deng Lu. Deng Lu, he who slept always with an axe or six at his side. One of these axes found its way quick into the side of the bearess... and then a deep roar lifted up the sky.

Leaping to his arches, Piss Dingle charged at Deng Lu and brought him to the ground, just as another axe was to be thrown. There was arguing, there was screaming, there was frantic sprinting about the camp. I apologize for the lack of precise detail, but it was the middle of night and I was surely a walking freak, as I always am when I am driven out of deep sleep so suddenly.

I do remember a very epic scuffle between Dingle and Deng, which ended in... the bear not being killed, but rather killing another of our own... and then going back to bed.

As it happened, the second fatality that the bear imposed happened to be Deng Lu's brother. Not a close companion, mind you, but an actual honest brother, and his only one I believe. This put something of a dent in the relations of all men considered.

"No... I didn't know you had a brother in this group," said Dingle, not knowing what else to say.

"His name was Skrodum Lu and he now belongs to the earth, thanks to you."

"Thanks to me? I'm not the one who provoked the bear."

"If you had not spoken of peace and forgiveness, I would have marched out and killed the bear when the chance was there. Had you not tumbled me over in the night, I would have finished her with a second axe. In all ways, this tragedy is of your making."

"I mean... yeah. How can I make it up to you?"

"You will name me as Leader of the Dingleites."

"All...right. Sure."

And just like that, Dingle had given up authority over the group he had given his name to, and Deng Lu was elevated to his first position of power.

At Deleras we stole some boats. It was thievery at its finest, but soon we remembered that Deleras lies at the bottom of the Del, and so we were hard-pressed to row our boats upriver. The currents raged against us, and we made very slow progress.

The walk from Deleras to Wesdel would have taken a few days; as it were, our rowboats made the trip in two weeks. We didn't mind though, we were so sick of walking. And the two-week sail upstream gave us all hideously large forearms.

At Wesdel, we dispersed so as not to appear a large body of forty men bent on snatching Tem Lomin and lynching him for his lynching of another. In whispers we spoke, hinting at wealth we did not have as incentive for the townsfolk to give up Tem's location. It did not take long, for the townsfolk had no love for Tem, and as it happened, Tem was not hiding at all. He simply owned a home in Wesdel, and was now inside of it.

The house of Tem was a modest little thing, square and compact, with just two windows on either side of the front door, and wood cross-hatching set against bumpy white plaster. The little home was set up against a steeply rising green hill, and this was enough to give some of our party alarm.

"See this won't end well," hypothesized Brooth Dimfether, "This guy's got a secret passage going out the back of his house into that hill, I can feel it. We'll run in, he'll run out, and then he'll have little douches of the hill come charging at us from under the slope!"

"Your imaginings are perilous," spoke the calm Deng Lu, "But your imaginings find no grounding on this plane."

And it was the plan of Deng Lu to break into the house of Tem Lomin by force immediate, without giving so much as a knock. But I and the Honorable Piss Dingle at length convinced him that we ought to lead by a kind example, that meaning not to employ the tactics of brute Skulfers when we had all been condemning those actions.

But Deng Lu only laughed and reminded Dingle that he was now the Leader of the Dingleites— Dingle had made it so himself— and he argued that as Tem Lomin had acted the part of a brute Skulfer, he ought to be given himself the treatment of a brute Skulfer.

Eventually it was negotiated that they would lure the man out by way of song. And so Brooth Dimfether, large and deep though he was, took stance at the head of the forty Dingleites, and was the dancer by which all others fell into place, and the loud singer by which all others found their tone:

Hear ye all!
This wondrous tale

Of why we
Came to the town of old Wesdale!
It is for the one who
In Fyninfer did slew
A man with seven arrows
And now he needs to fall.

His name is Tem!
You know of him
You know his
hiding skills are rather dim!
For he is in his house
Which we now will douse
To set things right with spirits
We'll sacrifice to them.

Tem Tem Tem, we sacrifice to them.
Lo Lo-min, we've come to take your skin.

When after nine vicious rounds Tem did not emerge, then Deng Lu led the charge, and the forty men descended upon the charming house, and destroyed it physically. Lomin they wrenched from his bed, with the giant arms of Brooth holding him up above the ravenous crowd.

"Spread them wide," spoke Deng to Brooth, and by this he was referring to Tem's cheeks. Once the cheeks of Tem had indeed been spread wide, Brooth held up a squirming squirrel, which he shoved deep in the mouth of Tem. And to secure the mouth of Tem, with his thick yet nimble fingers he stuck three needles between the Skulfer's lips.

A circle formed around the squirrel-and-needle mouthed man— he who had shot a Paleskin seven times through the back with no just cause at all— which Deng

Lu then made to be straight, for he liked things to be straight. He proclaimed himself "Lord" of the Dingleites, and thrust upon Tem all the disgusting deeds he was charged with (which really only amounted to one deed, but that single deed was filthy as we have made clear, and Deng elaborated to the full extent of its filthiness).

Then, for one animal in the body would be not enough for his crimes, Deng Lu lifted a snake up from his waist, one he had kept wrapped upon his belt. Handing the serpent to Brooth, once again Deng Lu Lord of the Dingleites uttered the title of this chapter, only this time he referred to cheeks of a different nature.

Brooth pushed Tem Lomin to the ground and ripped from him his trousers, then dropped the serpent down a crack, and into a dark hole.

"It was a bit much," said Piss Dingle as Deng Lu recounted his triumph over Tem Lomin to the people of Wesdale.

"And it was a bit much for Tem to shoot a man seven times in the back."

"Look, no one's arguing that. But if word of this gets out— of a Rich Mahogany being murdered in this heinous manner— it might just serve to get people more riled up. In fact it definitely will. You can't tell me that Skulfing's Deeplove are gonna take this and shrug it off. No, this'll give them more cause than ever to come after us— and not just us, all Paleskin and all Tanfolk!"

"You're one to talk," smirked Deng Lu. "You're one of them. A 'Rich Mahog.'"

"But I'm not with them am I? I'm with you!" exclaimed Dingle. "See, this is what they want. They want to make it all about the colors— they want to make men like you think it's all about light-skin versus dark.

246

But that's not what it is! It's about the oppressed, versus the oppressor!"

"And the Rich Mahogany are... the oppressors, of the lighter breeds."

"Look man, you're not grasping it. Not all—"

"Oh, not all, not all! But most. Listen to me Dingle, the Mahogany men are privileged. Each and every one of you. You must face the fact that you yourself have had a hand in building this system of oppression."

And Dingle was baffled. For near a year, he had walked the Lobes in ill cloth, searching of a way to help dismantle the systems of oppression. He had acknowledged fully they existed, and by the deeds of Rich Mahogany men. But he himself? He himself had never spread a word of hate. He had only lived a quarter century, while the oppressions of Tanfolk in this region had lasted a thousand years. How then, was this man— a friend, one who had joined his common cause— now so quick to denounce Dingle as part of the problem?

It was probably no more complex than the simple truth that Deng Lu was a passionate asshole.

"Alright, just put yourself into the place of the Mahogs for a second. And see yourself spouting all this talk of merciless revenge and grouping everybody into the same category based on their skin tone, saying everyone has the same level of guilt in your oppression, even the guy who's giving you aid!"

"I don't deal much with allephor and metagory," spoke Deng Lu, seamlessly fusing the words allegory and metaphor without realizing as he turned away. "We Tanfolk have been oppressed for many an age, and now is the time to rise."

"Oakay. So you don't... care about forming a society where folks are seen as equals."

"Folks are not equal, Dingle. There are strong and there are weak; I must be strong now for my people. Strong for we have been weak for far too long."

"Alright, how's this for strength?"

And without warning, Piss Dingle gave Deng Lu a mighty slap across the teeth. Violence ensued.

A nasty fight it was, not in the way of bloodshed, but nasty in the sounds of flopping body and jiggling fat upon the ground. Of legs and loins contorting themselves in a way that did not seem natural for these two wermen. All the Dingleites gathered round, and disgusted faces did they make.

"If only you could fight that way against our enemies. And not against men in our own camp," spoke the Lady Victory when the brawl had finished.

"Are you still here?" asked Dingle, for he had not seen her in a great spell of time.

"Yes. Either you have been avoiding me or I have been avoiding you."

"Which is it?"

"I think it's pretty obviously both. But now I feel the need to speak: why are you reluctant to deal out death to those who have dealt out death themselves?"

Dingle hesitated. He was tired of defending his pacifist ways, but a thought just then occurred to him:

"I think I know what it is. I think I'm a peaceful man on all ordinary occasions, but once I see oppression taking place— really see it— then I lose my peace most definitely. And I... I dunno, just something about the way that Deng was talking to me. He was oppressing me, so I hit him."

"So all you need to do is visualize the dark deeds of these Skulfers when we encounter them. Envision Tem

248

Lomin firing seven arrows into the back of an innocent man."

"Ya know... had I done that, I might well have been able to drop that snake down his arse."

"And that's the leadership we need! I have sensed a darkness in Deng too, a darkness that need not mar the purpose of our crusade."

"Deng Lu."

"Yes."

"You said Deng Too."

"I meant Deng as well, or Deng also."

"I see."

"I'm quite serious, Piss," continued the Lady Victory, "There must be a way for you to take back your role as figurehead. Dingleites do not belong under the thumbs of Deng, do you not see that?"

"Deng Lu."

"Yes."

"You said Deng Du."

"I was using his first name and then continuing on with my sentence. And you are merely avoiding what must be done."

"Look, Victory," and here they began to hump, "I already gave all my power to that Lu man, and it was all theoretical power anyway. I can't get it back, and quite frankly don't think I ever had it."

"No. You will have a chance to show your strength, and very soon. Dark Chevron's been sighted just to the north, in Pitidun."

And Dingle let out a mighty gulp, which then spilled drool down onto Victory who was under him. Those were the words he was dreading to hear. I know all this for I was lying in wait, packed in tightly with foodstocks in his tent.

We left Wesdale briskly the next morning, for all ears had been made aware that the location of Dark Chevron was now known. We would need to be quick, for unlike Tem Lomin, the Skulfer Dark Chevron— killer of Flod— was not simply staying in his house. He was truly on the run, a fugitive in the jurisdiction of the Lobes, now running about the sparse wilds of Garigal.

Since I was the only Dingleite who knew those lands intimately, all the company trusted me as their guide. In truth, there was a modest path that led straight from the woods on Wesdale's northern border straight up to Pitidun, but I did not wish to take it. Instead, I veered our party towards Kenetherin, deep swampland of the miserable sort.

"It's a bog!" exclaimed Rick Cottontree, to the aggravation of all when his leg first dropped into an oozy puddle of thick green fluid.

"Could you not see that fifty strides back?" shouted Deng Lu. "There's nothing obstructing your view. Not even mist."

"Well no one's said it!" shouted Cottontree ahead.

"You're beginning to talk much more than I should like!" replied Deng, and it was true that the time was coming when none of us should venture to speak more words than was necessary.

For flying bothersome creatures abounded from all directions, small buzzing insects that would quickly enter the mouth if left open for more than a moment.

"Are you sure this is the way to Pitidun?!" shouted Deng Lu at choppy intervals and waving his arms all about, waging war with the flies.

"This is a way to Pitidun! I mean, yes— the way. The way that must be taken." And as I had my long curved horn with me, I could speak without bother, and speak in a manner that made my voice sound tall, and sixlike. I rather enjoyed the sound of my own voice for once. And so I continued on, speaking at length on the Age of Enchantment when great covered shells would fly across the marshes bearing people and their goods, and then I recounted Snick Piggle's entire tale of Feenisall of Doncrethi, in the days when that glorious age came to its end.

"Would you fall silent for a whale?!" shouted out Deng Lu at last, and I thought I had misheard him.

"Fall silent for a while, you mean?"

"No. A whale. If I gave you a cosh-mikkin whale, would that be enough to make you fall silent? For it is the honest extent I would go to for your mouth to hold shut!"

And I took up Deng Lu on that offer, and my mouth remained shut all the remainder of our passage through the swamps of Kenetherin. Yet I am sadly yet to see my whale that was promised.

Night fell by way of swirling grey cloud, with bright streaks of violet and pink running round the horizon. And as the Dingleites waded out into the toxic black waters mixed with a slowly spiraling green, Piss Dingle said a thing altogether surprising and incomprehensible.

"We shall camp here tonight."

And Deng Lu was immediately up with the arms— "Sorry? This is the worst possible place to camp— ever."

"But I'm tired."

"Aye. I too," spoke I in simple agreement.

Most of our folk simply dropped, for the sticky hot march through bubbling marsh had tired them to no end. Rick Cottontree, however, allowed himself ten minutes of crying to himself before his dark rest. He was at one point, I noticed, illuminated by the vision of the lovely Tibsmith, lying on a patch of weeds o'er yonder. But mere moments later he was back with the tears, and even more so, for Deng Lu had taken up his place next to Tibsmith and was causing her comfort and laughter.

After hours of the failed search for sleep, Cottontree took up quarters next to Dingle, offering up juicy bits of knowledge.

"You know what they say about that Deng Lu?" whispered Cottontree most timid.

Dingle leaned in, admittedly wanting to know any dirt he could get on this rival Deng.

"They say he cums with axes."

And Dingle cocked his head and lowered his brows, knowing not at all what Rick meant.

"Have you not heard? When he tents alone, he will arouse himself greatly, but only if he holds an axe in each hand."

"This information is strange and telling," ruminated Piss Dingle, deeply tired, yet still interested.

"Yes, he is aroused by sharp blade, and those are no good things to have if ever he were to lie with woman."

"Lie with Tibsmith you mean."

And here the Honorable Dingle confronted Rick Cottontree on his very clear fondness for Tibsmith, which Cottontree denied fullfold.

"I don't, have any fancy, for Tib— whatever she's called."

"Don't act like you don't know her name, you both come from the same village of four people."

"Fair enough. I know her name. It is Tibsmith. She joined your party and I followed, but there is no cause in that chance. There is no fondness."

"Mm. Alright. Wo-kai!"

And Piss Dingle rolled over and fell asleep with those sarcastic remarks.

On the impending battle for the affection of lovely Tibsmith, I will say little but this: either Deng Lu or Rick Cottontree will succeed in gaining her favor. There will be passion of lips and loin. One will meet a terrible death, an evil fate at the hands of misfortune— while the other will gain unspeakable riches. Which destiny belongs to which man is, to you my reader, yet to be seen.

As all the men wished more than anything to skip over the crossing of Kenetherin, I will skip over it from here.

In Pitidun we found Dark Chevron and dispensed with him most heinously. His uproarious death was brought to him on the 20th of Sevallia, 3334. Did I skip over too much? Deal with it as you will. This chapter has grown atrociously long and I'm looking forward to ending it. Oh, oh dear.

Oh fecal shit.

They've come for me.

I see them now, rushing on the starline.

This is what I sought to avoid, why I endeavored to lead the men over hostile swamps, instead of taking the road.

I fear this manuscript will never come to see the lashing of pubes.

Oh, praise the giant woman we rest on. I have at this point recovered my pen and my liberty, and will retrace the days that have passed in my absence by the testimony of those I trust.

On that fateful day in Pitidun, I was rushed upon by cavalry, a branch of enforcement that was not satisfied with the sentence I had served for my previous crime.

"But I have paid for the crime!" I implored the lead horseman.

"Not nearly so long enough!" went the dumb bastard.

I turned to Dingle and those I counted as my friends— "Friends! Will you not explain to the cavalry that I was granted my liberty by a lawful court?"

"Uhh..." hesitated Dingle. "What is law anymore?"

And he shrugged, not wanting to wade into dangerous waters when he himself had just committed a heinous atrocity. I was carried away for a good long while, but the following conversation I am told transpired:

"Damn Dingle! I didn't know such a beast in you did lie!"

Those were the words of Brooth Dimfether, and other startled Dingleites who could not believe the gruesome manner in which Piss had recently disposed of Dark.

"What can I say? Dark Chevron stepped on the neck of Flod for the smallest of things... and stayed there for an hour. That's the heinous thing. What I did to Dark? It was dark. But it was over fairly quick."

"I liked the part where you dropped a huge boulder on his legs," giggled Tibsmith, moving close to Dingle.

Wanting to present himself as one of a similar mind, Rick Cottontree thrust himself up there in Dingle's pits too— "I liked the part when you fastened the rope around his shoulders and then pulled up, with the boulder still on his legs, until his belly split open by the pull."

"Split open by the pull," nodded Tibsmith, with wide eyes of adoration at the former leader of the Dingleites.

"Wait up, what was that you chanted after his belly split?" laughed Brooth.

"Oh, it was uh... 'there will be no pity in Pitidun!'"

"Yeah! No pity in Pitidun!"

254

"And then I said, 'no pity in Pitidun, only pits! And I rolled him over into the pit. And then you all buried him with hot coals."

"It was coal indeed," said Deng Lu.

"Watch out Deng!" laughed Brooth, giving his friend a slap on the back. "This kill's gonna make Piss a legend. I wouldn't be surprised if he took back the Dingleites yet."

And at that point, Deng Lu must have become burdened by a truth he had diminished. A great guilt washed over him, and as the Dingleites started the proper trek down from Pitidun, along the River Del, Deng came up to Dingle, timid and reserved. Night was falling soft through the cracks of the tall thin trees.

"Lord Dingle, I... have a thing to say."

"What is this? Rick Cottontree, have you stolen the skin of Deng Lu?"

"No, my lord... I just take on this timid and reserved manner for I am ashamed."

"There are many things for us all to be ashamed of, Deng. I am certainly ashamed, for playing no small role in the death of your dear Skrodum Lu."

"Well, this concerns Skrodum Lu, actually. My dear dead brother."

"A thousand sorries once again."

"But no— there is no need. I have no idea who was mauled by that bear. He was no man close to my heart."

"But you said—"

"Yes, Dingle. I told you he was my brother. And I told you his name was Skrodum Lu. Yet I have no brother, and Skrodum Lu is a name which no one holds."

"Praise goodness for that."

"Are you not upset?"

"Not so much, Deng. I came to know you as an arsepit quite early on. And when one is known to be an arsepit, such things that come naturally to an arsepit can

255

thus be expected of an arsepit. I just wonder why you confess this to me now."

"Because there is talk among the best of us that it ought to be Dingle at the fore of the Dingleites. If not only for the reason that your name is Dingle. Now I— I can start a group of my own. But I'd be a sore fit to lead a company of men with their name derived from yours."

"True. Perhaps your men could be Dengites. Though I hope such a thing lies still a far way off, for we must stay together for now if we are to achieve great ends."

Now they were all squinting in the dark, hardly able to make out shapes in front of them.

"When do we stop for the night?" asked Deng.

"When we reach the beds of the river," spoke Dingle with confidence.

"Very well. I do believe we've reached them," and he motioned at the sandy riverbed which lay just on the other edge of a grassy ledge.

"Those are not the beds I speak of."

"But they are beds of the river."

"How can you be sure?"

"Because streams always have visible beds, at all times, on either side— if they did not, the river would cease to be a river, and would rather be an ocean."

"Well if you're so certain that those are the river beds on which you'd like to slumber, go forth."

And so the company slept on wet sand, and was woken frequently by the rising tide.

In the morning, the Dingleites rose having had very poor sleep. They walked on, not but a mile further, and and then saw a row of seventy beds lined up against the stream bed. The former use of the word "bed" here denoting an actual man-crafted mattresses atop frames, the kind that invited a masterful slumber.

"What the hell is this?!" shouted just about everyone.

"I told you," smirked Dingle. "I wanted to walk the extra mile to the Beds of the River but Deng Lu here wanted to settle for the wet riverbed.

And all let off disgusted moans and exhales. "Deng Lu...!" For once they were all pissed, but not at Piss.

"Yes, the Del River is one of high luxury," smiled the Honorable Dingle. "Finest in the world one might think. On any other stream, one might expect riverbeds or riverbanks to refer only to sand or rock found on either edge of the stream. But not here. Here upon the Del, one finds the River Beds to be surprisingly rich and upheld quality, and the River Banks are fully stocked with coinage from all over the realm."

And so the Dingleites now walked in the stream itself, picking up currency from the River Banks as they waded along.

"So where do we go to next?" Asked Rick Cottontree, who was now fully onboard with this rash adventure now that his pockets were overflowing with silver. "Which Skulfer do we pick off next?"

"Skulfers? You think we ought to continue killing the bottom-most rung?"

"Well, they're the ones that cause all the injustice."

"But do Skulfers act of their own will? Well, yes. I suppose they do. So they are quite bad. But they are many, and to kill them all would be a task requiring thousands of men, and over a hundred years. No, Master Cottontree, I do not think we should go about plucking off Skulfers any longer."

And there were gasps along the River Bank, with the men ready to turn back to Deng Lu in a moment.

257

But Dingle spoke quickly, and saved his position at the forefront:

"Dingleites! Be you all that dense? Our enemy is known to us— he always has been known! That which we have searched for with years of uncertainty has always been before our nostrils. The enemy I speak of is clear and definable, a single foe what carries more weight than all the Skulfers combined!"

But no one could guess it.

"Who commands the Skulfers when present? Who employs them? Inspires them with talk of hatred and Lobian pride?"

At last Brooth called it out: "Url Skulfing!"

"Yes! It's Skulfing! The dick-tickler who gave his damn name to the Skulfers! How has it taken this long for his name to come up in all of this?"

"Well," shrugged Deng Lu, who now completely emasculated and submissive to Dingle after his blunder with the River Beds, "I suppose it's because we all thought that such a target would be forever out of our grasp."

"You would think that. You would certainly think that. And hey, maybe this will prove my greatest folly, but I think we should go for it."

"We would certainly win a great fame," said a frail old man nearby.

"Who are you?" asked Dingle, for he had not yet heard this voice.

"I am Urtain Piik," spoke Urtain.

"It's settled then. Urtain Piik says we all should go to Lakewood True, for I heard whispers in Pitidun that Url Skulfing holds his deepest army there."

"Ah, Lakewood!" Inhaled Brooth with a smile. "That spread of fortune. Twice have I laid lips afresh in the town of Lakewood."

258

"I'm happy for you Brooth, but we are not just speaking of the town of Lakewood. Lakewood True is where Skulfing's force resides."

"And what's not true about the Lakewood I know?"

"Have you not read Godsong?"

"You spent too much time with that man of the pen, Ward Geit Fung I fear. But tell me, what does the Godsong say of Lakewood True?"

"I would rather have you see with soup-risen eyes, Brooth," smiled Dingle.

"I desire to be swallowed by trees," spoke Rick Cottontree at some point in all this (you will remember I was not present, but rather languishing in jail).

"Do you not feel swallowed enough by trees in this instant?" Asked Deng Lu.

"No, I mean literally. Such is my newfound passion for these things called trees that think I would like to climb one, and then drop down the inside."

"You can play that game in Lakewood," assured the Honorable Dingle. "The magistrates'll take you high up to the tops of the hollow thick trees and when you're ready, they'll drop you in."

Cottontree's face lit up. "I do so like the forest better than I did the bare plains of Fyninfer, Lord Dingle. I am forever in your debt for these new woodland horizons, and will pleasure your cock whenever it does need."

"That... won't be necessary Master Cottontree. But thank you all the same. Now let us hasten on, towards the watered trees of Lakewood True. Many things we will carry, for many things we will need on this noble trek."

Chapter XIII
The Things They Carried

The following is a list of things that they carried, on their way
to Lakewood True in the middle of the Farlobe, plain and flat:

They carried axes, blunt and steep.
They carried dogfriends, large and deep.
They carried men, who could not walk.
Or those who just wished to be held.
They carried bread of Brunenfeld!

They carried ale, the kind that sucks.
They carried mail, to put on ducks.
For ducks of all, do need chain mail.
So that their bodies do not fail.
When swords of metal pierce their fluff—
They obviously need the chain mail in order not to be sliced
through entirely.

They carried books of words and deeds.
To keep them tickled in the weeds.
When nightly winds did make them bow.
The books gave solace, this is how:
To take their minds off of the cold.
With drawings warm of women old.

They carried spoons in cans of tin.
They carried knives for their foreskin.
They carried forks for all who live.
They carried corks for cups that give.

They carried greed within their coins.
They carried doom within their loins.
They carried freaks from other lands.
That carried beaks inside those hands.

They carried fingers, with their fingers.

Those which hung down by their arms.
Which shoulders carried in their turn.
They carried wood for which to burn.

They carried shoes, for they'd grow dirty.
Carried chairs to prove more sturdy.
They carried grass to lay their heads.
They carried asses for their beds.

They carried swords, for they weren't dumb.
They carried canes, for all want some.
They carried robe and carried cape.
All of them made to gruesome shape.

They carried heinous tools that cut.
They carried them to cut the nut.
They carried flame to cook the hawk.
They carried corn fresh off the stalk.

They carried girth, which kept them hungry.
Carried scents to make their lungs breathe.
Carried balls and carried games.
To scare off all the losing dames.

They carried fear, and carried wonder.
Carried beer, and all its plunder.
Carried hope, but not too much.
They carried blood and cocks and such.

They carried gifts for Horlio.
The Lord of Stars and All that Shines.
They carried gold to make her shrines.

They carried all these things and more.
To the the True of Lakewood, and its door.

—And all specifically in that order.

Chapter 14
Chambers of No Nourishment

Nobody really knows what they carried. But many have guessed over the years, and that game of guessing became so enthralling that an entire epic poem speculating on things they may have carried was woven, and included here in my account, though many have begrieved my telling it.

I have told it to provide some sort of transition from the tender scenes along the River Del to the heinous scenes of torture that we will soon find ourselves in, for other than that, there is none. They journeyed from that glorious river to the village of Lakewood in short order, where they immediately set about fulfilling Rick Cottontree's wish to be swallowed whole by a tree. I now rely on the word of my comrades for, as you remember, I was in jail once again, but I will continue to speak as though I was there, for thanks to the vivid testimonies put to me, I feel as though I was.

The young lad of Fyninfer, Little Risky as I called him, laughed like he was in some lewd situation as the tree-tamers lifted him high above our heads, to the top of some massive wide oak, and then dropped him into its hollow center. Many of us thought it was the end of Cottontree. We stepped slowly towards the oak, and all was silent and still. Then, to the startling of all, Rick's head burst up into the tree's deep hole at eye level, and he exclaimed 'Hoy Hoy Hoy' to which we all screamed in terror.

"Never before have I held such joy as when that tree swallowed me whole," sighed Rick Cottontree after he had been pulled back out through the oak's hollow. "Now I might die content, no matter what end I might face. This last spell of weeks has held more joy than all my years in Fyninfer."

But we were soon reminded that this charming village of Lakewood had been built around the charming Wood Lake, and therefore this was not Lakewood True. Lakewood True was a lake apart, where an ancient town had been, since submerged under muddied waters of a ghostly green.

There in Lakewood True they would find the men they wished to punish, so there in Lakewood True they would have to go, leaving the pleasant shores of Lakewood a mile or so behind. They all lamented this, for unlike Lakewood, Lakewood True was full of creeping things. A constant mist lingered about the place at all times. A haze so thick that one could not see the edge of the water when it was but inches ahead. And no shore to speak of, much less a beach— just an instant drop into a deep gloom.

The water was not entirely opaque; indeed one could look down and just barely make out the tops of trees. For this first settlement of Lakewood had been dry some thousands of years ago, with the trees stretching forth to the shore. But now the Lake had swallowed the Wood, and stood tall over the foundations of that old, old village.

All in the party were at a loss.

"So this is Lakewood True..." muttered Rick Cottontree in awe.

"How are we supposed to go about finding those we seek to punish? We can't even see past the haze," remarked the ever vexing Deng Lu. But he was not finished with his malcontent, "I mean, really. Are we supposed to dive down into the ghostly waters with the slowly drifting beams of light over the otherworldly dancing leaves on those... those tall submerged trees of ancient stock?! You think we'll find our men down there?!"

Unbeknownst to the Dingleites, there was actually a large network of underground tunnels and hidden passages beneath the lake. They would never have discovered this of their own ingenuity, and doubtless they would have here turned back for a pleasant night's sojourn in the promiscuous town of Lakewood proper.

They were ambushed, there in the mist of Lakewood True, on the 12th of Wethember so I have been told (or at least that was the date of greatest consensus among my sources), by a form of weapon that could be described no better way than excessive. For many in my land are content to fire arrows from their bows, but these attackers fired swords from their bows. Full-fledged, very real and very tall, these swords ripped through our friends like blazing comets ripping through dogs.

Siddlebok was hit first by one of these fast-moving sword projectiles, and he was hit straight-on through the chest. The sword flew so rapidly that it went in through poor Siddlebok's sternum and departed clean out through the spine, although clean is not how we remember it.

We all wanted to take several moments to show our teeth in nasty reverence of Siddlebok's passing, in order to digest the horror, but found that we could not. For the flying sword sent forth from a strong bow was not a single occurrence, as we at the time assumed it had to have been. No, an entire fury of swords soon struck through the air, whirling past our heads out of the fog.

Puup Gargeri was hit next; the flying sword struck his head so that it exploded in all directions, and that's when we all knew we had had enough. I and the others ran fast from the edge of that evil lake, and I know for certain that many more Unspoken souls were lost to those hurling bow-flung swords.

One may wonder why I have made no effort to mention Siddlebok and Puup Gargeri in detail before I wrote of their deaths. It is because they died. And therefore they will not be reading this account, and they will not care that their words are not recorded. I retain the privilege to let speak whom I desire to have speak, and to leave concealed the words of those I deem to be unnecessary. Siddlebok and Puup Gargeri were of the whole unnecessary, for they died, and I have spoken of their manner of death because that is the most important thing that they did in life.

Not all of the Dingleites escaped that dreadful attack. Piss Dingle did not, nor did Tibsmith, Rick Cottontree, Deng Lu, Urtain Piik or Dorak of Pagosa, and we for a great number of days thought they had succumbed to flying sword. And so we drank and made men in the town of Lakewood proper. But within the span of two years, we came to know that we were wrong — that Piss Dingle had lived. And the Trial of Flying Sword was not the crux of our adventure.

That was yet to come.

Piss Dingle felt a drip upon his scalp. Strange, thought he, for his scalp was well-known to be guarded by layers many of thick curly hair, making drips of an any kind doomed on the journey towards head-skin. Truly the tangles of hair were impenetrable. Truly no typical drip would find its way through. But yet, Dingle with his head hung low, felt a drip upon his scalp skin.

"Must be a damn well determined drip," he muttered to himself, waking himself from a rotten slumber, and lifting his head. He thought he had opened his eyes, and indeed he had, but he could not see. Instead of light gracing him with knowledge of his surroundings, he saw nothing but darkness. His eyes adjusted, sure, over the course of several minutes... but still this chamber of black stone was lit only by the flickers of faint torchlight.

His sense of hearing was thus heightened, and he could hear clearly a voice to his right:

"It's not the determination of the drips. It's the continuation of the drips. They fall, well, pretty consistently, pushing the failed drips down."

Piss Dingle knew that voice. He had heard it from the platforms of Harlobe. It was a famous voice, one that carried and one that stroked kind in the loin. It couldn't be— but no! It was! It was the voice of Jic Topper.

"Jic?" asked Dingle, half expecting no response. Half expecting to be fully alone in that dreadful dark dripping doom, wherein his desperate mind might have conjured up the voice of Jic.

But no, it truly was Jic Topper in this horrible chamber with him, and not just Jic, as we will soon see (or hear rather, for the place truly was quite dark).

"You surprised?"

"Should we tell him?"

"Oakay who was that?" asked Dingle, for a second voice was heard.

"You recognize Jic but not me?" said the second voice.

And with that clearly orated question, Dingle knew — of he course he knew— that voice too. There was a man of even more famous standing than Jic Topper, for that was the voice of Inder Sohn.

"Inder Sohn— sacred feeks! Who else is in here? Let's get this done."

And it was then revealed through whispers in the dark that Inder Sohn was farthest from Dingle, next to him was Kang Joon, and next to him was Jic Topper. These three were all prominent Tanfolk counselors from the land of Westlobe, where their breed was in supremacy. But they had done much to anger the fiery beast of Url Skulfing's pride, and thus became his prisoner here under the tunnels of Lakewood True.

"Is Dunly Moan in here too?" asked Dingle, showing a real joy as he discovered himself to be sharing a torture chamber with men of such high renown.

And indeed Dunly Moan was in there as well; he had remained silent as he was none too glad to be held up in a chamber of torturous intent, and had been none too glad either at any of the year's events prior. Before the election of Url Skulfing, this Dunly Moan had been an optimistic smile of a man from Westlobe, who had risen to the same extraordinary heights as his peers, despite being Mahogany in the Westlobe, where the Tanfolk held supremacy. Still, Dunly Moan's eyes shone with distinct brightness for several long years, and the world was amused by his chipperness.

Since the coming of Skulfing, all of this had changed in Dunly Moan. He had become tired, his eyes at a constant droop, with a cynical voice that lagged in low tones and dragged with the sting of sarcasm. Dunly Moan had suffered long in the time of Skulfing— suffered the hatred and disdain of his Rich Mahogany brethren in Harlobe and Farlobe, for they knew he was of the Westlobe, where his skin— although the same as theirs— was not among the supremacy. Also, Dunly Moan was just driven to madness by the simple fact that Url Skulfing's acts were so intolerable and nonsensical to any rational being.

"So what goes on down here?" asked Dingle with a surprising amount of casual calmness.

"We're expecting them to torture us," snarked Dunly Moan.

"The way you say that," rejoined Dingle, "Do you want them to torture us?"

"It'd be better to get it over with than just hanging around here day after day."

"How long have al'f'ou been down here?"

Dunly Moan looked to Jic Topper, a clear sign that they truly had been there for some great swathe of time, for their eyes had grown accustomed to the dark. "Two, three...?"

"Four years," spoke Jic Topper.

"Well, I can say with certainty you've haven't been down here four years," said Dingle. I just got here and you were seen above just months ago."

"Hey pal," condescended the ever-snark of Dunly, "You're gonna lose your sense of time down here too. Just wait."

"Dude, I've lost it already. Is it day or night?"

"Is it relevant?" barked Inder Sohn from across the way.

And here Piss Dingle knew that these lovable personalities of the Lobian political stage would not be so lovable in the depths of hell. Yes, he had been fortunate to be imprisoned with such a famous lot, but they were not the ideal circumstances he had hoped for, and so all then remained quiet for a very deep time.

Thenwhile, the free Dingleites had made their way to Derladan, south of Lakewood, between the land of Rolling Reed and Rock Meadow. They answered now to Carvin Cong, as both Dingle and Deng Lu were missing from their presence.

"It may be that the likes of Dingle, Deng, Tibsmith, Urtain Piik, Dorak of Pagosa and Rick Cottontree are either captured or lost, but we must be prepared to accept their passing. We should assume they are dead, so that any news of their actual state will not disappoint, but at best be a relief."

Carvin then sent forth Windal of Klontug, worldliest of their group, to report the events of the last several weeks to Fundrik Luber in Ho Spleen Ho. He was told to race with all speed and present himself as a humbled orphan, saddened by the loss of such friends, so that Luber might take pity on their cause and send more men.

Then all the Dingleites did the only thing that was proper and right of them: to mourn their lost companions. This they did til they got lusty, and then they set to a healthy rate of sin. Jernander Skug made right with Fi Fernin, tall and thin woman of our lot who was always mounting sprinting steeds with little effort, and all the wermen were jealous. For now the only available woman among them was Perfection, who was in reality the antithesis of her name.

But all was fine of the deep sort, for Swilly made all the girls of Derladan swoon and they satisfied the Dingleites in their turn, for the songs he sent forth from his flute made all in that town joyous for many long nights.

And in the caverns under Lakewood True, the old man Urtain Piik was hung from the ceiling by his penis. Many Skulfers watched from below, laughing the mean cackle.

But Urtain Piik never did cry out. He had gave a few miserable "oooohs" when they first raised him up by his aged flip, but aged and frail as he was, his body was so light that little resistance was given. Suspended in the air after a few minutes, he simply lost all sense of feeling. Saying prayers to himself, he fully resigned himself to death. This made the Skulfers sad, for it meant a great many of them had lost a wager— most had bet that

Urtain Piik would have screamed to be hung up by his genitals.

"Get him down, get him down!" ordered PARPINFOHZ, who was in charge of the proceedings in this chamber. He snapped his head back at a row of cages set in pits; therein were Tibsmith, Deng Lu, Rick Cottontree and Dorak of Pagosa. PARPINFOHZ licked his lips, trying to decide which one to try out next.

Dorak of Pagosa was chosen on account of his fat nature. As the Skulfers lined him up for the hanging rope, they laughed even harder, many of them taking turns at shaking the overhang of his belly. Then they fastened the rope hard around his genitals, and tugged hard on the rope, lifting Dorak high towards the crystalized ceiling.

This one did scream. But no Skulfer made a profit, for none had bet that he wouldn't.

In what must have been the most horrific moments of Dorak's life, he rose higher and higher, the weight of his body kept from falling only by that little sliver of muscle. Just before reaching the ceiling, the weight finally gave out. There was a ripping, and soon the meat-peak that connected the rope to the rest of Dorak's body was no longer connected to Dorak's body. With a valiant death cry, that large body of Pagosa came accelerating down to the platform, where it made the ugliest splattering thud heard in many ages.

Amidst the drunken revelry of the Skulfers, PARPINFOHZ stepped down towards the cages that held Tibsmith, Deng and Cottontree. He smiled most freakishly. What absurd torment lie in wait for those unfortunate bodies?

All the while, our man Piss Dingle was now in the hands of Leg Randy, in a more homely cavern of torment under Lakewood's southern shore.

"So why'd you do it?" asked Dingle, as soon as he made the connection that this Leg Randy was the very same Leg Randy who had assassinated the politician Piss Lip and never said why.

"You refer to my killing of Lip?"

"Dude. What else. Come on. Why'd you do it."

Leg Randy only smile.

"Come awwwwn," went Dingle. "You don't just kill someone of such high profile on a whim."

"Or do you though."

And there were several long moments of staring.

"Ah—"

"Ah!"

"Ah?"

Several long moments of that as well.

For neither of them were quite sure what would happen next. Dingle, in his heart, was terrified of Leg Randy, and half expecting him to suddenly lash out and gouge his eyes out or something of the sort; after all, he was now right down in the deepest pits of his darkest enemies.

But no such thing happened. Instead, Leg Randy and Piss Dingle passed a talk of quiet intellect.

"You came to Lakewood, no doubt, to strike Skulfing where it might hurt him most. But how can forty come against thousands?"

"It was never expected that we would raid Lakewood and topple Skulfing's regime at our first go. But my being here now is a mark of advantage for the Dingleites. For I am one of great fame; in this past year, folk have come to know of me and my dagger. To hear that I have been captured, to hear that there is truth in the whispers of an army under the waters of Lakewood...

this will hurt your cause in more ways than you can possibly know."

Leg Randy smiled at Dingle and shook his head, pitying the naivety.

"You believe that there are, on this day, more people in the Lobes that take your side than that of Skulfing. It is a foolish thing to think."

"No," argued Dingle, "For while there are more Rich Mahogs in number, many of them feel pity for the Tanfolk and Paleskin. And you can surely believe that all the Tan and Pale in these lands are against Skulfing."

"I hear those words all the time, but that is not true either. For just 31 years ago, Tanfolk were held in servitude here, and Paleskins in slavery."

"And Mahogs in Westlobe. Our fathers remember the days of Servitude well; they happened not long ago."

"Then that is all the more reason for you to halt these foolish insurrections. Your fathers should be pleased enough that their Servitude is finished. We have made great strides in these previous years."

"Strides there have been," Dingle admitted, "But still there are murders, and still there is evil. Your Minister Skulfing has shown himself time and again to be a ruler to unravel all the progress of this generation, and he must be stopped if such a thing can be done."

"If you wish to stop the High Lobe Minister Skulfing, I suggest you do it by legal means. Enough of this running around, uproot him by the proper channels of winning the Choosing!"

"The Choosing has been won! Twice did we defeat him. In 3330 it was Burden, in 3333 it was Burden again! But your man had him assassinated! That it the wrong we seek to set right."

Leg Randy snickered to himself. "Well. There is to be another choosing in 3336, two years from now! With luck you may live to rise out from here in time to cast your vote."

And here he took long lanky strides over to a cabinet of mystical chests, removing one and bringing it towards Dingle. Smoke rose from the chest of purple with golden decorations. It looked heinous.

"Ah Leg. After all our cordial conversing? Can't you just give me a few licks with the whip?"

"Your punishment must be more severe," smiled Leg Randy.

"Look, I've been hearing screams in these pits... sounding to be my companions Dorak, Deng, Rick and Tibby... I suppose it's only right that I as their captain face the same fate."

And it was soon after that Dingle's torment in that place was revealed: he would be made to drink juice of the driptop and droptips.

It confused him greatly.

"I'm sorry— what... do I have to do?"

Leg Randy explained once again, holding up a vile of liquid from the chest.

"We have captured you and intend on holding you for years. And in your stay you will be forced to drink THIS— the juice of driptop and droptip. The nails on the extremities of men... ground into a fluid for your consumption!"

He waited for Piss Dingle to plead the contrary, to weep in sorrow and offer up his life in submission, if only to be spared this pain.

But instead all Dingle said was "Oakay."

And he took the cup of Driptop Juice willingly.

"Just this?"

Leg Randy was surprised at the grand passivity in Dingle's voice.

"Well, it's... it's quite awful. Many have been repulsed beyond limit when shown that vile."

"You know what? It could be worse."

"You have not yet tasted it," smiled Leg Randy, growling with malicious splendor.

"Yeah I don't know, what does that taste like? Do fingernails even have— a taste? If they're made into a juice? I can't imagine it'd be good, but I don't think it would be that bad!"

"Well you will find out now."

"I mean it's not ideal, but sure, I'll take it."

And Leg Randy scowled, for he had never been faced with a prisoner of such bounding optimism and grand passivity.

"No. It could not be worse. This driptop juice will be the worst of all things, that you shall ever come to endure."

"I'll be happy about the fact that I didn't have to... well... drink a bunch of other stuff. As I've heard that many prisoners often must."

"Drink the Juice."

And Dingle drank the entire vile in one go, still the epitome of passive on his torment. After it was done, he looked around, expecting more torture to jump out and show itself.

"You're sure this is the only—"

"Yes." And Leg Randy's deep-toned 'yes' was blunt and tired of the conversation.

"You're sure you don't want to feed me liquid excrement, or mounds of pubic hair?"

"Just the driptop juice will do."

And Leg Randy left, disappointed that Dingle had found no pain nor even dissatisfaction at the torment assigned to him.

Simultaneously, Dunly Moan was being fed a piece of thorny wheat up the ure. Jic Topper had fresh excrement piled into his mouth, while Inder Sohn had aged excrement funneled down his throat. And Kang Joon was fed massive clumps of human hair.

All the while Dingle went about drinking cups of Driptop Juice, which he found to be fine.

Hearts were heated, tempers were riled. In the city of Ho Spleen Ho, riots filled the streets, fueled even by those who did not know what was happening. But Fundrik Luber knew; knew he did for Windal of Klontug had rode in with the dreaded news of Dingle's capture.

"Five hundred men... will five hundred be enough to perform a siege on Lakewood?" asked Luber.

"It is not Lakewood that we ought to sack," corrected Windal, "But Lakewood True. Please do not make that mistake again. For the town of Lakewood is merry and good. It is under the ghostly waters of Lakewood True that Skulfing's foundation of power does lie."

"But Skulfing's power stems from Essen."

"So we thought. But men around Lakewood see the Skulfers coming in and out at all time— thousands daily. Yet there is no fortress that can be seen. Our guess is they reside in the fabled tunnels running under the lake."

"Five hundred will not be sufficient then."

"No, but if we stay to ourselves for a reasonable spell of time, we could gather a force ten times that number, and strike at Skulfing when he believes that all opposition has been felled."

"Yes..." thought Luber aloud. "It would be unwise to wage open war when our numbers are so few. Rioters and screamers we have plenty of... but they are of no use to the greater cause. To defeat Skulfing we will need organized troops, those who can fight rationally and without blind rage. Perhaps we give democracy one final chance, and perhaps a new Minister will rise in two year's time."

"We can hope for that, but what chance do we have that Skulfing would give up his power when twice over he has not accepted defeat?"

"Then should he do the same in 3336, that will be our rallying cry. That will be the time for us to strike. By then, we will have built our army over the course of two years, and his refusal to stand down will be the perfect moment for us to wage a legitimate war."

And so it was decided. The next two years would be sent in the quiet recruiting of an army, bred for the purpose of wresting the Lobes from Skulfing in 3336 when he would almost certainly attempt to cling to his power once more. Of the poor captives under the Lakewood, nothing was said. They would serve their time as the spoils of war.

Back in the bowels of Lakewood True, Dingle was finished with his curiously simple torture, and left on his own to return to the deep round drop wherein he was suspended by chains around the wrists, in the company of those of the Council of Sound Logic.

Lowering himself down into the black abyss, Dingle cuffed up his own hands, and then dropped to a terrible jerk. Those members of the Council of Sound Logic had already been back from their tortures for many hours.

"This guy," smirked Dunly Moan. "Been gone a lot longer than we were."

"Hate to think what they did to him," mused Jic Topper.

"Oh, well I uh... I'm chained up right here," said Dingle. "You can ask me and I'll tell, but I understand if you'd rather whisper things of me. Go ahead, I'll pretend not to hear."

"The first day of torment is always the hardest," came the comforting voice of Inder Sohn.

"Ah, really?" replied the blunt Dingle, "Because mine wasn't even hard."

"No?" asked Kang Joon, surprised.

"No it was— it was whatever, man. They gave me a few cups of Driptop Juice. I guess they collect everyone's fingernails and drop-clippings and grind them all up into a juice. Waste of time? Sure. But it doesn't taste bad. Just... a little tickle in the throat where the stuff wasn't fully liquified. But not bad."

"You're... kidding," came the voice of Dunly Moan.

"I'm eldering," was Dingle's clever response.

A short silence there was, and then Dunly yelled out in frustration, "Do you know they do to us?! I have thorny wheat pushed my urethra! This guy is forced to eat pounds of hair, and these two are fed shit."

"Yeah! That's what I was assuming to be in store for me. But I'm not gonna lie to you guys. That's not what happened."

And in this way, Piss Dingle lost the friendship of all present in his doom, after a very short time spent together.

Windal of Klontug arrived back in Derladan after a spell of weeks. He found the Dingleites split in their manner, and in their manor. For they had acquired a lovely house with vines growing up the sides, and there they lived like a freaky family of thirty-some full-grown children. Split in their manner they were, for half of the company was content to stay in Derladan, for all time perhaps, while the other half was eager to get back on the tug.

"I gotta tell you Windal," growled Brooth Dimfether, "I'm just so hungry to get back on the tug! When and where are we off to?"

And Windal informed Brooth of Fundrik Luber's plan to slowly build a force, while the Dingleites remained in place, causing little trouble.

"Little trouble?" rumbled Brooth. "What are we to do if not raise Skulfers from their beds?"

"Well, see, you're not looking at the whole picture, Brooth. Tugging up Skulfers one by one was never Luber's intent, and it takes no real skill other than the element of surprise. We're not yet soldiers and we're certainly not ready for the deep fight. We must take these two years to sharpen our skills."

"And if we are all without skill then how are we to gain them? Skilless cannot teach skill to the skilless."

And he followed Windal around a corner, and there in the garden room stood a tall, cascading figure in flowing robes, turning around slowly and most awefully.

"I am here to make you godly offenders," spoke the voice, deep and clear. His eyes were old with wisdom and sacrament.

"This is Wi Tan Pree," spoke Windal of Klontug to Brooth, nearly blinded by the majesty of Pree. "He hails from Lidion, and we are undeserving of his knowledge. But we will take it, and use it well we will."

Moments turned to months, months turned to weeks, weeks turned to days, and days turned to years. Such was the mess of Rick Cottontree's mind in the Bowels of Lakewood.

Temporal distress was not the only thing that plagued him. Each day for multiple hours, he was locked in a long chest with thousands of insects. Now Rick the nature and feel of insects no less than any sensible man,

278

and this torture was a true torment. How much more so, then, when he looked across the pits and saw the dual torture of Tibsmith and Deng Lu.

Yes, Tibsmith and Deng Lu had been made to endure punishment together, in a very tight cage, suspended over fire. This too was an awful thing to endure on a daily basis, but jealousy did rage in the heart of Rick Cottontree all the same. For he wished that he had been given that torture, in place of the ghastly ordeal of the insect chest.

In the night, he longed for such a torture. He longed to be locked together with Tibsmith in that small iron cage, to have his breast thrust ever against hers, to have their necks ever intertwined. The sweat of the infernal heat would not bother him so much— oh, the sweat! How it should have been him to be that close with her, sweating most definitely, close as burning bodies can be. But it was Deng Lu that received that gift of a torture, which infuriated Cottontree all the more.

In short, it was a long two years for all three of those Dingleites.

By strokes of ingenuity, Rick Cottontree of Fyninfer was able to escape his prison in the Bowels of Lakewood, and free Tibsmith and Deng Lu as well. How it happened was as follows: after a full year of weeping the dry tear while his love abided so close yet so far, he devised a thing to do. Instead of lying still in his chest of insect, as he normally did, trying hardest to petrify his body— on a certain day in the middle of the year 3336 he instead let his anger flow large.

He thrashed about in the chest, killing nearly all the insects in one go. Not only that, but such was Cottontree's ferocity that he obliterated the bodies of the little creatures. Spiders were torn, roaches squashed, worms exploded, grasshoppers ripped. And so the contents of the chest were significantly lessened thereafter.

Not enough insects could be found to replenish the chest, and so Cottontree's three captors thought it best to clean it out and wait for new insects to arrive from Niswana. Yet they still gave him his hours in the chest the following day. Finding himself in the empty chest felt like heaven for Rick, but a greater heaven would he soon come to know.

With all his passion, he threw his bones upon the walls of the chest, and began to roll himself off his platform. Down and off the stairs he rolled in the chest, and then made a steep drop. It would have been fine if he had killed himself then and there, anything to get out of that heinous chamber. As it turned out, the best of all possibles occurred, and a cleaner of sorts came stumbling upon the chest, opening it with curiosity, only to find a rabid Rick Cottontree leaping out and slamming her body against rock and stone.

From a nearby arsenal, Cottontree gathered together various torture devices, and then ascended the stairs back to his chamber of pits, where he waited for the opportune moment to pounce upon his three captors. Pounce he did, and then did he crack off all their fingers with the devices he had found, and slowly took out their eyes by way of suction. Many things more was he set on doing to these monsters, but Deng Lu urged him to first ensure their escape:

"Rick! Now is not the time for vengeance!"

"Then what time shall it be? We will never again have the chance to settle scores with this lot!"

But then Tibsmith chimed in, "Rick! Now is not the time for vengeance!" And to Tibsmith Rick listened. He made quick kills of the captors, and then unlocked the cage of Tibsmith, pretending to hear a vicious noise closing in.

"Come, we must go now! There is sadly no time to unlock his cage."

But Tibsmith knew otherwise, and it is by her efforts that Deng Lu was freed as well. Deng would understandably be sore at Rick from this point on.

Hard feelings subsided rather quick, though, as the three of them rose up a steep set of stairs towards an grey opening. At the top of the stairs, a hatch opened up on a little island— could it be called an island? The three of them could not fit on it. It was merely an exit from the Bowels of Lakewood that here emerged on the waters of Lakewood True. All the same, the clouded light of day was heaven enough for them.

Liberation is the word, yet it does no justice to the feeling. For they all of them embraced at once, laughing the sweet and careless cackle, dancing the honest hop. And tongues came out, even between Cottontree and Lu, such was their absolute indiscretion and boundless joy at finding freedom after a hopeless captivity.

But coming down from Lakewood True, Deng Lu and Tibsmith grew incredibly ill in a very short time. The sun proved too much for them when it peeked out from the clouds, and their burns flared up, and eyes went blind, their legs unable to carry them— all very reasonable effects of having spent two years in a burning dark chamber of torture. The miracle was that Rick Cottontree had energy enough to keep going. It was the thirst for Tibsmith that kept him at a quick pace. Limping along, he came to a cottage on the edge of trees, and there he inquired of the Dingleites.

He expected to hear nothing, expecting that all in his party had been executed by that point. But to his surprise, Cottontree learned that the Dingleite whatever-it-could-be-called was growing quite fast but quietly, all around the town of Derladan. They were being trained for combat by the likes of Wi Tan Pree and his Tanfolk of Westlobe, and a great battle there would be.

Excellent, thought Cottontree. It was quite obvious what had to be done. And so it was done.

When Tibsmith and Deng Lu were well enough to walk, he led them straight to the Rock Meadow, where they would all become lost for years and years.

"Are you sure this is the way we ought to take?" wondered Tibsmith as they stood before the first great boulders, between which ran a narrow green walkway, bordered by stone all the way down.

"But of course. The town of Madriims is just along this road— in the center of the Rock Meadow actually, so there's no avoiding it. We must go through the realm of rock."

Cottontree had made up the town of Madriims, which sounded an awful lot like 'my dreams.' He was relaying all he had heard of the Dingleite situation, but simply lying about their location. It would be worth it, surely, for by losing themselves in the mazes of the Rock Meadow, they would all at once miss the great battle and he would have ample time to spend with Tibsmith. If only Deng Lu were not there too. Oh well, he could be dealt with. One way or another.

On the very first night of their stay in the Rock Meadow, Deng Lu became suspicious of Cottontree. He laid out many questions, all in accusatory tone, but here Tibsmith barked back at Deng.

"He's the reason we survived! He's the reason we're free."

"Oh but we're not free, are we Tibsmith? We're surrounded by miles of rock on all sides, and— contrary

282

to what this one said— there is not simply one road leading to Madriims. We have taken several each hour. Such a multitude of roads that we cannot hope to remember our way back. With no map, with no sense of direction, we become entangled in the deep web of this place. In all likelihood we have made enough errors on this one day to keep us lost in here forever."

"Ah... close up," said Cottontree. Tibsmith giggled, and it made Rick's heart beat double.

That night, Rick scooted towards the rock that Tibsmith leaned against, saying he could not sleep, and indeed he could not, for his parts were too eager with desire to find any hope of rest. Here was the great object of many year's obsession, alone with him in a maze of green grass and grey stone— alone excepting Deng Lu, but no matter, for now he slept.

"Did you enjoy your torture?" asked Cottontree in a quiet voice under quiet stars. It may not have been the most clever thing to ask, but under their circumstances, torture had been the one thing they had certainly held in common for the last two years.

"I did not," replied Tibsmith simplistically enough. "Did you?"

"I... also did not. But while I endured my torment, I could think of nothing else but you and yours, hoping with all my heart that you would find a way to manage."

"Well it seemed I managed well enough. Here we are now, in a peaceful place... lost, yes, but at peace nonetheless."

"It is peaceful," smiled Rick Cottontree, and he gazed up at the stars. "But if I could say one more thing about the torture, and then after the night passes we could done with it forever?" He looked to Tibsmith for her approval. "I would only have you know that, while I was sharing my company with roaches and worms, I longed to be in the place of Deng Lu. Close to you."

283

Tibsmith smirked. "You should not have longed for that. For it was not pleasant. Being close to me, yes, many say it is pleasant— but not like that. Not in a small cage, with no room to move about, all your skin burning and smelling of rot. I quickly came to detest being close to that man, and now that hatred follows me. Every time I look at him I am reminded of the torment. And so it would have been the same for you if you had been assigned to our torture."

And though he did not show it, Rick Cottontree's heart began to sing, hearing now that Tibsmith could not stand the thought of being close to Deng Lu ever again.

"Might we be close to each other now that we have room to move about?"

"Ask me again tomorrow."

"I will ask whenever we have a moment away from Deng Lu."

The next day was joyous like the jumping deer. The three companions rose refreshed, after sleeping nearly a full day, and relished in the perfect climate of the Rock Meadow. Perfect anything would have seemed, to a trio of tormented bodies just then escaped from their pits of hell. But the Rock Meadow was especially perfect, for the rock walls provided shade from the sun, and cool winds still did reach the higher paths of those passes. And Deng Lu no longer snarked about their being lost, so pleased was he with the pretty roads between stones. On that day, the three of them felt that they could go on like that forever, walking aimlessly down the valleys and up the hills, and so they all three joined hands and skipped along.

Each following day would grow ever less blissful, with the land of Rock Meadow providing diminishing returns. Deng Lu craved for purposeful encounters with other men, while Rick Cottontree longed for Deng Lu to get lost, and Tibsmith dreamed mostly of bowels.

Upon coming to a split in the road, Rick suggested that Deng take the left path, and then come back to the split to report his findings, while he and Tibsmith could take the right path, so that they could cover twice the ground.

"Oh no," shook the head of Deng, "This place is far too treacherous. We stay as one, we do not wander off. To fall prey of solitude in the Rock Meadow is to court certain death."

"Quite right, quite right," resigned Rick. And so he knew that the starlit hours would be those to make his talks with Tibsmith... but Deng Lu would always keep watch, staying awake far longer than Tibsmith, and so not even in the night did Rick have a chance to continue the courting of his love.

Perhaps it was the infuriation of waiting when his passion lay so close to him at all hours, or perhaps it was the madness that lingered and clung to all souls with the Meadow, but at any rate, Rick Cottontree did attempt to murder Deng Lu the next day. While Tibsmith was pissing, in a pile of rocks, Cottontree called over Deng, to a curve in the road, which then looked down upon a ravine.

"What is that?" asked Rick with the highest sense of wonder, and as Deng focused his eyes, Rick lifted a rock from behind, ready to pelt Lu into bloodied waters. But Lu swatted the rock from Rick's hand, and then laughed. Laughed they did both. And then suddenly Deng laid hands upon Rick, and brought him to the stony ground with chokes and spit.

Tibsmith ran over, condemning them both; Rick arose in protest of Deng's chokehold, Deng arose in protest of Rick's attempted murder.

285

"Quiet, the both of you," commanded Tibsmith, holding her head high. "It seems as though I have caught the eye of both of you, despite there being so many other girls to choose from in these endless parts. There will be no survival without peace, and so we will make it fair. You will take turns spending the night with me in private."

And so Cottontree wept that night, to wonder what lewd games Deng Lu was playing with the fair lady Tibsmith. He would know have to raise the level of his game, since he was now in direct competition with the fiendish Lu.

On his night, Cottontree held back nothing. He let flow all his feelings flow, all his feelings of pain and submission, and thus resigned all powers to the tall and lovely Tibsmith.

"Have you felt these things long?" asked Tibsmith.

"You have held the honor of my highest affection since first I saw you, but ever since my adoration of you grows with each day. So worthy and singular are you in my mind that I would give you anything I have. I do not say that merely because we now find ourselves all three without any coin in a desolate valley. I pledge to you, Tibsmith, that if any coin should ever again come my way, it will all belong to you. I will pay you tribute, whatever the cost, and with no desire for myself in mind, besides that which your magnificent grace should permit me."

"Don't be too quick to give up all your wants," laughed Tibsmith.

"Oh but it's all true," continued the whispering Cottontree. "I would not want anything but to lie by your side, doing for you whatever you might desire. I will want nothing but to be a slave to you and your will."

"Go on."

"If you asked it of me, I would carry you around on my back recreationally if ever you stopped wanting to walk places.

If you asked it of me, I would drink a tub of your sweat if you ever found means to accumulate such an amount.

If you asked it of me, I would spend fourteen consecutive hours sucking your extremities, stopping only for five seconds at a time to hydrate myself.

If you placed a platter of your own hair in front of me and told me to eat it, I would without question.

If you could not reach a stone pile in time and asked to use me instead, I would lend you my body as a receptacle.

If you asked it of me, I would even murder for you, as seen with my attempted assassination of Deng Lu."

And all this Tibsmith considered. They slept in silence, and the next two days passed in a terrible anguish for Cottontree, who believed he had gone overboard. For Tibsmith no longer spoke to him, and by Deng Lu she stood.

But on the next night when Cottontree was to hold her company, she smiled at him for an hour.

"I... I don't know what this is," shrugged Cottontree, but before he could finish, he was on his back, and Tibsmith had her fingers on his lips.

"I'm going to thrash you about. Is it oak to you?"

"As long as you don't draw blood. Or leave me debilitated on this stony meadow floor."

And just then, the long fingers of Tibsmith opened up Cottontree's mouth, and dove down the pipe of Rick.

A nasty sound of molested throat ripped through the soothing dark.

"Sorry, I've got a gag reflex," coughed Cottontree, taking a few swallows of recovery. "But it felt nice actually."

And Tibsmith once again put her long fingers down the throat of Cottontree.

"Maybe you shouldn't go down that far, or else I might puke on you."

"Stop talking."

"What was that?"

"Shhh..."

"Oh, sorry, I didn't hear you."

"Don't apologize."

And that is how they passed their nights.

Piss Dingle still passed his time in the Bowels of Lakewood, not in physical torment, but in philosophical exchange with Leg Randy. On the night I will record, however, PARPINFOHZ was brought into the mix, and this PARPINFOHZ was no great philosopher.

"It is not so much that the Rich Mahogany men hate the Paleskins," mused PARPINFOHZ, "As it is that the Rich Mahogany hates the idea of Paleskins rising. For much is the talk that the white-skinned folk have ambitions. Ambitions matching that of the Mahogs. Now you understand why we must not allow them an inch of breath. We must keep eyes on them always, so that their ambitions remain mere dreams... dreams that stop at the moment of waking."

How to deal with such a philosophy? How, wondered Dingle, might such a man ever be brought to break through such oppressive views? Finally he spoke.

"Imagine a world... PARPINFOHZ... where things were the other way around. Just stop to imagine it— don't tell yourself that it could never be, that you would never allow it to be... just envision it. A place and a time, where the pale-skinned man reigns as he would, and holds Us, the Mahogany, in submission. In the same exact manner as you hold the Paleskins. Never letting us sleep, terrorizing us always. How would you feel then?"

"Such a thing is folly beyond farce," smirked PARPINFOHZ. "In all worlds, the Rich Mahogany would prove themselves supreme. White is weak. Mahog is master."

"No. I take your words and I use them as a curse, a curse that in some other far distant star as we speak, the Paleskins will rise up and enslave your Mahogany counterparts."

PARPINFOHZ smirked again. "In that case, your kind would have become the villains. And then my people will be the pitied, the ones who are made to rise above oppression and be praised by the chronicles. Either way, the Mahogany Man wins in the end."

"Nay," spoke Dingle. "Nay to all your deeds, Parpinfohz. Such is your contempt that I strip you of your tall letters. From now on, when I speak to you, I speak to you as one who only has one tall letter. At the start of your name like the rest of us, and that's it!"

Leg Randy applauded Dingle, and then put in his own thoughts on the matter. "I do think Dingle has you conquered, PARPINFOHZ. For we can use the words you just spoke, against you. For in this world, the Paleskins are the Oppressed. They are those who are made to rise above oppression, and find everlasting praise in the chronicles. You're the one who just said it. It will always be— in any world— the place of the Oppressed, to rise and find victory."

"Sadly it is not that night."

"What night is it?"

"Tohzdee."

"Oh..."

And Dingle leaned in, not knowing what Tohzdee signified. He would soon find out—

"Brek laheg a khruoonk!" was roughly the sound Dingle recalled Jic Topper making, as his neck was struck by the axe of PARPINFOHZ. For Tohzdee— this night— was simply the night of his execution. Dingle was back in his round pit, suspended from chains, watching the strokes of the axe along with all the others there in chains.

For a moment after Jic Topper's head fell backwards, it looked as though he might miraculously recover and pull it back up. But it was not to be. The weight of the head continued to pull upon the tearing neck, seeking to follow gravity's will and find its way to the floor. After a sickening set of spells, Jic Topper's head tore away from the neck and dropped down the dark abyss, crashing with a smack on the stones below.

Kang Joon was mortified— though not to the extent that the topless Topper was— and rendered speechless. He looked to Dunly Moan for the words, in fact he had not to even move his head, for Dunly Moan was already in his line of vision, lying just beyond the body of Jic Topper. Now that Jic's head was gone, Dunly's head appeared to Kang Joon to rest on top of Jic's shoulders. Dunly was not rendered speechless by this unthinkable act, and after a few moments he let out a sigh, and spoke the words:

"Ugh... finally."

And at this Kang Joon raised his eyebrows, appalled and completely surprised at Dunly's choice of eulogy.

But Dunly Moan was not letting out a sigh of "finally" in response to the beheading of Jic Topper. He was— true enough— looking right in the direction of Jic's decapitation, but beyond that: a most valiant knight standing in silhouette, as a blinding light blasted in from over there.

290

Now believe me, I have made no mistake in relaying the deeds of Piss Dingle and Skin Toot as noble and heroic. They certainly were in their own right. I have been honored to have been chosen to transcribe their tales. But if I had a true and honest choice? If I could have chosen to write on the deeds of any soul in my time? Would I have still chosen Piss Dingle?

I'm obliged to say yes, and that may be something of a fact. But also there was this perfect knight who arrived to rescue Dingle and all the brave counselors of the land, who had been held there in the Bowels of Lakewood by Skulfing in a vengeful lustwind of fury. There was now this perfect Passian beast in their midst, who did no wrong in all his days, and defied all throes of danger to overcome the deafening odds in coming to save these men. Given the choice, would I not have rather put my quill to parchment on his deeds?

I am obliged to say no, lest my scrotum peel, and that Dingle was the more cunning figure, who wove a greater web of justice through those darkest days of Skulfing. But let us speak more on this dashing man.

He was Lord Cuomo, born of great blood and imposing stature, built of strong skin and bone divine. But it was not by body alone that he came to dominate the affections of all who beheld him. He was gifted too in the realm of speech, able to speak fast without losing any potency. Had any other character in this tale been tested to speak as fast as he, they would have fumbled into a land of dumb words. But Lord Cuomo spoke swift and still carried on with a song of truth, resounding with logic, wit and grace.

I had written long on the qualities of this Lord Cuomo of Costerwall, and it passed by unnoticed as Dingle did his read of my first draft, but Skin Toot caught it, and lashed me with bits of my own liver stuck on to a whip. My further praise of Lord Cuomo has thus been omitted in all subsequent copies.

But suffice it to know that Lord Cuomo did tear his way down the passages of Lakewood True, under the very waters of that murky bay itself, battling with word and sword all the course. He released Inder Sohn from his chains, and then Kang Joon from his shackles— was then disgusted to see the headless Topper— but then hurried on to release his friend Dunly before the Skulfers might arrive in larger number.

"Ay, what about me?" asked Dingle, when it appeared as though Lord Cuomo would free only his friends before departing.

"I don't know you," replied Lord Cuomo.

"But I know you! 'Let us obtain what's come to pass!'"

"That is my phrase," spoke Lord Cuomo, conflicted on whether or not he might take the extra moments to break the bindings of Dingle.

"Come along now. I'm fresh, ask Dunly, he'll attest that I'm fresh."

"Is he fresh?" asked Lord Cuomo.

"Ugh... I dunno. He's got no love for Skulfing."

"Well that's all I needed to know," and from that point Lord Cuomo lent Dingle nothing but broad smiles, and the affable persona that all across the Lobes had come to adore. Except for Skulfing and his Deeplove of course, who resented Lord Cuomo perhaps most of all others, for it is no secret that Skulfing held a profound hatred for all who bested him.

And Lord Cuomo had certainly bested Skulfing in all ways, as he continued to prove on this day.

"Hasten away, hasten today!" exclaimed the bold hero as he led Inder Sohn, Kang Joon, Dunly Moan and Piss Dingle up the narrow curving stone staircase, and out of the Lakewood Bowels.

Meanwhile, the Dingleites held their peace at Derladan by way of combat, training always under the wise tactics of Wi Tan Pree, who taught them well, until they were sufficient enough, and then he left.

"Where's he gone to?" asked Brooth Dimfether one sad evening, as he saw the vertical figure of Pree disappearing at the same pace as Anilthann on the red horizon.

"Wi Tan Pree... does as he pleases," spoke Windal of Klontug. "His job here is done. We will not be seeing him again."

"But I had offerings to give that man."

"He would not have wanted them. You were not his favorite, Brooth."

And the big man Brooth nearly cried, but Windal squeezed him hard— "You have become as a child in these years of rest. A more skillful child, yes, but your mentality has reverted into one of want. There is no want in war. In war, the only skill is to stay alive, and that we now stand a better chance of thanks to the teachings of Wi Tan Pree. So do not weep, you brutish Brooth, but give praise that Wi had come here at all. It was because of my dealings."

And Brooth whipped his eyes— "Thank you, Windal. You speak truth. We must now ride to battle."

"Not yet," sighed Windal. "The armies of Skulfing have grown tremendously in the past year while our force has lied stagnant."

"Then our time here in Derladan was wasted?"

"No. Still have I held talks with High Judge Luber from his quarters at Ho Spleen Ho. He too has been hard at work, building an army. It is ready now; they are called the Luberians, after some man's honor."

"Wondrous!" clapped Brooth. "Now we gonna rip off them Skulfing ass...!"

"Soon, Brooth, soon. First we have to join up with this Luberian force. They have told us to meet them at the Lone Oak."

And Brooth's face was blank. "The— lone oak? Is that a place?"

"It is a place of vague familiarity in the region of Athragal. It is labelled on a map in my possession."

"Windy, I've seen your maps. They are not precise."

"They're precise. They're simply not drawn to scale. So while we know that the Lone Oak of Athragal is between Elwood and Cricksend, we do not know exactly how far."

"Why don't the Luberians just come here?!"

"Now Brooth, this army will help us achieve our ends at no cost. The least we can do is meet them at the place they've chosen—"

"Everyone knows where Derladan is! Who the hell knows the Lone Oak-"

"But that is just the point. If the army or even any member of the force marches to Derladan, they will be seen on the Enterlobe by the keen eyes of the Skulfers and apprehended. They make now for the Lone Oak of Athragal, cloaked and by way of separate, little known roads."

"I still don't like the sound of this Lone Oak. Someone in our camp better be damn familiar with that tree."

"It is you who must go, Brooth."

And Brooth gave Windal the most critical eye as he looked down at him. "You serious?"

"With Dingle and Deng absent, you are debatably the figurehead of this movement. The Luberians will wish to hold their council of war with you present."

"What about you? You're the one who sets all this up!"

"Which is why it would be wise for me to stay back, in case any problems should arise—"

"I'll tell you, there are gonna be problems rising if you don't come! Pff, expect me to find a lone tree between Elwood and Cricksend, ten miles by ten miles! And not just a tree, an oak, whatever kind of tree that is!"

"I will teach you well in the arts of identifying an oak," smiled Windal calmly.

"You will come the ass up with me or I'm not going!" shouted Brooth, attracting the attention of all the Dingleites round.

And so it was put to a vote, with nearly all Dingleites concurring that Windal ought to go the ass up with Brooth to the Lone Oak, to provide support and help him find the tree. Windal at last agreed to go, on the condition that the girl Perfection come as well.

All the way to Athragal, Brooth complained about Perfection's presence. "Why'd you bring her? She's not perfect, you know that. Her name is a curse to her. She had proud parents, who thought they'd show their pride by naming their child Perfection, only to find the gods spiting them with each passing year as their daughter grew less and less perfect, until today she stands as the most awful of things."

"She is not so imperfect as you say," spoke Windal so that Perfection could hear from behind. But then, in a hushed whisper, "Fi Fernin was already conquered by the heart of Jernander. I do not claim to be a perfectionist, only that I take what's readily available."

"Look at all the Unspoken we have to choose from," laughed Brooth, and he motioned back at twelve

Unspoken warriors, who were also on their way to the Lone Oak to present themselves to the Luberian army. Windal was clearly prejudiced against and frightened of the Unspoken, so he grew silent and then walked in the back of the party with Perfection.

The road to Cricksend was one through the land of Rolling Reed, where tall grasses danced round their legs and bowed with the wind, which amused the Unspoken to no end. Windal and Perfection found the sights modestly joyous, while Brooth found no fun in the whole affair, and stomped along with mighty step, crushing as many reeds as he could.

Also meanwhile, Lord Cuomo— furry and grand— led his colleagues and Piss Dingle— all relieved to be out of the dreadful chambers under Lakewood True— towards a camp, where other folk belonging to the Company of Sound Logic resided.

One of Cuomo's old lovers, a wealthy jeweled heiress called Cabrana, ran out swift to meet the survivors. "Where were they held?" she asked with deep compassion.

"I found them in the ancient dungeons beneath the waters of Lakewood True," smoldered brave Lord Cuomo.

"But how did you come to release them?"

"By ways of steep cunning."

"How did you manage to escape the wrath of the Skulfers?"

"Dropped a lake on them."

And it really was as simple as that, for on their way out, Cuomo had broken a vital support beam, which started a line reaction of breaking beams, eventually bringing the whole of Lakewood True crashing down on the Bowels and drowning down all who resided under that ancient lake.

And so Cabrana turned her attention to the wounded Sohn, Moan and Joon, who were pleased to see a familiar face that was not so distinctly masculine as the Lord of Costerwall. But Dingle remained with the Lord of Costerwall, for he did not mind the distinctly masculine. He had seen hardly any of it in his own party. And so the two spent the day in broad talk, which eventually focused in on the pressing matters at hand.

"You hate Skulfing, I despise Skulfing," spoke Cuomo at last, getting to the core of things.

"Well, I don't know if I'd use the word hate," shrugged Dingle. "I mean, I've never met the guy. Sure, has he been the root cause of injust death and destruction throughout these lands? Has he inspired men to hate one another, while he grows rich off the devotion of those poor? Sure. He's the worst thing that's happened to these Lobes in all Lobian history. But do I hate him? Like I said, I've never met him. Maybe he's a cool guy."

And Lord Cuomo laughed aloud. "I think I begin to understand this Dingleite philosophy. You are of the same mind as I, yet cursed with indifference and passivity."

"Passivity is probably the word I would use. 'Grand Passivity' sounds better."

"But how can you indulge in Grand Passivity at a time like this?"

"Well... it's easy. All I do is recognize that our lives are not the only lives to exist. The world has gone on for thousands of years, and will for thousands more... each generation having its own problems, and each generation finding a way to cope. So yes, we have... tragedy. Terrible things going on all the time. But are we living in the time of the Horned King? Of Haegos? Of

Melizar? Of Caldar? The way I see it, Url Skulfing is just another incarnation of evil to be overcome. And overcome him we should definitely try to do! But do I hate the guy? Nah. He's just playing his part."

Lord Cuomo smiled— "And his part will be to die horrifically."

"Sure, why not."

And Piss Dingle and Lord Cuomo made a pact of the hand, to join forces combatting the sinister Url Skulfing, who had just then as they spoke conveniently stolen another election.

As Brooth, Windal, Perfection and the twelve Unspoken walked along the Rolling Reed, they came to a high hill overlooking a wide vista. To the east lay the village of Cricksend, and to the west lay nothing at all, for that was Flatfinger. Ahead, to the south, they could see the rolling gold turn to a rolling green, and that was Athragal.

"Our Lone Oak... lies somewhere in that region."

Brooth Dimfether huffed. "Ya should've just put your finger down and told them to meet us at Cricksend."

"Are you not enjoying the views?" asked the girl Perfection.

"The view of weeds up to my tits? It's not perfection. Neither are you, despite your name."

And it was clear that Brooth was drunk and sore. But a few miles on, the Rolling Reed died away and they were then in the wavy hills of Athragal, with the vivid green grass growing only ankle deep. Still Brooth found ways to complain.

"You ought not complain, Brooth!" shouted Windal, now with his arm draped around Perfection's shoulder. "Many would die for a chance to walk the hills of Athragal as we do now! They say this is the most perfect land in all Elaptirius."

"Do not speak to me of perfection, you clearly do not know its meaning," and here Brooth motioned to Perfection, "These hills would be pretty, viewed from a tavern at the top, but that is not our lot. We are made to walk in crooked lines, up and down and up and down! There is no purpose for these hills! They serve only to slow us! Can we not just walk through them?!"

"Enjoy the changing elevations, you brute of a Brooth!" chuckled Perfection.

"You are not perfect!" barked Brooth.

"Neither are you!" and all were shocked, for these words came from one of the Unspoken women, and it was the first time one of the Unspoken had ever spoken. Such was the annoyance with the bitter attitude of Brooth.

Hours into Athragal, at last trees began to show themselves. Windal and Perfection gave praise, but Brooth still muttered on, for these trees were in pockets, and none of them lone.

"How will we even know when we get to the Lone Oak? Is it really just gonna be one tree standing alone with no others around? And are there not several trees like that in all this land of Athragal?!"

Sparse clouds drifted in the sky, and a growing blanket of grey accumulated in the distance. But right below this blanket of grey, rested the customary strip of sunset: a warm and comforting orange, granting peace between the earth and sky.

As Dimfether's company rounded up over their next hill, they saw a single tree standing atop another hilltop, some mounds ahead.

"Well praise my mother!" smirked Brooth, his breath hard and tired from going up so many hills. "We've found it."

"Well, let's not get our hopes up just yet," exhaled Windal. "We can't even tell if it's an oak from here."

"It's an oak. I can feel it in my breast it's an oak. And anycourse, if it's not— doesn't matter! The Luberians will be passing through and see us fifteen soldiers sitting round a lone tree; they'd be cocks not to divert their course. They come to us! We've walked far enough."

And as Brooth was quite tired of walking, he took defiant steps towards this last hill where he would rest beside the Lone Oak and wait for the Luberians to come.

But this tree was not the Lone Oak.

It was the Lone Ash.

Chapter 15
Triumph and Nude

What could be so startlingly sinister about a mistaken tree on the vast expanse of Athragal? Well, nothing, at first glance. Nothing is inherently sinister about a lone Ash, but on that particular night, the mistake between ash and oak was a deathblow to our party.

For the men that met our friends at the Lone Ash were not the Luberians, but rather Skulfers disguised as generic friends.

A massacre of bloody embowelment followed swiftly.

Brooth Dimfether's organs were ripped from his waist and thrown high in the sky. Intestines, liver, colon, kidneys and more— all were flung a half mile in all directions.

But what of Windal of Klontug and the girl Perfection, you might be wondering? Luckily, they had grown tired of Brooth's negativity and snucken off to a stone grove behind a steep hill, out of sight from the others, where they partook in lewd ticklings. They managed to sneak away only for a cheap spell of moments, but when they arose and peaked around their hill, they saw their folk quickly encircled and then swiftly butchered. The speed in which it was all carried out was amazing! One moment it was just Brooth and the Unspoken, the next there was an army around them, and the next they were slaughtered.

Oakay, maybe Windal and Perfection had tugged on each other behind that hill for more time than they would like to admit. Hours can seem as minutes when held in a mischievous embrace. But it is the truth that they fled along the hills of Athragal in the gathering dusk, away from the tree that had caused so much peril and the death of poor Brooth.

They did not bother to find the Lone Oak, for it would have been near impossible in the dark anyhow. And even if the Luberians had assembled by that damned tree by now, they all were now endangered by the Skulfers roaming about those rolling prairies. They sped on to the east, out of Athragal and into the town of Elwood, arriving in the last hour of darkness, their legs having run all the night through. It was the 7th of Sexarion, in case you were wondering.

In the samewhile, Tibsmith and Deng Lu walked in unwilling meanderings about the monstrous Rock Meadow, between Derladan and Little Fools. But to Rick Cottontree it was all to plan, for it was he who had formulated their getting lost. But even he had now grown suspicious of these curving stone-lined ways, and held an eery foreboding in his core as they all came to realize they had not crossed paths with a single living thing. Two weeks it was, and yet no trace of man nor beast.

All of them felt its creeping truth, but Deng Lu was the first to openly acknowledge what they were all thinking. One could surmise that his open acknowledgement then brought about a change of course, for it was on that same night that they did come across traces of life in that highland (or valley; they had gone up and down so many times that they could now have no sense of high and low). But these traces of life were not those they were hoping to find.

It began with a single finger bone, skillfully spotted in the grass by Cottontree. He kept it, as a proud trinket, an honor for having such keen vision. But soon the sight of bones was all too apparent, and around a few more bends in the path there was a large skeleton ripped about in a thousand ways, a speckling of dried white upon the wet green.

"This must be a remnant of a bygone age," mused Deng Lu, not showing much concern. "An unhappy incident, probably at the fangs of some beast. But the fact that the bones have lingered so long means we are certainly out of harm. Clearly no beast resides here now, for the bones would have dispersed."

Rick laughed. "And here we were, hoping to find a sign of life. Now we find solace in the hope that there is none."

"Better to be alone than in the realm of a killer," nodded Tibsmith.

"Let's now hope that we continue this journey as before: just we three souls, in endless range of grass and stone, until we succumb to hunger."

"No," shook the head of Tibsmith, "That's not what I was thinking at all. I do hope we come across life. I just hope it's not stronger than us." And she began along again, turning her head, "So we can eat it."

Deng and Rick both lowered their heads in smirks, adoring of her spirit. They were already hungry—desperately hungry, though their thirst was halted typically once a day, when they would across a small stream. They would follow these streams in hopes of them leading to larger waters, that might eventually lead them out, but the streams always came to bad ends at murky ponds or simply disappeared under the rock walls.

But today there were no streams. Today they only found bones. And a startling number. As they roamed up their path, they grew not only more numerous, but more diverse. There were not only the bones of Passians, but also of a deep array of beast, and some preserved in full form. The eeriness returned.

Concern crept back into the hearts of these three men. Even Tibsmith, bold and daring as she was, with a ravenous hunger for any that would appear before her, began to give some shivers.

"I take back my earlier conjecture," said Deng, "This is clearly no accident. This is a place of purposeful ceremony: a dumping ground for the remains of those sacrificed to some heathen god, or perhaps just Passian hunger. And it is not by any means a thing left to the ancients."

And he motioned at the new bones in their path, these being moist and yellow, not at all the reassuring dried white remains that provided the reassurance of distant time. No no, these bones were quite fresh.

Windal of Klontug and the girl Perfection sat in the sole tavern at Elwood, for this town was merely a single street, with but a few stems of road branching out with its modest houses. They expected to find little aid here, but at least they were safe from the Skulfers. And so it was that they were discussing their predicament and toils at the bar, when they were ruffled on the heads by the bar's tender.

"I couldn't but overhear your vast toils," whispered the tender of the bar. "By the sounds of it, there's a gentle man that might be able to help you along. He himself is gentle, but he's capable of violence, if you catch my meaning."

And Windal of Klontug wanted to disregard the bartender fully, for he spoke like a poor man, slurring words and using childish pronunciation. But the girl Perfection told Windal to stop being so haughty, for his prejudice of small towns and smalltownfolk was flicking her in all the wrong places.

"Very well, we'll go see what this 'gentle man' has to say. It will be a waste of time, and we'll be no better off."

At first, it seemed that Windal and his large-city intuitions were proved correct. The bartender led them over to a disheveled figure in the corner, with a big crumbling hat that looked as though it had seen five hundred years. And with every smoke of his pipe, he coughed up little thumps and wheezes, and it sounded as though his lungs might soon just climb out his throat and collapse on the table in a miserable fit of exhaustion.

"Greetings," smiled Windal, uncomfortably. "I... have been directed your way by one of this tavern's staff."

"Ah, Fidledert. He's the only staff! Sit by my side."

"I'll stand," nodded Windal. But the girl Perfection took a seat by the stranger's side. The stranger immediately put his arm round the girl.

"Hey now," objected Windal.

"It's fine," spoke the stranger. "She's mine by royal right."

"Royal right?"

"I'm a King."

And Windal looked around the dark dilapidated tavern, and back at the stranger. "King of what? This tavern?" and he had to stop himself from cackling.

But the stranger's eyes were dead. Dead serious, sure, but also just dead. He was nearly blind and so he didn't put much stock in his eyes. Nor his voice, for it was quite weak, but he used it to its best: "There be more Kings in this land than the likes of Skulfing. He's of no line. His blood is pity. Ready toh be spilleth and dranked up by many a betther en he."

"I'm sorry chap, I can't understand you."

"I can understand him just fine," smiled Perfection, and took the old King's hand. "Do go on," and for the rest of the time, this old puffing King spoke directly to her.

"I'm the King of the Forty Knights! And I will have great triumph..." and here he began to speak so softly that Windal could here none of it.

To sum up, this 'King of the Forty Knights' pledged to fight alongside the Opposition of Skulfing, and granted all his knights to Windal and Perfection— all forty of them. With this force, the Dingleites were now doubled. Well, more than doubled, since the original forty Dingleites had been dwindled to sixteen with the all-too-recent massacre at the Lone Ash.

To Derladan they rode— only Windal and Perfection, for they had left the King of Forty Knights in Elwood to muster his forces— and there in Derladan, Windal was reprimanded to no end by his fellow Dingleites, who were outraged at the loss of Brooth Dimfether and twelve Unspoken, one of which had reportedly even spoken.

Windal accepted some of their rebukes, but objected most of them, pointing to his new acquisition: forty knights under the command of the King of the Forty Knights!

"So we are now up to fifty-six," calculated Jernander Skug, who was now promoted to the rank of Dingleite commander with the death of Brooth. "But many more would we have if you had met with the Luberian army as planned."

"That plan was ill-conceived. Forces of Skulfing now roam the Athragalian hills, and I fear the Luberians may be lost. Before we ride to their aid, we must consult the Council of Sound Logic; this is what Fundrik Luber instructed of us should we fail in convening with his army. They hold a camp on the southern walls of the Rock Meadow— I have their position drawn on a map!"

And at all the company moaned and gave boo, for so too was the Lone Oak drawn on a map, but their setting out to find it had led to the death of thirteen and the loss of an army.

"It will be far easier to locate a camp than a single tree!" assured Windal of Klontug. The Dingleites agreed and forgave Windal of his transgressions, but only after having stripped him of all cloth and having him walk laps around the whole of Derladan, carrying fruit about on his cock all the while.

As I was saying, the bones were quite fresh. Now we will wrap us this nonsense of the three journeyfolk lost beyond wit in the treacherous Rock Meadow.

Of course you must know that it is now only a matter of time before Deng, Rick and Tib finally encounter another lifeling besides themselves in the maddening stone maze. And when they did, despite all the tall talk, they each ran for cover behind a large boulder. Peering out, they saw the young werman walking towards them was of no great stature, and his skin was not bulging with muscle. He looked just as hungry and tormented as them. And he was disheveled, with a slightly crazed look in the eye, but again no worse than them. They almost decided to reach out and bid him join their company.

But then he began to walk with a slant, and whistle badly, and then speak in a strange tongue that none of them could comprehend at all. Best to just be done with him, they said aloud, before their sympathy came back.

'Twas Deng Lu that leapt out and gave the strange-speaker his final startle, for he then tossed a rock hard at his face. With a larger rock, he threw death down upon the grounded man, and then trampled the throat to make sure that all life had faded. Now there would be no chance of ambush, but moreover would there be food.

Tibsmith gladly took part in ripping the limbs from this prey, while Rick Cottontree looked away, now regretting this awful plot of his, wishing he had only been able to seduce Tibsmith in Fyninfer and thus save the trouble of two years' torture and a fortnight of starving wanders. Cottontree's spirits were soon revived though, for that night was one to be spent with Tibsmith.

"Do you grow tired of me sticking my long fingers down your narrow throat?" she asked him, as she did just that.

"Well it's... not my favorite," choked Cottontree. "But if it's your desire, I will gladly partake. It is now and always will be my greatest wish to follow your command."

"Well I have a new desire tonight."

Tibsmith jumped up, leading Cottontree past the fire, where the strange-speaker's meats had been cooked and devoured. On the other side of the rocks, there lay a fair pile of his entrails, which had been cast out of sight for the meal.

"Dance with me," ordered Tibsmith. And she picked up liver and lung, thrusting them against Rick's chest and rubbing them in well. "Do you like when I cover you with the insides of our cannibal dinner?"

Rick Cottontree did not. But he obliged Tibsmith in all her doings, and imitated her as well he could as she rained down intestinal joy on neck and shoulders. After dancing, they rolled about in the inners. And in the morning they were captured.

To the heart of Rock Meadow they were taken, dirtied beyond belief with another man's guts. Rick found it embarrassing; Tibsmith wouldn't have had it any other way. Deng was just relieved to now be in the company of other folk, for he had grown dismally tired of the two he was with.

The heart of Rock Meadow was certainly a highland, for they were led up a steep and straight path, with a terribly sharp incline. Once the land flattened out, it opened as well, revealing a circular camp with various structures of stone spread about. But these were not homes and shops of a stone craft; no, there was hardly any craft to it at all. Stones there were to make rooms of refuge, but they were just piled on top of each other. None of the stones were cut, none polished, and thus the whole place looked rather barbaric, especially to the tastes of Deng Lu.

"You look to be disapproving of our home," spoke the large woman who directed Deng's hands, bound with a rope.

"Oh, praise Horlio you speak the Arc Tongue. We came across one who did not."

"So you murdered him."

And the eyes of the captors were hard on Deng Lu, who was pushed to the ground.

"Well," he said, attempting to defend himself, "Would none of you do the same in our position? We've been walking these trails for weeks, just trying to get out!"

"Do you know nothing of our realm?" asked the large woman.

"I never claimed to! It's he who led us here!" And Deng motioned quick to Cottontree. Now on him was all the scrutiny of the gathering village folk.

"Oakay, let's have it," barked the large woman. "Why'd you lead them in?"

"Well, to— to search for our men. Is this not the way to Madriims?" And Rick Cottontree looked around in sincerity. But the eyes of all loomed on him heavy.

"You've been played for fools," said the large woman bluntly to Tibsmith and Deng after hearing the whole story. "I am from the world beyond and never have I heard the word 'Madriims.' It is not a place within our rocks, for the Heart of Rockdom is truly the only place with life left in all the Rock Meadow."

She then consulted with various other women, and it was decided that Rick Cottontree should be executed. They would kill him by means of uncut stone, which was no surprise, because they had much of it there, and little else.

But Tibsmith intervened on Cottontree's behalf, calling him her slave, which in many ways he was. "You cannot kill my slave!" she pleaded. "He is my beloved property!"

But these rock-dwellers were not as uncivilized as they may has presumed. The large woman spoke of their intolerance for slavery, and of their knowledge that slavery had been outlawed in the Lobes many years ago. Now it was time for Rick Cottontree to plea for his own life:

"I may not legally be this woman's slave, but I swear, serving her is all I have in this life! It is my pleasure and obligation to do all that she asks of me. To deprive me of life would be truly to deprive her of many things. And we have all suffered enough. Already at the point of madness we were when we first entered these rocks, for we were prisoners under the Lakewood. Deng Lu can attest to that—"

And there was a massive GASP all about the Heart of Rockdom.

"What— why are you gasping?"

But here the large woman disregarded the existence of Cottontree altogether, and put all her attention to Deng. "Is that truly your name?"

310

"Deng Lu? It is what my mother called me since birth."

"And who was your mother?"

"Tabritha of Lo Varna."

"That means nothing. Who was your father?"

"Deep Lu."

And again there was a gasp!

"And his father?"

"Can't recall."

"How about your father's mother?"

"Cunnis Lu, but don't ask me any farther than that for I shan't be able to tell you."

"No..." laughed the large woman. "Rather, it is we who will tell you!"

Deng didn't know what she meant. But before long she had disappeared into the largest stone structure in the Heart of Rockdom, and then emerged with a solemn, wrinkled figure in violet robes, rising with majesty and approaching solemn with the stars, which now showed themselves as the dusking clouds drifted away.

"Welcome to the Heart of Rockdom, dearest Lord Lu," said the old chieftain with a bow.

"Thanks! And you are?"

"They call me the Rockhard Werman, but that is not important. Seldom do I show my face in these days, but for one of your standing I would be a fool not to make exception."

"I— I don't know what's happening here. I just want to go home."

But Deng Lu was now surrounded by women, who led him to the talking place at the center of the Heart of Rockdom, where he and the Rockhard Werman would sit under starlight and share great secrets of the past.

"Have you no knowledge of your name?" asked he that was rock-hard.

"I... assumed it was a name just like any other. Passed down with the generations, not sure where it came from."

"There is a thing we are all suspecting. But it could be that you think yourself clever, and gave yourself that name. Or that your grandmother thought herself clever, and gave herself that name."

"I assure you it just a name."

"It is so much more."

And the large women in the Heart of Rockdom pulled Deng Lu right up out of his clothes, and gazed upon his physique. Then they heartily scrutinized him, and their awe of him grew more and more.

"All his features, all his proportions," sighed the women, "They are all as the book would say."

"Then there are no further doubts in my mind," smiled the Rockhard Werman at Deng Lu. "You are the Eternal King returned."

"The— I'm sorry, what? The 'Eternal King?' I don't think there is such a thing."

Now the Rockhard Werman was musing quietly, almost to himself, as he lit candles around the central circle.

"Many tales from this world are lost with the passing of time... a hundred may prove the death of all memory. But some tales are destined to go. Too powerful are they, too STRONG. A great sorrow it is that it ever faded from the world, but from now on it will remain. From its place here, it will once again take root, and take root so firmly that it will never again be forgotten."

Now the Rockhard Werman's scribe-boy came out into the stars, holding a book nearly as large as himself. Deng Lu caught a glimpse of the cover. It read, in bold letters:

BOOK OF LU

THE TALES OF THE ETERNAL KING
GREAT KING GRANDEST LU THE LARGE OF BESTLAND AND EXCELSIOR, OVERLORD OF ELAPTIRIUS AND ALL THE WEST.

It made Deng Lu laugh, for he thought this was some follycock pagan joke, held only here in the Rock Meadow, and nowhere else. But no, as the Rockhard Werman would have him know by the end of the night.

"This King Lu was the highest in all the West. Never before was a Passian man ever to yield such power in any land."

—And as he spoke, large women in cloaks paced slowly about the candlelit ring, humming darkly—

"From the Year 3001, he ruled from his home in Excelsior all the places southward and westward to the Sea. Nine Kings did he conquer in war, crushing their proud necks and leaving very few of them with heirs. He tamed these lands, and brought about such a peace as never was before. Nor never will be, until he again returns. For he will return. Perhaps he already has."

The Rockhard Werman stared Deng in the eyes. This was all a bit much information for him to take in so suddenly.

"What happened after the reign of this... this 'King Lu?'"

"His line reigned for five generations. After him, there was the Lesser Lu, Cinos Lu, Conis Lu, and finally Dang Lu."

The similarities in the names of these ancient royals to his own name and that of his grandmother gave Deng a chill. Surely these freaks must be making it all up on the spot? But no, the book was opened, and Deng saw the royal line written out for himself, in old fading ink.

"So this... this 'Dang Lu,' why did the line end with him?"

"He was murdered most treacherously by the King of the Twenty-Four Knights. Then did all the western world erupt in feuds and rival claims... giving rise to the Lawless Land of Lobes that the Hayamese Empire mocked, and they decided they had better bring their own mark of civilization to lands that had once known goodness. They suppressed the histories of all that came before, and now there are only two copies of the Book of Lu that survive. There is this, and one other. You may find the other in the Forest of Arches, two hours upstream from the town of Fishcunning on the Craun's western shore... speak at length with my large women on where to locate that manuscript, for it ought to belong to you. Perhaps the Line of Lu has not ended after all."

And so Deng Lu was suddenly made to feel as if he were descended from the most powerful King to ever rule the West. Knowing this did not help to ease his cockiness.

The next day, he and Rick Cottontree were led up to the peak of the tallest rock, where they could gaze down upon all the winding routes of the Rock Meadow.

"Alright, I see a way out. I'll try and commit the paths to memory, but it'd be best if you do the same, eh Deng?"

"How about Lord Deng at least."

"Sorry?"

"Oh it's just... well, let's get out of the rocks first. My, there goes Tibsmith."

And true enough, Tibsmith was now taking a path out of the Heart of Rockdom, very much alone. This whipped Cottontree into full blaze, and soon he was leaping down rocks, nearly killing himself to get to the bottom before he lost Tibsmith. Deng Lu took the path, and actually got to the bottom first, for Cottontree was rightfully scared of a high drop. But take a drop he did, out of fear that Deng would run off with Tibsmith and leave him stranded in the Heart of Rockdom.

"Why would she leave without us?!" yelled Rick as he fell on his ass.

"You're a bit overbearing, I suppose," spoke Lord Deng, making regal movements from now until the end of time.

"What's with you?"

"Like I said, I'll make a proclamation after we're out of the rocks."

And the two bolted like swine from the butcher, to get the hell out of that stoned haven.

The true path out of Rock Meadow was surprisingly simplistic once found. All it was was a single road leading from the Heart of Rockdom down a winding course, running alongside a brook all the while. The brook grew to a stream, the stream grew to a river, that being the Stone River, and this river grew into a massive bay, dotted with stony peninsulas. But oh, how lovely it was to see sky in multiple directions once more, instead of just upwards.

The sky lay all before them now, in addition to the camp of the Council of Sound Logic, wherein the folk stood amazed to see living beings emerge out of the fabled Rock Meadow.

Rick Cottontree was none too happy: he had led his friends into the Rock Meadow to avoid the great battle that was brewing; here in the camp he found himself faced directly with his old Dingleite brethren and a healthy crop of fresh warriors, ready to ride for Athragal that night.

Have you missed me? By me, I mean myself, Ward Geit Fung, author of this tale. Well, not so much author as accountant, one who takes the reliable words of others and sets them down on the page to be consumed as a single narrative. I now feel stronger in my narration, for from this point on, I am once again providing firsthand recollections, as I was a direct player in all of what follows.

If you recall, last you saw me I was captured near the Del and brought to imprisonment. I was brought first to Cricksend, famous for their jails, right in the middle of Farlobe. The seasons passed by, and at the annual rotation of prisoners I found myself by some happy accident to be a prisoner in the town of Aslut. Perhaps it was more divine course than happy accident — but it was glad whatever its cause, for also in Aslut there was residing an old young friend. An old young friend who, discouraged with the overwhelming plight of the world, had sought retreat in a place where the winds blew cool and rest was the great unending norm.

Yes, I speak of Skin Toot.

He came to me one deep day in Fevariat, I know not precisely when, but if I had the date in mind I would share it. Upon seeing him, I immediately asked for the date; he said he did not know it. But he seemed pleased to see me, so I made out that I was pleased to see him as well.

I was, thinking back. But my feelings of pleasure were trumped by surprise. How was it that my fortune had brought me to the very village that Skin had chosen for his retirement? I grew distrustful of the Universe and for a short time began to fear that I was sleeping, or all my life had been a long sleep. But as the conversation felt very real, and I still following the continuous flow that stemmed on that day, I will accept that sometimes the world simply does provide us with chance occurrences that can be hard to believe.

"I saw your name on the jill rooster," explained Skin, and by jill rooster he meant jail roster.

"I see," said I, "Do you habitually check the jail rosters in hopes of seeing old enemies?"

"I do and there's no shame in it. But tell me of your exploits."

"My exploits have been nothing short of languishing," sighed I.

"No, no— not these past years in prison, I care none for that. I'm inquiring about the short adventure of you and Piss and many others, when you left out of Ho Spleen Ho with the blessing of Fundrik Luber."

"Ah yes," muttered I, trying hard to remember, for near two years in little space and solitude had taken a toll on my memory, "We set out for retribution, and it was obtained."

I went on for an hour or so, choppily piecing together the fragments of my recollection. It was I, then, who was in for a tug when Skin Toot broke the news to me that Dingle and many others in party were killed near Lakewood in a dark ambush of sorts.

At this blunt news I was shocked a tremble. Dingle dead? Such a thing did not seem possible. Such a thing could not be possible, for my account of his life had no satisfying end whatsoever. Of course it was not true, but I was a woeful man indeed in those moments that I believed it. I recall saying, "If it is true what you have told me, then all prowess has been extinguished."

"I have not heard the tale directly," admitted Skin Toot, "For I have not left my place here in many over a year. I hear whispers around this town every now and next... whispers from Derladan, where the survivors of Dingle's men lay in wait. But for what I cannot know."

317

"They wait for the return of hope," mused I. "Dingle or no, that group of folk was hard in the way of vengeance, and ravenous for change. They'll see it done I'm sure, no matter how long it takes. Have you not felt the pull to go join them?"

Skin Toot laughed in my face from the other side of bars.

"You do not regret leaving the cause then?" I inquired further.

"So what? So that I could have fallen by his side? Cut down by the Skulfers of Lakewood? I knew such a thing was inevitable. You go up against the law— no matter how unjust the law may be— and you're only looking for trouble on yourself and those you're trying to help. You go up against a beast like Skulfing... my lord, what were they thinking?"

"Well, I'm glad you've not come to regret anything," said I, forcing a smile. "You look at peace."

"Best to live in peace when the option is there," exhaled Toot. "I am at peace, Ward Geit, for I am in Aslut. Do you not know of this place?"

"I know nothing of this place, save its jail," chuckled I.

"Well, here is not like other towns in Farlobe. Here we are free to go about on grand enterprises, unmolested by haughty men, and by 'we' I mean us of the light-skinned breeds."

"No? How so?" I asked, for I had the slightest remembrance on the progressive nature of this town of Aslut, but a well-kept secret was it in outer places.

"Well, for one, the town is predominantly comprised of Tanfolk; we outnumber the Rich Mahogs fifty to one. So there are no hurdles in the way of endeavors— that meaning there are no Mahogany institutions set up for the sole purpose of crushing our spirits. Here the banks and the taverns, the temples and the makeries, the shops and the courts... all are run by folk that look just like you and I. And so there is a profit to be made among us. Our monies do not dwindle, as in other Lobes where the Mahogs hold their supremacy. Here the Tan and Pale are allowed and encouraged to grow rich."

Skin Toot smiled at me with the grin of truth, and continued. "Grow rich we do, Ward. This place even has its own market made exclusively for the growing of wealth. It is not as large as that of the Mahogs, but the principle of the thing is exactly the same and there are just as many wealthings to be made."

"And how have you made out with your wealthings?" I asked, looking Skin Toot up and down, for he certainly changed from his old self. For one thing, he was wearing clothes.

"Ah. You have noticed I no longer wear naught but leaves. Well, my leafen attire was more a symbol of defiance than anything, back in the wild woods of Yonderlobe. A mark of my outer spirit. But here, I am accepted. Here I belong, and partake gratefully in society. So it would not be fitting for me to parade about in leaves and nothing else."

"If I recall, you still ran about in leaves and nothing else while we stayed for four months in the Harlobe capital town."

"Well that was different, Ward Geit. There I was a freak of the theatre. Here, I am a respectable business lord."

"Oh! My lord," and I bowed twirlingly for the good Skin Toot. "Tell me what is your business?"

"Such is the ease with which honest folk can make a deep living in this town that I've already come to establish my own makery. We make pipe and women happy."

I pondered this. "Well I understand the bit about making women happy— I think— but how does one make pipe happy?"

"Let me rephrase. We make women happy and pipe."

"Well how do you make women pipe? I hope you're not making pipe out of women."

"God strike you Ward Geit Fung! We make pipe, and we make women happy. There it is."

"Oh! In the same place?"

"Yes. No business should be stuck in the trench of only accomplishing one thing."

"Well said," spoke the mouth of me. "How many women are you currently making happy then?"

"You mistake me," shook the head of Skin Toot. "For my part, I will seek to make happy only one: the one called Danaria, she who is perfect beyond all others. I have not yet arrived at the glorious day when I might see her at will, and free of charge, but she allows me to cast eyes on her every few months."

Here I began to feel sad for him. And I felt sadder as he went on:

"She makes me pay, yes, but every week's wage I give to her it absolutely worth the toil. The last time I saw her, she allowed me to kiss the pit between arm and breast, and it was a thing altogether new and exciting for me. We have now agreed that this is all I should be permitted to do when we are together, but I am grateful. To spend eternity putting my tongue underarm of that fine lady Dan would be all that I ask in life."

I hurried to change the subject. "It's a great wonder that more Tanfolk do not make their way to this progressive place."

"It seems to be yet a place of quiet secret, and thank my goodness for that, for if there was widespread knowledge of the dealings in Aslut, the Rich Mahogany would surely not tolerate it for long."

These words held an air of deep foreboding, which proved to be more pressing and present than any could have guessed. For just weeks ahead, the thriving and progressive town of Aslut would be put to the torch.

Now we leap back out of the month of Fevariat, to the first of Sevallia, when Deng Lu, Rick Cottontree and Tibsmith emerged out of the Rock Meadow, and found the Council of Sound Logic's camp on the lovely Stone Bay. Many of their old Dingleite friends were there already, along with Dingle himself! They had feared he had become a gruesome casualty of the Lakewood Bowels, and at first they were pleased to see him. But then he told them of his simple torture of drinking fingernail juice, and they despised him for it.

"You may despise me to the world's ending," shrugged Dingle, "But now we gotta go. We got a... a war to go to, or something. Frup-frump!" And he gave a slap on the ass to his recently acquired horse Tirtramphiglu, or Tir Tram Phig Lu for folks who can't read good.

"Wait!" cried out Cottontree, who was fearful of riding to war on such short notice, and also riding to war at all. "How much time is allotted to a reunion of parted friends? Surely more than this."

"You're right, Cottontree. And according to the Dingleite Code which I have begun to ponder at the request of Lord Cuomo of Costerwall... the time allotted to a meeting of parted friends... is nine days. But that allotment of time may be sliced to four meetings, should the call for battle be made. To war, for the sake of more and the goodness of lore! To war with whore and shocking gore!"

321

That was the Dingleite Call to Arms, which would seldom be used, for as Dingle was now codifying his sect, he realized he was indeed a pacifist, and would only ride to battle in the most needful of times. Counseled by Lord Cuomo, Carvin Cong, Windal of Klontug, and now the risen-from-the-rocks Deng Lu, Dingle had indeed decided that this was one such occasion.

Nothing could stop the fury of the Dingleites joined together with the Council of Sound Logic. Together they rode to Derladan, on the First of Sevallia in 3336, and there passed the night in song and splendor, picking up the stragglers of their army.

The next day, they began the two day ride to Cricksend, where they planned to join forces with the King of the Forty Knights, at the behest of Windal and Perfection.

"Is it just me, or is anyone else thinking this King of Forty won't be of much help to us?" asked Dingle.

"You'd best not call him the King of Forty," said Perfection as they trotted along their southwestern road. "Nothing but 'The King of the Forty Knights' will do."

"Well, I have my own feelings about that. But I'll keep them fresh for when I meet this 'king' face to face."

The Dingleites reached Cricksend on the 4th of Sevallia, and sure enough, the King of the Forty Knights was waiting there, with thirty-nine knights.

Piss Dingle was not impressed.

"Oakay, what the hell is this? You're not a King. What are you king of?"

"Forty knights," replied the King of the Forty Knights bluntly, taking Dingle for an ass.

"Well for one, you can't even count. I've been looking over your shoulder for twenty seconds and I can already see you've only got 39 knights."

"More will come."

"Oh oakay, more. So... one more. Then you'll have all forty knights."

"I'm a proud line, and should rightly cut you from lung to liver, and out through your loin. But because your fight is of noble purpose, I'm prepared to ignore your insults and ride on."

"Oof..." whistled Dingle, looking the King of the Forty Knights up and down, "I don't think you should be riding anywhere. You look like your funeral was yesterday."

And thus Dingle and the King of the Forty Knights hurled insults at each other all the night through, until Dingle seriously began to question the old King's claims to ancient royalty.

"See, I don't get it!" shouted Dingle. "A King rules over land, not just knights."

"Land we had, Lands of the Dan! Until we, along with eight others of royal stock, were defeated at the hands of an almighty ruler. At the Battle of Deth! But even since then, those I rule over have grown in number."

"Yeah, by how many?"

"It was the King of the Twelve Knights who was killed at the Battle of Deth, but his children doubled that number! The King of the Twenty-Four Knights was born. And from that number I have grown the Kingdom to forty."

"See, but that's not impressive. Going from twelve to twenty-four to forty over the course of several hundred years is not impressive."

But the King of Forty differed highly, and this opened up an unexpected diversion into the realm of Luian mythology, whereby a dumbfounded Dingle learned of Deng Lu's supposed ancient heritage. Deng was brought over to explain, and the King of the Forty Knights nearly had a heart stopping to see a (possible) descendant of Lu in the flesh, but once he found his courage, began to yell curses and threats. At this, Deng Lu dug deep into his recently discovered past, and summoned up a rage of kingly fire that burst out in the loudest roar any had ever heard protrude from the mouth of Deng:

"So it is you that I have heard much about! You, King of the Forty Knights, with kin leading back to the King of the Twenty-Four Knights! He who cut off the Line of Lu until this day, severing that great house from its godly cause! Ending a dynasty which reigned with truth and valor!"

Needless to say, Dingle was puzzled by all of it. Last he had seen Deng Lu, he had merely been ambitious and arrogant, now he was the long-lost heir to a forgotten dynasty? Screw that. Dingle got up right between Deng and the King of Forty, and bid them to kiss and make a friendidge.

"Now kiss and make a friendidge."

"I will not kiss the offspring of the bastard King who ended my line," ground the teeth of Deng Lu.

"Oakay, if you claim to be part of that line, then the line hasn't ended. And say the dynasty hadn't ended! The chances of you being first in line to that throne would have been next to none. So give thanks to this King of Forty. He has given you the sacred chance of reforging the 'line of Lu'— even if Lu never existed! His ancestor literally gave you the chance to make a name for yourself, that you would not have otherwise had. So kiss him and make friends."

At the insistence of Dingle and all those backing him, Deng Lu and the King of the Forty Knights— aged and smoky of breath— kissed at great length. It was a humiliation for the both of them.

But now all was settled, and the next day the army marched into the shadow hills of Athragal, where they waved down the first Skulfer they could find. They swore that no harm would come to him, if he would go forth and summon the highest ranking man of that region to attend a Council of War, where the terms of battle could be decided.

It was Grandbor who arrived at the Council of War on the eastern edge of Athragal, surrounded by a host of many Skulfers. Dingle, Deng, Victory, Perfection, Carvin and Windal all rode up to him, and those who could manage bowed as a sign of minimal respect. At least the guy had showed up to the Council.

"Where is Skulfing?" asked Carvin Cong, his white beard showing exactly as he felt: too old to be held up in long talks of meandering words.

"We are not so stupid as you would think; we would not bring him here, for you would kill him."

"Tell him we wish to do battle on the third day from now, fine and fair," spoke the Lady Victory, plain and true.

"On a field of his choice. Here in Athragal," added Dingle.

Grandbor laughed at Dingle. "Do you find yourself lost in these parts, Piss Dingle? Never been to Athragal? Fields are hard to come by in this place. The country is plump on hill and slope."

"You can find a field," nodded Dingle slowly, with certainty.

"Very well," conceded Grandbor. "There is something of a field I know, in the center of Athragal. It's called the Tetful Rise, and I should think that will be the place of our battle. But look for the coming of my emissaries, for I will need to clear this matter with Lord Skulfing."

"Tell your ass Skulfing that he will show up to battle, or we will not!" shouted the ever rising voice of Deng Lu, to the chuckles of all.

"Well, in that case, I would think he will certainly not show," laughed Grandbor. "For he is not the one who wants battle. That would be you."

"We will fight regardless if your cowardly Minister shows his broad shoulders or not," smirked the Lady Victory, and with that Grandbor reared his horse and turned away.

But Windal remembered his sole question, and shouted out— "What has become of the Luberian army? That which was supposed to meet us at the Lone Oak!"

"We slaughtered them all!" yelled Grandbor, as he trotted away. "Do not wonder long how it felt, for you will be given the same courtesy in three days' time."

And so it was decided. On the 8th of Sevallia, there would be... something of an armed conflict. Piss Dingle gulped and hurried to his tent, to relieve himself by way of pumps.

The next day, Dingle's folk rode through the pretty shadowed hills, towards the Tetful Rise, where they would face the great battle of their century. Currently, the three great Dingleite women— Victory, Perfection and Tibsmith— rode together, speaking of their own lot.

"All this talk of Rich Mahogany supremacy and the oppression of the light-skins," mused Perfection, "But why don't wermen ever speak to the oppression of women? Are we not just as oppressed, by folk of our breeds even?"

"Perfection, you are so right," spoke Victory emphatically. "This battle is just as much about us women overcoming years of belittlement. After the Battle of Tetful Rise, we start on towards a new objective."

"One thing at a time, ladies," laughed Dingle, passing by on Tirtramphiglu.

326

"Um... are you kidding me?" asked Victory.

"Well," smirked Dingle, not realizing he was stabbing himself in the shin, "I mean, come on. You women don't have it bad. We've got a real thing we're fighting for here with the Tanfolk and Paleskins."

"Oh I see," continued Victory, now bitter, "So that goodness I gave you in the tent last night? It shall not be a thing recurring."

"I don't care if he is the leader of our cult," smiled Tibsmith, licking her lips, "Let's just have his bowels for a quick snack."

"What?!" exclaimed Dingle. "Just because I'm saying we should focus on the battle we all decided on years ago now that it's here— you're saying you won't give me goodness anymore and you Tibsmith are wanting to eat my bowels? You guys are sounding a little crazy right now. A little crazed. You won't get far in your ambitions of a matriarchal society by being this damn dumb."

As one might guess, those words did not get Dingle an apology from the women, nor did it win him any goodness. The only thing it won him was a swift exile from his own cult, whereby he was knocked from his horse and sent running through the hills, to perhaps meet up with them again by way of the Long Road Round, should he prove fast enough on foot.

It may sound like a punishment, to be knocked off one's horse and cast aside for an exile on the eve of battle, a battle of personal making and importance. It was certainly intended as a punishment by the women who inflicted it upon Piss. But as friend Dingle stood tall above a wide expanse of Athragalian land— virgin and pure— his feelings felt completely opposite than those expected of one resigned to some harsh penalty.

At last he had solitude. At last he had freedom from the constant scrutiny, and from the common strokes of the scrote. And as the sound of horses and chariots receded into the rolling distance, a soft wind tickled on Dingle's face. He lingered a few more moments in its softness, and the flavor turned to sweet. "Oakay, best to move on now," thought Dingle, before the sweet wind turned lewd in hopes of granting him orgasmic pleasure, for then surely he would be finished.

And so Dingle marched on down that gentle green slope, under vast grey cloud, songs in his head all the while. His pace waxed and waned with the speed of the wind, and at times he found himself twilling through the hills, with boundless strides and an energy that seemed endless. Though he had no horse, Dingle felt now to be covering deep distance at a faster rate than he ever had before.

The clouds curled round one another, and flew in restless waves, with more haste than he had seen in all his travels. Surely he must have been slipped a suspect leaf, or drank of some poisoned chalice the night before. Nothing else could explain the startling speed with which the sky now raced, and the swirling storm of clouds that danced hard but gave no rain.

In short, the Hills of Athragal had made this man taller than the very high peak of the Beltmar. And so, when he saw on the horizon a shape that looked very much to be the image of the good Skin Toot, Piss Dingle did not believe it to be real.

"Now I know I'm tall for sure..." trailed off Dingle, quite tall. "That ain't no Skin Toot. The spirit of Skin maybe. For he did love these hills, and told me I would too. I did not believe him. I did not think such wondrous lands could exist so close to Flatfinger. But how I repent of my pride! What I would now give to spend a day and night in the company of that Toot, roaming these slopes together—!"

"Hey man, let's go."

Dingle jumped and screamed, for while he was giving his monologue, he had completely missed Skin Toot's approach, and now the man himself stood right next to him. I was there too, and followed them throughout the rest of this account, but I do not think Dingle ever acknowledged it.

"Oh, damn! Good Skin Toot! What be lovely?"

"These hills, for one," spoke Skin calmly, astonished to see Dingle much, much taller than he had ever seen before. "Did you have a bad leaf?"

"Either that or a poisoned chalice. These hills are giving me deep. You feel that? The power of their rounded shapes? They're like tits. In all honesty. That's exactly what it is."

"Mm, yes. That's probably why they're making you so excited."

"But it's the clouds too!" Exclaimed Dingle, throwing his arms out to their maximum span. "It's the green, it's the grey...! Now I know why they call that place Greeningre; you know that place? Greeningre?"

"I've heard it's a very nice place to live, if one can afford it."

"We should go there." And Dingle gazed up and round, his eyes rolling about in their sockets. "But also we should never leave. We'll stall in Athragal for all times."

But Skin Toot reminded Dingle that there was a great battle to be had on the Tetful Rise, at daybreak on the 8th of Sevallia, and armies from all across the land were assembling to war. They must not miss it.

How, you may be wondering, did Skin Toot and I come to Athragal, once again intent on toppling the regime of Skulfing? Well, as I foreshadowed earlier, a great tragedy befell the progressive town of Aslut about a month after I had arrived in its jail.

The 'Ercassam' at Aslut occurred on the first of Sevallia, and even I— an intellectual— had not heard this word Ercassam. Apparently it is of an ancient dialect native to the region of Athragal; those survivors of the burning of Aslut told me simply to spell it backwards, and that would hold the clarification of my inquiries, but it only served to confused me more.

Anyway, the town of wealthy Tanfolk was put to the torch by envious Mahogs, who had found their simple prompt in the most awful of things. For it just so happened that on that day, a Rich Mahogany woman had been passing through the town, and dropped her pen. A well-intentioned Tanfolk picked up the pen, and rushed up to the Mahogany woman, tapping her on the shoulder to gain her attention when she would not turn about. The pen was returned and a smile given, but this Rich Mahogany woman was bubbling with horror. To be touched by one so tan! To have had her pen handled by such an inferior hand!

She returned to her home on the outskirts of Aslut, where Mahogs were in great number, and rallied all the town together in anger and boiling doom. Within hours they were all of them marching to the heart of Aslut, intent on doing away with that town altogether.

Now, does a shoulder tap really warrant the burning of a town? Does a returned pen, in all honesty, bring about massacres in civil places? I am inclined to think not, and that truly, the Mahogs living around Aslut had simply grown tired of living so close to the Tanfolk. And Tanfolk that were wealthier and more successful than them!

In their minds, this was not how society was meant to work. In the Farlobe, society was meant to work for the benefit of the Mahogany, and to the detriment of the

330

lighter breeds. They could not stand to see their Tanfolk neighbors leading peaceful and prosperous lives while they toiled in mediocrity, and so they were just waiting for an excuse— any excuse at all— to burn the town.

Skin Toot's makery was not spared from the flame, but thankfully he had been visiting me in jail when the deadly riot erupted. The sight of the violence in the streets proved to be the catalyst which revived the flaming spirit of the old Skin Toot. With ravenous spirit, the same which was born in Yonderlobe, he freed me from my bars, and together we raced through the burning roads of Aslut, rescuing children from their homes and chopping off loins of the aggressors.

Then we walked north to Athragal, and came across a badly wounded host of men calling themselves 'Luberians.' They spoke of a delusional old man, calling himself a King of forty knights or some such nonsense, and that he had held contact with a certain Dingleite, who would bring in more forces from the north and east, to do battle with the Skulfers ravaging the hills.

I asked Skin Toot if he might now wish to partake in the clashing of swords. Having been spared in Aslut, he said, when so many of his tan brothers had perished in flame, he now considered his life as forfeit anyway. His living was merely a gift from the divine, and he felt that he ought to use his remaining time in riding against the terrible injustice inflicted upon his oppressed peoples. For too long had the strength of the Rich Mahogany fist pressed down upon the Pale and Tan, and there would now be an honest uprising. Just as we were deciding this, we spotted a quick stumbling Piss Dingle up on the hilltop, and we no longer had any doubt. We ran straight for him, and somehow he did not see us coming, despite his spotting us first.

Thus it was that Dingle and Toot were reunited at last, and I was there too.

So we three Dingleites marched upon the long road to the Tetful Rise, happy to be once more free and in each other's company.

At dawn on the 8th of Sevallia, there was already a great thundering of clans upon the field of the Tetful Rise. The Skulfers, arrayed in colored armors and in strict formation, gave off haughty roars and hups. The Dingleites and their allies, wearing whatever they had and standing organically, gave off aggravating screams and yells of a virtuous political nature. It was ugly and disdainful all around.

But then the time for opening terms had arrived, and all were hushed at the behest of their lords. To the center of the field rode Deng Lu— now wearing a gold tiara belonging to the young daughter of Inder Sohn— along with Lord Cuomo of Costerwall and the King of the Forty Knights. The Skulfers sent forth their commanders: Miekpanse and Grandbor, with the master assassins PARPINFOHZ and Leg Randy closely behind.

"Where is Skulfing?" asked the child-crowned Deng Lu.

"He has sent me in his stead," muttered Miekpanse, not making eye contact with any of them. He was old and grey, with a face like that of an animal tired and slow, far too old to be riding into a battle of any kind.

"And do you wish to do for your Minister?" asked Deng, full of pity.

"Better to die for a true elected Minister, than for an imposter King!" put in the loud Grandbor, who felt the true spirit of war in his veins.

"I am no imposter," smiled Deng Lu. "Have you not heard of Greatest King Grand Lu the Large? His line was legendary in these parts. He was known to all, before the evil times when your Hayamese Empire stomped upon these lands and pushed aside all our wonderful traditions and tellings."

Here Miekpanse did raise his head, for this was an issue he felt passionate about: "Grand Lu was a myth. A myth of a lawless people who— in the year 3200— were completely uncivilized. Empress Caracos of Hayaman brought that civilization, so that we could stand here today and do decent battle!"

Here Lord Cuomo put in: "If your Empress Caracos had never brought your stamp of civilization, there would be no need for battle today! Today's battle is the result of generations of oppression, not because of the feuds of clans, but because of systemic prejudice, against an entire breed of people! You and your arrogance has brought this upon yourself, Meek."

The King of the Forty Knights began to speak, but Lord Cuomo turned and addressed his allies, much louder and better.

"Fellow Dingleites, members of my Council! Men of Luber, and those in the service of the King of Forty Knights! Today is not about the colors of our skin. Look around. You will see Tanfolk and Paleskin, as well as Mahogs in our ranks! For the Hayamese Empire has not rooted hatred in all who reside in these lands. They have rooted in a system of oppression and supremacy, and that is what must take its leave! As we charge these skulking Skulfers today, it is not you against whatever breed you are not! Take a look at your clothes! There is where the answer lies. We are the common folk, those who wish to live in peace, in a world that does not deem us inferior! We battle against them, not because of their breed, but because they have chosen a profession which encourages terror. They have been seduced by a cruel master, and by our sword today they shall perish!"

333

There were thunderous screams on the hilltops, and Lord Cuomo bowed gracefully in the direction of Miekpanse, granting him the field for a rallying speech. This proclamation of Miekpanse proved to be much more succinct:

"Win, and we will look back on this day with a deep grin."

And so the armies were ready, and a charge of cavalry commenced. Mouths were hung low, with roaring sounds bursting out from them, and lances held outright before the heads of horses. In a short set of moments, the insides of men would be flying hall.

But not yet. For just as the front lines closed in on each other, a fat little Mahogany man with an old temper came rushing into the middle of the field, throwing up his arms with cries of "Wait, wait! Wait damn it!"

And the riders of the front line stayed their horses.

A great silence took hold, as the riders all stared down at the old brown farmer.

"What the hell, old man?" said most of the riders on the front line.

"You'll call me Titch!" said Old Farmer Titch, putting his hands into his pockets proudly.

"Sir, what are you doing here?" Asked Miekpanse as cordially as he could. "Our front lines were just about to close in on each other. This is a battle."

"THIS... is my farm. You're on my land."

And for the moment, all hostilities were stilled upon revelation that they were on owned property. Proper deeds and documentation were provided, and the leaders of both sides agreed that the Battle of the Tetful Rise was never to be, for it rested on the tracts of Old Titch.

"Well, can we use the field next to your house?" asked Lord Cuomo politely.

"My land is vast. And even at a length of two miles, your screams and disembowelings would ruin my lunch. But at the same time, I would like to have some hint of the battle, for my evening entertainment. So go four miles to the west, where the valleys droop into low spots, and fight there upon the Titfall Dig."

Ah, yes... now history was showing its true course. The Battle of the Tetful Rise would be no more, forgotten to all who were not there to see its aborted charge, but this Battle of the Titfall Dig would be a thing to recall to for many an age.

Both Skulfers and Dingleites camped in the low circular plain of the Titfall Dig that night. Walls rose up gently on all sides, salted with little mounds that resembled breasts, often with sparse trees springing up between the mounds. To the surprise of many, there was a mingling of the camps, as sworn enemies laughed and drank together, upon the field where they would soon be murdering each other.

Lord Cuomo and some of the more intelligent men in that place were not surprised, for they were of the mind that all men could live harmoniously and in fellowship if their differences were not blatantly pointed out. They were also of the mind that a key person was missing from this scene.

"Where is Dingle?" asked Cuomo. "Is no one else thinking it?"

"The Lady Victory and Perfection told him to get lost," spoke Tibsmith. "He was speaking a bit too honestly for them."

"Ah come on. You make the guy leave this close to a battle of his own making? This battle, this is what his whole life's work has been leading up to."

Then Fi Fernin emerged out of a tent, after being pleasured by Jernander Skug. "I feel that he will arrive precisely when he is most needed."

"I have seen you but only very sparsely," spoke Cuomo, suddenly noticing Fi's great beauty, and lusting for it. "You are not outspoken like some of these Dingleite women. Why is that?"

"Because not all women are so. Do you wish to categorize me, to define me as those in Supremacy do with those who they deem inferior? Which side are you on, Lord Cuomo?"

And the Lord of Costerwall was embarrassed. "I meant nothing by the remark. I only meant to bid you favor—"

"The favors are mine to give," spoke Jernander Skug, now emerging out of the tent and covering Fi Fernin with all his tongue, to show Lord Cuomo that his flatterings would all be in vain.

So passed the night, and with the rising of the suns on the 9th of Sevallia, 3336, battle was joined.

The Battle of the Titfall Dig was primarily an affair of horsing and unhorsing, for the first six hours of the day. Instead of putting forth sweat into laying down romantic prose for the description of these things, I will simply relay what happened plainly and without much effort:

The Lord of Costerwall unhorsed Leg Randy.
PARPINFOHZ rehorsed Leg Randy.
The Lord of Costerwall unhorsed Grandbor.
PARPINFOHZ rehorsed Grandbor.
Leg Randy unhorsed Lady Victory.

336

Perfection rehorsed Victory.

Grandbor unhorsed Miekpanse, his own commander, by accident.

Grandbor rehorsed Miekpanse with a courteous apology.

Grandbor unhorsed Rick Cottontree, for he seemed to be an easy target.

Nobody rehorsed Rick Cottontree, for it would have been a waste of time.

Swilly unhorsed PARPINFOHZ.

Some peasant Skulfer rehorsed PARPINFOHZ.

PARPINFOHZ avenged himself upon Swilly, dehorsing him (differed from unhorsing in that he killed the horse of Swilly, so that he could not be rehorsed).

The King of the Forty Knights unhorsed someone, and this was impressive in itself since everyone had expected the King of Forty to die from exhaustion with seven minutes.

Miekpanse, old and frail, unhorsed the King of the Forty Knights, for he was evil like that and didn't think he would be able to successfully unhorse anyone else.

Deng Lu rode to rehorse the King of the Forty Knights, but accidentally killed him with fury instead, for the treacherous wrong his ancestor had done to his own ancestor, Dang Lu, last of the Luian dynasty.

PARPINFOHZ unhorsed Perfection, Tibsmith, and Jernander Skug.

Fi Fernin, tired of all the unhorsing and rehorsing, made a swift run for the horse of Leg Randy, leaping up onto it and throwing him to the ground. Now sitting tall upon a horse of her own, this most stunning of woman warriors went swift for Miekpanse and PARPINFOHZ, dehorsing them both at the same time. And she rode up to Grandbor with many others behind, and did swordplay with him upon beastback, besting him and casting him to the ground with a thrust to the breast.

Once he landed on the ground, all the surrounding Dingleites dismounted and made a swift go at the proud Grandbor, all of them focusing on this one deep foe so that he would be certain not to leave the field. This mob beat him with the blunt ends of their weapons, and then tore his limbs off halfway, so that they would hang painfully. When the blood of Grandbor covered them well, this mob of Dingleites at last tied him to a horse, which they sent off at full gallop, to drag the villain out of life.

Now it was that we— meaning Dingle, Toot and myself— at last came within earshot of the great battle. The sounds were all unpleasant, and we rightly considered stepping the other way for the sake of our soundlobes.

"But let us first catch a glimpse of the fight, and if our eyes are then as displeased as our ears, we might well turn back," spoke Skin Toot, and so we carried on.

As we came upon our final hill, suddenly the noises stopped. A thorny silence swept along the green; thorny in that it was a great relief, as a flower, but sharp with a sting for we all knew this silence should not be. Tremendous bouts of silence should never naturally occur so quick after an uproar of violence. Perhaps all on the field were suddenly brought to death at the same moment?

"I think the more likely explanation," said Skin with certainty, "Is that they hear us coming."

"Yeah. Let's be real here," expanded Dingle, "They can sense us, now a mile away, and they have halted the fight, so that they can acknowledge the coming of Piss Dingle to the field of battle! It's the only thing that makes sense."

But as they rounded up over the hill, they saw all the lines facing away from them, towards a new army that had come: that of Skulfing's Deeplove, passionate townsfolk and villagers who had never known a deeper cause in all their days than to lay down their lives for one they deemed superior to all men.

"Well this is stupid," remarked Skin Toot.

"Are these people... really that dense?" wondered Dingle aloud. "That they could admire this evil regime from afar I can almost understand. I don't agree with it, but I get it. I grasp it. This I don't grasp. How can they love this Skulfing that much? How can they love his lies and deceitful ways more than they love their own lives?"

"It is a dark and evil mind that has swept over these lands. Let us move forth at once then, so we might at last rid it from the source, and these poor misled souls can be guided then by a new light."

But Dingle held back Toot as he started down the hill. "Yes, but let us wait a moment. It appears as though PARPINFOHZ now gives a speech in a funny purple hat, and all eyes are on him. Our entrance will not be grand if we make our approach now. It will be overshadowed by whatever vile words this one speaks."

And they certainly were vile. For PARPINFOHZ did sit astride a massive steed in a large (frankly fat, in all dimensions) purple hat, pacing between the lines, giving an impassioned speech on why the armies of Url Skulfing would triumph then and forever, and why prejudice between the breeds would and should never die. The amusing thing is that he spoke not to the Deeplove which had just assembled to fight— no, they already knew this rhetoric by heart, and needed no further goading to bring angry violence to the field— but to the Dingleites, Luberians and the Army of Sound Logic.

The entire speech reeked of cock and circumstance, and although I asked to hear a rendition of it retold, none would ever venture to repeat any of what was said. For an idea, I would reference any of the numerous recorded speeches of Skulfing, Miekpanse, Grandbor or Poomp Yu. Speaking of Poomp Yu, he had been gutted from Skulfing's administration some years ago, but even that was not enough to silence his hate for the Opposition, and he reappeared now as a soldier in the newly come civilian Army of the Deeplove, and he would mark his fair share of havoc in the second stage of the battle.

Anyhow, PARPINFOHZ may have gone on for days, spewing pride and condescension, if he was not suddenly and discreetly silenced by a strike of flame, which it is said came from Deng Lu, for he had apparently stolen a flamebow from the Skulfers of Lakewood and kept it concealed for years.

The goal was to silence PARPINFOHZ, certainly, and this was achieved for a moment, mostly on account of the surprise— after all, none of Dingle's lot were presumed to be in possession of such high-grade weaponry. But nonetheless, the quick burst of flame shot of from the crowd and struck his lower cape, which quickly ignited and consumed him whole. Then he was no longer silent, for he did scream as loud as one can, with his horse beneath both terrified and rampant, sprinting this way and that with the flaming purple lord — now purple, orange, and red— strapped to his back.

As soon as the blazing PARPINFOHZ left the field, the Deeplove would wait no longer. They charged and smashed against the unready lines of the Dingleites, and it was then that we made our bold descent onto the plain of the Titfall Dig.

No one noticed our coming. Dingle said we would be just as well to turn around leave since we were given no great welcome, but Skin and I bid him to continue on. We then complained of the lack of song on the battlefield.

"I mean, is it really too hard to have a single band on the battlefield?" yelled Skin Toot over the deafening clashes of furry and sharp iron fury.

"Right, the soldiers are miserable enough. At least give them some music to die to."

But I was quick to point out the memory of Lay Pork, terrible battle of old where an entire orchestra had been swallowed by rock upon a plateau, and suffered arguably worse deaths than the warriors.

"That was a one-time deal!" argued Dingle. "What are the chances of that happening here? You could put the band right up on that bluff over there— Athragal is a place of beauty and wonder, not a place of evil rocks that swallow men by way of some dark enchantment!"

"It does look like a very good place for a band," nodded Skin Toot. "I'd certainly be able to fight better if there were songs playing atop the hills. It would grant me the inspiration to carry on, or to begin in the first place."

And by chance, they noticed Swilly, wounded on the ground, bleeding out of thigh and shin, but with his flute still tucked within his breast. Gladly did Skin Toot run up to him. He was moaning and grinding, but Skin spoke of all the ways in which they could make the battle better.

"Come now. I do not ask you to stand, but merely to find the strength of mouth. You're of no use as a spearsman! Your calling always was to flout about. So join me, Swilly. Join me in bringing song to the Battle of the Titfall Dig."

Being convinced, Skin and I carried Swilly under the shoulders, up a bluff overlooking the field of fight. Once there, we began to serve our part. Warriors we were not, but for either grace or ill, we would inspire others to the arts of war ere the day ended. With a legendary rhythm I pounded mallet on rock, and Swilly blew upon flute longer than he ever had, and the voice of Skin Toot thundered down upon the valley, our trio never to be outdone in all the history of those hills.

"I Would Have It Be of That Manner" was the song we chose to perform, all day long, and never did we stray from its simple and famous nature. It was a well-known tune of the young and handsome Lowroad Folk, and all upon the field knew it well. For those who admired it, the battle grew vastly more enjoyable, and they fought well. For those who despised the song— and there were just as many if not more— the battle grew ever more hellish, and because of it they also fought well. And so our rendition served exactly as we intended.

Many things hellish could be spoken of, but I will relay just one for this segment of the battle, for in doing so, for Tibsmith has offered to allow me her extremities should I report on her great kill. She has great extremities and so I do so gladly: long had the eyes of Tibsmith been planted on Poomp Yu, infamous in the administration of Skulfing as one who had ended years of agreement between nations pertaining to the preservation of virgin lands. Poomp Yu had pushed an agenda of clearing away trees, of polluting rivers, of cutting away rock from stone to drive the ever-growing hand of industry's makeries. And for this, Tibsmith lured Poomp Yu over to a little valley within the valley, by taking off her armor, and even a patch of cloth.

Poomp Yu set down his axe, and with wobbly legs stumbled down to the dried-out ravine where Tibsmith swayed sensually. She placed her arms around him, and he closed his eyes amidst the sounds of war. Did he actually think he was about to get some amidst all this death and savagery?

In reality, he got none, but rather had much taken from him. For Tibsmith grabbed him and gave him a spin through the air, landing him on his back. She then ripped his shirt off and laid her sharp teeth into his mid-section. Soon she was tearing into his bowels, biting them and ripping them out. So ended the deeds of Poomp Yu.

On the valiant deeds of Dingle in this moment of war, I will speak short, for his time on the field was four minutes. He walked out slowly, picking up a bloodied sword of the fallen with leisure, and he swung clean out of his hands at a passing horse. I assume he was several strides off from hitting anything. Then one bulky and unshaven of the Deeplove landed with a growling axe just before our hero and founder. But Dingle was completely calm, and shrugged, lifting his daggers with a second shrug. This was not one the Deeplove warrior wished to combat; in fact, he would have been disgraced had he struck down this defenseless, most Dinglish of all Dingleites. So the Deeplove warrior moved on, to do battle with Marc Tempull.

So Dingle moved freely about the field, looking for those he might put out of misery. He came across a middle-aged woman Skulfer, whose entire left side was mangled, with arm and leg bent egregiously. She coughed up blood and could speak no words, so Dingle took a guess and thought that maybe she would rather be killed than endure more moments of pain. So he drove his sword slowly into her heart.

Just then, Windal of Klontug came galloping up to Dingle, with Luberians and Unspoken wermen swift behind. "So this is the man we follow!" He yelled mockingly, casting eyes down on Dingle. "One whose only kill would be that of a wounded woman upon the ground."

Dingle tried to explain himself, saying it was a merciful killing, and that he— never having been trained in war by Wi Tan Pree as his companions had— could not hope to kill anyone fairly.

"You are a defecant warrior, that cannot be helped," went Deng Lu, freshly ridden up to find joy in calling out the flaws of Dingle, "But the way you treat women is appalling. How dare you show your face on this field."

"How dare I show my face on this field? I'm the reason we're here! If you're talking about the passing comments I said to Victory and Perfection—"

"I am, and those things will not be forgotten nor forgiven!" now yelled Lord Cuomo of Costerwall in a deeper voice than any had known him to harbor. "You do not speak to women like that. No, you look at me. You do NOT speak to women like that."

"Do you even know what was said?" Asked Dingle, for he suspected that through rumor, that which he had actually said might have become twisted and worse. But still Windal screamed and chastised, strange for the battle was still raging, and soon Dingle had had enough:

"Look, what do you expect me to do? I will not take back my words, for I feel they were reasonable at the time. I feel that you are trying to dictate my own actions, and set your own virtues as superior to mine, and that kind of thinking is what I strove to fight against when I started this Dingleite movement. But I see now that the faces of my own men are staring down upon me as if I have done more wrong than Skulfing. Ya know what? I don't need this. Screw all of you. I fight for your skins no longer. The Tanfolk cause is a dead one. I no longer fight for any breed, regardless of how oppressed they are, for you do not appreciate help when it comes to you. From now on—" but by that point they

344

had all gone back to fighting, leaving Dingle alone— "I fight for only those who would put an end to fighting."

Sad and frustrated, Dingle walked up the nearest hill, abandoning the fight, and gaining the high ground, from which he could sit and enjoy the bloody dismemberings without being at risk of such things himself. They were all fools, thought he, and they would surely all perish by the falling of night.   T h e n he looked up, and saw a strange beast on the far bluff: a tall figure, narrow and blue, with broad violet pads upon his shoulders. It was Url Skulfing, come at last to witness his admirers die for his cause. And beside him sat Fundrik Luber, other architect of that battle, he too cowardly as well to join in the bloodshed. "Surely that it where I belong," thought Dingle.

As so Dingle walked along the circular ridge above the Titfall Dig, glancing down every now and again to see the furry and swift cuts of iron fury below. The sounds of wrath and rage still lingered in the valley, but were now intertwined with our bold rendition of "I Would Have It Be of That Manner." Before he knew it, Dingle had come to the other bluff, and stood now face to face with the great evil figure, whose politics he had hated since first they appeared in the Lobes. And, as he suspected, he was kind of a cool guy.

Very relaxed, very much in good humor, and of a decent composure, Url Skulfing sat there with Fundrik Luber. Sworn enemies they were, cursing the name of each other behind their own doors, but here above the field of battle they were getting on quite nicely. There is always such a mutual respect among leaders of men. That even if the hatred of ideals be silently bubbling over, there can yet be found the curious capacity for the enjoying of a beautiful day, with friendly conversation, while their respective armies murder each other down below. This is much the same phenomenon that occurred on the 9th of Sevallia, 3336.

"Hey, can I join you guys?" asked Dingle to Skulfing and Luber. They looked surprised at first, surprised that any not of the noble class would dare to climb the bluff and stand amongst the architects of war while the battle lingered.

"Oh, I do recognize you," said Fundrik Luber at last. "You are the one... whose name was given to this venture, was it not?"

"Yeah. I'm Dingle," said he, not impressed. "You granted me full right to go out and kill Skulfers." He looked up into Skulfing's eyes, with no fear. This nearly brought out Skulfing's temper, but he remembered where he was... sitting in the circle of architects, above his vastly superior army which would soon be victorious. And so he thought it best to feign courtesy for the time being, and it was he who invited Dingle to sit.

"I hope you will accept my apology," spoke the voice of Skulfing. The voice was not at all as Dingle would have imagined; for such an imposing figure, there was something of an obnoxious twang or drag in its quality, and the cadence of his words was not at all eloquent or inspiring of any sort of awe. "For your days, of imprisonment, in the Bowels of Lakewood."

"Oh that," shrugged Dingle. "Yeah I'm over it. I was fine. All I had to do was drink stuff, mildly unpleasant but far from torture. Now... my friends on the other hand. Them you'll have to apologize to."

Url Skulfing smirked. "The Council of Logic, you mean."

"Right. Jic Topper was beheaded, but you can still apologize to most of them. I'm pretty sure you had thorny wheat shoved up Dunly Moan's urethra. He wasn't a fan."

346

"I hate to say this..." trailed off Skulfing, "But I don't think many of your friends, I don't think they'll be looking for apologies tonight. Some of them... won't be looking. For anything."

And the battle certainly appeared to be dire. The Skulfers and the Deeplove was in the vast majority. The Luberians, Army of Sound Logic, Knights of the Dan, the Unspoken— all these were dwindling like paper in flame. The original Dingleites held strong by the grace of Wi Tan Pree's training, but not by much else.

"I have to admit, the wild savagery of that tall Tan... barbarian, for he was a barbarian... it shines. It shines like a dying light of primitive innocence in your followers. But they don't follow you, do they? For they are not up with us. They are not enjoying the peace... that they could be. You're a man of peace, and I respect that. You respect the quiet. And because of this, you will not be killed. None of your men... will be killed— well, how's this. I'll spare, I'll spare any three— any two— of the people on that field. Just name it. Name two people, they will not be killed."

"The good Skin Toot, and the author of my tales. They stand upon that rock yonder, singing a proud rendition of the Lowroad Folk's 'I Would Have It Be of That Manner.' But all others, I do not care for. I thought I did, but they are quick to exile their captain, and slow to accept him back when he returns," spoke Dingle with remorse.

The wicked smile of Skulfing formed on that creature's face.

"So you are beginning to see what we in the Supremacy has always seen. Sympathy for the lesser breeds brought you down to a... pitiful place, Lord Dingle. As it did, for many in the Lobes. But now you see again. Mahogany is rich, mighty. Tan is tattered,

347

white is weak, pale is pain. These sayings, they do not come to be by chance. It's truth."

And for a moment, Dingle almost agreed with him. Perhaps Skin Toot and Ward Geit were the sole anomalies. Perhaps Paleskins and Tanfolk truly were of an inferior disposition. But then he remembered the hospitality of Wi Tan Pree and all his people in the heavenly place of Lidion, and connected it with a thing Skulfing had said.

"You spoke of Wi Tan Pree in the past tense," observed Dingle. "For what cause?"

"For the cause that I killed him," spoke Skulfing, bluntly. "Burned him, really. Took his skin. And the skin of all those in Lidion. The place is now an ash-filled mess, and I don't mean trees. I mean the ash that comes from fire and smoke."

And with that gruesome revelation, the hatred of Skulfing came back to Dingle. But he did not break away in anger, with harsh words. No, he retained his famous Dingleite composure, and sat among the leaders, even when a new King approached to take up their company. This was King Mothi of Hendik, and his coming would prove to be the final earth upon the already-nailed coffin of the Dingleite cause.

"Join us, Mothi!" clapped Url Skulfing as the Hendik King took a seat. "The sun will soon be setting, as will the opposition to my reign."

Few were the deeds memorable enough to be recorded after the dimming of day, but there is one that comes to mind. Windal of Klontug, setting his gaze fierce of Miekpanse— cowardly subordinate, blind follower of evil— began to ride hard for that frail old man in glistening armor. At the last moment, he turned away, giving Miekpanse Marcunnel an awful fright, so awful that he then called for a line of forty-four riders to

348

be assembled behind him. He then rallied a charge, and rode hard for the one who had given him that fright.

All of this was exactly to Windal's cunning. For Miekpanse Marcunnel now rode at the head of forty-four Skulfers, with a stupid little grin and eyes lifted fiendishly upward, intent on running down Windal. But Windal threw up his spear and once again rode directly at Miekpanse. Now the face of Miekpanse was familiar: one of fear, of his head trying to dive down into his neck, and looking back at the bluff where Skulfing sat, his eyes cried aloud for his master, wondering he had forsaken them! That he would sit and watch the battle from afar while his loyal men put all on the line for his glory— whatever Miekpanse's thoughts, they must have been short, for Windal was soon driving his spear right on his breastplate, and knocking him hard from the horse.

Windal veered away just in time, but for Miekpanse, nothing could be done. He landed hard on his back, and would have survived by grace of his armor. But now a stampede of forty-four horses rushed over him, having no notice of his fall, and not even his glistening plates of steel could save Miekpanse from that. The hoof-fall struck him at least twelve times, and each time his body was decimated and blood shot up and out. This was the end of Miekpanse Marcunnel, first subordinate to Lobe Minister Url Skulfing.

The retribution for this blow came promptly. Black-robed Mahogs of Hendik, fresh with many arrows, fired a sky of sharpened birds at Windal of Klontug. There was little chance that any could have escaped that volley without receiving at least a handful of stickings. The fatal blow struck our Windal through the back, with the arrowhead piercing just out of the nipple. He fell there upon the Titfall Dig, and I rushed down from my rock, halting the music for the time being.

He could speak but little by the time I had reached him, but I begged him to share final words, so that I could include them in the tale. He spoke as follows, though I had to make some guesses, for every other word was covered by blood:

"Woe, that I would spend my whole life searching for perfection! Only to find her, and find that she was not perfect at all. But adequate, oh my was she adequate! Adequate beyond all measure. Acceptable beyond glory. Yes, she would have done fine. She would have been... just fine."

And with that, he said no more.

I hurried to inform the girl Perfection what was said in the dying breath of Windal, and it served to rally in her a great and mighty fury. At length she cried into the heavens, and grabbed her sword, bent on charging down every last archer of Hendik. Curiously, as this perfectly adequate girl rode towards them, the archers of Hendik stood down. For there was one newly returned to the field, who had claimed this one as his own.

It was PARPINFOHZ, his fair Mahogany skin now charred and black. A body of burns could not hold him back from his fight. And now, as the sun lay down large on the rim of the hills, with his one unmelted eye he lifted a bow of pure devilry, that which had been seen near Lakewood, that which would launch an entire sword at his target. And so it was: the hideous candle PARPINFOHZ launched a blade at Perfection as she rode past, from the side, and that blade split her right in half, the upper half flying high off the horse. I will speak no more on this, for it was a grizzly thing to behold.

350

As the sun dipped lower and lower, and evening's dim grew large, we worried. No number of song could save us from the impending doom that now stared us down true, tangled among us in a valley of slain warmen. And as we looked up, we could see it clear enough: the one we once called Lord, seated next to our most heinous enemy. Piss Dingle himself, dining himself in laughter among Url Skulfing and Mothi of Hendik, with Fundrik Luber there as well. War meant nothing to these. It was just a folly to them; all the lives of us on the field were merely numbers against numerals, any consequence for them being null.

This angered Fi Fernin more than any of us, and so she boldly rushed up the hill on horseback. To the architects of war seated atop that bluff, it must have come out of nowhere. One moment they were safe in their jovial talk, the next there was a horse flying up to slay them. As I'm told, Fi Fernin brought her sword down upon Mothi of Hendik's clavicle, continuing straight down and then carving the meat out of him. She then merely gave harsh glances to the others, and then rode back down into the valley. Such a deed must certainly be eligible to be counted as boldest and most grand in all of this account.

When the sun had shone its last and the faint afterglow filled that cool Athragalian evening, there came the penultimate surprise of the night: another army stood now, rounding up and halting at the top of the green ridge, a line of silver-armored horsemen shining in splendor, and a golden-crowned king in their center.

"Endoth the Third!" shouted Jernander Skug, for he was a deep lover of all things Ilandian.

Yes indeed, Endoth III of Ilandia had made the long journey from Metrikall, crossing the Andiloth, riding along the woods of Piglandium, down the borders of the Sashites, over the Bloody Foreskins and finally on through Harlobe, Yonderlobe and Farlobe until he found them at last upon the Titfall Dig. The ride would have taken weeks.

And suddenly we all despaired. There was no hope of victory on our side now. Only a crushing defeat, for we dragged on with little strength, and now a fresh army — grander and more accomplished than any we had ever seen— now stood upon all ridges above. Their armor reflected the sun's final rays, their swords clean and shimmering silver, sharper than the tongue of Deng. And their King stood tall upon his horse, both arrayed in precious gems, jewels of the Royal Isilunian Line!

These then were far beyond any of them. Even the Skulfers— whom had contacted Endoth with pleas of aid— nearly got down on their knees to bow before the Ilandians, such was their apparent majesty. But as it happened, nothing happened.

Endoth III did not join the fight, nor did any of his proud Ilandian forces.

For in the mind of this high and mighty King, such a thing was not worth the effort. He took one look at the pitiful sight below— of peasant soldiers in tattered garb, tearing at each other's flesh before reverting to blunt blades— and he realized that he was above it. He had come all the way to Athragal to see for himself the plight of Skulfing's war, and now would do nothing but laugh at it.

And so the King of the Ilandians yawned and rode away, refusing to even sit for a moment with the architects of that miserable excuse for a war, let alone have a drink. He was a veteran of the Thirian War, for the sake of God! He had served most nobly in the Battle of Rockspyn Bending, and would thus not waste his time on the Battle of the— he cackled when he said it— Titfall Dig.

"Well, there goes the High King of Denderrin Othim," remarked Jernander Skug.

"What a prick," added Tibsmith.

"But I do believe this spells out better things for us," said Rick Cottontree, wiping the sweat from his brow and balls. "For now we will feel better about our position, knowing the immediate defeat we would have been in for. With Endoth riding away, the Skulfers ought to feel humiliated! And with that dent to their pride, we may yet take the night."

"Oakay, you can tell yourself that," said Victory, who was wholly unprepared for victory.

But miraculously, her name came true.

Miraculously, victory did come to the Dingleites in the valley of the Titfall Dig, in the deepest hour of dusk. For it just so happened that naked tribesmen of far and distant Garigal had just arrived.

You should remember the disparaging remark that Dingle had made to the King of the Forty Knights, days before the battle. He had counted only thirty-nine knights in his retinue, for that is truly how many were present. Had Dingle only known the whereabouts of the fortieth knight, he would have done well to fall on his face and kiss the shins of the King of the Forty Knights of the Dan.

For the fortieth knight had ridden far, far into the West, where they lived yet a King unknown to all others. King Di Panguish of the Garigs, he was called, and he lived at the foot of the Sestarions, in a village where all were nude, for none ever came to that far end of the world to tell them about clothes. But Di Panguish of the Garigs knew of the King of the Forty Knights, and they held an alliance of old, still remembered from the days before Grandest Lu broke the old dynasties and declared himself Overlord of Elaptirius.

In short, King Di Panguish rode in like thunder, he and all his naked warriors streaming down the slopes of the valley on enormous bison, the likes of which had been thought to have been extinct for an age.

Their weapons were crude, but their bodies were naked, and this terrified the finely-dressed ranks of the Skulfers. Skulfing's Deeplove and the archers of Hendik were molested by these pale skins, their rich bodies then forever marred with shame. And so Di Panguish and his Garigs feasted on the flesh of our foes, and we Dingleites called it a night, for it was one.

Chapter 16
The Battle of Lidion

Or the Second Battle of Lidion, as it should be called, if we are to pay due respect to ancient legend. For one should not forget the tales of Gildebrak and the children Adium and Luminthred that were entrusted to him, whether they be historical or fabricated for a greater cause. Either way, "Stirring of the Oak" is a phenomenal tale, and the grounds of Lidion forever immortalized by its telling, but it has no place here.

Here we track our heroes, fresh from victory in the hills of Athragal, south to the town of Fishcunning on word that Skulfing had fled to his newly taken refuge at Lidion, but not before they made a notable smoke in the midnight air near to the field of battle. Even the dark did not loom so terrible in those hills, for stars could be seen in all places, wrapping around from low up and down to low.

With great care, the surviving Dingleites together with the surviving Skulfers and those naked warriors of farflung Garigal carried the dead to resting spots arrayed equally distant to all their fallen brethren, and then set the bodies alight. For miles, the outstretched corpses lit up as candles, making that rolling land glow with song and memory.

By first light of dawn, the song had stopped and the fires were put out, but the bodies remained, to serve as feast for many happy birds and beast.

Along the southward road to Fishcunning we rode, along the Road of the Shady Ridge, which at one time stretched back behind them all the way to the rumored shore of Peace Haven. It was certainly a place several hundred years ago in the Age of Enchantment, but its condition now is in doubt; tidings never come from that far to the north and west. But I speak of far-off lands of age and ruin, when I should be focused on relaying the mark of age and ruin that we soon encountered ourselves.

After kissing our sweet dear horses until God's reuniting us, we purchased a handful of canoes from the merchants of Fishcunning, and set off down the River Craun. We had not far to go, for our first stop was a place which had recently grasped the interest of Deng Lu.

"I think we might be a navigational wrong," noted Jernander Skug, who sat in the same boat as Deng Lu. "If we ride the Craun up to Triagor, it is but a double hop to Lidion. Getting off the river where you suggest will cost at least a day."

"What is a day?" said Deng, as if he were about to continue, but was cut off by Jernander.

"Very much time when we're dealing with the Skulfers and their fortification of Lidion."

"What is a day when compared to all the years we've traveled!" Finished Deng Lu.

"I understand this, this 'forest of arches' is tempting to you Deng, but one single day may truly be the difference between an easy siege and a dire one." Many ears in the canoes now turned to hear the reasoning of Jernander. "If we do not use every minute to our advantage, it may mean that Skulfing has the time needed to arrive at Lidion before us, and to erect walls and station men behind them. Why not rush to take the place back before our enemies arrive?"

"Our enemies be there already!" noted Deng. "You remember what our hostages from the victorious battle said. A month ago, Lidion was taken by force, such a force that shook the rocks and broke through to the strongholds of Wi Tan Pree himself. We go to a likely anyhow... I would have the secret of my forefathers be known if my life should soon end."

Jernander continued to argue, on how all their enemies of war would be pursuing on their heels and amassing at Lidion to destroy them, but the deeds of Jernander were then few, while the Deeds of Deng were already growing famous. All throughout the Farlobe, folk spoke of his bold dealings at the Battle of the Titfall Dig, wherein he— with not a word— lit the famed assassin of Skulfing all ablaze. So the party followed the will of Deng Lu.

As this was all being decided, Piss Dingle, Skin Toot and I rowed ourselves in pity, far behind the rest of our group. We had become the outcasts, more so than before. I, for my part, had always been so, but now word of Dingle's sexist leanings took hold, and he was shunned, as well as Skin Toot for remaining loyal to his friend.

"I'm pretty sure I've been slandered," spoke Dingle to Toot and I in our pitiful rowboat.

"Every wicked word and fell glance that they bestow on you," noted Skin Toot, who was the weakest rower of we three, and so he mostly just relaxed, "Stems from one or two things. The harsh words that you spoke against the woman Dingleites—"

"They weren't harsh! I still they were well-called for, that we need to focus on defeating Skulfing before we worry about defeating the enigmatic shadow of... belittling women. I mean how do you even confront that?"

"It is not a thing that we rode to war for. Yet. But it is either that, or the regrettable tale of you stabbing a Countess."

"Again!" Cried Dingle. "I stabbed no one! It was a poke! And she was no Countess, she was a serving wench at the Deep Tickle who did the counting. That's why they called her a Countess."

"Oakay, might I add something?" asked I, this being one of the few times I was permitted to speak. "Perhaps phrases like 'serving wench' only serve to exemplify your ill feelings towards the finer sex."

"Well it's just because I'm getting so sick of this!" Defended Dingle. "You say one thing, your meaning is mistook— you tap a girl on the shoulder, when you think things are getting on with her, and it becomes a tale of me stabbing a Countess with a knife, a full inch down!"

"That does sound implausible," nodded Skin Toot.

"Because it never happened! Someone is out to get me. Deng Lu? Can we all agree this is Deng Lu?"

"He has coveted the permanent role of Leader of the Dingleites from the start," added I.

"Thank you, Ward Geit! Thank you."

"But we must make peace, for it appears the boats are landing."

"Whatever. Let's just keep sailing. They don't want us anyway."

"True, but the sigh of the Arch Forest is not a thing to be missed."

And so we landed on the beach, where paths and plaques of knowledge had been erected, but were now so overgrown they could hardly be made out. There was idle chatter among many, but such was my desire to see this place proper that I made a full announcement, the likes of which I never make:

"I believe here that our three remaining Unspoken friends have the right idea: to say nothing at all. For this place is a sacred place, arguably more so than Lidion which we seek to retake. For this place has much history —"

Here they all began with the chatter again, and walked up into the Forest of Arches with little reverence.

"It's fine," said Dingle. "Let them go... and we'll take up the silent rear."

And so we did. Slowly and deliberately, we admired each and every arch. From the first— being a broad stone arch, still relatively smooth compared to others which had lost their fine polish of prior centuries, and bearing welcome marks— to the last, which was here debatable as to what constituted an arch, but I said that it was two stumps protruding from the ground. Clearly they had been crafted by man, and surely many years back these stumps had risen and joined in the form of an arch— what other cause could they have had to have been laid there?

Of the numerous arches in that primeval wood (of which I counted four hundred, and then lost track), there can mostly be grouped into five types. There were the Wooden Arches, which had surely made up the whole of the woods back whenever man first decided to put arches in the place. None of these now survived, for they would have had to have been thousands of years old. But there had been various revivals of the Wooden Arches, perhaps in the same places where the originals had once stood. The Wooden Arches were now primarily marked with death and decay, where they remained standing. In many spots they were but pitiful remnants.

Arches of Rock were a step above those of wood— the rocks still survived, but many lay toppled about the ground, time having worn away the adhesives and sculptings that had once held them in place.

The Stone Arches still stood, and in greatest number. These were of a great craft, especially considering their making over two millennium past. Their making can be traced as early as the Starling

Alyin's bidding, who championed the cause when she and Mandle founded the Kingdom of Alyinen around the Year 931. Of all the arches of any kind, I should say that stone arches are certainly my favorite.

And of course there were Golden Arches, and Steel Arches, primarily the work of the Sixth Age, or that of Enchantment, somewhere between the Years 2600 and 2800, before all went back to creeping fingers of vine and earth. Now in 3336, out of every five arches, four were covered near complete with wrapping vines, leaves and branches, with tall mounds of earth often covering their lower reaches. Yes, the world had swallowed much of this old site, but it was all the better for it, in the mind of Skin Toot.

For while I was there lamenting the loss of the old world, Piss Dingle gave lamentations of his own: "I look up and all around, and can't help feeling this is a very awe-filled place. So filled with awe that we do not deserve to be part of its story. I believe there were once great things that happened here... perhaps the greatest of things. Or perhaps the greatest lies yet ahead, belonging to some far distant tale in the future.

"But wherever greatness lies, it is not here. It is not with us. Our story is not as remarkable as stories that have already come and gone, and cannot stand as anything at all compared to what will certainly come after. It makes me sad."

But Skin Toot reprimanded both of us amid the overgrown arcs of stone. "I've had enough of it! Not of the arches— keep them coming, they are glorious! But of you! You two sorrowsucks. You, feeling remorse for a time you never knew; you, feeling somehow that this incredible journey cannot compare to what came before or has not yet come to pass! But I say this is the perfect time in which to live.

"For us, no time could be better. We are seeing the Forest of Arches in their gloomiest, eeriest prime! Never before has the overwhelming might of the earth shown itself so strong in these parts! The earth has literally crawled up to consume these ancients marks of man! And in the future, I fear they will be swallowed and broken completely, so by then there would be nothing left to see.

"And you, Ward Geit, do you really think you would be happier living in that haughty age? Look at all they did. Everything they did, crafted to such precision! It must have been an age of much labor, and you know it must have been strict. I suspect that the Masters of that age drove folk like us insane, toiling and working more than any time before, with less time and monies to enjoy anything at all! So what if they could travel great distances and record their own voices, and faces. They must have been miserable; we live lives that are carefree, or at least can should we choose to. That is what I will choose to do. After we take back Lidion, of course.

"But who is to say our tale will not gain the same strokes of immortality as, say, Gildebrak, or DANE, or Fingerlobe, or Robber Jon, or Feenis of Donc? The finer tellings of those tales are all wiped away now, and all that's left are the written words. And that much we have! Thanks to you, Ward Geit, our story is now being told in written word, and that puts it on the exact same level as all the tales that have come before!"

And thus our spirits were uplifted. So we walked along, coming to a stacked steel tower of arches, where Marc Tempull climbed up the many steep tiers, bidden to do so by Deng Lu, who held sway over Marc.

"Bold work!" Applauded Deng Lu. Now within the top center arch, the book should be hidden within a drawer."

Upon seeing that Marc Tempull was not apt at finding drawers, Deng Lu grunted and began the climb himself, for fear that Marc Tempull would do something rash and damage the sacred manuscript he was searching for. Once atop the top center arch, Deng Lu cast Marc Tempull aside and began feeling the metal walls for ridges. At last he found a crease, and slid his dagger through a crusted-over crack. Cleaning the crack of a century's residue, Deng Lu then busted down to the opening to the hidden compartment, revealing a set of ancient manuscripts.

The dust of three hundred years puffed up, assaulting Deng's face, and he grew aggravated with these old books. He threw down the pages that he knew not to be those he was looking for, and at the bottom of the pile, found the object of his quest: the sole known surviving copy of the BOOK OF LU, save for that in the Rock Meadow of course.

Now, Deng Lu finding the BOOK OF LU is fine. It's worthy of mention. But it is not the highlight of this section. The highlight is that which Deng so carelessly cast down to earth: one of the other books held in the hidden compartment, which floated down to Piss Dingle as if on angels' wings, graceful as a book falling out of the sky can be.

Now, Piss Dingle and Skin Toot had always wanted to read a book freshly fallen from the sky, and this fallen book was one of the greatest fortunes that ever befell them. They had me read it to them, starting that night, and we were amazed at the treasure we had found.

"Bounds of Mediocrity and the Seeking of Highest Flame: An Account for The Sorry Days of Domis Foke, by Fokinthote Wardindade" was its name, although I took to calling it simply "The Lost Book of Domis Foke." For certainly it had been lost all these; I had never heard of it, no one I knew had ever heard of it.

But here it was, found again by chance! A tale that immediately grabbed us, one of an outcast, longing for the old glories of the world that had long been lost. Needless to say, I saw much of myself in those opening chapters, as did Dingle and Toot to a degree.

It washed a sense of calm and reassurance over me, the finding of that book. For often had I feared that my own works might be lost... that years spent following my Lord Dingle and good Skin Toot, recording their deeds... might have all been in vain should not a sufficient number of copies be made of my writings. But with this sole lost book now in my hands, I came to believe that the world never forgets. That which is meant to be told and retold, passed down through the centuries, will survive. Even if it be by the plain and simple fortune of one day being unexpectedly cast down through the air.

That night, we camped at the edge of the Forest of Arches, for four of our party had wandered off, and we did not endeavor to leave them behind. Here we at last heard from Carvin Cong, who had been weary for much of the journey, his age holding him back from speaking where he otherwise might have. But now he felt the true pull to speak, and share what he deemed to be wisdom only an elder could share, almost as if giving some sort of farewell address.

"Now if there's one thing we cannot do... it's go out looking for them. We have no idea which way they even started. The ways they could have gone are endless, so we have, to stay, here! They've got wits enough! Good ones for Paleskins at least. They'll find their way back, you'll see! And if they don't, we'll have to go on without."

And at the mention of Deng Lu, he muttered a few obscenities in line with racially derogative terms. For though he had been fighting years for the progressive cause of breed equality, still he had been ingrained from an early age that there were undesirable traits in Tanfolk, and especially Paleskins. Of course this is no excuse for his behavior, but realistically one could never expect one of his generation to fully change to suit the views of the young. Progress was made within the heart of Cong, but the core of his old mind could never be remolded completely, and this a thing that each new generation continuously fails to accept about those of the previous century.

And as it seemed that Carvin Cong moved slowly to his tent, so I moved over to Swilly, whom I had always envied for his ways with women, and, garnering the nerve, I asked him a question that had long been on my mind.

"Speak at length on the Skirmish of Bottom Lass Peat. I wish to all know."

But Swilly only laughed as he inhaled leaf of the Cudnut, "Ahhh... you will know none. For now. But I'll tell you someday. Someday you'll know."

And to serve in making me only more curious and enraged, he started singing the song that we all had known well from our days in his theatre troupe. All around the good fire, voices sprang up:

> It's the skirmish! The skirmish!
> Of Bottom Lass Peeeeeat.
> The skirmish! The skirmish!
> Of Bottom LASS Peeeeeeeat.

And then the Unspoken, this being the only thing they ever were to sing:

> It's the skirmish! The skirmish!
> Of Bottom Lass Peeeeeat.
> The skirmish! The skirmish!

Of Bottom LASS Peeeeeeeat.

And I cursed the heavens, for we had sung that song so many times but knew not of its meaning. None had ever been able to gather any knowledge on the topic of Bottom Lass Peat, despite Swilly writing an entire play with its title and song as trademarks. The only thing we knew is that the "skirmish" had cost him three fingers. I resolved to let the matter pass though, for the mood of the night was fair.

As we all sang the chorus to the Skirmish of Bottom Lass Peat, the Lady Victory approached my Lord Dingle at the edge of the camp. Still was he sitting quietly on the outskirts, none of his companions willing to converse freely with him. We reveled on, but Dingle sat alone.

"They do not despise you as you may think," reassured Victory, standing by his stump.

"But they believe me now to be a lesser man. One who holds an arrogant heart, when it is words and slander that have betrayed me."

"I know," whispered Victory, and took a deep breath, grabbing Dingle's hand.

"Don't you fricken grab my hand!" he said, snatching it back. "You're part of this. Tell them you were mistaken, that I hold no thoughts of superiority over women, or anyone, because I don't!"

"I've tried; their minds are made up."

"Mm. Perhaps there is some truth in the saying that the lighter breeds are stubborn in their thoughts.

"Are you regretting taking up your company with Tanfolk and Paleskins yet?" asked the Victory to Dingle, motioning over at the camp full of drunken companions.

"No, their fight is a noble one. Even if they spit in my face I would continue to support their strides towards justice."

365

"Why's that?"

"Well, I put myself in their place, which is very easy to do. I was born in
Westlobe, and had I stayed, I would've felt the same pain of prejudice that they have felt back home. I would be in want of those to fight for my equality, and so it's just as important that I assist in fighting for theirs."

"Equality? Do you think it will ever come to that?"

"It may. Every generation seems to draw closer. But there are ghosts from the elders, words that stick in the mind... grasping fingers that won't let go. Look no further than my cousin Cong. And it's these sickened souls that will go about killing and condemning, and once again the Tanfolk won't stand for it, and the Mahogs will not stand their lack of compliance with the evil system, and the fighting will break out again."

"Is that why you truly sit here in the shadows? Here on a quiet stump, away from the shouting and rallying?"

Piss Dingle took a breath of contemplation.

"I wish I could be part of a more simple tale. One where it felt so unmistakably right to fight for a winning cause. I long for a tale of good and evil, where forces of darkness creep out of the forest and we ride to meet them, for there is no question in that. There is no pondering what course of action to take, or whether to take action at all. There is only what is so clearly right: to ride out and destroy that which is bad. And we would shout our cries of victory into the moon and stars, and all would embrace in knowing what we did was good and pure.

But what of tonight? The people we go out to fight against are the fathers and mothers who reared us, their siblings and kin. Those who mean to slaughter us are none other than the friends of our grandparents. They have done wrong, and continue to do wrong, but what judgment do we give them? Do we slaughter our opponents now because they gave in to a system of thought that rang through their ears since childhood? On one hand we cannot go about burning their homes, for they will only gather in greater force and purpose. And yet if we do not destroy them outright, still they will rise up strong and carry us all to torturous fates."

He sighed again. "I wish very much that we were in a simpler tale."

And Victory sat down next to Dingle on the stump, and began to show an old fondness for him, that which she had not shown him in over two years. "The tales you wish for happened long ago, and that is why you crave them: they are removed from you, an escape from the world you were born to. They are far-off fantasy and crafted to be appealing, full of grand heroic images, the kind of thing that makes you feel alive. They are to be enjoyed, in easy times, for their consumption is one of life's pleasures.

"But tonight is not meant to be easy. Tonight is the beginning of another true fight, and true fights are not easy to consume. They are hard things, things that men were not made to enjoy. But it is the fight of your time, and your world. It is here and now, and it is all very real. You are not simply a figure of legend, to be told to children around good fires. You are a real man in a real time, who will very soon rise up to do real deeds... whether they come to be seen as heinous or pure."

And Dingle rose. "You speak right, Victory. Now go tell your friends I did not stab the Countess."

To the surprise of none, it was Deng Lu, Rick Cottontree and Tibsmith that had wandered off and gotten lost, much as they had done in Rock Meadow. Marc Tempull was with them too. And as they walked circles in the southernmost ring of the Arch Forest, they at last came across the Craun.

"Well, it'll all be spring legs from here!" exclaimed Marc Tempull. "Now all we've got to do is follow the river north."

But Rick and Deng were not listening. They had been at each other's throats again, as of old, for Deng's heroics on the field of battle had swayed Tibsmith more towards his side.

"You cannot be jealous of the High King," thundered Lu.

"You are High King of nothing!" Barked back Rick. "You have found a questionable book, of questionable origins— and even should it be fact, who is to say you are heir to that throne! Look to your own family! Surely there are others who would be farther up the line of succession than a young fool like you!"

"My family does not care for such things! If they do, they'll be purged, I assure you."

"And this is why you'd be a lousy lord!" And Rick Cottontree shoved Deng Lu. "You hold sway over so many men! Why can you not be satisfied with holding sway over little Marc Tempull! Why most you take Tibsmith too?! You don't even fancy her!"

And a battle of shoves and whinnies took hold, until Marc Tempull ran up with a simple "Where is Tibsmith?"

And Rick Cottontree fell to his knees, fearing that he had lost the great love of his life and was now stranded in another maze of creation, this time only with Deng and Marc.

But there was a rustling in the leaves, and all were hushed. Anticipation drew upon them... if it were her, Rick resolved to leap upon her with loads of kisses.

But it was not the fought-after Tibsmith. It was the old, grey-haired mild Raycist, Carvin Cong.

368

"What are you doing here?" Asked Cottontree.

"I've come to save your pitiful pale pouts. Come on, there should be four of you, no?"

"We've lost Tibsmith," pouted Marc Tempull.

"My lord, even when you're lost you can't stay together. What a waste it was that men ever lost their pigment."

"We will not follow you back to camp if you seek only to deal us insults," spoke Deng Lu, proud and rising up. "There is fair honor to be found in the Pale, just as in the Rich Mahogany. One day they might again call us the Proudish Pale."

"Well that, young Master Deng... is a day I hope to never see."

And Carvin Cong led them north with a smile, really not meaning to be facetious. Soon they were getting on quite well, and he had forgotten that he was in the company of those of a different breed, especially as he led the group and heard only their voices. They spoke of old tales, places along the road, goats and foxes, women.

Such a conversation as this was what the old Cong had been hoping for, last night when he snuck out of his tent. He had felt old for far too long, and on this day was resolved to feel young. He certainly did feel young as he found himself shedding the chains of prejudice that he had held on to for so many years, and felt as though the paths of life were opening up before him. He forget his age completely.

"Do you ever miss Wi Tan Pree?" asked Marc Tempull of Cong.

"Hmm..." he said to himself. "Didn't care much for him when he was with us in Derladan. But I suppose I didn't give myself a chance to get to know him. All I saw was colorless flesh. Thinking back on his words though... yes. I miss him. He seemed to be a lovely man."

369

"I think, if Pree had lived," continued Marc, getting sentimental, "We had not have any more trouble, at all. If he could have held on to Lidion, and met us in Athragal... we would've lost no men, and Skulfing today would have been vanquished."

"You speak of Wi Tan Pree as if he were Thala himself," laughed Deng.

And this talk of Wi Tan Pree went on, until— to the joy of all— they saw Tibsmith, sitting on a pebbly beach, her legs outstretched to meet the little waves.

"Why Tibsmith! We thought you had gone the way of the Garloly!" said Marc, and by the time that was said, Rick Cottontree had already run up for an embrace.

"How is it that you sit here so calm?"

And there was a voice from beyond, filling all their heads, as if by sorcery...

"She came across one she never hoped to see again."

They all knew that voice... it was luscious, tasty even, filled with life. The voice felt as a rush of smooth and sweet water, filling their mouths and running down their throats, but never were they wanting of breath.

The heads of Cong, Deng, Tempull, Tib and Rick all turned on their hinges, and there they saw him. There, atop a grey stone arch, stood the one they all dreamed of seeing again, but only in their dreams.

"It cannot be," spoke Marc Tempull in wonder.

"But it is, you see," spoke Pree, with his tender bottom words. For it was Wi Tan Pree, and he emerged in glorious fashion, splendidly descending down the stairs of the arch as light streamed along his robe through the trees.

They embraced long, for best of an hour. And Wi Tan Pree assured them that Skulfing's words were false. Lidion had not been taken... the attempt had been futile.

"The sacred realm of Lidion will never fall," smiled the wise Pree, and comforted all who were in need. "There is nothing to fear... not now, not ever. And so we will eat and drink, here in the woods, until nightfall. And then we will rest."

He was so effortlessly persuasive, that all five of them abided his words.

They sang songs of light and passing, of Thala and Thiru, the death of Alyin and the defeat of old Cromentor at the hands of Bastard Lu. Here, Deng Lu would have typically cried out in defiance, but such was the soothing voice of Wi Tan Pree that he merely nodded off in a daze, and fell asleep.

"I think I love you most passionately," confessed Marc Tempull, when he was the last one awake. "What do you say to that?"

"Hmm..." thought Wi Tan Pree, "Do you remember what was it you said when you laid eyes on me atop the arch?"

"It cannot be, is what I said."

"Yes, yes. 'Cannot be.' Indeed you were right. Indeed it could not be, for Wi Tan Pree is dead. For I, am... despite what you now believe..."

—He changed in an instant—

"Not Wi Tan Pree."

And it was Url Skulfing that sat in his place.

Now it so happened that the Dingleites moved west from the Forest of Arches, deciding that Deng Lu, Tibsmith, Rick Cottontree, Marc Tempull and now even Carvin Cong would not be returning to them in a timely manner. So they now consisted of Lord Cuomo at the fore, followed by Inder Sohn, Kang Joon, Dunly Moan, Swilly, Jernander Skug, Fi Fernin, Lady Victory, three Unspoken, Ward Geit Fung, Piss Dingle and Skin Toot.

371

A final obstacle of natural standing assaulted them shortly after passing by the westernmost arch, this being a great wall of earth and granite. The wall was tall, but not so tall as to completely rule out its climbing. The jagged quality of the granite would even provide outcroppings for hams and pies, but many were wary of making such a risky climb, especially when there appeared to be a tunnel just a mile down.

"Oakay, there's something you guys should know, so I'm just gonna come out say it," spoke the Lord Cuomo, proud even when admitting of shortcomings, "I have a terrible fear of tunnels, so much so that I'd rather climb half a mile than just walk on through. See you on the other side."

And with that, he mounted a granite bulge at the base of the rising hill, and began to climb with skill.

"He knows he's at least ten times more likely to kill himself making an unnecessary climb than by walking through a tunnel, right?" asked Jernander of us, not seeing the logic in Cuomo's choice.

"For some, the deep feelings of the core will always outweigh that of logic," pointed out I. "If he feels more at peace making a treacherous climb then walking under hill, then let us let him and not mock his choosing."

"I'll mock his choosing til the sun grows cock," laughed Jernander. "Because we're short of men the way it is. We don't need one falling to his death when there's a tunnel right here."

"I think it's fine thing to be suspect of tunnels," said Piss Dingle, "If not straight-up fearful. It's unnatural for men to walk through mountains. We're not moles."

Skin Toot was quick to agree. "The toil taken to forge a tunnel is far beyond that of a single man, and therefore brings to mind dark times when industry crushed the spirits of all. The entire concept of a path through unpassable reaches smells of evil, and marks the craft of devilry."

"Guys. It's a tunnel. Let us use it," reiterated Jernander.

"Nope, no— I'm terrified of tunnels too," admitted Dunly Moan.

"But you're not scared of scaling a ninety-foot granite wall?"

"Well, I'm equally frightened of that," went Dunly, "So I'm just gonna go around. That's all there is to it. Just gonna walk around the hill. Bet I'll beat at least half of you to the other side too."

And so the Dingleites were once again sundered for bad reasons, for it was Jernander who was then too stubborn to respect Dunly's fear, and bade them all to go into the tunnel. Truth be told, Jernander had the opposite of fear for tunnels; he liked them a bit too much. So as he approached the mouth of this tunnel, he became bubbly and joyous.

But there were foes guarding the mouth of the tunnel, and as soon as we realized this, we had all wished we had either made the climb, or simply walked around the hill, as Moan had done. But it was now too late for that, for Leg Randy and a squadron of Skulfing's Deeplove fell upon us, binding our arms, legs, and chins to our bellies. What made the matter truly worse is that these members of the Deeplove were dressed as actual goblins. They had been scary enough without masks and costumes of mangled flesh.

"Ah, little boy Dingle," spoke Leg Randy, fiendishly. "You're a little boy. You're a boy, Dingle. And once again I find you in my legs. I will show to all that you're a boy, and a little boy truly. All at Lidion will find you humorous, for I have been instructed to put new forms of torture to you there!"

"No! You listen to me, Leg!" countered Dingle, as the goblin-dressed Deeplove wrapped cords again and again around the beams which forced his chin down to his belly.

Leg Randy let out a huff, and then corrected him: "You may not call me Leg, for that is my name. Leg Randy, or nothing at all."

"Then I will call you nothing at all! For I never found you deserving of the name you hold. Randy? Be you of sound mind? Such a name is far above your worthiness. Do you realize the outrage you inspire across all the world?"

"Go on."

"You ruin the name Randy! Such a strong and awesome name, carried on by proud men before! Do not pull the name along with you into a resting place of rot."

And by all accounts, none present seriously thought that this method of reasoning— insulting one's name, or rather saying they do not deserve their name— would have any good effect. We all thought that Dingle was making a serious wrong, that this would only serve to provoke and trigger Leg Randy, and that our torments would soon grow worse and worse. But in a happy strike of chance, Leg Randy began to wet, and then flow tears, culminating with the deep weeping. Intertwined with this process were the following words:

"So you have said that which I've always suspected, but none in these camps would ever dare say. My name is wrong."

Here he unsheathed his mighty scimitar, and we all bit our tongues in worry and doubt. Leg Randy continued:

"And I do not wish to go on, tainting the memory of better men. I would not choose to soil the name, for I know it is not my name alone— that other Randys in the world will not wish to be associated with the evils I have

374

done. Let the name Leg, then, stand in for my heinous deeds, and let me leave them all behind."

And to everyone's surprise, Leg Randy cut off his own leg, without a single breath of hesitation or drug to ease the pain, and let that leg fall to the ground. The freshly one-legged man then kicked his horse with the only leg he had left, and as he came riding up to Dingle finished his speech—

"I will take with me the Randy, for now that is all I am, and let it be told that with that singular name of glory I changed my course in the final hours of life!"

And there were legs raised by all in the presence of Dingle's Company then, to celebrate the monumentous occasion of Leg Randy— one so formerly loyal to the cause of Skulfing that one didn't think a change in him could ever be— casting his Leg and his leg, to become only Randy, and randy for a brighter cause.

Randy led the Dingleites through the tunnel, which rose up and let out upon a flat stretch of prairie. We walked until we came to a small stone grove surrounded by a few trees; surely such a place had been designed as a singular place to launch an attack in old days, for all around there was nothing but grass until one came to the boulders and tiers of Lidion. The goblin-dressed freaks of Skulfing's Deeplove had all fled, and this was disconcerting, for they now ran straight for Lidion, and would surely raise the alarm against us.

"It is fine, those that hold Lidion number no more than sixty."

A sobering silence washed over us.

"That's not fine!" spoke Jernander with volume. "We're twelve! And now you have one leg."

"Yeah, really," yawned Skin Toot, "You could've made your redemption speech and set us free without chopping off your leg. We still could've just called you Randy regardless."

"I think you will find we are yet thirteen," smiled Randy, as he motioned his head up at the granite hill, which Lord Cuomo of Costerwall now strode down.

"Great," said Jernander, feeling all the powers of the sarcastic voice on that day, "The glorified messenger counts for at least fifty soldiers, wouldn't ya say?"

"He is certainly worth nine of theirs, perhaps more," nodded Randy, quite serious.

And as the Lord of Costerwall approached, we told to him the story of Randy's Redemption, and of his casting of the Leg from his name and body.

Cuomo didn't care much for the tale, but instead handed Piss Dingle his own sword, one of shimmering steel and long blade, that he might use to cut down the Skulfers who stood guard over Lidion. For now the time of our assault was drawing dangerously near; none of us wished to stretch our tales of war past that day; if we must die, then we resolved to die soon.

"Is this an arrow?" asked Dingle, who was still confused as to what constituted an arrow after the scarring ambush at Lakewood True.

"It's actually a sword," replied Lord Cuomo. "Are you unfamiliar with this very basic type of weapon?"

"He's never used one," chimed in Toot.

"Never used a sword?"

"It's true," admitted Dingle, "I think it would be best if I were to go on using daggers, and you the sword."

"But that's where you're wrong," argued the Lord of Costerwall. "You are naive. So I will always counter what you believe to be best."

And by this logic, which turned out not to be entirely sound, Lord Cuomo convinced Dingle to take up the sword, while he in turn took Dingle's daggers, for he had always coveted them, and the weapons would thus be switched in the hands of their typical bearers for their siege upon Lidion.

But there is one thing more that occurred before the siege: scared faces, and flailing arms, running forth towards our stone grove on the prairie.

"It's Tibsmith," squinted Fi Fernin, as she crushed Jernander's hand in a tight grip, as she always did to warm her hands for battle. "And Cottontree and Marc. But no Deng Lu... nor elder Cong."

The trio slid into our stone grove, their bodies quite crushed with exhaustion, their breath too weak to gasp. Their faces were pale beyond nature.

"I believe they have seen a most terrible sight..." said I, feeling the full extent of their plight without knowing the specifics.

"That's the look I had on my face when Cong showed me his dark parts," said Dingle quietly, at last releasing a haunting memory he had kept tucked away for many long years.

But eventually the truth was told. Rick Cottontree told of what passed:

"It was Wi Tan Pree! Standing tall upon the arch... a blazing figure against an awesome backdrop. He gave us words of comfort, and lured us to sleep... singing softly, and sweetly..."

"I don't like where this is headed, considering the way you came in dread," whispered Cuomo.

"I'm scared," said Skin.

"And you should be. For it was Skulfing!"

"No!" erupted many of us. "No— Gah! What! Ahh! Oh my— deep and horrible goodness! You cannot speak truth! The devil's loin! Save us from all damnation!"

Such were the cries that I recall hearing there in our small stone grove in the center of the prairie, mingled with incomprehensible, disgraceful gutturals. At last, Cottontree was allowed to finish the tale:

"When at last he revealed himself, for he wore the skin of Wi Tan Pree, he cast off that skin with a sudden blast, and we all made the woods tremble with the high pitches of our lungs. We ran as fast as we could, but for all his boasting, speed was apparently not passed down through the royal line of Lu. Deng took up the rear— by quite a surprising distance if I should say— and so Skulfing pounced down upon him, as he leapt through the air as if through water.

Looking back for the briefest of glances, I saw the Minister Skulfing feasting hard on Deng Lu's leg, and the teeth sounded like grinding razors. Like... more grinding saws than I have ever before heard put together. I saw flesh fly off the bone."

Tibsmith winced.

"To the great shock and dismay of everyone, I should say that we will not be seeing Deng Lu again," and as he looked away, Rick Cottontree made a little smirk and grin to himself.

"But you've left out the best of parts!" pointed Marc Tempull. "For a long branch was then thrust into the backside of Skulfing's neck; this is further proof that he's not of our race, for if he had been any sort of Passian, such a blow would have debilitated him. But as it was, he only turned away from Deng, to see the maker of the blow: dear old Carvin Cong... whose memory would now be plastered in goodness if not for the all-too-recent revelation that he had shown Dingle... dark parts, in the past?"

"Ah, forget I said that, that was— that was nothing," coughed Dingle under his breath. "That never happened."

"Anyway, Carvin Cong saved us all! Perhaps. For Skulfing then put his whole terrifying body towards him, and as we sprinted down the path, the last thing we saw were his terrible shoulder pads rising up, revealing something that looked heinous, but we dared not stay around to scrutinize what it might have been. With any luck, we will never know."

"So Cong and Lu have fallen too," lamented Kang Joon, putting his hat to his chest. "And Dunly Moan must have gotten lost walking around that hill. May Thala watch over us, as we sixteen men now try to take a place guarded by sixty. We're not done yet."

Once all plans of the siege were made and settled, we sent out our first man past the trees, into the great naked sweep of the prairie. All had unanimously decided that Marc Tempull should be the one to take these bold steps into potentially dangerous territory, for he was the least skilled at fighting among them, and the role of this first walker was foremost to see if the open prairie was safe for such a charge. Turns out, it was not, and sending out Marc Tempull to perform such an errand was a death sentence.

As soon as his reached the middle ground between the boulders of lower Lidion and the trees where the Dingleites hid, alone on that wide open expanse, Marc Tempull was blasted with arrows from afar. Lord Cuomo winced as the brave sacrifice of a man fell with an easy plop, and at that point they had come to know the wide open expanse was not welcome of their approach.

Then did arrive the further tossing of ideas, as to how they might go about crossing the dreaded expanse without coming to the same dark end as Marc Tempull.

"We might go retrieve the ancient trebuchet from yonder town of Sesterball," offered Skin Toot, "and with that we may fling ourselves over the sharp boulders, and destroy what villains we find there by way of both surprise and falling upon them from out of the sky."

Skin Toot's idea was met with the nine cheers.

But "I don't think you're being a lamb of truth," objected Lord Cuomo. "There is a reason Passians have never been thrown by a trebuchet in place of stones. And it is because Passian bodies will not withstand being flung from a trebuchet—"

"You yourself have just said that Passians have never been flung from a trebuchet, and therefore you can't know— not for certain— what the outcome will be."

Here Lord Cuomo nearly choked on his own scoff. "I know that our bones are not strong as stone! Even rocks will crumble and crack when thrown such a great distance. You cannot advise this to these men. Even if the town of Sesterball should be generous to lend their trebuchet, it would all be in vain! More suicidal than the brave march of Marc Tempull we all just so horrifically witnessed."

But Skin Toot had a rebuttal: "We will dress those to be flung in great suits of armor, and I will be among them to show my true faith in this endeavor."

"Well if we had this armor that you assume we have, why wouldn't we just walk forth in the armor?" asked Cuomo. "Why wouldn't we have put it on Marc Tempull before sending him out to his death??"

"Then we will pad the Flung with many, many layers of cloth."

"Won't be enough."

"Many, many, many layers of cloth."

"Won't be enough, Skin."

"How many 'many' would you advise, Lord Cuo?"

"Don't call me Cuo."

And so the bickers raged, until so quietly did Jernander Skug and Fi Fernin sneak away and return

380

with the ancient trebuchet of Sesterball, that none had noticed their absence.

"Fine," renounced Lord Cuomo, "We've got a trebuchet. But I swear Skin Toot, if we lose anymore men on account of this follycock scheme, I'll have your skin."

"Then I would just be Toot," lamented Skin Toot.

But there was no time for lamenting. The scheme was put in motion, and the first volunteer was dressed in much cloth. Of course it was Swilly, never to be outdone in brave and sexy deeds. This would merely be another chapter in his lifelong list of feats and endeavors, which made a meal of him to forty women at any given time.

But here it all ended, for Swilly was flung, and then lay still on the grass, most likely a great deal of many vital bones broken. We called out to him, but heard nothing but a great moan, which only grew louder as Skulfers crept out from Lidion, and set their torches down on Swilly's body. I cursed them, for now I would never know any of the details surrounding the Skirmish of Bottom Lass Peat, and that enigmatic event would pass out of all knowledge.

We did not let the Death of Swilly deter us from trying the same thing again. This time, three volunteers were dressed in many, many more cloths, then many more and many more on top of that, and bound all up in strong rope. The three to make the Fling this time were Skin Toot, Kang Joon, and Randy, for without his second leg, he wouldn't be much good for the charging.

We can only imagine how the Skulfers on the other side of Lidion's boulders passed the time as this ambitious trebuchet plan was carried out, but it is likely they had assumed the Dingleites had gone home and were no longer paying much attention to their watch, for when the trebuchet launched and sent Skin Toot soaring across the plain and over the boulders, the few Skulfers stationed there were very surprised indeed.

The Fling set Skin Toot out of his wits a great deal; already from his point of launch and as he flew across the sky, the winds and speeds put his mind into a state of ethereal distance. The harsh landing had brought him abruptly back to his duty, but his body was so badly cracked upon impact that he wished to lie in place for the span of twenty lives. But as the four Skulfers stationed as boulder guards turned with mouths of wicked intent, dropping their bows and picking up swords, Skin Toot felt a sense of urgency.

His legs roared up a burning pain as he attempted to stand, and within moments he would have been slashed to the ground by the boulder guards if it were not for the fortune of the Second Fling. This Second Fling hurled Kang Joon to the ground, and it came to shake the boulder guards even more, for they now looked to the sky in horror, as if at any moment it might again open up in a fierce downpour of men. The Third Fling was not to come for another fifteen seconds, but these moments of fear were enough for Skin Toot to recognize his opportunity, and so like the awesome heroes before him— Fingerlobe, Domis Foke, Old King Wilderfrant and the like— he put aside all notions of pain and charged forth with his own little blade.

From Kang Joon Skin Toot would receive no further help: Kang Joon would never again stand. The force of the Fling had broken him. Indeed, his distracting had been just the thing that was needed to give Skin Toot a momentary advantage over the boulder guards, but now things looked quite grim. Skin Toot could not face these four men all by his lonesome, even with all the padding and elements of soup rise in the world. It would be up to the Third Fling then—

And alas his fears were in vain! For then did Randy fall from the sky with such a glorious thud that he took down one Skulfer full to the ground, killing him instantly, and knocking over one closeby with his outstretched falling leg. Skin Toot quickly stuck his sword down into the neck of this fallen Skulfer, and that left only two who had been stationed at those boulders. Two against two, Skin Toot and Randy prevailed by means of their great padding, girth and vigor.

"Skin! The signal!" shouted Randy of the One Good Leg.

And then did Skin Toot scream a broad-pitched cry into the air, for this is what he was to do upon clearing out the archers, so that Lord Cuomo and Piss Dingle would know it was safe to run out across the field.

Oh what a happy day it would have been if those four archers stationed at the boulders had been the only foes to overcome in that sacred place called Lidion. But very shortly were Skin Toot and Randy to realize that the Bowels of Lidion were now being shot up, raging right for them, alerted to their presence by the obvious sound of Toot's cry.

Soon Skulfers and members of the Deeplove were swarming about Randy and Skin, and the fallen Kang Joon as well. One especially abhorrent Skulfer walked up to the fallen Joon to finish him.

"We're not done—" started Kang, but he was unable to even complete his famous phrase, for the abhorrent Skulfer's boot smashed his fallen face in whole.

But then came the sound of hope from beyond the rocks: the thundering of sweaty cries, flowing deep and good through the windy field, now visible on the horizon. Leading Skulfers frantically shouted out orders, and a line of infantry was assembled behind the rocks.

The line of soldiers numbered forty; the oncoming Dingleites numbered only twelve.

'Twas Lord Cuomo leading the charge, followed swiftly by Piss Dingle and myself, the Lady Victory and Fi Fernin, Inder Sohn and Jernander Skug, Rick Cottontree and Tibsmith, with three nameless Unspoken warriors taking up the rear. Perhaps they had names, but they never told us, for they were unspoken. Anyway they shortly died, for it is the place of the nameless to die first in all great battles wherein they find themselves outnumbered.

The Battle of Lidion was a great affair of true and right men showing their strength to be three times that of the wicked Skulfers, who were by that time coming to know they were wicked in their own hearts, and this can be used to explain the unexpected circumstances of the fight.

For even though the Skulfers number forty, they were brushed aside within minutes by the Dingleites who numbered twelve (fourteen if Skin Toot and Randy are counted, but they by all accounts were wasted after their Flings from the trebuchet). The Dingleites fought hard with the sense of obligation that they were fighting not just for themselves, but for the justice of all the Lobes, and for the avenging of Wi Tan Pree.

The Skulfers, on the other hand, became discouraged, having known for some time that they were on the side of a losing evil cause, and now seeing that their rivals held such fury and passion, they resigned to protect their post at Lidion with as little effort as possible. Thus the twelve was mightier than the forty, and after five minutes of fight, all of the named Dingleites remained afoot while did only fifteen of the armed Skulfers.

The Skulfers called for a retreat, and ran swift up the curving Stairwell of Joy, stone steps upon the heaps of Redrock, which led up to the top of Lidion.

"Dingle! Follow them! Up the stairs! Let none escape!" yelled Cuomo, as he laid into his opponents— for he still held Dingle's daggers, while Dingle in turn held Cuomo's sword.

And with that famous sword, Dingle leapt up the Stairwell, knocking down Skulfers as they now flooded down the stairs. It is true Dingle was not skilled with Lord Cuomo's sword, and while he appeared to knock the Skulfers down, it was only by their treachery that they fell. For the Skulfers were only feigning pain, and would then— rolled over upon the steps— reach out their arms to grab Dingle by his legs, and pull him down upon the stones, delivering true pain unto him.

A group of three Skulfers then pummeled Piss Dingle with their fists upon the Stairwell of Joy, and they enjoyed it thoroughly. Until, that is, Lord Cuomo ran forth upon the top of the Redrock, positioning himself firm at the top of the stairwell. He aimed Dingle's daggers, and one by one threw them down upon the Skulfers who pummeled him.

One by one, the daggers missed their mark. And so the Skulfers looked up, and seeing that Cuomo of Costerwall had no more daggers, they looked back down and continued beating all earthly fluid out of Piss Dingle.

Cuomo could no longer help. Victory, Fi Fernin, Rick Cottontree and Tibsmith had all pursued the fleeing Skulfers along the lower trail which led to the Water's Fall of the Harl; Inder Sohn and Jernander Skug were engaged with Skulfers far along the ledge of the Redrock. It was then the place of Skin Toot, Randy and myself to charge up the Stairwell of Joy, where halfway up the body of our lord Piss Dingle was being flattened out by the grimy hands of dirty men.

Skin Toot was the bravest of us, charging up the stairs fast, though his jaunt was awkward with the padding of cloth he still held around his bod from the Fling. All the grimy Skulfer had to do was to hold out a hand and push him over, and Skin Toot came rolling back down the stairs; crutch-wielding Randy and I had to jump over his tumble as we ourselves leapt up to the aid of Dingle.

There was a clashing of swords, we against the higher-held blades of the Skulfers who stood some steps above us. Randy was wise and struck at the Skulfers' heels and ankles, bringing one to the ground and chopping one's foot clean off.

I was not so wise, and I was regretfully sliced across the neck. I then sustained cuts across the waist and punctures in the chest, followed by or preceded by a straight stab through the middle of the face. This, needless to say, killed me.

I do not wish to distract the reader from this glorious climax that I am now in the middle of, but to avoid further confusion I must lend this quick aside. Yes, I am your author. Yes, I have written all that you have read, and all that you will continue to read, in this manuscript.

It is true that I am Ward Geit Fung; it is also true I am not Ward Geit Fung.

For in the time leading up to the Battle of Lidion, while Lord Cuomo and Skin Toot wrestled out the details of the Trebuchet Scheme, I was led aside by Ward Geit Fung, who at that time I was not. For at that time I was Jernander Skug, Skug being pronounced in the same fashion as "great lewd rabbit." And it was then that Ward

Geit Fung informed me— should the unfortunate incident arise that he be killed in battle, or brought to captivity or some other horrible fate— that I should assume his name, that I should absorb his person entirely, and thus become Ward Geit Fung.

I continued to be Jernander Skug for the first portion of the battle, but as I battled with Skulfers on the ledge of the Redrock, I saw with that encompassing view the moments when Ward Geit was struck down upon the Staircase of Joy. And when he had breathed his last, his spirit fled that pale white body, and came directly into mine, so that it was in a way Jernander Skug that died, and Wart Geit Fung, who lived.

(I was heavily coached on how to write the proceeding passages, so while I have relayed what I swore to relay, let me— Jernander Skug— briefly say, that yes, Ward Geit Fung is dead, I am Jernander Skug, Jernander Skug is alive, but he has sworn to now be Wart Geit Fung until Jernander Skug himself finds himself dead. Long live Ward Geit.)

We hasten back now to the battle. Aided by the clever strikes of Randy, Dingle found the will to rise, and give the grimy Skulfer a few fast punches of his own. Bringing him to the ground then, he and Randy held him there with knees in his back, and smashed his head against the steps until there ceased to be a head.

Lord Cuomo applauded as he descended the stairs, but Piss Dingle was in no mood for his claps. "What the cosh! Don't you know how to throw a dagger?"

And Cuomo apologized. "It looks as though you were perhaps right, Dingle. You should have held your daggers while I my sword—"

"'Perhaps right' my ass. I don't know how to use a sword, you can't use daggers. Switching weapons was your idea. We will now forever be enemies, and the fault is yours."

"Are you sure you wish to make me your enemy when you might at least use my aid for the remainder of the day? Lidion is not yet won. I see Skulfers down yonder up the Rise, engaged with Inder and Jernander. Down below, Rick and the women pursue their number to the Falls of Harl."

"Don't try and be smart with me, Lord of Coster-fall. You know damn well I'm not going to declare you an enemy until the present battle is won; why would you even waste time in your musings."

But this bitter talk between Dingle and Cuomo was cut short as Randy tapped them both on their shoulders, averting their attention to the Redrock ledge in the distance, where Inder Sohn dueled with a Skulfer called Grauhnshuh, awfully close to the edge. A forty-foot fall lay two strides away from them both, and as the swords clashed and steps were taken, Inder Sohn found one shoe bracing the very end of the ledge.

"You have him!" yelled Lord Cuomo, providing the support he felt Inder Sohn to be in dire need of.

"You think your screams are gonna help him?" asked Dingle. "Just let the dude concentrate."

"I'm just providing the means for him to rally."

"Yeah? You know what else would've rallied us all? A band."

Cuomo scowled at Dingle, looking away from yonder duel for only a moment. When he looked back, Inder Sohn was visible not.

"Where did he go?!" yelled the Lord of Costerwall.

"That Grauhnshuh guy cast him off the rocks," said someone else.

And Lord Cuomo gnashed his teeth together, finding a moment's resolve, snatching his sword away

from Dingle, and racing towards the Skulfer
Grauhnshuh.

With livid rage did Lord Cuomo engage, not
bringing to mind that he now stood in the exact position
that Inder Sohn had been in mere moments before,
which had caused him to be cast off the ledge to his
doom. Now the brave Lord of Costerwall stood on the
same ground, steps away from the infamous cliff, fencing
with Grauhnshuh the Skulfer.

Skin Toot saw the potential for devastation, and
hurried on to Cuomo's aid. Dingle tried to stop him—
"He's a broad wank, that lord!" he said, for one too many
arguments had erupted between them. But Toot was
ever eager to display his prowess, and knew that thrilling
rewards would lie in wait should he save Lord Cuomo
from a dark end.

Toot's hurry was in vain. For Grauhnshuh soon
stepped forward with broad steps, forcing Cuomo
backwards off the ledge, in the same manner as Inder
Sohn before, and with a yelp of soaring pitch that Lord
fell.

But it was not to be a dark end.

Rather, it was a dark mid, for yes Cuomo fell, and
landed hard upon his back on the stone path below, but
there was life in his eyes. He had fallen forty strides and
lived, landing right next to his friend Inder, who had so
clearly died.

Moments later, Victory, Fi Fernin, Cottontree and
Tibsmith came rumbling forth on the trail, leaping over
the fallen Lord— lamenting over the corpse of Inder—
and pursued by a line of ravenous Skulfers. Up the
Stairwell of Joy they raced, reaching the top of the rise
just in time to see Grauhnshuh throw Skin Toot down
into one of the narrow crevices between the Redrocks.

Dingle hid under a mass of leaves, waiting for all to
pass, and then biding his time, he followed them down

the path atop the Redrock. With wisping sounds he hopped across the crevices broken between the Redrock, and with one hop was startled to hear the voice of his friend from below.

"Dingle!" laughed his lifetime companion from his unfortunate spot below. "I have escaped death for a time, but my brave loins brought me here, where I can no longer feel them. Indeed this is a fate worse than death. To be trapped like this, in a narrow crack between monumental stone, unable to move my limbs. Woe to the Crack of Doom! If you should be able to fish me out, kindly do so. If not, please lend me a dagger to the neck, and let this nightsweat be over with. I have made my peace."

"Nah," said Dingle. "I'm not gonna kill ya. But it'll be a minute. Just hang down there."

"Dingle I demand you! Rescue me now or end me! I will gladly take the darkest end over this rock-hard black middle!"

But Dingle was already gone, for there was no way he alone could have rescued Skin Toot from that crevice — he was too far deep. But he would not so easily murder his friend, for perhaps his other companions might lend some support. And thus it was that Dingle strode cautiously to the single-foot path that wound around the Great Boulder of Peace, wrapping around to the Falls of Harl, seen then through low-hanging leaves.

The Dingleites and the Skulfers fought there in the shallows of the Dan, just before the fall, and the company threw up the Nine Cheers in terrifying vigor, which sent the Skulfers tearing off for the far bank.

The obnoxiously loud Dingleites pursued their foes into the green, where Lady Victory and Fi Fernin, in a joint effort, tore the skin from his neck and strangled his bare throat tight with hair ripped from his head. Victory then stood with her boot on his neck, to stand watching him die as she sprinkled modest bits of glass down onto his eyes. Fi Fernin, meanwhile, ran back to the Redstone ledges, and it was by her flexibly good-looking graces and agile diving skills that Skin Toot was grabbed nimbly out of his rock chasm.

In the misty Danwater, then, it was only Tibsmith and Cottontree that remained, lusty and wet amidst the shin-high waters of the Dan. Tibsmith looked up into Cottontree's eyes, with a smile as to say many things, but to most clearly say that the chance of a dark end was behind them. There would be no dark ends now— only ends creamy and warm, soft and fleshy to the touch.

"Well, I think you've waited long enough for this," smiled Tibsmith, looking down at the innocent face of Cottontree.

"You know I have," sighed Rick. "How long have you known? Known that you were all I desired, in all this world, and that had it not been for you, I would never followed Dingle out of Fyninfer?"

"I have always known," whispered Tibsmith sensually. "Your heart is an open leaf. And I finger it now, feeling all the colors... all the edges... all the life."

As Cottontree puts his hands around the waist of dear Tibsmith, he caught a glimpse of Dingle in the leaves. Our friend Piss only grinned and put up the mangled four-finger salute that is to say, "I will not interrupt this warm and creamy end."

And it seemed as though all the spirits of the wind were breaking out in joyous merriment, with smiles stretching miles, and hearts full with the contentment of all, as Rick Cottontree finally stood before the glorious reward of his valor, and the end of his quest.

Then Url Skulfing leapt up over the forty-stride waterfall, in a single bound, further adding to the suspicion that this man was really never a man at all. In a single moment, Rick Cottontree went from feeling completely secure in all the promises of a happy life— as though he had conquered all conflict in existence— to feeling as though all the world was nothing but a never-ending terror. In that very same moment, the dread Skulfing landed in front of him with a harsh displacement of water, which cast Tibsmith to the side. She hit the water forcefully, and then lay under the shallows for several sickening moments. Of course Rick Cottontree would have turned to lift her up from the waters of the Dan, but...

Piss Dingle gagged. From his position behind the leaves he saw the thing that no man had ever lived to report. The broad violet shoulder pads rose up, revealing a thing altogether sinister and unexpected, but most of all gross.

There were tape worms.

Monstrous tape worms, the length of a goat, all curled up now rising up straight! With holes all across, which spat out little sharp tongues and creeping drowned eyes, all then turning towards the tips of these Dreadworms, where sharp spear-like teeth slowly extruded out of the tight twisting red gums. The sound was of a dying gulp, of a disgusting old man choking on his own blood, or trying to spit out loads of thick sliming maggots, the kind that are longer than the throat the seek to escape.

And so, the eight tape worms attached to Skulfing rose up, up from the broad broad shoulders that bore them, and down, down unto the face of Rick Cottontree.

Bloodlashing screams of pain and anguish, for Cottontree had in a single moment gone from master of all the world, to he who was now losing everything. Losing the flesh from his face, losing the battle at hand,

392

losing the blood in his skull, losing Tibsmith, losing the form of his bod, as the Dreadworms worked quick with their teeth.

To allow such a scene of horror to play out unimpeded would have been a right damn sin, and so Piss Dingle sloshed on in a rush, stomping into the waters of the Dan, throwing daggers at his greatest foe; he had by now decided resolutely that Url Skulfing was not a "cool guy."

Quickly, he lifted Tibsmith up out of the waters and removed her, throwing her down upon the sands of the bank. This rescue lent Dingle a single moment to clench his eyes, take a breath, and then run towards this villain supreme, to engage in what would be the defining fight of his life.

The Four Accounts of the Climax

Now, throughout this true telling, I have tried most thoroughly to take the various tales and evidence I have seen with my own eyes to form one singular narrative. Here, however, the paths must diverge, for there are four separate versions of the climactic chapter in this tale. There is, as of yet, no consensus on which Account is most accurate. Clearly it is mine, but others are not so sure. Read them through thorough, and after you have pondered them amidst the six winds, judge for yourselves.

My Own Account

My own account of this ordeal is certainly my most favorite, and perhaps it is because I find it to be most true. After all, the events which I am about to describe were witnessed by my own true eyes, from my stance atop the far bank of the Dan, standing with a clear view of the pool at the base of the Harl below me, and thus I am at a loss as to how so many alternate versions have sprung up (three of the most popular I have recorded hereafter).

Noble Piss Dingle ran towards Url Skulfing with a mighty cry of war, ramming into him with the force of strong loins, and lifting the great freak right off his feet — sending them both over the edge of the Falls and plummeting through mist, forty strides down.

Landing with a roaring splash in the pool at the base of Harl, Piss Dingle and Url Skulfing rose up drenched, there in the lower Dan. The worms of Skulfing hissed, while Dingle unsheathed two daggers, sliding the metals off one another and holding them out in valiant pose. Never was a more legendary standoff brought to my eyes. There is none that can top the picture I so vividly recall in my mind, with the worms on

Skulfing's shoulders twirling slowly, readying for assault, and Magnificent Piss Dingle, standing firm with daggers stretched across his breast.

At last, Skulfing's Dreadworms leapt forth, and Dingle dropped under the Danwater. A moment later he shot back up, sending a rapid dagger right between Skulfing's eyes. This would have been a noble launch, had not the worms of Skulfing all merged onto the point, saving Url's face from decimation. But this provided Dingle with an almighty revelation: the worm that had stopped the dagger shrieked out, as the blade tore through it, and in that moment, Skulfing too took a wounded step back.

In that moment, Godly Piss Dingle, Mighty Piss Dingle... knew how he would come to vanquish this beast. And so Dear Beloved Piss Dingle let the six winds fill him with peace and purpose, and Url Skulfing rose up tall, readying his worms. The shoulder worms launched another assault on Dingle, but this time, Dingle did not drop. Instead, he held out a firm hand— hard as it must have been— and clenched it upon that horrific worm.

The wailing of the worm was horrific. The feel of the worm was horrific. The seven fellow worms that now all attacked at once were horrific. But still did Brave and Valiant, Awesome and True Piss Dingle hold on tight to Skulfing's worm, and smashed upon it with his dagger, severing its bod fully.

Skulfing fell to his knees, but only for a moment. For he knew he could not give away the true weakness that was just imparted upon him. But it was too late— the Grand Fiend of Yonderlobe knew exactly how the severing of his shoulder worm had ailed him.

And so he grabbed another, and severed it. And another.

After severing four of Url Skulfing's tape worms, the Lobe Minister began to sprout a forest of dead skin atop his head— hair, some might say— which flowed fast like waves in the wind as did the ghostly weeds of Lakewood.

Still Dingle felt no remorse. He half-severed another worm, and with this Url Skulfing began to cough up bone.

It was clear at this point that Almighty Piss Dingle was on a straight path to victory, and so he spoke like the gods, reprimanding Skulfing for all the evils he had done.

"This is for all that you have allowed to transpire, rather encouraged, in your reign of darkness—" he cut off another worm— "Know that the Lobes will never again fall to one who cares not for its people. For one who claims to love justice but then lets evil pass by. For one who revels in corruption and then accuses his opponents of that which he himself is guilty of. For one who starts fires with words of hate and literal flame, and then does nothing to put them out, but rather fuels it. There have been enough fires in these Lobes. Now it is time, for this dark time of crying demon, to be at its end."

And he grabbed the last three remaining worms at once, and severed them all with his dagger. "I speak of you, Lobe Minister Skulfing."

And Skulfing— his cheeks sinking into their sockets— fell back slowly into the Dan.

"The bitch I speak of is you."

And upon hearing these words from the tongue of Mighty Piss Dingle, Url Skulfing fell under the misty waters of the Dan, at the foot of the Harl, with one Dreadworm falling after him, to give company in the watery grave.

Dingle shivered to think of all that had taken place there that day. All who had lost their lives, all whose lives would be forever changed as a result of those great trials.

And, trembling, he looked to the dagger in his hand, that which had only moments ago done such vile cuttings.

"Goddamn gross," said Dingle out loud, and dropped the dagger full of worm guts into the Dan, never to be seen again.

Here ends the Account of Ward Geit Fung.

The Account of Piss

The story told by the protagonist himself is incredibly different, though not so entirely different as those to come. In this telling, the outcome was largely the same: Url Skulfing was defeated, and defeated at the wet hands of Deep Piss Dingle, him Deep. But, in the words of our protagonist, never did he lift a dagger to the man.

"No, I never cut off his tape worms," spoke Dingle to me once in great confidence. "Rather, we got down and had a time of great doings, to the extent that one may with a long-scowled adversary.

"It is true that he came at me with thunderous eyes, and broad arms raised high as he lifted the lining of his shoulders, revealing the hideous nature of that which was concealed: tape worms! And my first thought was— and still is— WHY? Nasty. That's all it is. My first instinct was to take out my dagger as you assume I did and cut the worms forever from those disgusting burrows in the flesh of Skulfing— perhaps this is where your mind veered unintentionally into fantasy, for I can see how the vivid scene would take hold of one with an imagining spirit like yours. But I held that instinctual hand with my other, and asked myself, what would I be solving? Surely this tall beast of horrendous stature would not simply let me cut the worms from their place of plantment. He was clearly fond of them, or else he would have parted with them himself.

"And so I did a thing altogether unheard of, and here you must have fainted in a spell of disgust, where I imagine you dreamed of my triumph, to the tune of your own vision. But no, Jernander— or, Geit Fung? Am I calling you Geit Fung now? Sure. I did not charge in with blades of steel. I charged forth instead, with warm fingers and a splendid tongue."

And so the Lord Dingle, right honorable and saintly, has tried to tell me many a time. But I will not have it. I know what I saw— and it was not the image of a noble hero bending down to the heinous Lobe Minister in sexual servitude.

No. My Lord Dingle did not arouse that villain and persuade him to denounce his evil deeds by means of physical passion. We should not even consider it for a moment. It is beyond folly, and farce.

Yet I am obliged to include it in my manuscript, for I am currently held before a large tub of excrement, to be dumped down my open throat should I not give it a page.

Here ends the Account of Piss Dingle.

The Account of Lady Victory

The account of Victory was that the whole affair was a failure.

Yes, she witnessed events the same as I, looking down in the same set of moments, albeit from the other side of the Dan. Still, it was not more than thirty strides that separated us. But I will include her telling as well, for she has promised me extremities to suck should I comply.

Dingle wrestled around with Url Skulfing down at the base of the Harl Fall, until of a great sudden Skulfing lifted a leg— and shot forth a projectile of the cold blue fluid that his legs so famously seeped.

Upon this, Dingle's head fell back in a spell of sleep, and Url Skulfing caught him. His hands held Dingle at a slant, inches above the foaming waters. He looked up with an earth-shaking malice, locking eyes with those who viewed the horror. Contemplating whether he ought to end the ordeal with a slice to the face with Dingle's own dagger, or simply to lower his adversary's face into the sacred river and carry out a drown, Url Skulfing relished in his win.

Skulfing's Dreadworms, however, took no time for relishing. They rose soon after Dingle's consciousness left, and began to devour him whole. They brought endless ravage to his face in the same manner as they did to poor Rick Cottontree.

The worms then spun a rapid web of silk, which slowly took the form of Dingle as he was in life. A perfect "Clohn," as they would have said in the Age of Enchantment. And as the hideous worms sprouted new mouths all along their long sectioned selves, they sang out in an otherworldly choir. The song rang all about, shaking the trees and shimmering in the air, giving rise to mist and faces on the wind, a most peculiar form of devilry never ever mentioned before or seen since.

It is my conjecture that Victory was here drunk on the most supremely lewdest of fruits. There is no excusing this absurd hallucination, for nobody else noticed even the slightest hint of any of these things happening. But I resign, for the Lady Victory does have fine extremities, and I will soon be with them.

So yes, the true Piss Dingle fell dead in the waters of the Dan at the foot of the Harl. His Clohn took in a breath of life, granted by the ethereal sounds of Skulfing's shoulder worms, and then began to walk about the earth in perfect resemblance to the one true Piss.

If any of you reading in our time should come to see Piss Dingle roaming the fields, or walking the streets... know that he is an imposter. Know that he is a construct, made of evil design and placed upon our world by the Url Skulfing, who was— sad as it may be— the true victor in the Battle of Lidion.

I was present recently on a day when I read this passage aloud in the company of our main folk.

Upon hearing it, my friend Dingle turned and said "What the goddamned hell Victory?"

And we all laughed, albeit reservedly, for small doubts in our minds did linger that the Piss Dingle who now sat before us may in fact be an actual imposter, a worm-molded counterfeit forged by Skulfing to do his bidding upon earth. We tucked those thoughts to the backs of our minds, for facing such a possibility in earnest would make our lives too terrifying to endure.

Here ends the Account of Victory.

The Account of Lord Cuomo of Costerwall

And at last we come to the words of Dingle's rival, who here tries to rob him of all glory he might rightfully deserve. For of Lord Cuomo, the claim is that Piss Dingle never defeated Url Skulfing, nor even met him in battle at all for that matter. In this account, all the markers related in My Own Account come to pass all the same, but by the hand of Cuomo, with Dingle resting cross-legged and out of water's spray.

For, as you may remember, Lord Cuomo had been thrown from the ledge of the Redrock in the same manner as Inder Sohn. Whereas the fall had killed Inder, Lord Cuomo lay on his back, badly hurt but very much alive. And when Url Skulfing had leapt up the Falls of Harl to murder Poor Rick Cottontree, Cuomo heard his cries of anguish.

400

Setting all pain aside, he pushed himself up from the corpse of his dearly departed Inder, and limped with haste towards the base of the Falls. From his vantage point, he could see Skulfing's back atop the waterfall, as his worms feasted upon Poor Rick Cottontree. Still having held one of Dingle's daggers, Lord Cuomo decided to put an end to this freak then and there, and let fly he did that bold dagger.

The dagger flew up over the Falls of Harl in the same way that Skulfing himself had, and struck the dread Lobe Minister in the back. Livid, Skulfing turned to lock eyes with Cuomo below. Our saintly Lord of Costerwall merely locked eyes back, delivering a smug little face.

And so Skulfing leapt down the Falls, and Lord Cuomo went rushing in, with sword drawn, to massacre the sinister Minister.

When pressed on the discrepancies of his tale from all others, Lord Cuomo to this day will maintain that it was he in all versions of the fight, and that Dingle had spent the entire duration of the combat sitting down behind the leaves on the Near Bank, diddling with twigs.

"Well sure you'll believe the Mahog," says Lord Cuomo to any who ask. "Of course Piss Dingle will take the glory. He says it's all his doing, and you all believe him, for the Rich Mahogany love in all ways to lift up their own. And so the glory is his. This book is about him— Piss Dingle, and not I— because he is of the Rich Mahogany breed. And I, alas, am no more than a mere Tanfolk."

Sounds like he's just jealous.

Here ends the Account of Lord Cuomo.

I will not impose my will upon which account you ought to be believe, although there is a clear choice. Anyway, there is little discrepancy as to the ultimate outcome of the battle, unless one is to believe Victory's Account, wherein Piss Dingle died and was replaced by a Clohn of himself, while Url Skulfing stills roams the deeps of this earth.

Otherwise, the tale confirms that Url Skulfing was vanquished, there in the shallow waters of the Dan at the foot of the Falls of Harl on the First of Wethember, 3336. It was done either by Dingle's dagger, the sword of Lord Cuomo, or the passion of Dingle's loins.

And for that we true Lobians will ever be grateful, for already indeed the Lobes appear to be on the mend. With the sinister ranks of the Snake Affiliate made leaderless, there was no great power to render the peoples voiceless. The Choosing of the Reign was thus upheld in the Glorious Year of 3336, after being thwarted by Skulfing the previous two times, by way of the courts in 3330 and by way of assassins in 3333.

Now there would grow to be true justice under the joint-rule of Joon Lu and Tung No, Joon Lu being of mutual relation with the recently departed Kang Joon and the dear Dingleite Deng Lu, who— surprise incoming— did not die in the Forest of Arches. For old Carvin Cong's diversion had done its sacrificial part, and given Deng Lu the chance to crawl down an old hollowed-out tree, so deep that Skulfing could not hope to reach him.

And so the Line of Lu was saved, to perhaps be brought forth in old glory with the coming days. Whether Deng shall ever establish himself as a King in the image of his forefathers, I make no predictions, and speak with no prejudice. He did many great things in our company, and I will leave it at that.

Together the new powers in our land now work to undo the evils of the Skulfers, who were expelled to distant lands north of the Urf, Moysinthy as it is known collectively, that meaning "Lands of the Unknown." Despite their name, those parts are not entirely unknown to us, for we know many Skulfers still linger in Moysinthy as of this writing. But we in the Lobes of Hakamena are working to dispel them further. Our efforts will be the tale of a later date.

Disgraceful Epilogue

I apologize in advance for any shortcomings in this book, of which I know there to be many.

As earlier noted, the author was killed in the Battle of Lidion, although I am the author, and therefore he— or I— could not revisit some of the earlier chapters in an effort to polish them or bring them to flawless seam. Indeed, I know there are many things that Ward Geit Fung meant to go back and expand upon before publishing this account of the now Noble Piss Dingle. Although I am charged with relinquishing my former name and carrying on the soul of Ward Geit, I was not at that time Ward Geit, so I have no way of knowing what he intended to fill in. I will not attempt to guess; rather, I will let the old words of the old Geit speak for themselves, even if their inclusion sometimes seems to be going places which lead to nowhere at all.

All hope is not lost though, for Piss Dingle and Toot still live upon broad tracts of the Lobes. They are quite wealthy now, and have shown considerable interest in learning to read and write themselves. In which case, the possibility of them accounting for their own deeds may not be such a laughable thing in the future.

For the time being, they continue to crusade against intolerance in the Lobes, albeit with words instead of steel. However, I have heard that they are now beginning to feel the itch of raw brutality once more.

The last time I saw them, Toot was in conference with Lord Cuomo as to how he might recover his Skin after their deal made on the field outside Lidion— whereby he was fated to lose his Skin— so that he might come to be Skin Toot once again. At that conference I

404

heard Piss Dingle speaking long on the clear injustices of Lord Hirreldohf of Dorwein, in that heinous land of Moysinthy, where it is custom to sacrifice the lives of fifty-six boys every time a King is laid to rest.

Noble Lord Dingle said that there is an enemy he would like to face, now that all the lines of absolute good and punishable evil have so often been blurred... now that it is no longer certain which course of action should be taken to help rid the world of injustice. With the heinous Lord of Dorwein, whose villainy is so absolutely deep, he would feel no remorse in again giving rise to his famous dagger.

Is that what days to come have in store for the Lobes? Will we yet come to have further tales of Dingle and Toot, tearing out the bowels of evildoers? Many lament that they have since fallen to the realm of kind social politics, and long to see the day when they will seek combat as in days of old. Will this come to pass with Lord Dingle's proposed venture into Moysinthy?

We may yet see.

1717171717171717171717171717171717171717171717171717171717

Made in the USA
Monee, IL
07 August 2021